TOUCHED BY LIGHT

ALSO BY BERNA HUDSON

THE HAND OF REASON

Touched by Light
Rule of Reason (coming Summer 2026)
Shadow of the Hand (coming Late Summer 2026)
Rise of the Five (coming Autumn 2026)
Dawn of the Light (coming Winter 2026)

CIRCLES OF MEYAN

Circle of Mists (coming Winter 2026/2027)
Circle of Secrets (coming Spring 2027)

BERNA HUDSON

TOUCHED BY LIGHT

HAND OF REASON BOOK 1

TUMULUS PRESS

First Published in Great Britain in 2026 by Tumulus Press
Suite 1, 7th Floor, 50 Broadway
London SW1H 0DB
United Kingdom

A CIP catalogue record for this book is available from the British Library.

ISBN 978-1-9192877-1-3 (UK paperback)
ISBN 978-1-9192877-0-6 (UK hardback)
ISBN 978-1-9192877-2-0 (ebook)

Map Design by Elyot Veillon and Frederick Kroner in collaboration with Stardust Book Services.

Illustrations by Jonas Spokas in collaboration with Stardust Book Services.

Cover Art by Fakel Barros in collaboration with Stardust Book Services.

Typesetting by Book Polishers and Fakel Barros in collaboration with Stardust Book Services.

Printed and bound by CPI Group.

For my father, who
taught me that changing my mind is an act of bravery
and that true freedom lies in choice.

Uncharted
Harbourview
Cuttstone
Elekan
Merchant Landing
Extrachange
MEYAN
Tradesburg
Lukur
Freetrade Port
KLAEVA
Ginval
Tinderport
ROHIN
Dorchet
Sauka
Simbar
Retan
Sylvale
Sintra
Stonehelve
Teakport
Amberil
Eldermoor
TAMADAL
Kalmat
REO
Doubletree
Entres
Vilar
Gyllia
Mylia
Ilia
Ros
Kiras
Retan Waters
Lyra Point
Quzal
Fisten
Mirah
Fallya
Gallya
Eldermist
Erin
Lis
Owestry
Velan Strait
Arya
VEL
Erian Waters
IBYSSANIA
CELENTRA
MERIDIANA
SERAPHIA

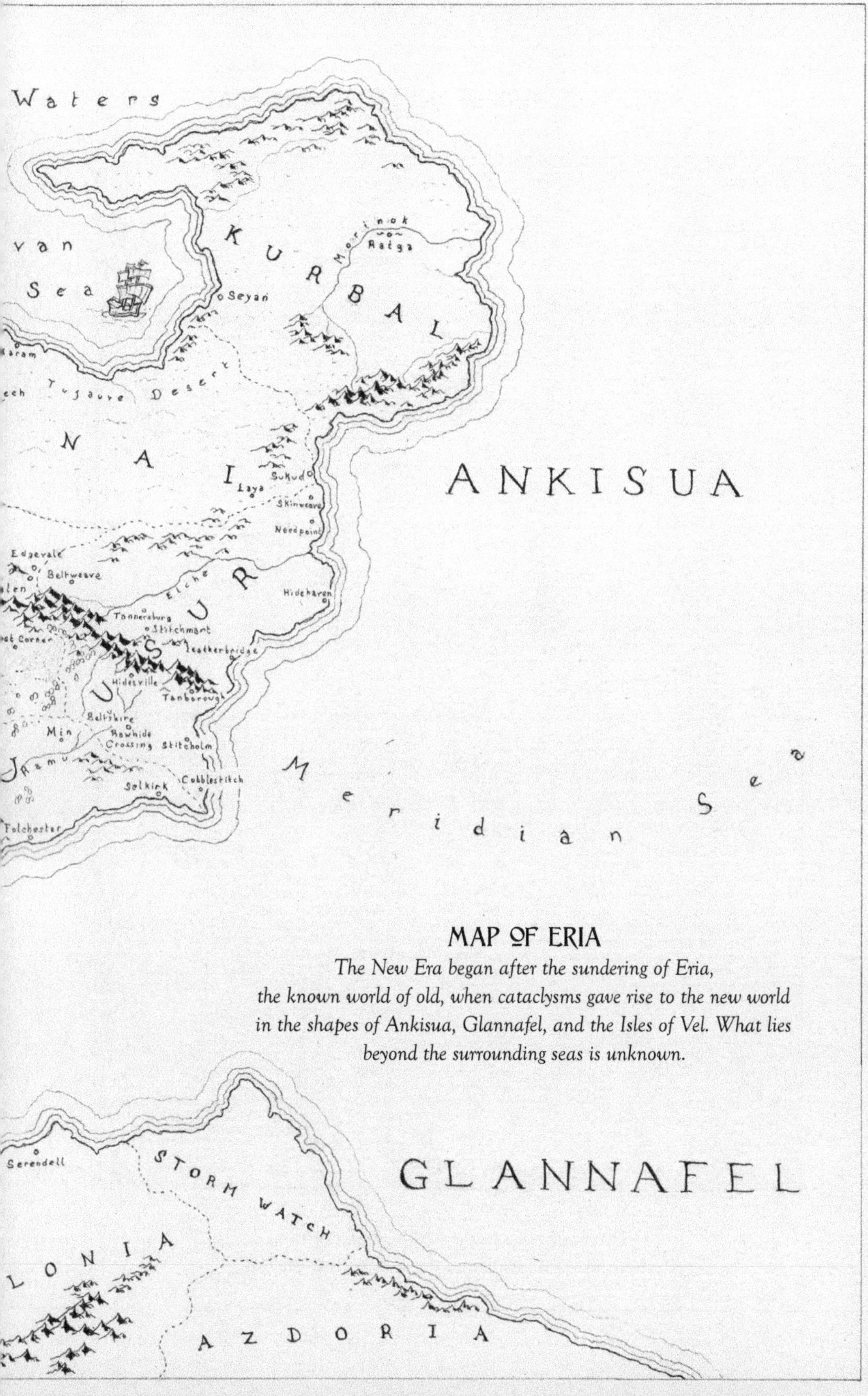

MAP OF ERIA

The New Era began after the sundering of Eria, the known world of old, when cataclysms gave rise to the new world in the shapes of Ankisua, Glannafel, and the Isles of Vel. What lies beyond the surrounding seas is unknown.

SECTION OF MAP OF SOUTHERN ANKISUA

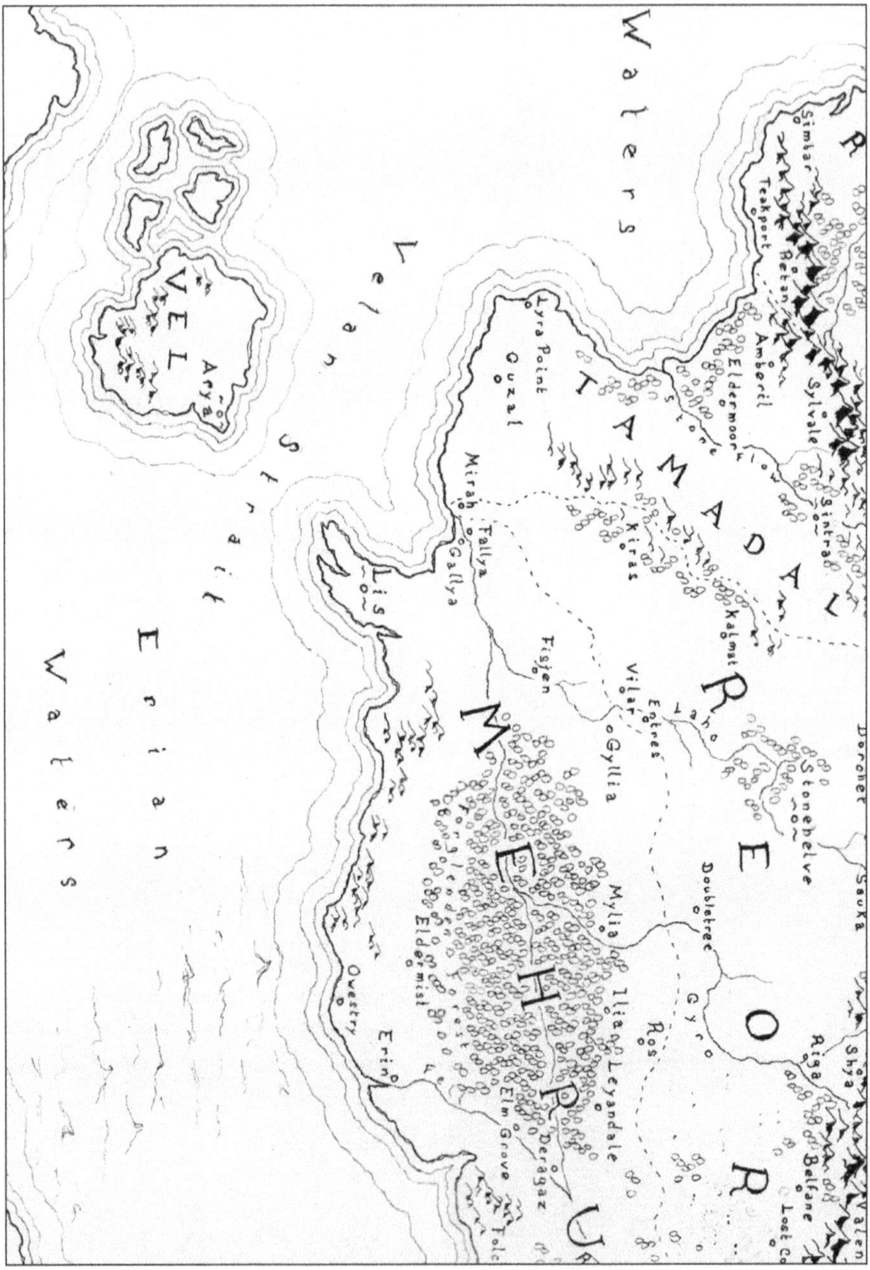

This book is set in the fictional land of Eria,
where all speak, spell, and think in British English.

CONTENTS

PROLOGUE

YEAR 5161 OF THE NEW ERA – SUMMER

FELIM GUIDED HIS cart down the West Way. The sound of his old horses' hooves pounding rhythmically against the hard-packed earth was soothing, and the late-summer sun on his back was pleasant. He relished the solitude since his travelling companions had turned off into side lanes, and the monotony of the gnarled bushes disappearing into the distance pleased him. He'd soon be home.

Felim was brought out from his enjoyment of the placid afternoon by the sound of hooves behind him. Twisting in his seat, he searched the road. A cloud of dust rose in the distance, heralding a rider coming quickly. Felim guided his cart to the verge to let them pass.

As they came closer, Felim admired the spirited roan horse galloping easily in his direction and the large grey dog loping along at its side. He paid little attention to the rider till the man reined in and came to a standstill by the cart.

'Felim! I was hoping to catch up with you.' A tall man stretched a hand towards him.

Felim squinted up. 'Peryst? Is that you? What a surprise! What are you doing here?'

'Searching for you. I've been following in your tracks since Belfane. I arrived when the Lithe Fair was wrapping up and was told that I'd just missed you. Where's my sister?' Peryst, his wife's twin, asked in barely accented Reordan.

Utterly surprised at his brother-in-law's presence, Felim answered quickly. 'She didn't come to the fair this year. Our twins are too young for such a trip.'

Peryst wore a haunted expression for a moment. 'Marie bore twins? How old are they? And more important, how are they and Marie?'

Felim glanced round before replying and was relieved there was nobody to see him conversing with a Klaevani. Being married to Marie was one thing, but talking to a leather-clad man with weapons on his back was a whole other. He forced himself to smile as he replied in the friendliest tone he could manage. 'Six months old and growing quickly. They keep Marie busy.' He changed the subject. 'How is it that you're here? We haven't seen you since Marie and I left Klaevan! How long has it been?'

'Almost sixteen years since I hauled you out of a snowdrift, half frozen.'

Felim squirmed at the memory of his time amongst the northerners. How different his life would've been without it.

Forcing out a smile, he said, 'A very long time indeed. I wouldn't have recognised you if you weren't so much like your sister!' There was no mistaking the startling green of those eyes.

Peryst lowered his voice to little more than a whisper. 'I had a feeling that Marie might need me.'

Felim grimaced with distaste at the mention of any *feeling* that could denote a hint of Touched power. He'd had enough of that from Marie since the twins were born. Caring for Raf and Reba had been hard on her, and she'd become more sensitive than usual about her Klaevani heritage, seeing hints of power everywhere and obsessing that one of their children would be discovered to be Touched when tested by the Hand of Reason. The night before he left for the fair, she'd panicked about it again. A gust of air had moved the wooden animal mobile he'd carved for the twins. Bells had tinkled and figures had pranced above the delighted children, and Marie got it into her head that it was one of the children making them move. As if that were possible! Not even Klaevani were born with developed powers.

'She is well,' he said curtly. 'Just busy with the twins.'

At Felim's tone, the grey animal at Peryst's side let out a low growl, and Peryst leaned down to place a calming hand on its head. Felim forced another stiff smile as he recognised it as a wolf. A wolf! Civilised people had dogs. He asked mildly, 'How are things with your family?'

'As usual. I'd like to visit Marie if that's acceptable to you?'

'She'll like that. She misses you sorely,' Felim said grudgingly. It was true. Marie had struggled never seeing her family again, particularly her brother.

He studied the lean grey wolf. 'And who is this?' He stretched out a hand for the animal to sniff.

The wolf turned to Peryst, who made an affirmative gesture, before sniffing at Felim disdainfully.

Peryst lay a gentle hand on the wolf's head. 'This is Nela. She's guarded me through many lands since we lost her mistress.' He patted his horse's neck. 'And this is Roan.'

Felim nodded, knowing the importance of animals in the life of nomads. The roaming life of his wife's family was incomprehensible to him. They travelled the lands across the Kunlan Range, where the Hand of Reason hadn't yet ventured, hunting and hiring themselves out as mercenaries throughout the warmer months and retreating to their clan's fortress for winter. Felim had been returning from Genai, where he'd been studying glassmaking techniques, when he'd become lost in the heights of the Kunlan Range. After Peryst rescued him, he'd recovered from his ordeal amongst the wintering Clan de Arranu. There'd been something magical in the glimmering light, the smoke-laden atmosphere, and the tunes that sang of gods and legend. And he'd loved Marie of the mesmerising green eyes so deeply and so completely that come Spring—and despite her family's objections—he'd led her down to the southern flatlands and into Reor of the age of reason.

Felim shook his head, banishing the memories. It was so long ago. He glanced round nervously again, hoping that he wouldn't encounter any who knew him while Peryst rode by his side. He kept the conversation easy and avoided the divisive subjects of the Hand of Reason or the Touched. Thankfully, Peryst was more interested in the intricacies of glassmaking and the Academy's inventions powered by the glass vials like those he made, and Felim gladly educated him, knowing that Klaevan was a backward nation that relied on Touched powers like the old Reor. The two nations had once had a close relationship, but current exchanges between them were fraught because some clans had become more vocal in their objection to the Hand of Reason's tentative expansion in southern Ankisua.

'Do you and Marie come to the Lithe Fair every year?' Peryst asked.

'We do. This is the first year that Marie didn't come. I'm a purveyor of glass vials for the Academy.' Felim couldn't keep pride from his tone. 'I manufacture three types, the gold vials for storing sunlight, transparent for wind, and pale redz for water, in three of the sizes set by Stonehelve.'

'And Marie helps with this?'

'She does. Marie's got an infallible intuition for the proportions in the materials we use. This last year she spotted an inaccuracy in the batch of sand, soda ash, and minerals the Academy provided for the wind vials. Only because I'm careful with my supplies and had saved batches from previous years was I able to fulfil my required quota.'

'And your Academy was satisfied with the replacement?' Peryst asked with what Felim sensed was a tinge of irony.

Fighting his annoyance and without hinting at the trepidation he'd felt when the brown-clad Guardians held samples of his vials up to the light, tapped them with metal rods, and placed them on trays over open flames as he waited, Felim said, 'Not only were they satisfied, they also granted me conditional approval for the manufacture of the most expensive kind of vial: the silver ones for storing lightning. Only the smallest size, but it's a start.'

'What does that imply?' Peryst asked curiously.

'A team from Stonehelve will come to inspect my facilities and advise on the renovations required for their manufacture. Once that's done, I'll be given a trial contract for fifty vials. If those are accepted, I'll deal in them for two years. The contract will provide extra income with which I'll modernise my kilns and save enough to ensure that my children can lead comfortable lives if they're not selected for an education at the Academy.' Either way, his children would honour their Reordan roots and name despite their green eyes.

Peryst raised his brows. 'That is what you would desire for them? An education with your Academy?'

'Of course. It's what any true Reordan wishes for his children.'

Peryst made no comment. 'And Marie makes vials, too?'

'Marie makes jewels with leftover glass and clocks, like your grand-mother, she says. Despite having the twins to care for, she made this year's clock more intricate than any she'd made before, depicting a scene from the Lithe Fair itself. The Udal of Belfane, impressed by its details, paid above the asking price to display it in the village's town hall.' Felim was proud that its workmanship showed off his own glassmaking skills.

'And it gives you a good living? This glass business?'

'It does. In the old days, we Lengahrs were farmers.'

Peryst glanced round at the parched ground and low yellow bushes that graced the land as far as they could see. His doubt was clear.

Felim let out a chuckle. 'In the days before the Hand of Reason, the land was manipulated by unnatural Touched powers and forced to yield as if fertile. Afterwards, when there were no longer Touched, my forebears remained, surviving thanks to those bushes, and proving to be as resilient as them.' He pointed at the twisted plants. 'They have little need for water, the berries can be made into jams and wines, and the wood carved into furniture.'

'So, it was you who shifted to glassmaking?'

'My father. He saw the advances elsewhere in Reor and realised that Lost Corner could join the march towards progress. The farm had the infrastructure needed, with barns and silos that could be easily reconfigured into workshops.' Felim didn't tell Peryst that his father had waited for his own mother's death; she'd grown up on stories of Touched burnt on village greens and hadn't loved the Hand of Reason. Not a day after her passing, Felim's father sent an application to the Academy in Stonehelve and then placed Lost Corner firmly back on the Reordan map. 'By the time I took over, we were known for the quality of our glass.'

'This new contract cements that for you and Marie?'

Felim nodded. He didn't say that when negotiating the new contract he'd realised that Marie's absence played in his favour. For the first time, there were no sidelong glances at her from the Guardians, no raised brows at her accented Reordan, and no frowns at her forthright negotiating. Hiding his nerves, Felim had discussed the matter easily and had been given the highest increase in percentage he'd ever received plus the approval for the new vials.

When he turned his cart into the lane that led to his ancestral home, Felim was, as usual, filled with pride. The house, a long and squat building made generations earlier of thick straw walls and mud bricks, covered in clay and whitewash, lay at the end of the lane. Its bright blue shutters were open, and—oddly—smoke rose from the central chimney in the warm evening's waning light. On either side of the blue front door sat large glass pots, each holding a small olive tree, a sign of prosperity and plenty. Behind the house, just visible a quarter mile away, lay the old barns and stables, now modern glassmaking workshops.

Marie must have been listening for him because the door flung open when Felim's cart was still a distance from the house. Dogs ran out, barking their welcome. As he stopped and climbed down, rubbing his lower back, Marie came flying at him without even noticing the rider who had stopped a little behind.

Felim held her tightly, burying his face in her dark hair. He was too happy to have his wife in his arms again after more than two weeks to notice much else. When he tried to pull back and see her face, he realised that she was crying quietly into his neck.

'What are these tears, Marie? Joy at having me back?'

Marie lifted a ravaged face. 'Oh, Felim. How I wish it were that.'

His beautiful wife, only just thirty-one, looked exhausted. While he'd been gone, her warm complexion had turned sallow, and her cheekbones had become sharp.

'My love, what is it? Have you been ill?' Foreboding dried Felim's mouth.

Tears streaming, Marie shook her head.

Behind them, Peryst approached and cleared his throat. Marie turned.

'Peryst?' Sobbing even louder, she moved to hug him. Her brother held her close and murmured old words of childhood comfort. Jealousy tightened Felim's chest as Peryst's words calmed Marie when his own had not.

She wiped her face and darted glassy eyes from one to the other as she uttered words to her brother in Klaevani, a tongue she'd never used in front of Felim and that he'd never wanted to learn.

'What's the matter, Marie?' Felim insisted in Reordan as he twisted her back round to face him.

She didn't reply but led them to the house. Felim followed, a knot of vague fear growing in his chest.

The front door opened to the cheerful great room, kept warmer than necessary by a roaring fire in the hearth. Decorative logs had lain there for years because no fire had been set since Felim's early childhood. There was no need: they had solar-powered heaters for warmth. The heavy wooden trestle table and benches stood near the arch that led to the kitchen. Shelves held Marie's books and glass ornaments, and pride of place was given to a clock depicting a mountain scene. Opposite the fireplace and between two armchairs sat the large wooden pen he'd made for the twins. Reba and Raf lay on their backs babbling, kicking their legs, and waving their arms in the air. The room was illuminated by the typical Reordan solar lamps that cast dancing shadows into corners. It would've been the usual cheerful—and normal—domestic scene of any afternoon if not for the pots, pans, and spoons spinning and swooping above the pen and every now and then banging together.

Felim stopped just inside the door and gaped at the scene.

'It was a little chilly this morning, but I had no intention of lighting a fire. Why would I? We have heaters for that.' Marie's voice had a slightly hysterical edge.

'But you did anyway?' Felim made himself focus on the fire. Only the fire. He couldn't deal with the pots and pans. He scrambled to make sense of what was happening as the crackling heat struck his face. '*Why*?'

Marie shook her head. 'I didn't.' Her voice broke. 'Reba.'

Felim warily approached the pen. 'Hello, little ones. Do you have a smile for your papa?' He injected his tone with forced cheer.

Upon seeing him, Raf turned onto his stomach and pushed himself up enthusiastically. Reba remained on her back, babbling up at her father. The floating cooking implements fell slowly to the ground and landed gently with barely any noise. Felim lifted Raf and held him close as he ruffled his dark hair. *My boy. This is my boy.* He couldn't think beyond that.

'Raf, meet your Uncle Peryst.' He passed the boy to his brother-in-law and then turned back to the pen where Reba was stretching her little hands up to him and pouting. As Felim studied her, she wrinkled her brow crossly and thrust a hand towards the fireplace. The flames flared and licked the upper edges of the mantle. She waved her other hand at the pots. They crashed against each other in a deafening racket. Horrified, Felim had to force himself to touch her, to take her into his arms. The flames immediately lowered, and the pots stilled. 'Reba, have you been making Mama cry?' He tried to sound jovial despite the panic gripping his throat. *This cannot be my child. This cannot be my beloved daughter. It's a monster with ungovernable powers that will doom us all.* He strove to hide the mix of terror and revulsion that made him want to gag.

Reba grabbed onto his collar tightly with one hand; with the other, she waved at Marie, whose long, dark hair began to flit about her face. Reba and Raf giggled.

Marie turned a haunted face to Felim. 'It's been like this for the last two weeks. Yesterday, she made Raf float above her.' Her voice rose steadily as she said, 'I was terrified that she'd drop him suddenly. I can't leave them for a second. I don't know what to do.'

'You teach her, Marie. That's what you do,' Peryst said shortly and traded children with Felim. As he took his niece in his arms, he waved a hand at the fire, which guttered down immediately. 'No, Reba. We don't use our powers on others without permission.' He pushed Reba's hand down, and Marie's hair fell to her shoulders. Reba made a sound of protest and raised her mother's hair again, but Peryst took the baby's hand and said gently but sternly, 'No, Reba.' Reba pouted but lowered her hand. 'Good girl, Reba.' Peryst smiled and blew a bubble into her neck, which made her giggle.

Felim took a faltering step back. 'You're *Touched by Light*,' he whispered hoarsely, voice filled with repugnance. He turned to his wife in horror. 'Why didn't you tell me?'

'I didn't know.' Marie's gaze shot to her brother and then back to her husband. 'You were there, Felim! You met many of the Touched from our clan. You only survived thanks to a Mender healing you after we brought you in from the snow.' She shook her head. 'But I didn't know about Peryst.'

'My pains started a few weeks after you left, Marie,' Peryst said drily.

'Pains?' Felim repeated. *What's the man talking about?*

'Most Touched suffer headaches when their powers come in and their sixth sense expands and settles behind their eyes.' Peryst rubbed between his brows. 'It can be excruciating. I was overwhelmed by sensations I couldn't control. Da and Mama took me to Genai where I learnt to focus my mind's eye at will and control my powers,' he explained. 'So yes, I'm Touched, and so is your daughter. One of the Arranu Touched.'

Marie placed her hands on her hips. 'Arranu Touched? She's too young. No power manifests this early!'

'But it can. Don't you remember the story about the de Arranu adventurer who brought a bride back from Glannafel? Since then children can be born in our family line with a fully open mind's eye and developed powers, like the children in the Isles of Vel and Glannafel.'

Marie twisted her hands. 'A story, Peryst! That was only a story!'

'Perhaps not,' he replied.

Marie turned to Felim, who'd been shifting from one to the other trying to grasp the implication of what he was learning. 'If I'd known, Felim, if I'd known it was true, I would've ...' Her voice trailed off.

She would've what? Felim raked a hand through his hair. He was honest enough to admit that, had he known, his sixteen-year-old self would've done nothing different. He'd been so besotted that hordes of Touched—with tails, even!—could've marched through the mountains and he wouldn't have cared.

He'd wilfully ignored his father's warning. But now all their lives were at stake. 'Does anybody else know? Has anybody seen her during my absence?' he barked.

Marie shook her head. 'I've let it be known that the children are ill. I've allowed no one in the house.' She clasped her hands and, voice trembling, said, 'I never know what she'll do, Felim. I'm terrified the Hand will find out.' Her voice broke. 'And that they'll burn her.'

'They will if they do,' Felim said.

'No, no, no!' Marie wailed. 'They won't take my child. I won't let them!'

Peryst tickled Reba and made her giggle. 'You must teach her, Marie. She's too young to know control. To her, moving things and lighting fire are activities no different to using her hands or eyes. Like any infant, she'll experiment with what she can do.'

'Experimenting will cost her life,' Felim said sharply, 'and our livelihood.'

Her face in her hands, Marie sank into one of the chairs. 'How could this happen to us?'

Peryst replied drily, 'How? You come from a family with power, as Felim must as well. Otherwise, you couldn't have made a Touched child.'

Marie went to her husband and shook his arm. 'Felim? Who had power in your family? If I had ever thought—if it had crossed my mind—I wouldn't have tried to have a child in Reor.'

Felim rubbed shaking hands over his face. 'I don't know of any Touched in my family. Both my parents were only children.' He paused as a memory suddenly came to mind.

In her last hours, his great-grandmother had rambled about the early days of the Hand of Reason, when the Five and their first followers rose against the existing regime and travelled from village to village rooting out the Touched and burning them, regardless of age, in large pyres on village greens. She wailed about hiding Touched friends in the garret and of a daughter taken by the Hand amidst screaming children and crying parents while the scent of burning flesh permeated the air. With a voice loud for one who was dying, she raved against the Hand of Reason for taking over the land with more death and pain than had ever existed in the Reor of the Touched. A child at the time, Felim tried to quiet her, terrified that someone would hear, disgusted that she voiced such heretical ideas. And when she'd expired soon after, he had been relieved, even grateful.

'There was a great-aunt taken by the Hand of Reason in the early days. I was told that she was taken in punishment for her parents hiding a Touched neighbour. Perhaps that wasn't true,' he admitted.

Peryst intervened. 'It's of no consequence. What does it matter who was Touched in either of your family trees? What matters is how to protect Reba!' he added, cradling the yawning baby.

'Nobody may know about her, Marie. Nobody! Ever!' Felim cried.

Marie nodded, sniffled, and turned to Peryst. She stretched out her arms. 'It's time for bed, Reba. Come to Mama.'

Reba yawned sleepily and nestled into Marie's neck as her mother reached for Raf as well. Felim controlled a shudder as he watched them. *So small, so seemingly helpless, but truly a monster.*

While Marie put the babies to bed, Felim went out to store the glassmaking materials he'd brought from Belfane in the workshops, and Peryst rubbed down the three horses. As Felim tidied his workshop, he struggled to make sense of the nightmare he'd come home to. He knew full well what it meant but dreaded to think of what would happen. There had to be a way out. There had to be a solution in which they wouldn't lose everything. He just needed to find it.

In the outhouse by the kitchen, he met Peryst but avoided his gaze as they washed off in silence. Peryst was Touched. His daughter was Touched. Despite their normal appearance, they were unnatural beings who tapped into powers that destroyed lives and realms. *Reba, my little girl. Reba, my princess. Reba … is a monster.*

He led Peryst back into a quiet house where Marie, appearing more like herself despite her thinness, was heating a meal. The cooker, powered by combined solar and lightning power, gave out no smoke, so the house was rich only with the scents of herbs and lamb. Trying to clear his head, Felim went to the pantry and brought out a bottle of wine made from the same berries that had kept his grandparents alive and poured three generous glasses.

As the meal cooked, Marie asked about the fair. *How can she act as if she can forget that our daughter is Touched?* Felim couldn't understand her, especially when their whole lives were in the balance. Knowing that the moment to discuss Reba would inevitably come, he replied to her questions mechanically as she toiled at the cooker. Marie expressed pride at her clock decorating the Belfane Town Hall and was pleased at the news of the lightning-vial contract. But when he mentioned that the inspectors from Stonehelve were coming in two weeks, he knew from her sudden paling that Reba was back in her mind although she'd never left his. And despite Peryst trying to distract her with news from their family in the North, Marie reverted to the scared and trembling woman from earlier.

She spooned the lamb smothered in sauce into colourful bowls and placed them on the table in silence. Felim stared into his glass and took a deep drink, the liquor warming him as it went down. He turned to his brother-in-law, seeing him differently now that he knew he was Touched. Unable to keep repugnance from his tone, he asked, 'When were you able to control your … powers?'

Shrugging off the slight, Peryst said evenly, 'Touched power generally manifests during puberty unless you choose to become Touched and have your mind's eye forcibly opened, in which case powers can manifest immediately. But at first, no Touched, whether born or made later, will have much control. All need training that takes days or even weeks. In my case, my senses of sight and touch went wild, maddening me with sensation. I even lit involuntary fires when my emotions ran high,' Peryst added wryly, 'which isn't unusual for adolescent boys. But with help, I learnt to gather enough mental strength to pull away. Afterwards, I was taught to sharpen my senses at will and use my Primal abilities to manipulate fire when I wanted to.' He nodded at Marie. 'Those in our family tend to combine powers of different kinds, so I'm both a Sensal and Primal.'

Felim didn't even try to hide his horror. What Peryst was saying was so unnatural it made him sick.

Peryst then added quietly, 'Like any other of your senses, the abilities that stem from the mind's eye can be more developed or less, more attuned to different aspects or less. And, like every other ability, that power is neither good nor bad. It's no different to having a good ear for singing or sharp aim.'

It's nothing like that! Nothing! How can he even suggest that abilities that disrupt nature can be likened to singing?

Felim opened his mouth to reply, but Marie's wail stopped him.

She put her face in her hands. 'There's no way we can keep this a secret unless nobody ever comes into the house and I never leave again.'

'We'll have to find a way.' Felim placed an arm over her shoulders.

'What would happen if someone learnt the truth about Reba?' Peryst asked.

Felim hesitated and then replied in a flat tone, 'We'd be denounced to the Udal or to the constabulary.'

'Are there such institutions in Lost Corner?' Peryst asked. 'It's such a small village. Aren't most homesteads, like yours, spread out, all far away from each other?'

'Yes. But there are both in every village, however small. It's usually the Head Defender of the constabulary who deals with these matters. Machrot is his name,' Felim said.

'So, whoever finds out will tell Machrot. What then?' Marie asked.

'He'll send notice to the capital. Guardians and Defenders will come immediately from Stonehelve instead of waiting till the twins turn one. They'll examine and test them.' Felim stopped.

'And?' Peryst asked.

'The testing won't be pleasant, I imagine.'

'Why? What do they do? Is it different to when they test adults?' Marie asked in a whisper. 'They gave me something that made me sleep when they tested me before they allowed us to marry.'

'I don't know. Parents aren't allowed to watch, but I've heard that children scream,' Felim replied. Marie paled even further.

'And then?' Peryst insisted.

'If they find her to be Touched, which they will, of course, they'll either take her away immediately or burn her on a public pyre on the green. But either way, she'll be …' He gulped, overcome by guilt for earlier thinking that his little Reba was a monster. He could now only imagine his baby daughter being snatched away by a black-and-purple-clad Defender.

'She'll be what, Felim?' Marie asked.

He replied harshly, 'Killed, either here or in Stonehelve.'

'What determines one or the other fate?' Peryst asked.

'I don't know,' Felim replied. 'Lost Corner has produced no Touched children in my lifetime, but one was burnt in Belfane five years ago. Last year, a Touched child from there was taken instead. I don't know where or why.'

Marie lowered her head onto her arms as Felim continued. 'Once she's taken or burnt, all our contracts will be cancelled, and we'll be declared enemies of the Hand. None of our children, our children's children, or even their children will be eligible for the Academy or for contracts with the Hand. Our lands will be taken, and we'll become beggars, going from village to village scrounging for work and scraps, exiles wherever we go.'

'I saw this, Marie,' Peryst said softly. 'I saw it in a dream. It's the reason I came to Reor.'

'What do you mean? How could you—' Felim stopped himself. Peryst couldn't mean he'd known that Reba was Touched, *or could he*? He passed a hand over his face.

'I have a whisper of our mother's ability to sometimes see truth in dreams.' Peryst smiled wryly. 'Mama insists that alongside Glannafel ancestry, we also have Rohinian somewhere in our bloodline.' He paused. 'You owe your life to such ability, Felim. If Mama hadn't dreamt of you lost in the snow, you would've perished. And now, perhaps it'll also have a hand in saving your daughter.'

Deep silence followed, broken only by Marie's soft sobbing.

With his arm still over his wife's shoulders, Felim stared into his glass as Peryst paced back and forth in front of the hearth, a deep frown between his thick, dark brows. He finally stopped and turned to his sister, who was slight where he was tall but dark haired like him and with the same features and stubborn chin. 'Pack your things now!' he ordered. 'Pack everything you need and value into Felim's cart and come with me. I'll lead you east into Usur, and we'll take one of the mountain passes to the North. You can make a new life in Klaevan.'

'Make a life? How?' Felim replied sharply. 'I'm no Klaevani monster hunter. I have no skill with weapons. Nor can I master the fancy glasswork of Genai at this point in my life.' As he reminded his brother-in-law of how real people lived, Felim watched wild hope flare in Marie's face and then slowly dull. 'I'm a glassmaker of Reor and can only work my kilns for utilitarian purposes as a faithful son of the Hand of Reason.' He lifted Marie's chin and addressed only her. 'There's been a Lengahr on this land since the founding of Reor, Marie. We Lengahrs are not like you Klaevani. We're not wanderers with no ties. We *belong*, Marie. We have *ties* to our land, to the earth under our homes. I have ties to this land, to every bush, to the old and gnarled apple trees in the yard, to the cracked earth. My forebears held this place through lean times and plenty. When the land yielded, they took, and when it didn't, they survived from it in other ways. And now, building on my father's efforts, you and I have made our glassmaking business into what it is. How can we abandon it and become beggars, scrounging for charity? *This* is our home, Marie. This is *my* home. I cannot just walk away and turn my back on who I am. I'm a Lengahr, and I belong here, as do *all* who carry my blood.'

Tears ran down Marie's face as she asked, 'What are you saying? What about our child?'

The hair on the back of his neck rose at her words.

No. A Touched child cannot be mine. Will never be. I won't sacrifice everything generations of my ancestors fought for because of a monster.

But before he could utter the words that Marie would never forgive, Peryst stopped pacing, utter disbelief on his face.

'You would choose these stones.' Peryst kicked at the fireplace surround. 'Stones? Over your own daughter?'

Felim clenched his fists. 'You can't understand!' He stalked up to his brother-in-law. 'How could you? You're a wanderer, a tramp who's never had a home. How can you ever grasp the meaning of stones and mortar? Of knowing that every time you wake, you do so where countless of your name did so in the past?' His voice throbbed in uncontrollable anger as he grasped the taller man's forearms and shook him. 'It's not just stones, Peryst, it's my *roots*. My family settled these lands at the time of Reor's founding. They defended them against invaders, beasts, and drought. They trusted these lands to give them a living, generation after generation after generation. I owe it to them to do the same and to preserve these lands for any who come after me!'

Growling at the aggression aimed at her master, Nela pushed her lean body between them as Felim's dogs started barking and Marie rushed forwards to grab at both men. Felim shrugged to dislodge her hand digging into his arm.

'Stop! Both of you! This doesn't help and you'll wake the children. Stop it! Now!'

Felim let go of Peryst and took a step back, hands raised, still furious but striving to control himself.

'I may not have a home of stone, Felim, but I do have a home in those who share my blood. And Reba shares yours. She, too, is a Lengahr.' Peryst spun to Marie and grasped her upper arms. 'Marie! Come with me! The Marie I remember would do so. You can save the children! We can take them to Mama.'

'The children?' Felim was so angry he spluttered. 'They're *my* children, and you'll take them nowhere!'

Marie placed a shaking hand on Peryst's arm. She held tightly as tears rolled down her cheeks. Her voice lowered to barely above a whisper. 'The Marie you knew was a child. I barely remember her. I can't hold a weapon today. I can't spend every night camping in a new place. This is all I know.' She waved her hands, encompassing the house. 'This is what I've built. Here, with Felim. I sleep in the same bed every night, and I never have to worry if I'll find shelter or warmth or food. I'm a clockmaker, Peryst, and a glassmaker. And I can't leave Felim and what we've made together. I can't.' Her voice broke.

'There could be another way,' Peryst said slowly, rubbing his arm where Marie's nails had dug through his sleeve.

Felim sighed in frustration as wild hope danced over Marie's face again.

'You're not going to like it,' Peryst added.

'What is it?' Marie asked eagerly as Felim's temples throbbed dully.

'Reba's six months old and can light fire and move heavy objects. She has exceptionally strong powers. And that's only what she's shown so far,' Peryst said.

'Do you think I don't realise that?' she snapped.

'I know you do, but I'm setting the scene. My powers didn't manifest with such strength, and it took training before I could control them. Yet this child was able to light fire and keep pots and pans dancing with no appreciable effort. She was also able to bring everything down gently instead of dropping it when distracted. She has incredible focus for one so young.'

Marie frowned. 'I *know*, or do you think marriage, motherhood, and abject terror has softened my brain?'

Peryst grinned. 'Maybe a little.'

Balancing the heavy glass in her hand, she said, 'I may not have your and Reba's powers, Peryst, but there's never been anything wrong with my aim. In fact, it was always better than yours.'

Felim interrupted. 'Can't we close her mind's eye?'

Marie shook her head. 'Once open, the mind's eye cannot be closed. Ever again.'

'What about stopping her powers?' he insisted.

'There's no way of doing that. And if there were, it'd be like cutting off her arm or blinding her. It's who she is, Felim. The only way to stop her powers would be by killing her.'

Felim sighed. 'What about sedating her? Till she can control her powers.' He added quietly, 'If she lifted Raf as she lifted those pots and pans, she's a danger to him and to us.'

With disgust, Peryst said, 'Sedating her wouldn't fool your Guardians. And she's no more dangerous than any child in the Isles of Vel or Glannafel. And anyway, didn't you say that Guardians are due to test the twins when they turn one?'

Marie's hand flew to her mouth. 'I'd forgotten that!'

Felim asked Peryst, 'What were you going to suggest, then?'

'Reba needs somewhere safe where she can develop, where she won't be curtailed or harmed,' Peryst said. 'I can take her to Klaevan, where she'll be out of the Hand's reach.'

Marie gasped. 'Away from her family?'

'No, Marie, *with* her family and *to* her family. Or do you forget that I'm family and that the whole of Clan de Arranu is her family as well?'

'You know what I mean. You're telling me to forsake my daughter, to take away her life,' Marie whispered.

Peryst shook his head. 'No, I'm telling you to give her the life she deserves. In Reor she's a monster. She'll be despised and reviled, and that only *if* she's allowed to live. In Klaevan she'll be my beloved daughter, a respected and proud member of Clan de Arranu. She'll develop and hone her powers as she was born to.'

'And what of Raf?' Marie barely mouthed.

Felim answered, 'We'll give him the life he deserves, too. The life of a respected son of the community of Lost Corner, with comfortable circumstances and strong connections to his family's land and past.' *This is it! This is the solution!* 'Think about it, Marie. Think of what Raf will lose if Reba is discovered.'

Marie's face twisted with horror as she whispered to Felim, 'You're telling me to choose between my children.'

Felim straightened, real hope running through him at last.

Peryst's right. This will solve everything. The Reba of before was my beloved child. Today's is a monster. But she carries my blood, and I'd struggle to watch her burn, even though I know she should.

It was different for Marie, so he used a soothing tone to voice the platitudes she would understand. 'If we leave, we lose everything, but if we stay, we also lose everything. More, we lose our daughter as well. Whatever we decide, there'll be pain, Marie. There's no good decision here. None.'

'Why? Why did this have to happen to us? What have we done to deserve this?' Marie tilted her face up and pleaded to the god she'd grown up with. 'Why, Ilu? All I've done is work hard! What did I do wrong?'

Peryst laughed mirthlessly. 'Nothing. Things simply happen, Marie. This isn't your doing.'

Marie clutched at Peryst's arm urgently. 'Will you love her like she's yours?'

Peryst smiled softly. 'She is mine, Marie. You are mine, and she is yours, so she is also mine.'

She nodded. 'She can never come back here as my daughter. Never.'

'She won't,' Peryst said. 'She'll be my daughter. None—not even our own mother—will ever know that she's not.'

'And when you have a child of your own, will you still love her?' she asked.

'I'll never have another child,' Peryst replied with an expression of desolation. 'It's not six months since I buried my Sanjia and our newly born twins, also a boy and a girl. They didn't survive childbirth in the wilds. My soulmate is dead, and none other than she will bear a child of mine. Reba will be the daughter I lost.'

Marie nodded curtly.

Shaking his head as he tried to think through the confusion of hope and horror that flooded his spirit, Felim turned to Marie. *I can't leave my home. I won't. So, the only solution is to give away Reba.*

He remembered the night of their birth: both tiny and squalling, squirming with life. He thought of Raf. The idea of him floating above his sister made his stomach cramp with terror.

How can my beautiful Reba suddenly be a monster? How did she become this terrifying creature? How is she no longer the daughter I adored? Or is she still? There has to be a way to stop it, to turn things back. To erase the last few weeks.

'No. Wait, Marie! Wait! We must think about this. There must be a way to cleanse Reba.'

'No, Felim. There's nothing to think about. And no way to change what we have. What else can we do? We can't leave, so we have only two options. With one, both of our children live and have the chance to thrive, each in their own way. With the other, one will die, and the other will live a life of poverty and shame.' Marie's expression was empty of emotion, and her voice was wooden. None of the warmth that usually suffused her face was there, as if she had been made of glass manufactured in their workshop. 'Can't you see that there's no choice?'

Nothing will ever be the same again. Will Marie ever forgive me for not abandoning everything I've fought so hard for? Will she ever forgive me for forcing her to choose between our children?

They would never dare to have another child. And everywhere they would glimpse Reba's shadow. Every waking hour they'd know that they'd sacrificed one child for the other. That they'd chosen the life they had over Reba. That *he* had chosen his land over Reba.

Can anyone survive such a decision? Can we?

'I'll pack her things for you tonight and explain her care. You'll leave come morning, Peryst,' Marie said.

'Wait!' Felim said, holding her by the arms, trying to stop time, trying to reverse it all in his mind to before the fair, to when they'd had two normal children, to when they'd been happy. 'Wait, Marie. This is too sudden. It's too much.' His voice shook.

'The Guardians come in two weeks, and in two days the glassworkers will return. I can't bar the doors to the house forever,' Marie said. 'We can pack up everything and leave with Peryst or give Reba to him. There are no more options.'

'We can't leave. You know we can't, but we can make up an excuse. You can be ill. I can be ill. The children can be contagious!'

'For how long? No, Felim, they'll come as usual and will find that I've lost weight and am pale and wan.' He started to protest, but she waved him down. 'It'll be consistent with a first-time mother who has lost one of her children.'

Felim gasped out a reply. 'Lost? How?'

'I've cried alone for two weeks, Felim. I'd resigned myself to losing my child to the Hand of Reason's flames. And now I have the chance of saving them both and giving each the life they deserve. How can I not take that chance? During your absence, I let it be known that the children were ill. Reba, despite my knowledge of herbs and cures, won't have survived. Raf will be unsettled at her absence and so will seem like a child recovering from the same illness that took his sister,' Marie said flatly. 'You will have come home from Belfane to find this horror and will have helped bury our daughter where the orchard used to be.'

Felim struggled to grasp how their lives could change so quickly, how his child was no longer the child he knew, and how they were faced with impossible choices. His mind had been so clear when he was angry, but now, faced with his wife's implacability, he could barely think. 'There must be another way.'

'We lose Reba, your ancestral lands, and all we've worked for, and condemn Raf to squalor, or we run away, exiling ourselves, and you lose what's most important to you,' Marie said bluntly.

He chose to ignore the accusation in her voice and said wearily, 'We'll dig the grave tomorrow once Peryst has gone. And we'll mourn and remember Reba as the beloved daughter we lost so young.'

'Raf will forget he had a sister, and he'll never know the truth,' she whispered and then, as if the cord that had been holding her gave way, she lay her head on Felim's lap and sobbed uncontrollably as he held her and muttered words that wouldn't comfort her. No words would comfort her now. Or ever, he realised.

Early the next morning, Marie packed two waxed cotton bags of her own milk, dried and then powdered in preparation for the following winter. She explained that Peryst would need to boil water to mix with the powder before Reba could drink from the glass feeding bottle. 'Infants sicken from dirty bottles, so boil the bottle to clean it.'

'I will.'

'Reba's never had anything other than milk. When you run out of the powder, you can start to mash food for her.'

Marie gave Peryst so many instructions, rules, and care tips that Peryst told her he was feeling faint. She packed innumerable cloth squares for changing the baby, ointments for face, hands, and bottom, herbs for ailments, and all the clothes she could fit in Peryst's saddlebags. She taught him to change her and to strap Reba to his chest with a long stretch of material. She had him strap and unstrap the child ten times before she considered his efforts acceptable.

Finally, when Peryst was mounted on Roan with Reba strapped to his chest, Marie removed the green glass jewel that Felim had given her the day of their nuptials and that she'd worn since then. She passed it to her brother. 'Give it to her when she's old enough. Tell her that her mother loved her with all her soul and that the green glass holds all that love.'

Peryst bowed his head as he stored the jewel. 'I will. She'll be loved by me as if by you, Marie. Never fear for her if I live.'

Through tears, Marie smiled. 'I won't.'

Felim held Marie and Raf as they watched Peryst ride out of sight with the wolf running alongside. Then, filled with relief he would never admit to his heartbroken wife, Felim took a spade as Marie collected anything of Reba's that was left. They chose a spot far from house where there were a couple of very old twisted and bent apple trees that still faithfully produced a half-basket of fruit every summer. Between the trees, he dug a deep hole into which he placed all of Reba's remaining belongings. He covered the hole with a tidy mound on which Marie placed a bouquet of glass flowers she'd made when she was expecting the twins. Felim would make a glass headstone once the workshop was up and running again. It would say *Reba. Ever in our Memory.*

REOR

YEAR 5161 OF THE NEW ERA – SUMMER

PERYST HAD POURED over Felim's maps the night before leaving. Though he had spoken of going north, his true aim was to reach the southern border as soon as possible. While still in Reor, both he and Reba would be in danger, so he'd avoid villages and settlements till he was well versed in caring for his new daughter. He rode down the lane and veered left once out of view of Marie and Felim's house. Instead of heading east, he went towards southern Mehru, where he would complete the painful errand of communicating his wife's death to her father in Lis. He hadn't thought beyond that.

Peryst calculated four weeks of riding hard to the border with Mehru but knew the trip would probably take longer because Reba would need time off his chest.

As he rode, he thought briefly of the tiny babies he had wrapped so tenderly and carefully before placing them in his beloved Sanjia's arms when laying them all to rest in the southern cliffs of northern Usur: those children he had lost before they'd even drawn a first cry. The pain took his breath away, as always, and he tried with everything he had to dull it by conjuring other, happier memories of Sanjia. He was unable to do so and could only see her pale, pained face as she slowly died in a pool of blood while he was helpless to save her. And suddenly, he was beset by anger towards his sister. She had let her daughter go; she had not fought for the child who lay on his chest. Peryst would have done anything—*given anything*—for his two dead babies, but Marie hadn't for this one who lived. She'd given in to her husband instead of fighting like a wolf for both her children.

Peryst sighed, wiping a hand over his face as the memory of Marie's stricken expression and shaking hands came to him. He was being unfair. Marie had done what she could. Giving him her daughter was her way of fighting for her child, and he knew the decision would haunt her. It had to. It would have haunted him.

He spoke down to Nela, who walked calmly by Roan, her pads barely making a sound. 'What shall we call her, Nela? You and I are giving this girl a new life. Reba's dead, like Sanjia and the babies. So who, then, is this to share in our wanderings?'

Nela kept walking impassively but made a sound like a purr deep in her throat.

Peryst smiled tenderly and peered at the little face fast asleep against his chest: curly dark hair like his own and golden-brown skin that reminded him of Sanjia's but was the product of the mix of Felim's darker Reordan skin and Marie's lighter Klaevani. The small, straight nose and determined chin were also like his and Marie's, as were the bright eyes of the unusual shade of green they owed to their Glannafel ancestry.

'Who will you become, little one? Who will you be, my daughter?'

My daughter. The words sounded easy on his tongue. As if they belonged there.

This child was bringing him out of the daze in which he had existed—not lived—since Sanjia's passing. Barely eating or drinking, he had wandered aimlessly through northern Usur in a living nightmare. With hindsight, he knew that if the dream hadn't come, he would've succumbed on a mountainside and let himself be taken by hunger, thirst, or wild animals to wherever it was his Sanjia dwelt. The dream—a whisper of his mother's power in which sometimes a dream told a truth—beset him almost three months earlier when he'd all but given up as he sat against a rock, covered in dirt, gaunt and feeble from lack of sustenance. He'd heard Marie crying. He'd seen her fear and despair. And he'd seen more: the Hand of Reason taking a baby from her mother's arms as Marie fought and screamed. He'd seen his sister slapped away and then humiliated and hungry, another baby in rags, Felim's lands appropriated, and the family begging their way along Reordan streets as doors slammed in their faces. He'd seen a baby girl, like his daughter, set on a pyre by cloaked strangers. The child's wails and her terrified green eyes, like his own, had woken him up. Peryst had been unable to save his own daughter, but he could save Marie's. He *would* save Marie's daughter from the Hand of Reason.

Without any other thought, he'd begun the journey southwards. He'd cleaned himself up along the way, growing stronger with every step he took towards his new purpose. Peryst had known full well what he would find when he reached Lost Corner with Felim and knew what he would say. He'd spent the weeks it took to reach Belfane thinking of what he would do. And now Reba was his daughter. He vowed there and then that he would never again think of her as anything other than that: she was his daughter, and only his.

Whimpering, Reba stirred against his chest and then woke hungry, uncomfortable, and cross.

'Shhh, little one. We'll stop soon. There should be a stream ahead.'

Reba squirmed and cried, a high-pitched wail of confusion that terrified Peryst. He realised that she wouldn't recognise this new world without her brother and the usual wood and glass toys hanging above her. She was constrained, wet, and hungry, and her cries grew, as did Peryst's alarm.

'I know, I know, little one. You want milk and your mama, but you'll have to be satisfied with me. I'm all you have now. We'll stop soon, and I'll feed you. Shhh.'

Peryst used one large hand to stroke her hair and spurred Roan through the arid plain in the south of Lost Corner with the hope of reaching the ravine he'd seen on Felim's map. Though he had enough boiled water to prepare milk for the baby, he wanted shelter to screen them from strangers as well as stream water to wash her well and clean the bottle afterwards.

Roan's gallop settled the child again, as Peryst had hoped. Knowing it would be short-lived, he sighed in relief when he spotted a slight change in the landscape ahead. The ochre earth and low-growing, grey-green shrubs persisted, but a ribbon of darker green announced the ravine, a deep gully with slightly more vegetation near the trickle of water that snaked through its depths. A poor excuse for a stream, he thought, but better than none. After dismounting, he led his horse carefully down by the stream. The ravine wasn't as deep as it had seemed. He examined the area carefully, searching for tracks and any sign of danger. Once sure that there was no living being other than him, his beasts, and the child, he placed a blanket under a tree by the water and then unstrapped the baby, who woke up again and protested louder than before.

'You are Maia. You have the force of worlds within you, my daughter, or at least in your voice.'

Peryst placed the child on her back on the blanket. Maia ended her cry abruptly and shifted her head from side to side. It amused Peryst to see her surprise at the unfamiliar surroundings. Maia turned her head to stare at the leaves above and at the reeds that swayed near the water. The air was cool, and there were sounds of a light breeze and of water trickling and splashing over rocks. The scents of the wilderness would also be new to her—of green, growing, and life—unlike those of Lost Corner: hot, dry, and of glassmaking fumes.

After three unsuccessful tries during which Maia squirmed and grumbled, Peryst managed to change her competently enough, he thought, after washing her carefully and covering her in the ointment Marie had given him. But he was always alert to unknown sounds and danger. He then washed the soiled cotton square in the stream and hung it to dry on a pair of sticks. He set a small fire to boil more water to take with him, waving his hands over it to make sure that the smoke dispersed before it rose enough to be spotted from afar. Then he carefully mixed the milk powder with the water he'd carried from Lost Corner. Everything arranged, Peryst sat with his back against the tree and Maia nestled into his strong arm, with his sword at hand just in case. He fed her from one of the glass bottles Marie had packed. She'd never drunk from such a contraption before, but hunger gave her enough of an impulse to figure out how it was done.

Once sated, she lay on her back, one hand grasping Nela's ear as the wolf lay by her, head on paws but alert, while Peryst cleaned the bottle and then boiled water so he could cool, pack, and take it for later feedings. He shared with Nela the supplies his sister had packed and wondered how his hunting reflexes would change with a child strapped to his chest.

Peryst was warmed by the sight of Maia waving her fingers and making the leaves above rustle and twist while still holding tight onto Nela, who nuzzled her gently.

Nela had been Sanjia's, a year-old wolf hand-reared from a pup. She had howled mournfully during Sanjia's endless labour and, like Peryst, hadn't eaten for days after he buried his wife and children. Nela, however, had recovered first. Following what Sanjia would surely have wished, in the darkest moments it was Nela who had protected him, weak and despairing as he was, from wild animals; it was Nela who had nudged him to find streams, who had brought dead animals and scraps of food to him. Nela had kept Peryst alive till the dream came and woke him. And now, Peryst saw, Nela had discovered a new mistress in Maia.

'Maia,' Peryst said. The child ignored him. 'Maia,' Peryst said again, crouching and gently turning the baby's head. He smiled at her and repeated the name, 'Maia.' The baby gazed at him, bewildered, and then back at the twirling leaves.

'Maia,' Peryst said again, gently turning her face back to his. He needed her to answer to the name before they encountered anyone. 'Maia.' He repeated the name over and over till, out of understanding or frustration, the baby responded. Each time she did, Peryst blew her neck, tickled her, or otherwise made her giggle.

He changed her once more and packed everything back into Roan's saddlebags. He hated the idea of strapping her to stare at his chest again. It took some time, but he manipulated the cloth till he managed to securely strap her facing forwards.

'You shall see the world with me, Maia. We'll make our way to Klaevan the long way. You'll see everything I see, and I'll teach you everything I know. You'll speak every language in Ankisua, as I do, and learn every culture and custom, as is the Klaevani way, because you are my daughter.'

Peryst led Roan and Nela across the stream and up the other side of the ravine. Beneath the early afternoon summer sun, they set off in the direction of the southern forests where the border with Mehru was blurred amongst the barely visible trees.

As they went further south, dry flatlands gave way to rich reds and browns, soft green grass mounds, and taller trees, making hunting easier and giving him more cover from prying eyes.

Peryst soon realised that the trip would take much longer than his planned four weeks. He needed to stop every five to six hours, if not more often, and give Maia time to roll on the blanket. His water supplies needed replenishing much sooner than expected, and it took time to boil and then cool the water for storing. He ran out of his own supplies by the third day and had to hunt with Maia strapped to his chest. The first couple of tries ended in failure when Maia squealed in excitement at the sight of a rabbit or wild goat, but Peryst, with smiles and coaxing, taught her to be silent till the deed was done. He struggled changing her and despaired when she cried for no reason he could fathom.

I'm a monster hunter, a soldier, and a talented Touched. That's what I know. I've never been a father. I've never cared for a child. My only experience of fatherhood was burying my children. How can I care for this child? He lay awake, afraid to sleep in case danger beset them, worried about all he was doing wrong. Exhausted, he wondered if he'd made the right decision. *Will I be able to fulfil my promise to Marie? Will I be able to give Maia the life she deserves?*

YEAR 5161 OF THE NEW ERA – AUTUMN

After six weeks of travel, Peryst was feeling more competent and had developed a rough routine. Leaving Nela to watch for danger, he learnt to sleep lightly at the times when Maia slumbered as well. But he stirred at the least sound, never resting fully. The few hours of sleep provided him with enough energy to function and made him feel that, maybe, he'd be able to become the father that Maia needed.

A few days from the border, so much later in the year than he'd expected, and already well into autumn, he came across an unexpected spring in a light grove littered by fallen leaves and settled near the water but just outside the trees. Maia fed well and managed to pull herself up on hands and knees on the blanket. She hadn't used any powers in the previous few days and seemed intent on developing her physical prowess. She rocked back and forth on the blanket, babbling and squealing, as Nela lay watching over her.

Peryst, his back to the child, was startled by new sounds coming from Nela—a combination of guttural growls and rough, low, frenzied barking—accompanied by a high-pitched cry from Roan. Reaching for the weapons on the ground beside him, he turned to see Nela poised in front of Maia, jumping and snarling at a creature the likes of which he'd never seen before.

A beast with red-feathered wings stretched to a span twice Peryst's height hovered above silently then swooped down and screeched. Its dull copper body was long and snakelike. It reached for Nela and Maia with two long, clawed paws. The creature's birdlike head moved from side to side as it tried to bypass Nela and grasp at the soft, crying child. Without stopping to think, and barely aiming, Peryst grabbed his bow and shot an arrow straight at the animal's head. He missed, but the creature turned its attention to him. The sound of the flapping wings, the animal's screeches, Nela's growling, and Maia's crying raised an infernal racket, but Peryst heard nothing, concentrating all his attention and power on the arrow and the beast. Still as a rock, he watched the creature turn to him, its long beak open to show a triple row of sharp teeth. He waited till it was flying straight at him before focusing his mind's eye to find the weakness that every living being had. Seeing it was one he could conceivably reach, he aimed straight at the spot in the centre of the animal's brow. The arrow hit true, burying itself halfway up the shaft into the beast's brain. The animal tossed its head, gave a strangled cry, and collapsed to the ground a foot from Peryst in a heap that made the ground shake.

Nela stopped her noise and took to nuzzling Maia as Peryst sprinted towards them. With shaking hands, he examined first the child and then the wolf. He breathed in relief at finding them both unharmed. He held Maia to his chest, whispering words of comfort as he knelt in front of Nela, stroking her and thanking her for protecting his daughter. Then he turned his attention to the creature lying dead on the ground.

'The Alkaid of Ros will give you a bounty for killing it,' a voice said suddenly in Common, the vernacular spoken throughout the continent.

Peryst turned without a word, grabbing again for his bow.

A pudgy, tawny-bearded, ruddy little man walked out from the trees. 'Don't shoot me.' He raised his hands. 'I'm not after eating your child like the previous foe.' He poked at the creature with his shoe. 'Very impressive shot, to be sure. Close and true.'

Without lowering his bow, Peryst growled, 'Who are you and what do you want?'

'Golfen Nimbleknees, at your service.'

The man made a sweeping bow. A halfling from Rohin.

'I merely wish to observe the cockatrice up close. I've never seen one before, and I'd much rather approach a dead one, wouldn't you?'

Peryst frowned and swivelled slowly. He could see nobody else close by, and Nela, though alert, didn't seem overly concerned about Golfen.

'Is that what it is?' Peryst asked. 'I've never seen such a beast myself.'

'They're quite rare,' Golfen said, crouching by the cockatrice's head and opening its beak with a shaking hand. The terror was apparent on his face as he tentatively exposed the three layers of teeth.

'It's dead. It won't bite,' Peryst commented.

Golfen coloured slightly and handled the beast with more confidence. 'This one's been lurking in the area for a few weeks, taking livestock and children. The Alkaid offered a bounty for its head. You'd be entitled to claim it, seeing as you killed it.'

Though coin wouldn't go amiss, Peryst shook his head. 'I'm not from hereabouts and would rather not call any attention to myself.'

Golfen nodded. 'I saw your arrow and would have assumed that.'

Peryst raised an eyebrow.

'I avoid calling attention to myself these days,' Golfen said. 'Though not strictly of the Touched'—he cleared his throat—'like others, in Reor I'm doubly damned. I'm a halfling connected to the Dreaming.'

Halflings had the usual six senses but their mind's eye was fully open from birth. Unlike humans and elves, whose Touched abilities could vary widely, halflings were all dreamwalkers who saw events in their dreams: some trivial and others not so.

'Why doubly?'

'I dabble in potions.' He sighed. 'Not only the healing kind, I'm afraid. The Hand used to tolerate us, but a couple of halfling alchemists I knew were, very sadly, recently toasted.'

'Toasted?'

Golfen frowned at Peryst. 'Burnt. To. A. Crisp. Together with their potions.' He grinned wryly. 'That was a miscalculation on the part of the Defenders, of course, because many were flammable, and some even explosive. The fire spread beyond the green and consumed the town hall.' He chuckled. 'A well-deserved consequence, I thought.'

'This happened in Reor?'

Golfen shrugged. 'Reor or northern Mehru? Who knows which is which these days? It was right on the border in a small hamlet a way to the west,' Golfen replied. 'I'd lived nearby for many years but deemed it was time to move before the Defenders came a-visiting my cottage.'

Peryst picked up Maia and strapped her to his chest carefully as Golfen observed him curiously.

'I've never seen a man carry a baby like that. Where's its mother?' Golfen peered at the nearby shrubbery. Peryst realised he was expecting a woman to jump out of a bush.

'Dead,' he said.

'So sorry. I didn't mean any offence.' Golfen bowed again.

'None taken.'

Peryst rolled up the blanket and placed the last few things in the saddlebags.

Golfen spoke mildly. 'Dour, aren't you? If you're not going to collect the bounty, I'd advise you to do as I will and at least collect feathers, teeth, and some scales. They can be sold for a pretty price beyond the border, in southern Mehru.'

Peryst saw in Golfen's face a recognition of his situation and an inclination to avoid others lest they be sympathetic to the Hand. Reor was now a land of distrust, where strangers were never welcome and even friends were considered with suspicion before being invited to share a hearth.

'Thank you. I didn't know that. What do they use these things for?'

Golfen knelt by the cockatrice's wicked claws and reached to touch its scaled body. With a small, curved knife, he started lifting the iridescent scales with care. 'I'll do the scales. You're strong, so you do the teeth. Here.' He passed Peryst a small set of pliers. 'The teeth and scales are used for potions. The feathers are strong, warm, and waterproof and can be used to fashion garments.'

Peryst shook his head in disbelief as he knelt by the creature's head. He first tried to recover his arrow, but it was wedged into the beast's skull and wouldn't budge. Instead, he decided to follow Golfen's advice and started pulling out teeth, each about as long as his little finger.

'You'll have to take care in this area. I'm small, so, provided they don't have tracker dogs, I can hide easily. But you have a lot with you.' Golfen waved his hand absently at Roan and Nela as he carefully detached scale after iridescent scale into two piles.

'Dogs?' Peryst asked.

'The Hand offers bounties for anyone with more than a hint of power who is brought into any of their border posts. Few are born Touched these days in Reor, and those few tend to be dealt with when discovered at the testing, so young enthusiastic marauders with tracker dogs have turned their attention to the likes of travellers like me. And you, should you come across them. Is the child also Touched?'

'None of your concern.'

'You're right. It is none, but it should be of yours. Any child makes you vulnerable; a Touched child makes you dead.' Golfen moved over to the cockatrice's wings and started plucking the longest and most colourful feathers. Then he started plucking of the shorter feathers. 'You can make a cape with these to protect the child from the rains you'll face later in the year.'

'I'm done here.' Peryst divided the teeth into equal piles and placed one by Golfen. 'It was a pleasure talking to you, but I must get going.'

Golfen jumped to his feet, his head reaching halfway up Peryst's thighs. 'Wait! If you carry on the way you're going, you'll run straight into a band of marauders that's established itself as a border patrol. I know this area very well! I can guide you safely to Mehru. Safety in numbers and all!'

Peryst sighed. He could see in Golfen's beseeching expression that he was trying to convey his trustworthiness. Peryst could deal with bandits, monsters, and soldiers on his own, but he wasn't sure his reflexes would be the same if holding Maia. Without Sanjia, life had lost all value, so he'd been happy to risk everything. But now he had Maia. He was all *she* had, and so he simply couldn't die. He was loathe to add another seemingly helpless being to his care, but if Golfen could really help him avoid meeting patrols he would be an asset. All he wanted was to get out of Reor with Maia as quickly as possible. Once in Mehru, he'd decide what to do. Travelling rough with such a young child was proving far more difficult than he'd expected. And he had only a few more days left of powdered milk!

'So be it,' Peryst said as he took his share of feathers and scales. 'But we leave now.' He hoped that Golfen didn't intend to run along by his side. 'Where's your mount?'

Golfen held two fingers to his lips and let out a low whistle. To Peryst's immense amusement, a saddled goat approached through the trees.

'A goat?' Peryst spluttered.

Hands on hips, Golfen angled his face up at him. 'How would you expect me to mount a horse on my own? And while I'd obviously prefer a crystalhoof, ponies native to the Retan plains are hard to come by in the area, so I make do. To each, his own size.' He patted the goat fondly and then leapt onto its back with alacrity, adding sternly, 'If we're to travel together, I would know the names of my companions.'

'I am Peryst de Arranu, from Klaevan.' He placed a protective hand on Maia. 'This is my daughter, Maia.' He pointed at the wolf. 'Nela, our protector, and I ride my faithful Roan.'

Golfen bowed his head and rubbed a hand over the goat's head. 'Well met. This is Rosie, my goat. We'd been living in a cottage near the River Gyro for a few years now, undisturbed, but given the rise in purges of halflings and Touched discovered nearby, Rosie and I decided not to wait our turn. It seems as if the Hand of Reason constantly needs to remind Reor what happens to those who are Touched. It needs to show them that the Hand never forgets its hatred of power and will stifle it with flames when it can. So, Rosie and I head south to find a boat to take us home to Rohin.'

Peryst tried hard not to laugh at the sight of the well-saddled Rosie but let out a noise somewhere between a cough and a snort.

'Allergies,' he said in answer to Golfen's suspicious gaze.

'Follow me, Peryst de Arranu. I will lead you so that we will meet none who could hurt your child.' He reached up and touched Maia's loose, dangling foot. Worn out by her physical exertions and the cockatrice episode, she'd fallen asleep, her head leaning sideways on Peryst's chest. 'How often do you stop with her?'

'Every five or so hours,' Peryst said. 'Sometimes more often. How long till we cross into Mehru?'

Golfen considered. 'If you were alone, I'd say five days hard riding because we could sneak through the patrols. On the border, the Hand recruits the young and enthusiastic who haven't been given places at the Academy to do their hunting, but that's much to our advantage as passion is no replacement for skill. Given the child, however, we'll need to take a longer way and hopefully be in northern Mehru by two weeks, maybe even three.'

It had been six years since Peryst had last been in Mehru, and memories flooded through his mind. It was in southern Mehru that he first met Sanjia. Though he couldn't bring happy memories to the fore of his mind yet, he longed to be in the white villages of southern Mehru, with their beautiful, singing people. Maybe there he would be able to see Sanjia smiling in his mind again instead of wan and dying.

Golfen gave Peryst a glance. 'How long since you've been in northern Mehru, Peryst de Arranu?'

'Northern? Twelve years or thereabouts,' Peryst replied. 'I've spent most of my time since in southern Mehru and beyond the Kunlan Range.'

Golfen nodded. 'You may not find quite the land you remember, lad.'

'In what way?'

'The reach of the Hand of Reason has grown long in recent years.'

Peryst stopped Roan and turned to stare down at Golfen. 'Six years ago, they were reaching tentatively beyond the border, but I can't believe they've established themselves all over northern Mehru yet. The High Luk wouldn't allow it.'

'Only in the most northern towns, for now. The Hand is like a disease that spreads very slowly, but once it does, it takes hold.'

'In Mehru? Are you sure?' Peryst thought of the Mehru he remembered: friendly villages rich in music and lore and full of respect for the local Mas, every village's wise woman. It was a land where the Touched were always welcomed, where someone like Peryst could earn coin with his powers by killing vicious beasts or simply putting on a light show to delight children. He remembered being in a village in his early days in the South, before he joined the Southern Mehruvian Army, and teaching a boy with seeds of power how to light a candle. He recalled the delight on the lad's face when he figured out how to focus the energy that had arisen inside him and the mother's gratitude as she realised that she would no longer have to deal with accidental fires.

He shook his head. 'Not in Mehru. Not yet.' They had feared this, he and Sanjia. When they were training with the army in Kurbal to learn the methods needed to establish an Idhan in the Southern Mehruvian Army, they'd heard the rumours swirling in the North that the Hand of Reason was spreading and had planned their return to Mehru early.

'Northern Mehru is not what it once was. It's not just the sidelong looks and extensive questioning that us halflings are subjected to, Peryst. Very often, we're asked to leave inns and taverns. The famed Mehruvian welcome is no more on this side of the Ramu as the Reordan Defence has begun recruiting locals into their guards. It's a matter of time before we have squads of Defenders setting up constabularies and Udals replacing the Mehruvian Alkaids.'

'Are you sure you're not confusing it with Reor itself?'

'Northern Mehru is a land that's following the path set out by Reor, where an accident of birth spells disgrace. It started as it did in Reor, and we all know how it evolved for them.' Golfen sighed. 'Reor started by offering solar energy in the form of simple lanterns to northern Mehruvian villages a few years ago. All they asked in exchange was for Guardians of the Hand to be tolerated in their villages.'

'Mehru has always been welcoming to all travellers,' Peryst said, shrugging, wanting to disbelieve that the High Luk's fears had come to pass.

'Yes, but these travellers came bearing the gift of doctrine. The Hand aspires to a world without Touched, and they start by giving away solar lamps and heaters, followed by explaining why a world without the likes of you and me is better for everyone. They've spilled over from Reor, Peryst.'

'Mehru wouldn't fall for that,' Peryst said, thinking of his father-in-law, who took no nonsense but, like his daughter, was cheerful and welcoming with a keen wit.

'You'd be surprised,' Golfen said mildly. 'All they need is for a couple to swallow what they see, and that's enough to divide a village. Soon neighbour is suspicious of neighbour, child is suspicious of father, and then they convince someone with authority—maybe the Alkaid or perhaps the head of the local guards—and the stage is set for the Hand. The whole of Mehru will fall, as Reor did. It's simply a matter of time before the fear that thrives in Reor covers the South as well.'

'They're so clever in their approach. Loathsome, but clever,' Peryst said, spurring Roan to keep up with the goat, which was surprisingly swift.

'Very,' Golfen agreed. 'Many villages by the Reordan border in northern Mehru are very nearly under the Hand's complete sway, though they don't quite realise it yet. Some are closer than others.'

Peryst touched the sleeping Maia's damp hair, which was plastered to her head. 'I should have gone north,' he said quietly.

'It's the same everywhere, Peryst. Now that the Hand is completely established in Reor and with new, more ambitious leaders, their fingers are stretching out in every direction. I've heard there are already Defenders in southern Usur and that they'll start testing infants in Gyllia next year. That should tell you how entrenched they've become. So, the best you can do is make your way to Lis without calling attention to yourself and find a boat to take you north, beyond the mountains, where the Hand cannot reach.' Golfen paused. 'Yet.'

'Easier said than done when I carry a baby strapped to my chest and am running out of milk,' Peryst grumbled.

Ros

YEAR 5161 OF THE NEW ERA – AUTUMN

THOUGH PERYST HAD not really believed Golfen, the reality of his words hit him upon crossing the northern arch into the white-washed town of Ros at sundown on their third week together.

'What business in Ros, foreigners?'

Two armed guards with suspicion written all over their faces and with the insignia of the Hand of Reason on their chests and sleeves—a hand holding a solar torch—barred their way into the village. As Golfen had said, they weren't Defenders but local Mehruvians who were taking on the Hand's mantle.

'None. We're passing through on our way to Lis,' Peryst answered mildly in Mehruvian, 'and have been craving the legendary Mehruvian welcome after many days in the wilderness.'

'We've grown careful with our welcomes, foreigner. Not all who come to Ros have its best interests at heart. Do you?'

Peryst smiled easily, but inside his stomach tightened. 'I've long been a friend of Mehru. My late wife was one of you, and so my child is one of you. Mehru has been in my memories throughout my travels. We only seek accommodation for the night and to replenish our supplies. We'll be on our way by daybreak.'

The guards shared a glance. Peryst knew that unless they were Touched themselves, they'd have no way of telling a traveller's nature, but that anyone coming from the direction of Reor would probably be suspected of being a fugitive from the Hand. One of them fixed his gaze on Golfen and spoke after waiting a beat. 'The Waning Light Inn takes in travellers of all kinds. They're by the southern arch. You won't find accommodation elsewhere.'

Peryst hid his shock, resisted the impulse to reply that it was the legendary Mehruvian welcome that was like a waning light, and simply nodded in thanks. With a quick gesture at Golfen, he spurred Roan down the road to the town's southern side, thinking that it had been a mistake to even enter. But he had no option. He needed more milk for Maia.

Ros hadn't changed physically since he'd last passed through so many years earlier, but it had a different feeling. The Ros he remembered was, like most Mehruvian towns and villages, surrounded by low walls with white arches marking the four cardinal points. Set in the shape of a cross, the main roads led north to south and east to west and were lined with white buildings with domed terracotta roofs that gleamed in the setting sun. Front doors had stood open and life was lived outside, children were brought up by the community, the elderly were cared for by all, and joys and heartbreaks were shared on street corners.

The central green, where the four roads met and where each corner held one of the main town buildings—the town hall, from where the Alkaid governed; the guard house, where the Ros Guard had its headquarters; the Temple of Gal, devoted to the goddess worshipped in Mehru; and the Ros emporium, the trading centre—was unrecognisable. The temple was closed, its door and windows barred, and the emporium was empty. People walked with purpose, looking down, with few lingering to talk to others. Though Peryst and Golfen saw sidelong and quickly masked glances of curiosity, no one called out greetings or asked for news from outside; instead, they got out of the travellers' way and avoided catching their gaze.

Peryst and Golfen rode in silence; Peryst in the silence of disbelief, and he recognised in Golfen the silence of fear.

The Waning Light Inn was a small, three-storey building under the southern arch's shadow. Its walls were thick, and sunken rounded windows were protected by shutters stained a faded red. The front door, of the same colour, was open as Ros's doors had been in days past. Above the door, a guttering candle shone from a wrought-iron lamp and illuminated the name of the inn carved into a faded wooden sign that swung slowly, creaking.

After dismounting, Peryst went in, leaving Golfen with their mounts. Inside, it was dark, so it took Peryst a moment to be able to see the empty wooden tables covered in a layer of dust, an unlit fire, unlit candles in candle holders peppered round the room, and a narrow staircase at the back. The only other door was a swinging, stable-like door behind a narrow, empty bar. The glasses that hung above it, like almost everything else in the room, were also dusty.

'Hello,' Peryst called out. 'Is there anybody here?'

'Do my ears deceive me? Have the heavens sent me guests to warm my beds or yet another fool coming to try and convince me to use unnatural lighting or sell my vineyard?'

A tall, grey-haired, and very thin woman stalked out of the swinging door and studied Peryst, hands on hips. 'You're not a Guardian of the Hand, unless they've expanded their recruiting to large, baby-carrying brutes.'

'You were expecting a Guardian?'

'All the gods protect me! No, a thousand times, no! But some come a-calling regularly, as does the Alkaid.'

'No doubt they're friendly people.'

The woman snorted and studied Peryst with interest. 'Who would you be, and what do you want in my humble establishment?'

Peryst bowed. 'Peryst de Arranu, at your service. I am passing through Ros with a travelling companion from Rohin and my daughter. We have two'—Peryst paused, wondering how to define Rosie—'mounts that need care for the night and a wolf. We would also be grateful for beds and any food you could provide for the rest of our journey, particularly for my child.'

The woman shook her head. 'Guests! Who would've thought? Haven't had guests in months. If I'd known you were coming, I'd have dusted this room.'

She turned back to the swinging door, yelling, 'Metis!'

A slow-moving hulk of a man with hair growing low on his forehead and a blank expression came out. The woman spoke to him gently. 'Metis, this man has two horses and a wolf outside—'

Peryst cleared his throat. 'One horse and one goat.'

The corner of the woman's mouth quirked but she carried on without comment. 'A horse and a goat, Metis. You're to take them to the back and make them comfortable. Brush them down and feed them well.'

The man's inexpressive face transformed, and he nodded enthusiastically. Peryst followed him out to remove his saddlebags and call Golfen and Nela into the inn. The huge man approached the animals carefully, joy apparent in his expression. He started at a respectful distance, placing his hands out, and slowly came closer, making animal noises and stroking first the horse and then the goat.

'Metis has sorely missed having animals to care for. I took him in as a young child when I discovered him wandering the wilderness. He cannot speak. Who knows where he'd been or what had been done to him. Animals are his only joy. He'll care for yours better than I'll care for you.'

Golfen bowed grandly. 'Mistress Innkeeper, Golfen Nimbleknees at your service. Any care we receive shall be met with gratitude.'

The innkeeper grinned down at him. 'Amanda Callaman, at yours.'

She held open the door. 'Come inside. It's not a good idea to talk outside these days.' She peered up and down the wide and empty street and led them back into the dark room before bolting the front door securely behind them. Peryst again tried to adjust to the dark as Amanda took a rag from under the bar and started dusting swiftly, lighting candles as she went. The gloomy place was transformed into a warm wood-panelled room of some charm. Peryst found it easy to imagine it as a cheerful tavern full of patrons.

'I've been more diligent in keeping the beds aired and rooms clean upstairs.' She knelt by the hearth and set a fire going. 'I'll take you to your chambers and have Metis bring hot water and logs for your upstairs fireplaces once he's finished with the animals. It's proving a chillier autumn than usual.'

'Thank you, most gracious mistress.' Golfen bowed his head as he and Peryst followed her to the rickety, narrow stairs in the back of the room.

Amanda chattered as they climbed. 'It's been a long time since anyone stopped in Ros. Most want to get through to southern Mehru as quickly as they can.'

'Why is that?' Peryst asked.

'The Hand's been tightening their hold in the area.' She grimaced.

'As in many places,' Golfen said.

'Indeed.' Amanda raised her bony shoulders in a shrug and shook her head, then stopped on the stairs and turned back to face them. 'They start slow, bringing us lanterns to replace candles, cooking ranges, constant running hot water, all things that make life easier and more comfortable. Then, they start spreading rumours, making everyone afraid. First, they forced out our Alkaid and then stories began rolling six or so years ago about how the Mas in some town north of the border had been poisoning people with one hand only to charge for curing them with the other. How someone using powers caused disease in locals. How some Touched had taken his neighbour's lands with his power. All silly stuff with no names and no evidence, but repeated often enough it got less silly.'

Golfen nodded and mouthed *I told you* to Peryst.

'What happened?' Peryst asked.

'People stoned our Mas and her partner, who wasn't even Touched. They fled with their adopted daughter after the people they'd known all their lives burnt their belongings on the green.'

'Lucky it wasn't them that burnt,' Golfen said.

Amanda smiled sadly. 'Lucky indeed as further to the west, in Gyllia and villages nearby, the Mases have not been so fortunate. Ours fled, bloodied but alive. After that, most of our Touched followed her to the forest, but three refused to leave. Ros was their home, and they couldn't believe that friends and neighbours would turn on them.'

'Surprise, surprise,' Golfen intervened with bitterness.

'Indeed,' Amanda said. 'We were all forced to watch them burn.' She sighed heavily. 'Good thing I'm short and stood in the back, but despite not being able to see, I could hear and smell enough, and I won't forget either in a hurry. There are no Touched in Ros now, and none with even a snippet of power will admit to it.'

'Yet you don't use Reor's lanterns,' Peryst said.

Amanda frowned. 'No. I won't accept the Hand or their inventions. We never had Reor's power struggles. Small a town as we are, we did well. See us now!' She stamped her foot on the stair. 'Our Alkaid, a mild-minded woman, fair above all, fled after they almost killed her daughter, Touched like her. Now we have a lackey of the Hand, like the Udals of Reor.' She spat in disgust. 'Even the joy of Gal has left Ros since they closed the temple and forbade worship.'

Peryst had always admired Mehru's belief in Gal. Mehruvians believed Gal had made the world by a happy accident and had given it to its inhabitants with no strings attached. Gal set no rules and made no demands. That, Mehruvians thought, was for people, not for Gal.

Amanda continued climbing the stairs and speaking over her shoulder. 'From what I hear, towns to the east are still resisting, led by the Alkaids and Guards of Leyandale and Min. Those to the west, however, are exceedingly like Ros.'

She came to a stop by two doors facing each other. 'The one on the left is for you, Master Golfen. The one on the right for you and your daughter, Master Peryst. I have a cot somewhere. Metis will bring it for you.' She passed a gentle hand over sleeping Maia's head. 'Where is the child's mother?'

'Dead,' Peryst said. 'I travel to deliver the sad news to my father-in-law and introduce him to his granddaughter.'

'The child is a daughter of Mehru?'

'She is.'

Amanda frowned. 'But you are not. Some up here will think that a daughter of Mehru should remain in Mehru. You shouldn't share that information lightly.'

Maia woke suddenly, hungry, wet, and wailing.

'No, no, little one,' Amanda crooned as Peryst removed her from his chest strapping. 'Here, give her to me while you prepare her things.'

Amanda rocked the child against her shoulder. 'It's all right, little one.'

Peryst took Maia and changed her swiftly and competently. Then he sat her on the floor against one of his bags. More comfortable, the child inspected the room in interest as Peryst prepared her milk.

'You still feed her milk?' Amanda asked, picking up and examining the cotton bag where little of the powder was left.

'Yes. I know she needs to start on food, but we've been in the wilds, and it's been difficult to prepare anything other than this. And I'm running low on milk as it is. I have only one more cotton bag left.'

Amanda put down the bag. 'Give her that. I'll see what I can find downstairs. A growing child needs more than milk.'

Maia drank her milk urgently and furrowed her brow so like his own when finished that Peryst couldn't help laughing. As he considered preparing another bottle, Amanda returned.

'Bring the hungry one downstairs, Master Peryst. In the meantime, Metis will carry up hot water and the cot.'

Amanda had set a bowl and small spoon on a table in the front room by the roaring fire. She took Maia from Peryst and sat her on a chair. With a length of cloth, she secured the child so she wouldn't fall. Then she draped her in a further length of cloth.

Placing a third length of fabric over her own lap, she explained, 'Feeding a young one is messy business.'

'What's in the bowl?' Peryst asked, suspicious of the beige puree.

'It's a biscuit dissolved in water. Our Mas used to prepare them for infants. They contain everything a growing baby needs, according to the Mas. I have yet to find one who doesn't like them.'

Maia confirmed Amanda's words, messily gobbling each spoonful and leaning forwards with her little mouth open, begging for more. Peryst thought the guilt at the child's obvious hunger would suffocate him.

I haven't been caring for her as I should. Am I a bad father? What else have I done wrong? What else will I do wrong? Am I making the right decisions by Maia? Will I? Will I be the father she needs?

Amanda spoke quietly, seemingly sensing his dark thoughts. 'It's difficult for someone to raise a child on their own. This is why we live in communities, so that family and friends can help when needed. You've done very well by your daughter so far, Peryst de Arranu. She's strong, alert, and healthy, but now she needs more.'

Peryst nodded curtly, dismissing his fears for now. 'Where can I get more of those biscuits?'

Turning to him, Amanda sighed and put the spoon down. 'You can't get any fresh ones. I already told you about our Mas. But I have some of her stock stashed away. I'll give you that, and with the milk you still have, you will—' She stopped abruptly as she watched a gust of air raise the spoon from the bowl.

'Maia!' Peryst spoke sharply. He grabbed the spoon and placed it back in the bowl.

Maia puckered her face and whimpered.

'We do not do that, Maia,' Peryst said firmly.

Amanda turned from father to daughter. 'She's Touched,' she said quietly.

Peryst lurched defensively towards Maia as Nela leapt up growling, but Amanda placed a calming hand on his arm.

'Stop, you'll upset the child and the wolf further.' Amanda took up the spoon and carried on feeding Maia as if nothing had happened. She spoke in a normal, calm tone. 'I was saying that with your stock of milk and the biscuits I can give you, there'll be enough till you reach your father-in-law.'

Peryst didn't reply but, like Nela, remained on full alert.

'I had meant to tell you to stay till you mastered the art of the new food, but that's no longer a wise course of action. I don't interact with my neighbours much, but they all know I'm critical of the Hand. Your daughter is too young and will use her gift to satisfy her needs or whims as most babies do. It will be dangerous for her here.'

Peryst nodded wearily as he sat back down. 'I know.'

'I'll watch her while you do your ablutions. Bring down whatever needs washing. It'll soak as you and Master Golfen eat then dry overnight in front of the fire. You'll enjoy a good meal.' She winked at him with a wide grin. 'And sleep in a bed, probably for the first time in months.'

Peryst rubbed the back of his neck. 'I've forgotten what a mattress feels like.'

'If I were a few years younger, Peryst de Arranu, I would help you remember, but those days are sadly past. While you sleep, I'll pack food for this young one and whatever provisions I can spare for you and Golfen. You leave tomorrow at dawn.'

Peryst felt himself redden as Nela pushed her head under Amanda's arm and rubbed her head against the woman's chest.

'Thank you, Mistress Amanda, for your words and generosity.'

Amanda shook her head. 'Bah. Mehru has been known for its hospitality for generations. I will not let Reordans break that.'

'What softness of mattress, what bliss of hot water, what an establishment, what glory to the owner!' Golfen declaimed from the top of the stairs and, after he descended, finished with a deep bow aimed at Amanda. 'I see the princess feels as I do,' he added, observing Maia's clear enjoyment of the food.

'Go! Clean yourself and bring down all that needs washing. I have a tub in the back. Metis will help.' At Peryst's hesitation, she added, 'Your daughter will be safe. The wolf and Master Golfen will undoubtedly make sure of it.'

Peryst passed his big hand over Maia's small head of dark curls, avoiding the mess of her face, and climbed the stairs. Removing the leather cuirass and trousers he'd worn since he crossed into Reor was blissful indeed, and the hot water added to the pleasure. He washed thoroughly, shaved, and discarded the clothes he'd worn for weeks, vowing to do the same for Maia. Dressed in a clean white shirt and his only other pair of trousers, he set the fire going in his room and cracked the window open slightly before he made his way down the stairs with his and a bundle of Maia's soiled clothes.

Maia sat against cushions on the floor in front of the fireplace playing with Nela and an articulated wooden toy in the shape of a dragon. She waved her arms and babbled when she saw Peryst.

Golfen, from his comfortable position by the fire, smiled beatifically. 'I've been left on princess duty. Our lady, Mistress Amanda, left message that you take all that through the door behind the bar.'

Peryst crouched by his daughter. 'I'll be back soon, little one.'

He pushed the swing door with his shoulder and walked into a large, well-scrubbed kitchen where another fire roared.

Amanda faced a brick stove, occasionally stirring a heavy pot and giving instructions over her shoulder to Metis, who stood at a door open to the back of the inn. 'Bring a further basin of water in here for the child and pour the used water from upstairs onto the vegetable patch.'

Metis filled a basin, laid it in front of the hearth, and went past Peryst as Amanda noticed him waiting with a pile of clothes. She laughed deeply. 'You make a lovely domestic picture. Put it all in that tub.' She pointed at a large tub of water sitting above the fire.

As Peryst placed the garments in the water, he caught a strong whiff of herbs rising in the steam.

'Another recommendation of our Mas. The combination of herbs cleans clothes well, leaving them stain free and lightly scented without the need to scrub. After you bathe the child, bring the rest of her clothes to soak, too,' Amanda instructed. 'Metis will hang it all to dry overnight so that you can take it tomorrow morning.'

He took the basin filled with herb-infused water and then Maia upstairs and bathed her. She gurgled and splashed joyously as he sponged her. Peryst carried her, clean and rosy, back downstairs and set her on the rug in front of the fireplace before going into the kitchen to drop the remainder of the clothes in the tub.

Amanda ladled a thick and hearty soup with chunks of meat into deep bowls.

'If I'd known you were coming, I'd have made something fancier, but at least the wine will be of good vintage. Take that bottle, Master Peryst. It's one of the last made from my vineyard.' She pointed at a dusty brown bottle on a shelf above the cooker. 'Maia ate half a biscuit. I suspect you'll be able to feed her that amount and milk for a few weeks, but her hunger will grow as she does. The biscuits will do for her till she can chew. Our Mas insisted that infants needed a varied diet, so if you come across fruit, mash it for her and add it to her meals.'

Peryst spoke gravely. 'I am truly grateful for your help and advice, Mistress Amanda.'

Amanda smiled sadly. 'It's been a pleasure, Master Peryst. It's too long since I've had anyone other than Metis to care for.'

She placed the bowls and a loaf of bread on a wooden tray and then added a meaty bone. 'Your faithful wolf will feast as well and have a warm hearth to sleep on.' Amanda smiled and gestured at the door with her chin. Peryst obediently held it open as Amanda sailed through to the table closest to the fire, where she set down the tray to place the two bowls opposite each other.

'Will you not join us in our meal, Mistress Amanda?' Peryst asked politely.

Amanda placed the bone in front of Nela, who sat by Maia, and turned to the counter for three thick glasses. 'I will join you for a glass of wine but will eat later with Metis.' She smiled down at Maia, whose drowsiness mirrored Golfen's. He was sprawled on the chair with his ruddy face and ginger hair even redder by the firelight.

Peryst turned to Golfen. 'I'll be leaving tomorrow morning, Golfen. You're welcome to carry on with me, or not, as you see fit.'

Golfen started abruptly. 'What was that? Leaving tomorrow? We should rest a few days before starting again! The princess likes it here.' He gestured at Maia, who'd fallen asleep against the cushions.

'It's because of Maia that I'm leaving, Golfen,' Peryst replied quietly.

Golfen opened his mouth and closed it again. 'I see.'

Amanda took a sip of the wine. 'This is good wine, though I say it myself. Made from my own grapes.'

Peryst tasted his and sighed contentedly. 'It is excellent wine, as is the food.'

As they ate, Amanda spoke quietly. 'There are no halflings in Ros, Master Golfen. There were a couple of alchemists and potion makers who would assist our Mas. They left even before she did, following the warnings of their dreams.' She sighed. 'My days here are numbered as well. For now, I won't leave. Everyone knows that Metis and I have no powers. I secretly help people flee under cover of darkness. So far, they've left me alone, but my lands are good, my vines yield well, and my inn has been profitable in the past. I see the greed in the Alkaid every time he comes by.'

'What do you mean?' Golfen asked between bites.

'That the time will come when I'll be accused of some trifle against the Hand. They'll confiscate my lands and send me into exile if I'm lucky. If not, I'll be dead, and the Hand will take all I have.'

Peryst put down his spoon. 'Come with us, then. Come to Lis. I don't know what welcome I'll find with Sanjia's father given that I bring him the worst news a father may hear and a letter with his daughter's last wishes, but I cannot imagine southern Mehru ever willingly siding with the Hand.'

Amanda smiled sadly. 'That is a kind offer, Peryst de Arranu, and maybe once I would have dropped everything and followed you on your travels as I'm sure your Sanjia did, but I have Metis to care for, and I love my lands. I'll resist as long as I can, and only when I see no hope will I go.' She seemed haunted for a moment. 'I was born in this house, as my mother before me, and my grandmother before her. This house has belonged to a Callaman woman since it was built, and I'm the last of them.'

Peryst had a fleeting memory of Felim talking about Lost Corner and his family's lands with the same fervour and sense of ownership. He had no such feeling for any parcel of earth. Like most Klaevani, he roamed, always adapting to new ways and never clinging to one place. He believed land was the realm of Ilu, god of earth, sky, and water, never to be owned by anyone but merely to be used for a time before moving on. People were another matter. As he'd told Felim, to him, like to all Klaevani, people, blood, and his clan were his home. Lands could change, but family was forever.

He glanced down at the slumbering Maia, knowing that she would have no lands to call her own but a wealth of humans to call upon should she ever need to do so.

Amanda caught his look and misinterpreted its meaning. 'If you're done with the meal, you should take her up and get some rest yourselves even if it's still early. You'll need to be gone before a delegation from the town hall arrives to ask about your intentions in Mehru.'

Peryst nodded and collected his and Golfen's bowls.

'Leave them there, Master Peryst, and care for your child. Metis will have left a cot in your room. She, too, will have the luxury of a mattress.'

Peryst bowed his head. 'I am grateful.'

'To bed with you! And to sleep! You may feel regret or relief that I am not younger,' she said with a saucy grin that made her lined face seem decades younger.

'Regret, always regret,' Peryst replied gallantly with a bow before crouching to pick up Maia, whose little hands tightly clasped the wooden dragon's tail.

'Take the dragon with you,' said Amanda softly. 'She likes it.'

He nodded and climbed the stairs with the sleeping child, knowing full well that he had lied. He could feel only relief that Amanda would remain downstairs. His loss was still too raw for him to be able to even think of another woman, and he was quite sure it would ever be so, but he would've hated to offend Amanda in any way.

He lowered Maia gently into the promised cot and covered her with a blanket, then stoked the fire before stripping and throwing himself onto the bed. For the first time since taking Maia, he enjoyed a deep, carefree sleep without nightmares or fear. He woke before dawn feeling rested and at peace. Maia lay in her cot, kicking and chattering in the darkness.

He changed her and carried her downstairs. Expecting a sleeping house, he was surprised to find Amanda and Metis in the kitchen.

'Ah, good morning!' Amanda pointed at tidy piles on the scrubbed kitchen table as she served a bowl of leftover soup for Peryst and soaked half a biscuit for Maia. 'There you have the dry laundry, a pack for Maia—I came across a little extra dried milk—and supplies for you and Master Golfen.'

'Thank you, Mistress Amanda.'

The innkeeper smiled and turned to Metis. 'Go and wake Master Golfen. If he's to travel with Master Peryst and Maia, he'll need to rise quickly. They need to leave as soon as they've eaten.'

Metis nodded and left the kitchen as Amanda stretched out her arms for Maia, who greeted her with a smile. 'Come, young one, let us give you a hearty meal so that you let your father make good progress away from Ros this morning.' She secured Maia to the chair and fed her quickly and efficiently. 'I've also packed a map of northern Mehru for you, marking villages and hamlets where you should be safe. Bear in mind, however, that my information may be out of date.'

'I intend to avoid inhabited areas, Mistress Amanda.'

'That would be very wise till you cross the Ramu. Southern Mehru is very different. They are a stronger people, governed by the wisdom of the High Luk. I doubt the Hand has even a foothold there.'

'I fervently hope not.'

SOUTHERN MEHRU

YEAR 5161 OF THE NEW ERA – AUTUMN

After carefully analysing Amanda's map, Peryst led his charges through the wilds of northern Mehru, avoiding all populated areas. They soon adapted to their new wanderings, with Maia more alert and vocal and the soft and hilly landscape growing ever greener. It was easy to spot inhabited areas from a distance and, thus, avoid them. Peryst and Golfen took turns keeping watch at night, each sleeping a few hours at a time, but hadn't run into any trouble almost two weeks into their travels away from Ros.

'Have you always been this quiet?' Golfen asked as he lay against a tree. Maia grumbled as she rubbed the wooden dragon's tail against her swollen gums.

Peryst kept studying the map and merely grunted in reply.

'We've been travelling together for weeks, Peryst de Arranu, and I know close to nothing about you. Were you as silent with Sanjia?'

'Sanjia didn't know the meaning of silence. When not talking, she sang,' Peryst said, feeling somewhat lighter at the thought of his wife's off-key singing.

'How long was she with you?'

'I met her when I was twenty, eleven years ago,' Peryst said shortly.

'Where did you meet?'

Without planning to, and for the first time in almost eight months, Peryst began talking about Sanjia. 'She served from behind the bar of her father's inn, opposite the promenade in Lis. She was so beautiful, Golfen, that I was lost when I first saw her.' But even as he painted her in words for Golfen, he still couldn't see her smiling in his mind.

'Was she as lost as you?'

Peryst grinned. 'She had the whole Southern Mehruvian Army professing their love for her, men and women alike. Later, I became a captain serving under Agazi Anil, the High Luk's daughter, who commands one of the nation's six battalions. It was an unusual feat for one who'd started as a Klaevani mercenary but the only thing that kept Sanjia's father from tossing me out on my ear as Sanjia kept me guessing.'

'How long till she gave in?'

'Long enough to almost kill me. In 5155, I was ordered to leave for Kurbal by Agazi Anil, who wanted to set up an Idhan in the Southern Mehruvian Army.' At Golfen's expression, he clarified, 'A section of the army made up of Touched who use their powers to aid the rest of the troops. From what I was told, the High Luk was growing concerned about Reor and wanted to strengthen southern Mehru's defences. I went to take my leave of Sanjia, but she said she loved me and would come with me. It was the happiest day of my life.' Peryst smiled to himself, thinking of his joy and the feeling that nothing could ever go wrong for them. 'We took a ship north to Kurbal, where I shadowed an irascible elven Idhani for four years to learn the methods she used in training her troops. Sanjia, who was also Touched, practiced with another Idhan. It was on our way back south that we learnt that a baby was coming.'

'The princess,' Golfen said.

Peryst shook his head.

'Sanjia carried two babies. She had such an easy pregnancy. We travelled through southern Kurbal into Usur with the intention of settling in Skinweave for the birthing before heading back to Lis for a few years—at least till the children were four or five. In that time, they'd learn that they were Mehruvian as well as Klaevani, and I would train an Idhan under Agazi Anil.'

'What happened?'

Feeling his stomach knot at his only clear picture of Sanjia, Peryst rubbed his face. 'Her pains started suddenly and early in the northern Usur wilds, only a few days from Skinweave.' His voice broke, and he couldn't control the tears that slid down his face as he saw her distinctly in the only images that still came to him: her fear and her pallor as she screamed in pain. 'There was nothing I could do, Golfen. She wouldn't let me leave her to go for help, and we were too far for any to arrive in time. I could only hold her helplessly as she shuddered and cried, giving birth to a boy and girl. With her last breath, she made me swear to care for our children, to make sure they knew they were both of Klaevan and Mehru.'

He leaned over Maia, tears wet on his face, and kissed her softly on her forehead, seeing not the babies who had never drawn a first breath and who lay buried with Sanjia but Maia and only Maia. His mind had pushed those children so deep that he refused to face them even in the privacy of his thoughts.

'The boy?' Golfen whispered as he placed his hand on Peryst's.

'With his mother,' Peryst said and even then wondered which boy he meant. The one who lay bundled in Sanjia's arms? Or Raf?

'Will you make your home in Mehru?' Golfen asked quietly.

Peryst shook his head and wiped his tears before leaning back onto his hands and angling his face up to the leafy canopy to breathe deeply and steady himself after the onslaught of memories. 'Not eternally. I'll take her to her grandfather as I promised and remain till she's a little older. I'll rejoin my company and see what my Agazi needs from me and perhaps spend my time in Lis training an Idhan for Mehru's defence against what I'm starting to believe will be an inevitable battle with Reor.' He was distracted by Golfen's doting look at Maia and was suddenly overwhelmed with gratitude at his presence, not just for the company but for the help with Maia. Caring for a baby was far more difficult—and lonely—than he'd expected. He smiled. 'It would've been very difficult for me to care for her on my own these last few weeks. You've been a great help, Golfen, and good company. Thank you.'

Golfen beamed. 'I've always had a weakness for little ones. And the princess is special. It's been a joy to spend my time with the two of you. But you'll need to talk more. A child needs to hear words to learn words.'

'I'll try,' Peryst replied, recognising that the comment came from concern for Maia and, therefore, he was grateful for it.

Then he pointed at Amanda's map, which he'd placed on the ground between them, out of Maia's reach. She soon gave up trying to grab it, turned onto her stomach, and brought herself up to rock back and forth on hands and knees, exclaiming and babbling loudly.

'We're still a way from the Ramu and have two choices.'

'And they are?' Golfen asked as he picked his teeth with a stick.

Peryst placed his finger on the map above Forglenden Forest. 'We're about here.' Then he moved his finger to the right. 'If we go this way, we'll come very close to the vale of Leyandale: one of the larger cities in northern Mehru, which had a powerful and well organised town guard last time I was there. Like other towns and villages in northern Mehru, Leyandale governs itself.'

'Is it different in southern Mehru? I've never travelled beyond the Ramu.'

'Very different. The Hand will have to go piecemeal in northern Mehru. Some towns and villages cooperate with each other, but most don't. Each is governed in its own way with its own institutions and laws, though they all do have a picture of the Mehruvian king in their town halls, or at least they used to.'

'So, they owe fealty to a king?'

Peryst chuckled. 'The last king of Mehru died at an advanced old age in 5122, almost forty years ago, leaving a handful of sons and daughters who'd grown old themselves waiting to inherit. Each wanted a throne, so they agreed to share Mehru in their father's name, choosing their areas of power in order of age, thus fragmenting the kingdom into many small realms, some stronger and some weaker. Three of the original heirs divided northern Mehru amongst themselves, but they all passed away in the first ten or so years. The one who ruled the west had no heirs and the second, based in Ilia, had two daughters, but neither survived childhood. Only one descendant of the bloodline remains as a ruler in northern Mehru: the Alkaid of Min.'

'So there's a king in Min?' Golfen asked. 'I didn't know that.'

'No. When the rest of northern Mehru eventually settled into a series of independent city-states and towns, he declared himself as Alkaid for Min and the East, but does have far more influence in the region than the Alkaids of the other towns in northern Mehru.'

'And the South?'

'The heirs of the South chose the youngest amongst themselves as High Luk. He was a young boy at the time, vastly younger than his older siblings, who've all been dead for years now, though some of their offspring remain scattered round southern Mehru. The current High Luk was the child of the previous High Luk's old age with a much younger wife. He's been based in Lis ever since, where they established the central government. A few matters of limited importance are devolved to the southern towns, but everything of import is decided by him.'

'I see.' Golfen studied the map. 'So, Leyandale is a city. Do we know if the Hand is there already?'

'Amanda didn't think so, but we can't know for sure, so we'll assume it is. Going through the vale means we can cross the Ramu via the bridge south of Leyandale, but we'll certainly meet others who may or may not be under the Hand's sway.' Peryst moved his finger to the left on the map. 'If we go this other way, we'll cross into Forglenden Forest. From what I know, only bandits make their home amongst the trees, but we'd hope not to meet them. We might encounter beasts, and we'll need to ford the Ramu and then cross more forest on the other side. The way will be convoluted but may end up being safer.'

Peryst sat back and leaned onto his hands again.

'What? You want me to decide? So that I'm to blame when it all goes wrong? No, no, Master Peryst. Good try, but no.'

'I'm not asking you to decide, Golfen, I'm merely asking your opinion,' Peryst said patiently.

Golfen scratched his head and then glanced down at Maia, who had fallen sideways next to him and was trying to reach his beard. He put his small hand in her smaller one and gazed at her with adoration. 'We should take the Forglenden route and not place the princess in danger of meeting those who would do her harm,' he said firmly.

'So be it.' Peryst stored their things in Roan's saddlebags as Golfen played with Maia.

'When you're old enough, I'll let you ride Rosie, Princess.' He crooned over her as she gurgled and finally, to her delight, grabbed hold of his thick red beard.

'But you're not old enough yet,' Peryst said, disentangling her fingers from Golfen's beard. 'Come, Maia, the way goes on.'

He held her high in the air and made her fly as she giggled. Now that she was bigger, generally awake when they travelled, and more awkward to carry on his chest, he'd switched to carrying her on his back. It had taken a few days to get used to his new sense of balance, but he was enjoying having more freedom in his arms. Hunting had become easier, as had riding, but he struggled having his weapons on his side, like Mehruvians, instead of in his weapon harness on his back, as was the Klaevani custom.

YEAR 5161 OF THE NEW ERA – WINTER

Forglenden Forest started at the bottom of a ravine and stretched as far as he could see. Though the Ramu was invisible though the trees, Peryst had a vague idea of where they'd meet it in a few days. He knew they'd find no bridge in the forest and hoped the waters wouldn't be too deep to ford.

Once they zigzagged carefully down to the bottom of the ravine, they were faced with the dense forest, dark under the canopies and lush with vegetation rich in ferns and shrubs.

Lifting his arms but not reaching close to the top of the tall bushes and shrubs over Rosie's head, Golfen gulped. 'Maybe we should have gone the other way.'

'Too late now, my friend.' Peryst saw Golfen's worried face but knew by now that Rosie was sturdy and determined. 'Roan will flatten the brush for Rosie, Golfen.'

Golfen chuckled. 'She'd better, or Rosie and I will become lost in the undergrowth.'

The way through Forglenden Forest proved to be far more than convoluted. Peryst chose the way forward, always considering Rosie and trying to trample the vegetation he rode through till it was flat enough for the goat. A few times it went quite wrong when a bush bounced back and hit Rosie in the face, causing her to startle. With nowhere to bolt, her reaction was an unexpected buck that sent Golfen flying backwards. The forest's thick undergrowth was then a blessing as it cushioned a fall that would otherwise have broken bones.

It was dark and damper than he'd expected under the thick canopy, so Peryst dressed Maia as warmly as he could, knowing that somewhere beyond the trees winter had started. There were no paths and few clearings. Though they came across numerous streams, places to rest and stretch out were scarce amongst the tightly knit trees. They made camp where they could, taking turns to sleep and watch against thick trunks and under dripping branches, surrounded by ominous creaking and rustling.

After another shift during which Peryst kept watch not only to the backdrop of forest noises but to moans and groans from Golfen, who tossed and turned wrapped in his blanket, he asked whether his dreams were plaguing him.

Golfen blew into his daily cup of thick warming drink made from the tokoa paste that Amanda had packed for them. Peryst brewed it each morning for them as it helped to shake off the chill. 'I only wish they were.'

Peryst sipped his own tokoa, gratefully feeling the warmth spread down his body. He knew halflings were connected to the Dreaming and that they could see much while they slept, so was confused by Golfen's answer.

'I've been alone too long, Peryst, far from others like me. We can only access the Dreaming when there are more than one of us. We halflings are meant to live in community, not alone.'

'So, you're not dreaming when you toss and turn in the night?'

Golfen rubbed his temple. 'I'm sorry if I've disturbed you. I hope I haven't woken the princess.' He pressed the heels of his hands to his eyes. 'No, I don't dream. My mind's eye tries to connect to the Dreaming, as it's meant to, but it can't. The attempt hurts me, and it gets worse the longer I go without joining.' He pointed at Peryst's pack. 'You wouldn't carry nigella petals or hirim grass, would you?' Then he smacked his forehead. 'No, no. Even if you did, I wouldn't let you take it. We couldn't both sleep and leave the princess unattended.'

'I'm sorry, Golfen. I carry neither.' There were herbs that could connect others to the Dreaming alongside halflings. Genaians sometimes used them, as did the elves of Kurbal, but Peryst had never tried them.

'Well, the sooner we get to Lis and I find more halflings or a boat to take me home, the better!' Golfen said, tickling Maia's chin and then bending to roll his bed mat.

Peryst also tidied his things, wondering at Golfen's cheerful demeanour despite night after night of pain. Golfen was always chattering to Maia, to Rosie, and to Nela, smiling and filling Peryst's silence with stories and laughter. Peryst knew he couldn't have done the same given such circumstances, and his respect and appreciation for Golfen grew.

'Why did you leave Rohin in the first place, Golfen?'

'Perhaps there was a Klaevani in my family tree.' Golfen chuckled. 'I cannot say. One day, after a dream that showed me far-off lands, I decided I needed to see them.' He mounted Rosie with a flourish. 'But now I think I may have wandered enough. It's time for me to be amongst my own.'

TEN DAYS INTO the trees, they came across a gauzy white substance covering the ferns. Peryst turned east without a word.

'Why? What is it?' Golfen asked, twisting in his saddle.

'Webs, I think. But for them to cover such a large area, the creatures that spin them must be enormous or a great many in number.'

Golfen dismounted, approached the stuff, and sniffed at it while studying the plants underneath. 'I know of creatures that could produce this kind of web, some with venoms that are useful. It may be no bad thing to come across them.'

'Any such creature is one I'd rather we never come face to face with,' Peryst said shortly and guided Roan through particularly heavy vegetation, where the rustle and crackling of bushes and undergrowth made it impossible to carry on a conversation. Once through, they came to a small clearing with a faint path ahead and stopped to take their bearings.

'Was it a bad idea?' Golfen asked. 'We've been wandering through trees for days.'

'Was what a bad idea?'

'To come through the forest?'

'I'd say it was,' a third voice intervened.

Peryst reined Roan and clasped his bow in one movement as Nela growled at the voice coming from a tree.

'Put it down. You wouldn't know where to aim and, in any event, you're well surrounded.'

Golfen spun desperately in his saddle, whispering, 'Where are they? Who are they? Bandits?'

His heart thundering in fear and frustration, Peryst slowly lowered his weapon. 'It would be polite to show yourself.'

A laugh sounded. 'Call off the wolf, and I'll come down.'

'Nela. Stay.' Peryst spoke aloud but knew the wolf would obey his mental instructions as well and remain alert to defend Maia with her life. He sent a grateful thanks to Sanjia, who'd taught Nela to obey mind commands. Ears cocked, Nela growled softly and sat down next to Roan.

The crackling of leaves heralded the appearance of a young man who jumped down from a tree a few yards in front of Roan. Mehruvian, dressed in brown and green, he'd been perfectly camouflaged amongst the branches. 'Who are you, and what is your business in Forglenden?'

Before Peryst could reply, Maia, who'd been drowsing on his back, started protesting loudly at the lack of movement that had been rocking her to sleep.

'A baby? You carry a baby on your back? Whatever for?'

'Why we cross through the forest and why I carry a child is not your concern.' Peryst was furious at the questioning and even more at his helplessness. Anything he did would put Maia in danger, and he couldn't afford that.

The young man tilted his head. 'Ah, but it is, you see. None pass through the forest without Mistress Thallya and Mistress Fiona's leave, so you can either tell me your business here or tell it to them yourself.'

'I know none with those names,' Peryst said. 'Nor do I know yours. It's a simple courtesy to introduce oneself to strangers.'

'You'll know them all before the day is done.' The young man placed two fingers to his lips and let out a low warble. A young Mehruvian girl appeared, hanging upside down from a branch. 'Here's a name for you! Sacha Valekeep will blindfold you, and we'll lead you to the camp. Otherwise, we'll make you sleep. Your choice.'

In another situation, Peryst would have dismounted with a jump and run his sword through the insolent youngster, but his hands were tied. He couldn't afford to lose consciousness and be unable to defend Maia. Filled with pent-up anger, he grudgingly accepted the blindfold but focused his mind's eye before Sacha lowered it over his face. They were, indeed, surrounded. Fifteen others emerged from behind trees and bushes. Not all were as young as the speaker, but they were all armed with arrows at the ready. And though he sensed weaknesses in them that he could conceivably reach, he'd be vulnerable against so many with Maia on his back. Biting his lip in frustration, he let himself be led.

Concentrating, he was able to keep track of the path they took. No one spoke, but he heard the fifteen proceed, some on the ground and some in the trees. As Roan started moving, Maia settled again, sleeping heavily against his back. The way became easier and quicker as they moved south. Soon, Peryst recognised the slight warmth of the winter sun on his head. He wondered where they could be.

'I made the wrong choice, Peryst. We should have gone through Leyandale,' Golfen said.

'A bit late for regrets now,' the young man intervened, 'but you can be sure that we're much nicer than any you'd meet on the roads.'

Before Peryst could reply, the young man spoke again. 'You may remove your blindfolds.'

As he removed the dark material, Peryst was blinded by the most light they'd seen in days. It took time to adjust, but when he did, he blinked as he took in a bustling camp in a large clearing surrounded by the forest on every side.

Tents and wooden shacks were set in a circle and shelters made of branches and wood were balanced up in the trees. The inhabitants were varied, mostly Mehruvians but some undoubtedly Reordans. There were halflings and humans, and Peryst was surprised to see even a couple of elves peeking down from one of the arboreal shelters.

'What is this place?' he asked as he dismounted. Nela sat at his side pushing her head under his hand.

A voice shrieked, 'Golfen Nimbleknees!' and a Rohinian woman streaked across the clearing towards Rosie, who startled and would have bolted had a young lad not held her firmly. Instead, she bucked again, but Golfen, used to her antics, leapt down and opened his arms to the runner, who fell laughing into them.

'Neeva! What are you doing here? What is this place?' He held her from him and turned her to face Peryst. 'Peryst, this is Neeva Turraneel, a good friend from my native Rohin.'

Peryst bowed his head in greeting, but, before he could speak, the young man who'd led them interrupted. 'You know these people, Neeva?'

'I know Golfen, Tam. We grew up together. He had a real knack for odd potions.' Her gaze shifted to Peryst. 'The man I don't know.'

'The man is Peryst de Arranu, a valiant man and a good friend,' Golfen said, making Peryst's chest swell in gratitude. 'He saved me from a cockatrice in northern Reor, and since then we've travelled together.'

Tam turned to Peryst. 'You were the one who killed the cockatrice near the Gyro?'

Peryst nodded once.

'You gave the Alkaid of Ros great joy. Not only did you rid him of a pest, but you also neglected to collect the bounty. Double joy for him,' Tam said. 'We heard of it even here!' Then he bowed his head. 'I'm Tam Ashweaver.'

A lean Mehruvian woman approached with another, also Mehruvian but slightly older. Their hair, lined with grey, was tied back and both wore brown, like Tam and many of the others round the camp.

'Are you Touched? Is your child?' the younger of the two asked, and Peryst reached for his sword.

She lifted her long-fingered hands. 'Leave your sword, Peryst de Arranu. Most of those here have power or are otherwise of an origin or appearance that doesn't please the Hand of Reason. None will hurt you or your baby, not here. Like the rest of us, you may find refuge in our camp amongst the trees.'

Peryst slowly loosened his grip on the hilt of his sword. 'You know my name, but I do not know yours.'

'I do apologise. I am Thallya Thornglen, once the Mas from Ros.' She gestured to the other woman. 'And this is Fiona Hyden. We're partners in life and in the managing of this camp.'

Golfen interrupted by asking, 'You're the couple from Ros whose belongings were burnt on the green?'

'Unfortunately, we are,' Thallya replied. 'But how would you know that?'

Peryst bowed his head. 'From Amanda Callaman. I owe you, Mistress Thallya, a debt of gratitude. It's thanks to your biscuits that my daughter has survived.'

Thallya sighed. 'Amanda is still in Ros?'

'She is.'

Thallya and Fiona shared a look of exasperation as Thallya pushed a stray strand of grey hair behind her ear. 'Stubborn woman, so attached to her vineyard that she cannot see the fisted Hand over her head.'

'She can see it well enough,' Peryst said. 'But she'd like to pretend it isn't there. I asked her to come with us, but she refused.'

'She'll be lucky if she's driven out,' Tam intervened. 'Those opposed or even merely less enthusiastic about the Hand burnt last week in a village near Gyllia.'

Peryst glanced at the settlement and its people. 'What is this place? Why haven't you gone further south? Why not settle under the protection of the High Luk?'

'Because we're like Amanda, loathe to lose our lands and angry that we've been chased from our homes. So, we'll take them back, one by one, and drive the Hand of Reason back to Reor,' Fiona replied evenly.

'You're planning a revolution?' Peryst asked. 'From here?'

'Every uprising, every revolution, starts with a seed, however small, however lowly. We are that seed, but, like a tree, we'll grow till we are the forest that covers Mehru,' Thallya said, her hand on Fiona's.

Maia had started stirring against Peryst's back, so he unbound her and, with one arm still entangled in the cloth, brought her to his front to face yet another new world. She blinked up at the sun and moaned as she placed her fist back in her mouth.

'The child is breaking a tooth,' Thallya said. 'Who is she?'

'She's my daughter, Maia.'

'Welcome to our camp, Maia,' Thallya said, touching the baby's cheek before turning her attention back to Peryst. 'She resembles you but has golden-brown Mehruvian skin. Where's her mother?'

'Her mother is dead,' he replied, wondering how many times he'd need to say it, how many times he'd be reminded that Sanjia was no more. 'Sanjia was a daughter of Mehru. I travel to introduce Maia to her grandfather in Lis.'

'Ah, Lis.' Fiona sighed with a slight smile on her lips. 'Southern Mehru is still free from the Hand.'

'You'll be safe there, then, Peryst,' Golfen said as he caught Fiona's last comment.

'Perhaps,' Thallya said. 'But now we welcome you to our camp. Follow me, Peryst. Maia must be hungry and would benefit from more than dried biscuit. We have more infants here and cook proper meals for them.'

The camp was like a well-organised village made up of the most varied population that Peryst had ever seen. They lived in apparent harmony, halfling next to human, human next to elf, Touched and not. From what Thallya told him, the conflicts that arose were no different to the usual conflicts based on personal chemistry (or lack thereof) and petty grievances of any society. Though seemingly led by Thallya and Fiona, every decision was agreed by the Gluok, a committee made up of representatives chosen from each group that dwelt in the forest. Everyone had a voice, and everyone had a chore: there was hunting, gathering, cooking, training, making of weapons, caring for youngsters, and caring for elders, as in any populated area.

As Thallya led Peryst and Maia, with Nela tagging along, to an area where older men and women of all origins cared for the youngest children, she made her case for them remaining in the forest for a spell. 'Maia will break her first tooth soon. She'll be in pain and difficult till she has her first four. Stay here till then and help us. In exchange, we'll assist with your daughter. She'll soon learn to eat solid food, which will make your travels easier, and will learn to sit unaided, enabling you to ride more comfortably with her.'

Peryst, thinking deeply, said nothing as Thallya threw what he was sure she believed was her winning shot. 'In the next three or four months, near other children, Maia might even learn to speak. Olli Farbow and Tandy Fewmare's son, Ren, is a little older but would be a good companion and role model.'

There was a lot in what Thallya suggested. Travelling with a child who could eat what he did would indeed make his life easier, but he again suffered a flood of guilt at relinquishing the child into the hands of others, even for a short time.

She was his to care for; it was the promise he'd made. He held Maia so tightly she yelped in protest.

Thallya stopped and placed a hand on Peryst's arm, making him turn to her. 'Your commitment to your daughter is admirable. She is lively, curious, and thriving, all testament to your care. But there's no shame in receiving assistance from others. Every single member of this camp can share knowledge with her and you, just as in every other corner of the world. Let your daughter learn from many so that she may be richer and know more than any one of her teachers, including you. It is the Klaevani way, is it not? And she is also of you.'

Peryst sighed, recognising the truth of Thallya's words. The Klaevani travelled the world to learn from others, so he should allow his daughter to do the same.

Though he knew he needed to return to Lis, he also knew that till Maia was a little older he would be as vulnerable as when they had been ambushed earlier in the forest. Once he no longer needed to carry her on his back, he would be able to defend her with both hands and shield her from dangerous beasts and humans alike. So, he gave in.

'We'll make a home here till Maia's at least a year old. Then we we'll travel south to Lis.'

Thallya nodded and smiled. 'So be it.'

Borders of Forglenden

YEAR 5162 OF THE NEW ERA – WINTER

THE NOISE CAME again: a rustling of sodden leaves and a little whimper. Peryst crept in its direction, wary but not overly worried. In his experience, small noises belonged to small creatures. He didn't know all the animals that dwelt amongst the trees of Forglenden Forest, but so far they had been the rather typical beasts that fed the camp: rabbits and larger rodent-like mammals. But this was a sound he didn't recognise and given the season, an animal that didn't hibernate. He'd been tracking it for some time, but it wandered aimlessly amongst the wintery forest in no recognisable pattern, turning back on itself and going in circles, almost as if lost.

Peryst hoped it would be a creature he could take back to the camp as, other than the brace of rabbits that hung from his shoulder, he'd caught nothing larger for the evening meal. Perhaps the creature he followed had scared all other animals into hiding.

The noise just ahead between a clump of bushes became constant. Peryst approached carefully, bow in hand, making barely any sound, just as Tam, who was also hunting that day, called out from beyond where the animal hid. The whimper turned into a yelp, and a small person running as fast as their short legs could move emerged from the bushes.

Peryst had just enough time to sheathe his bow and straighten before the person crashed headlong into his legs and fell onto their backside.

'A child!' Peryst exclaimed.

It was indeed a child, a small girl: six or seven years old, dirty, with matted hair filled with seeds and leaves, scratches all over, and with streaks where tears had left clean canals down her face.

Empty hands raised, Peryst crouched by her side. The child tried to back away, scrambling on her rear, a terrified expression on her snub-nosed face.

'I won't hurt you,' he said in Mehruvian, given the little girl's looks. 'Don't be frightened.'

The girl stopped moving, her dark eyes enormous and chest rising and falling with her too-rapid breaths.

'Are you lost, little one?' he asked in the gentlest voice he could manage.

Staring, the child shook her head and then nodded before shaking it again.

Peryst smiled. She would never have seen a Klaevani before and so would be shocked at his appearance. 'I'm Peryst. I'm from Klaevan, which is far, far, away across the mountains. That's why I have such strangely coloured eyes. I have a little girl, too. She's younger than you. Her name is Maia. What's your name?'

'Does she have green eyes, too?' the little girl whispered.

'Yes, she does, just like mine.'

'They're pretty.'

'Thank you. Yours are pretty, too. They look like my wife's.'

'Is she here? Is Maia's mama here, too?'

'She's not,' Peryst replied. 'Maia's mama is gone.'

'Did the bad men take her?'

Peryst forced himself not to frown. 'Why do you ask? Are there bad men nearby?'

The little girl sat up straighter and nodded. 'They came home. Mama said they were coming to get me. She told me to lie very still and piled hay over me,' she said with a slight tremor in her voice.

'What's your name?' he asked her again.

'Cali.'

'Where's your home, Cali? Where's your mama?'

'At the farm with Riki and Bas. Dada's away with Feli at the fair, but he said the three of us were too young. When we're like Feli, he'll take us to the fair.'

'Is Feli your brother?'

Cali nodded. 'And Riki and Bas.' She puffed out her chest. 'I'm the only girl. I'm six.'

Peryst took his water bottle and held it to Cali's parched lips. 'Have some water, Cali. Just a little bit.'

She guzzled at the bottle, water spilling onto her clothes in her haste.

'When was the last time you ate or drank, Cali?'

'I don't know, but I'm hungry. And cold.'

Peryst had no food on him other than the dead rabbits, but he took off his cloak and wrapped it round the little girl snugly. 'Let's get you to camp and find some dinner.'

Cali shook her head vehemently. 'I can't go to a camp. Mama said to run into the forest till I found Mistress Thallya or Mistress Fiona. She said that they'd see me amongst the trees and look after me till Mama could come.'

'I can take you to them, Cali. They found me when I was lost in the forest.'

'Was Maia lost, too?'

Peryst smiled. 'She was with me.'

Cali's bottom lip trembled. 'I wish I could be with my Dada.'

'Why did Mama tell you to run into the forest, Cali?'

'Because of the bad men,' Cali said. 'They came to the farm to find me because I'm like Grandmama, but Mama says I might not be able to move things like Grandmama. She says maybe I'll hear very well, and she'd like that very much because then maybe I'll do what she says.' Cali giggled.

'Did you come into the forest all alone?'

Cali leaned her head to the side and considered before replying. 'When the men left, Mama took the hay away and brought me to the trees and told me to run to Mistresses Thallya and Fiona and tell them that a hand is coming.'

'Let's go to the camp and find Mistress Thallya and Mistress Fiona so you can give them your message and have some food.' He bent over. 'Would you like to ride on my shoulders?'

'With the rabbits? Dada sometimes brings rabbits for Mama to roast. Does Mistress Thallya roast rabbits? Does Mistress Fiona?'

Peryst grinned at the idea. 'I'm sure they do, but these will be roasted by my friend Golfen, who's a magnificent cook.'

'Is that good?'

'Very good.'

He placed Cali on his shoulders and held her shins as he retraced his steps back to the camp.

'You were meant to bring a deer, Peryst! Only you would bring a child instead!'

'Cali, this is Tam. He was the one who brought Maia and me to the camp.'

Thallya approached. 'What have we here?'

'A hungry Cali. Thallya, this is Cali. She brings a message from her mama. She's been searching for you in the forest for days.'

Peryst set Cali down in front of Thallya, but Cali flinched back against his legs and grasped his hand convulsively.

Thallya crouched in front of her. 'Are you hungry, Cali?'

Cali nodded.

'Shall we ask Peryst to come with us to find some food and warmer clothes?'

Cali nodded again.

'How many days were you in the forest, little one?' Thallya asked as they walked to the hut that housed the camp kitchen, where the Tamad in the camp reigned over pots and pans and occasionally allowed Golfen to join them in preparing meals. Thanks to their cooking skills, Peryst had eaten better in Forglenden Forest than he had in years.

'I don't know,' she said. 'Lots.'

'How many times did it get dark?' Thallya asked.

'I think two times or three. I thought animals would eat me. It was dark. I was scared.'

'The child seems to have been in the forest for days,' Peryst said. 'The mother packed some food and water for her and sent her into the wilderness alone. How could a parent do that?' He tucked Maia's blanket more snugly while, as every night after the camp meal, she slept soundly on his lap. The mere idea of abandoning Maia to fend for herself made him feel sick.

'If the alternative were worse, any parent would do that and more,' Thallya replied from across the table where Peryst and Golfen sat nursing their evening gell, the Usurian wine drunk all over Ankisua. Cali had been accommodated with the other youngsters without parents and, like them, had been asleep for hours.

'I'm assuming that Defenders came for the child?' Peryst asked.

'It seems so. From what we've pieced together, Cali belongs to a family that owns a farm by the fringes of the forest east of Ilia,' Gena Ringdell, Thallya and Fiona's adoptive daughter, replied.

'Did Tam mention that there were purges in Ilia?' Peryst asked, trying to remember.

'Not quite,' Gena replied. 'The Alkaid sees what comes, but instead of resisting, he's trying to ingratiate himself with the Hand of Reason to avoid ending up like the one in Ros.'

'What do you mean?' Golfen asked.

'The Alkaid in Ros was replaced by a puppet of Reor. Amanda told us that,' Peryst said.

'Indeed. So, the Alkaid of Ilia seems to be trying to avoid that by presenting the Hand with an already *cleansed* town,' Fiona said.

'Not much difference for the Touched to be burnt by a Defender or an Alkaid,' Golfen muttered.

Thallya smiled grimly. 'But much for us. If the purges are Defender led, the town will be angry, and anger can lead to rebellion. But if town led, it becomes more difficult. Reordans are very good at inciting people to turn on each other. When they do and it leads to live burnings, the population tends to find ways to justify their actions to avoid facing the guilt and horror of what they've done. It's much harder to sow seeds of rebellion in a population that feels guilt as well as fear. If just fear, it's easier.'

'What we know for sure is that Cali's bad men were after her because she's Touched like her grandmother,' Peryst said.

'And that her mother hid her, telling them that she was with her father at the fair,' Gena added.

'What fair would that be?' Golfen asked.

'Who knows?' Fiona replied. 'There are numerous annual fairs, some in Reor and some in northern Mehru. I don't keep track of them all.'

'What will happen when Dada returns with no Cali?' Peryst asked.

'Hopefully, they'll come up with a convincing story. If they were indeed Defenders, they won't like being duped,' Thallya said drily.

Peryst shook his head. 'The Hand is truly like a disease that spreads slowly.' He turned to Golfen. 'Your phrasing was very accurate, my friend.'

'Well, we'll leave you to your drinks, but I'm very glad you found her when you did, Peryst. The child wouldn't have survived much longer on her own. It's a wonder that she wasn't devoured by beasts.' Thallya rose to her feet and stretched before turning with Fiona to their hut as the tables slowly emptied and the camp retired for the night. Gena bent over to touch Maia's forehead, said goodnight, and followed.

Peryst shook his head. 'Cali's mother must be frantic worrying for her daughter.'

Golfen snorted. 'Cali's mother must be grateful that she's saved her child from the pyre, Peryst.'

Peryst sighed, thinking of Maia alone in Forglenden stumbling upon beasts and poisonous plants. Yes, Cali had been lucky. How many more children would face such dangers on their own to avoid being taken by Defenders?

'The northern realms think Reor won't attack its neighbouring lands, Golfen. They don't see the Hand of Reason as a true enemy, nor do they see the horror of their ways. I fear they'll wake up to their danger when it's too late.'

'They're sadly mistaken. Perhaps they're not yet making bold and noticeable moves, but they're inching beyond the Reordan borders! Your northern realms are in for a shock. We Rohinians have seen what comes.'

'I know. I heard the Dreamscribes of Rohin have been worrying about a dream that keeps repeating.'

Golfen swallowed noisily. 'It was the first dream I had in months, when I joined the halflings here in a communal dreaming session.' His expression was haunted. 'A large hand was spread over a map of Ankisua. It lowered slowly, covering the South in its shadow till all colours were erased. Then the hand clenched for a moment and moved north.'

Peryst tightened his lips. 'Will there be nowhere safe to raise my child?'

'Unless someone manages to stop the Hand, no,' Golfen replied. 'Maybe Fiona and Thallya have a point and what we need is a seed of rebellion that will grow. It must start somewhere.'

Peryst took a sip of gell and waved a hand to encompass the ramshackle camp. 'Maybe. I should think you need more than a seed.' He shook his head. *An army is what's needed: an organised and disciplined army to prevent Reordans from sneaking south armed with poisonous words sweetened with lamps and cooking pots, piping systems and cisterns.*

Golfen sighed. 'All life starts with a seed. Even the largest trees—whole forests—start with seeds.'

Peryst raised his tumbler. 'May the seed of rebellion flourish and grow strong, then!' He placed it back on the table. 'What will you do, my friend? You had planned to sail back to Rohin, but I see you and Rosie very comfortable here in the forest.'

Golfen clasped his hands over his belly and leaned back in his chair. 'I'm thinking I might become part of the seed of revolution. Tumultuous times are coming, and here I am once again connected to the Dreaming and can contribute. Where do you think Reor will go first? I'm guessing they'll try to take southern Rohin even if it is but a barren corner of our lands holding only the herds of crystalhoofs and the Retan Pass. But if Reor controls the pass, it controls incoming and outgoing trade with the North.'

'You must have more of the Klaevani in you that you think,' Peryst replied drily.

Golfen shrugged. 'Or desperate times call for us to do what we would never have imagined. What about you? The princess thrives here. She has cut three teeth already and crawls at top speed.' He beamed. 'I'm waiting for her first word to be *Golfen*!'

Peryst smiled as he thought of Maia sitting herself upright in the cot, babbling and leaving little teeth marks on the tail of the wooden dragon she carried everywhere. Then he leaned his forehead onto his hand. Not used to sharing his feelings since Sanjia's death, he lifted a face he knew to be strained. 'It was so much easier before, Golfen. It was easier when I was alone. Then, I would have simply rejoined my company without further consideration. It was even easier when Sanjia and I decided together. But now it's just me, and I'm afraid for the first time in my life. I'm a father now and cannot risk everything when I have Maia.'

'True. But being a parent doesn't mean that you forget yourself and your own needs, Peryst.' Golfen hesitated. 'I've noticed you get along with Gena. She's a charming young woman. Do not deny yourself companionship or even pleasure because of Maia.'

Peryst gaped, shocked into speechlessness. When he could finally utter a word, he said, 'I do get along with Gena. She's an able fighter and a powerful Touched, excellent as a partner on the night watch. Nothing else, Golfen. My loss is too recent, too raw, and I truly wonder if I'll ever be able to touch another woman with desire after losing Sanjia in such a way.'

Golfen smiled. 'The day will come, Peryst.'

'Maybe, and maybe not, but now my focus is my daughter.'

'She can't be your only focus. You must do what you feel is right, but you must find a purpose beyond her. How else will you teach your daughter to be the woman she's meant to be?' He clapped Peryst on the back. 'On that thoughtful note, I will retire to my dreams.' He beamed. 'It's so pleasant to sleep amongst images once more.'

Peryst followed him thoughtfully with his gaze and then laughed softly to himself. *How else indeed? I've been so wrapped up in caring for Maia that I've almost lost myself. Before losing Sanjia, my purpose was to improve the Southern Mehruvian Army so they could face the Hand. But it all toppled in that cave. Since then, I've been too overwhelmed keeping Maia alive to think beyond the next day.*

As Peryst carried Maia carefully to the hut they shared, he recovered a purpose of sorts, not just the culmination of the mission charged by the High Luk through Anil. He would help train the Idhan. Later, he'd head North and raise awareness of the Hand of Reason. The northern realms needed to see the danger that would come from Reor, they needed to be aware, and they needed to wake up before it was too late so that there were no more children fleeing for their lives like Cali.

The day watch brought in a young couple they found wandering amongst the trees. They carried bundles on their backs and the girl was heavily pregnant.

'They say Defenders are coming to test the babies like in Reor. My Ma was Touched, and her grandmother was, so our baby might be too,' the boy explained, a protective arm over his wife's shoulders.

'Who says?' Thallya asked.

The boy and girl stammered over each other to reply. 'People in the villages. They say Ilia is being cleansed of Touched and Defenders are coming from Reor. There are Defenders in Ros instead of guards.'

'Rumours, rumours, rumours! I need facts,' Thallya said crossly. 'Tam, we need someone to head out of the forest and find out what's really going on.' To the couple, she said, 'We'll shelter you till the birthing, but you must decide what you intend to do. If you choose to remain in the camp, you'll join us in the resistance against Reor. You'll train for a battle that will come and fight for the soul of Mehru. If not, you can settle in southern Mehru or find transport across the mountains to the free North.'

At Thallya's words, the girl grasped her husband's arm nervously.

'I'm a baker. I'm not fighter,' he replied.

Thallya spoke with the steel that Peryst had come to recognise and even admire. 'Perhaps there will come a time when even bakers find they must raise their mixing spoons to resist the Hand. But that time is not yet, so you still have the luxury of choice.'

'Thank you, Mistress Thallya. We'll go south. I'm sure there'll be a need for bakers there.'

Day after day, more stragglers were brought in from the forest. Young and old, most had fled upon rumours alone, fearing that what had happened in Ilia would spread. Some, mostly younger, chose to join the camp, but the majority rested for a few days and then continued their way into southern Mehru.

'Nothing much has changed,' Tam explained when he returned from his reconnaissance. 'I spoke to Gavrel Kingslight, who's a member of the Mylia Town Guard. He's sympathetic to our cause and has vowed to keep us informed. From what I gather, there are a few Defenders in Ros who've taken over duties from the Ros Guard as has happened in most northern Mehruvian towns where the Hand has moved in.'

'And Ilia?' Fiona asked.

'As we'd heard, the Alkaid was facing opposition from some of the town worthies and decided to conquer approval by violence. Once he had eliminated his opposition—by hanging, not burning—he decided to prepare the town for the advent of the Hand by doing a cleanse.'

'The Mehruvian Alkaid initiated purges?' Peryst asked. 'And so it starts.'

'Not yet. No purges have occurred in Ilia so far. But the Touched have been incarcerated.' Tam shrugged. 'Rumour has it that they'll be transported to Ros where purges will occur.'

'Rumour?' Thallya asked through gritted teeth. Fiona placed a calming hand on her arm.

'It's the best I could do. None know what the Alkaid plans, though he did send a messenger to Ros a week ago,' Tam replied. 'No answer had come by the time I left.'

A shrill cry pierced the air as Cali, who'd been with the other children playing, tore across the camp and into the arms of a bedraggled woman. With her came a boy of about twelve and two younger ones. All were weary and bent under their packs.

'Mama! You came. I knew you'd come for me.'

The woman sunk to her knees to hold Cali, kissing her face and touching her desperately. 'You're safe, you're safe, Cali,' she whispered brokenly as she wept.

Peryst approached and took the woman's heavy pack and placed it on the ground beside her.

'Cali was very brave and did exactly what you told her to do, madam. You can be very proud of such a daughter,' Peryst said quietly.

The woman raised a face stained with tears. 'I was so afraid for her. I didn't know what else to do. They wanted to take her.' She sobbed quietly into her daughter's hair. 'I could only hope that she would be found.'

'She was. And is safe and well, as you can see.'

'But now they've taken Father,' the older boy said.

Peryst turned to the boy and held out his hand. 'Feli, I assume. I'm Peryst. Who has taken your father? And why?'

'The Alkaid's men,' Feli spat. 'They're going to burn him and the others in Ros.'

Thallya had approached unheard. 'Is this another rumour?'

Cali's mother lifted a ravaged face. 'If only it were. The Alkaid is brave enough to imprison all the Touched in the area but not brave enough to burn them. He knows Ilia won't accept that.'

Peryst wondered. He rather thought Ilia would accept that and more given the right circumstances. Reor had, and not all Reordans were evil; most simply wanted to live their lives and feed their families. 'How many are they taking to Ros and when?' he asked.

'Ten. There were never many Touched in the area,' Cali's mother replied. 'From what was announced, I gather they'll be leaving in two days, at dawn. To avoid leading them to Leyandale on foot, they're repurposing the butcher's cart as a prison wagon.'

Peryst turned to Thallya. 'We have time to intercept and free them. We can't stand by when we know they'll be handed to Defenders.'

Thallya frowned. 'I'll assemble the Gluok.'

Peryst and Gena waited amongst the bushes on the right side of the road from Ilia to Ros while Tam and Olli waited on the left. They'd chosen the spot carefully:

close enough to Ilia to be able to reach the forest swiftly but far enough so that any kerfuffle would not be noticed by the town guards.

In Gena, Peryst saw what would have happened to Raf: her younger sister had been born Touched and taken by the Hand in her native Reor. The rest of the family had been disgraced, their belongings requisitioned, and their lands snatched. With nothing but the clothes on their backs, they'd made their way south, begging and taking odd jobs when Gena was barely seven. Her parents had been killed by bandits while Gena was at the river washing their ragged clothes. She'd returned, arms full of soaked laundry, to find their little camp destroyed, everything of value taken, and her parents slaughtered. That day, the child became a woman. She dug graves for her parents with her hands, and, once she'd buried them, she walked till Thallya found her, skeletal and frail, wandering the woods near Ros. She and Fiona had taken Gena in, helped her to open her mind's eye and become as Touched as her sister had been at birth. Despite the horrors that lay behind her, Gena was cheerful, and an agile and well-trained warrior with a quick wit. Peryst discovered that they complemented each other well whether hunting beasts, bandits, or Defenders.

Cross-legged on the ground, Gena spoke up to Peryst. 'Can you see them yet?'

'There's a smudge on the road, but that's all I can make out for now.'

'We'll need them to be relatively close for the plan to work.'

'I know.'

The butcher's cart came into view slowly. Led by two old horses that trudged along the pocked dirt road, the cart had been covered and turned into a makeshift prison wagon. Two members of the Ilia Guard rode up front.

'They don't seem to fear an ambush,' Peryst remarked. 'They have no mounted escort or further guards, unless there's a guard inside the cart.'

Gena snorted. 'An Alkaid who tried to get a run on the Hand won't be the brightest. He must be feeling he's the king of his little kingdom and that nobody would dare thwart him.'

'He's about to be thwarted,' Peryst replied and leaned to pull Gena to her feet. 'Time for the games to start.'

'They promise to be quick ones.'

'We do it at the same time, Gena.'

Gena made no reply but winked quickly at Peryst before turning her attention back to one of the cart's wheels. Peryst had his mind's eye focused on the one opposite. It wasn't enough for them to slow the cart down. They planned to immobilise it completely. But the cart was solid and the axle sound and would survive ruts and irregularities on the road. Peryst had only found a slight weakness in one of the main bolts attaching the wheel to the hub. Concentrating on the bolt, Peryst nocked one of his metal-tipped arrows and let it fly to that exact spot as Gena—a Matter Primal who could manipulate all manner of things—shifted the ground under the opposing wheel, creating a rut where the road had been smooth.

As the bolt shifted under the blow from Peryst's arrow, the wheel wobbled alarmingly as the other one sunk into the rut, putting inordinate pressure on the axle. The cart tipped sideways. The driver pulled up the reins abruptly, scaring the horses into rearing and pulling so violently that the axle cracked. The two guards had no time to react further before Olli and Tam jumped out from the left.

Peryst left them to deal with the drivers and ran with Gena to the back of the cart, which was fastened with a large padlock.

'Can you deal?' Peryst asked.

'With pleasure.' Gena had the padlock in pieces in seconds. Sitting inside the cart on benches that had been fitted on either side, ten people leaned back against the walls. Some were barely more than children. Their expressions were terrified but, tied to the benches and to each other, they couldn't move.

Dagger in hand, Peryst jumped into the cart and started slicing through the sturdy ropes. 'We've come to liberate you.'

'Why? Who are you?'

'We're from the forest,' Peryst replied. 'We serve under Mistresses Thallya and Fiona and aid any who oppose the Hand of Reason and Reor.'

'My, my, my daughter,' a man stammered. 'My wife sent her into the forest alone to save her. Do you know anything of a young child?'

'Cali? She's safe and well. I found her,' Peryst told the man, who was rubbing his wrists where the rope had left deep welts. 'She's at the camp with your wife and boys.'

The man stretched his hands and grasped at Peryst's arm, shaking it and repeating, 'Thank you, thank you, thank you.'

'Come, follow us.'

Peryst helped the frailer of the prisoners down onto the road and gave them all water from his bottle.

Tam came back. 'Ready?'

'When you are,' Peryst replied. 'The guards?'

'They'll sleep for a spell and wake to an empty cart and broken axle.'

'The least they deserve,' Gena muttered.

'No, they're not responsible for this,' Cali's father replied. 'They were threatened into submission. The Alkaid swore he'd take their children.'

The four led the prisoners off the road and into the wilderness where they'd be safer. They'd expected to make a swift getaway to the camp, but, seeing that one of the prisoners was very frail and the rest weak from lack of food and water, Peryst led them to the site where he and Golfen had camped with Maia just before reaching the camp. He wouldn't be back in time for his daily ritual of collecting Maia for the evening meal but had charged Golfen with doing so, like he did on the nights Peryst was with the watch. His child would be made a fuss of by Golfen and his companions, cared for as well as when he cared for her himself.

It was a night later that Peryst saw Cali snuggled in her father's arms as Maia lay asleep in his own when they all sat under the glow of the evening fire. Of the ten rescued, all had vowed to join the rebels except for Cali's father. He would lead his family across the mountains to the free lands of the North where his Touched daughter could flourish.

Peryst smoothed Maia's tousled locks and wondered. His purpose had been so clear the night after he'd brought Cali to the camp. But now? He glanced across at the sleeping Cali. *Should I go North, too? Or should I listen to my gut that tells me to fight for a world where my daughter can go safely where she chooses?*

He lowered his lips to Maia's head. He didn't have to decide yet.

FORGLENDEN

YEAR 5162 OF THE NEW ERA – WINTER

SCREAMS WOKE THE camp. Sword in hand, Peryst jumped up from his mattress and rushed to the door. People ran in all directions, weapons in hand, lit by the embers from the central communal fire. It was difficult to make out what was going on.

'Stop! Everybody, stop!' Thallya's grave voice boomed as Maia, startled by the noise, wailed behind him.

Peryst wrapped her snugly against the cold of outside and soothed her against his shoulder as he walked back out, weapon in hand.

'Who screamed?' Thallya asked calmly as Fiona came to stand by her side. The turmoil died down and questions rang out.

Focusing his enhanced sight, Peryst saw no immediate danger in the darkness. He could see no obvious attackers and no injuries, so he leaned his sword against his thigh and, with both arms, rocked Maia till she relaxed against his shoulder, half asleep.

A girl they'd rescued from the butcher's cart, little older than fifteen or sixteen, came forwards, head bent. 'It was me,' she said quietly.

'Why, Fyla, what happened?' Thallya asked gently.

'I couldn't sleep, so I went to sit by the stream.' Her voice shook. 'I was just sitting there enjoying the reflections on the water when it suddenly went dark.'

'What did you see?'

The girl shook her head repeatedly as she tried to speak but couldn't get the words out. Thallya turned and spoke softly to someone behind her.

A few moments later, Golfen approached with a glass, which he gave to the girl. 'Drink it all, Fyla. It will calm you.'

Fyla grimaced as she drank. Peryst had had the pleasure of one of Golfen's potions one morning after he'd had an ale too many the night before. Its effect had been excellent, but the taste foul. Golfen cared little for taste aesthetics. He left that to the Tamad, he said to Peryst. He cared only that his potions were effective.

'I'm sorry, Thallya,' she whispered.

'Was it the Hand, Fyla?' Fiona intervened. 'Or bandits?'

'No, oh no, it wasn't human, it was an enzidia. A huge one, bigger than a horse!'

'Did it hurt you?'

Fyla shook her head. 'I ran back here. I thought it was following me, though.'

Thallya sighed. 'Where was the night watch?'

'They heard me yell and went to try and find it.'

Peryst, who'd placed the sleeping Maia back in her cot, approached Thallya, who was talking quietly to Fiona. 'A little before Golfen and I arrived at the camp, we came across an area west of here that was covered in webs. I thought it was a very large spider or a vast colony of small ones. I'm assuming this enzidia is a type of spider?'

'Southerners tend to use the term spider or enzidia indistinctly, but, in reality, the enzidia is a sub-species of spider: highly poisonous and about the size of a large nut,' Fiona replied.

'The girl spoke of a much larger creature. Probably not an enzidia then.'

'Probably,' Thallya said. 'But it'll need to be dealt with. We cannot have the threat of a beast as well as the threat of the Hand. But first, we'll need to hear what the night watch has to say.' She pushed Fiona's shoulder. 'Go back to bed. I'll wait for them.' Then she turned back to Peryst. 'Will you wait up with me?'

'No need.' Tam emerged through the trees leading his mixed band of fifteen. 'We're here.'

Peryst had learnt that the night and day watches should not be underestimated, however young the humans or however small the halflings. They fought together like gears of the clocks his grandmother and then Marie had made, each with a particular strength in battle. All were dangerous, but together they were deadly, very like the flawlessly run Idhans he'd seen in Kurbal.

'What happened?' Thallya asked.

'There were traces of a sticky substance. It's like that produced by an enzidia, but there's much more of it than we'd expect, and it's killing the plants. The creature must be huge, so it's not an enzidia but some other kind of spider. We didn't see it but heard it rustling. The ground shook as it escaped.' Tam spoke grimly. 'Whatever kind, it's abnormally large and poisonous.'

Thallya shook her head. 'Everyone, get back to bed and sleep if you can. Come morning, we'll discuss how to deal with this creature.' She turned to Tam. 'Be alert tonight. It may have simply feinted and be preparing to return for its prey.'

Shrinking, Fyla blanched.

With a nod, Tam turned to his troops. They all made their way to the perimeter of the camp to keep watch.

Weapons at his side, Peryst lay back down next to Maia's cot. He didn't expect to sleep so leaned back against the wall to think about the previous couple of months.

They had all adapted well to life in Forglenden. Peryst spent a portion of his days training youngsters to use weapons. He also assisted in training those who came into their Touched powers whether they'd been born Touched or had their mind's eye opened by Thallya. Learning to harness powers came easier to some than to others. Peryst taught them practical things such as lighting a fire, moving the air to aid the flight of an arrow, and sharpening and releasing their focus.

Because the Rohinians were usually busy collecting potion ingredients in the forest and brewing all kinds of concoctions, Peryst had seen less of Golfen during the days, but they sat together every evening to talk. Only a few days after Golfen had reconnected to the Dreaming, Peryst noticed a difference. Though always cheerful, Golfen had carried a weight that Peryst could no longer see. And he was glad.

Maia had displayed few powers since they arrived, only occasionally moving a toy but little else. Peryst wondered about this. Maybe when she underwent physical change, the power was dampened? Or maybe it was that she was seeing and learning so much that she'd forgotten that her power was even there. Or perhaps she simply didn't need her powers when her needs were met. She spent part of her days with the other young children under the care of those who could no longer wield weapons and received Peryst at the end of the day with shrieks of joy.

He woke to the light of the pale winter sun and muted sounds from the camp, surprised to have slept at all. After rising with Maia, he joined Thallya and Fiona at the communal table.

'We hadn't expected to have to deal with a beast, so didn't account for that last night when planning today's schedule,' Thallya declared. 'Our original plan was for Sacha and May to go to Leyandale, which hasn't yet fallen but lies two weeks from Ilia, where the Hand is now truly present. This will still happen but not yet. Though we cannot plan if we don't know the situation in the city, we must first deal with this new threat.'

Peryst intervened. 'I know where to find the webs I mentioned last night. I've killed many monsters in my life so could try my hand at this spider.'

Thallya nodded. 'Not alone.' She turned to a tired-looking Tam. 'Tam, make a team for Peryst of those who weren't on guard last night.' She patted him on the arm. 'And then get some sleep.'

Tam considered and then named Tandy and Olli, the young couple who Peryst knew from the night watch, another man Peryst hadn't met, and a male elf, a Kurbali with dark skin and black-and-white-streaked hair. Peryst was pleased that Gena was included in the team.

They set out walking west soon after he settled Maia with the children's group. As they walked, Peryst fell in next to Gadryl Tideswell. 'Though less unusual where it comes to Kurbali, it's still uncommon to find elves south of the Kunlan Range. How do you come to be here, and why do you fight the Hand when it has no reach in your lands?' he asked.

Taking his time to answer, Gadryl turned serious blue eyes to Peryst. 'As you say, it is more common for us Kurbali to travel than for our Sahari kin to do so. But I wished to see the world. I was in northern Mehru, heading towards the coast to find a ship to bear me home, when I came across Sacha in Gyllia.' He made a gesture between a shrug and a nod.

'Ahh,' chuckled Peryst, 'the sparkling Mehruvian eyes. Yes, my friend. I, too, was struck by eyes like that.'

'Gyllia was a fair town, but elves are no longer welcome there, so I left, and Sacha took my hand and led me here.' He shrugged again.

'And you've joined the fight against the Hand?'

'What would you do for your sparkling Mehruvian eyes?'

'If she were alive, anything,' Peryst said fervently.

Gadryl gave an obviously rare smile. 'There is your answer.'

Light-footed Gena, who walked ahead, stopped suddenly and lifted a gloved hand covered in a sticky substance. 'What's this?'

Gadryl and Peryst caught up with her. The bushes and leafless trees were all covered in something that was killing them.

'When I caught a glimpse of this, I thought they were spiderwebs, but now I'm not so sure,' Peryst said, touching the silvery stickiness with one gloved finger before bringing it to his nose.

Gadryl pointed ahead at a dense pattern that covered trees from the ground up. 'Those are webs, but this isn't.'

Peryst crouched and cleaned his finger against the earth. 'It might be some kind of venom. The trees don't seem to like it. Try not to touch it with your skin, just in case. Do any of you know anything about enzidias or spiders in general?'

Gena wrinkled her nose. 'Other than that they're a type of highly poisonous spider with eight legs and disgusting? No, I'm afraid not.'

Gadryl spoke up. 'There's a sub-species of enzidia in Kurbal, the sprinossa, which spins a web and then coats it in venom. Its prey loses consciousness when in contact with the web, so it's easier to truss.'

'Could this stuff come from one of those?' Tandy asked.

Gadryl frowned. 'I've never seen one larger than my hand.'

'From the size of all this,' Peryst replied, gesturing at the grove covered in webs and venom, 'either we have one giant creature or a huge colony of smaller ones. Neither a pleasant prospect.'

'Fyla said she saw one huge creature,' Gena said.

'What Fyla said doesn't mean there aren't more spiders,' Peryst replied. 'She was scared out of her wits.'

'If it's a sprinossa, I doubt it's a colony,' Gadryl said.

'Why?' Gena asked.

'The sprinossa is a loner. A female will eat its mate after becoming impregnated then travel to wherever it means to make its lair and release its eggs weeks, months, and even years later,' Gadryl explained.

'So, this could be the lair of a female and its young,' Gena said.

'No. The female will give the young a day from birth to get away. If they're within her proximity the next day, she'll eat them,' Gadryl said.

'Charming and loving mother.' Gena rubbed her own glove in the dirt to clean off the poison.

'How could one have grown so big?' Peryst wondered.

Gadryl shrugged. 'I wouldn't know. I've never heard of one doing so. I suspect it's something else.'

The six crept through the grove carefully, making their way through withered bushes and dying trees smothered in webs and venom.

'Whatever species, it seems to have moved away from this area,' Peryst said.

'Not surprising,' Gena replied. 'Nothing can live here with every plant dead or dying, so it'll have little chance of finding prey.'

'And so, it'll move to another area and kill the trees there as well,' Gadryl said sadly. 'We must find and destroy it before another swathe of forest dies.'

Olli hadn't said a word till then but spoke up quietly. 'We should start from where Fyla saw it and radiate out into the forest. Maybe it was scouting for a new area last night.'

'It would be dangerous to have it so close to the stream where we do our washing,' Peryst added as they turned back in the direction of the camp.

From the point where the stream was shallow and children came to bathe in the warmer months, they scouted out slowly in a fan shape. After six hours of searching, they had almost given up when Olli called out. 'There's some venom here, and it shines.'

'Wait.' Peryst held up a hand to stop his companions. 'My Sensal abilities will be useful when we find the creature but won't tell me much till I can see it. Do any of you have an ability we can use?'

'Fire Primal, so not much use for now,' Olli said.

'I'm an Air Primal and weak Mender so can't do much yet either,' added Jai Mayvale, who hadn't spoken since they left the camp.

'I'm a Sight Sensal,' Gadryl replied.

'And I'm a Hearing Sensal,' added Tandy.

'What can you tell us?' Peryst asked as he watched Tandy and Gadryl focus their mind's eyes and scan the area carefully.

Sight Sensals could see the world differently when their mind's eye was focused. For some, colours became brighter, and things that were otherwise hidden were revealed. Others saw more detail than a normal mind could take in, such as the track left by a rabbit a week earlier, the seeds from which each plant and tree had grown, and a trail. Some saw truth, and some, like Peryst, saw weaknesses. Hearing Sensals could hear a faraway whisper, rustling underground, or the thud of footsteps where there was nothing to be seen.

Gadryl whispered, 'The creature passed through here a short time ago. The trail is fresh.'

Tandy, mind's eye focused, added, 'I can hear it. It's straight ahead and injured. It drags two legs.'

'Once I can see it, I'll be able to gauge any weakness it may have. Wait here,' Peryst said and crept along the trail carefully.

The faint trail curved to the right. Ahead, dragging one of its back legs, moved a spider as tall as a grown man. It struggled to make its way down a narrow forest path better suited for small mammals, turning this way and that in an effort to coax its huge bulk through the trees.

Peryst focused his mind's eye on the creature. Its body and the top sections of its legs were covered in a hard, dark-red carapace, marked and scratched but otherwise intact. Six of its legs were sound, but two hung limply: the back one and one in the front. Its head, also hard, had eight eyes; four on the right side were damaged and unseeing, as was one on the left, but the remaining three on that side scanned the path. Unlike spiders he'd seen before, it had no fangs but a wide, toothed mouth and a pair of short and seemingly malformed arms dangling from its chest. With his mind's eye focused, Peryst could clearly see the venom conduits that terminated in the pincer-like endings of those two extra limbs. It had few weaknesses, Peryst saw, thus explaining its ancient age. Though its eyes were vulnerable, its hearing made up for that loss and, unlike the cockatrice, an arrow through one of them wouldn't reach the brain, protected as it was by a chitinous layer. The only way to kill it would be to pierce the soft space between the two venom-bearing arms where the carapace failed to join completely.

Peryst melted back into the shrubs and returned to his companions waiting along the curvy path.

'We were debating whether to come and rescue you,' Gena said drily.

'No need.'

'What's your verdict?' Olli asked.

'It's going to be very difficult.' Peryst relayed what he had seen.

'That doesn't sound like a sprinossa at all. How big is this soft area?' Gadryl asked.

Peryst raised both hands, uniting index fingers and thumbs to demonstrate. 'About this big, but it's between the two venomous arms. The shot would need to come from the front and at a low angle.'

'You said the legs were soft at the bottom,' Tandy stated.

Peryst nodded. 'They appear softer but may not be, and two of its legs are useless.'

'We should lure it towards us,' Gadryl said. 'I assume your aim is excellent, Peryst? And that, like any self-respecting Klaevani, you carry maqtarum arrows?'

'My aim is good enough,' Peryst said and removed an arrow from his quiver. The telltale blue of the metal tip marked it as maqtarum, a toxin-laden metal that Klaevani mined and used to forge weapons for monster hunting.

'Then I'll try to blind it,' Gadryl said, 'You aim at its vulnerable spot.'

'And we'll go for the legs to stop it rushing us,' Gena finished, speaking for the rest.

'Beware of the arms. I don't know if the pincer shoots poison or merely injects it on contact, nor do I know whether it's lethal, but considering the size of the beast, any of its venom will probably be quite harmful,' Peryst warned. 'Are we ready?'

At the silent nod from the others, Peryst led the way, this time making as much noise as possible, bow in hand and mind's eye focused ahead.

He wasn't prepared for the monster to turn and charge at them at top speed, faster than they could've expected such a large creature to move, with its armlike appendages wrapped tightly over the vulnerable area on its chest. With a leap, Gadryl swung himself up to sit on a low branch and started shooting arrows at the spider. Like most Sight Sensals, his aim was excellent, and soon the beast could only see out of the leftmost eye, which made it falter and turn its head at an awkward angle, upsetting its centre of balance. Peryst hoped Gadryl would stop at that to prevent its strong hearing from taking over and it becoming more assured. He was relieved that Gadryl then joined the others in aiming arrow after arrow at its legs, though without much effect. The arrows just slid without a bite. Then Gena made the ground under the huge spider sink enough to destabilise it. As it stumbled, she jumped forwards with her sword and hacked at the front legs with Olli and the others close behind.

'Watch out, Gena!' Gadryl and Peryst yelled in unison as the appendages unfurled from the creature's chest and aimed at the woman.

The moment the vulnerable area was visible, Peryst shut out the screams of his companions, the fear that this enormous beast would get him and leave Maia stranded in Forglenden, and the feeling he always had that one day his powers would fail and he'd be like any other non-Touched man. He focused his attention on arrow and target, and, just as the monster dug its pincers into Gena's thigh, he shot true, straight into the vulnerable soft spot.

For a moment nothing happened. Gadryl, still hanging from the branch by his legs, kept shooting at the creature, while Olli and Tandy screamed and tried to wrest a shuddering Gena away from the pincers as Jai hacked at the creature. Then, suddenly, the giant spider shook and emitted a low whistling sound before collapsing in a heap.

'Make sure it's truly dead,' Peryst said to Gadryl as he leapt to aid Gena who lay shaking with her eyes open but senseless. Pink foam dribbled from the side of her mouth, and her nails and lips had gone blue. Peryst turned to the others, feeling once again the helplessness he'd suffered when faced with a dying wife. 'We need a Mender.' He shook his head in frustration and then remembered that Jai was one. He turned to the boy expectantly.

'I'm not very powerful,' Jai said, focusing his mind's eye on Gena and then taking a step back in horror. 'There's nothing we can do. The venom is too potent and too fast. Maybe Thallya, who's more powerful, will be able to help, but I doubt it. Gena's organs are already dissolving.'

Tandy took off at a run in the direction of the camp as Olli and Jai waited with the same dejected helplessness as Peryst.

From behind them, Gadryl spoke quietly. 'The spider is dead.'

By the time Golfen, Neeva, and Thallya arrived trailing Tandy, Gena lay dead in a pool of pinkish fluid. Peryst crouched by her side, overwhelmed with sorrow. He was joined by Thallya, who fell onto her knees beside him, a look of devastation on her face.

'Don't touch her or the fluid,' Golfen panted, hands on knees as he tried to recover his breath. He placed a bulging bag at his feet.

'Why?' Olli asked.

'A venom so powerful will have suffused her organs, Olli, so if you touch anything, it will pass to you.'

Olli took a quick step back.

'Do you know what this creature is, Golfen?' Peryst asked, angling his head at the spider.

Golfen nodded, keeping at a distance and without the urgency to approach he had displayed with the cockatrice. 'It's a thoxutria, one of the most venomous creatures you can find. They can live for hundreds of years, usually in dark and humid caves.'

'What would it be doing in Forglenden Forest?' Gadryl asked.

Golfen shrugged. 'I can't imagine. They normally live underground.'

'There are a few caverns further to the east,' Gadryl replied. 'We haven't explored them in detail, but perhaps they are deeper than we thought.'

'Where the spider came from doesn't really matter,' Peryst said heavily. 'What matters is that we've lost Gena to it.' He placed a gentle hand on Thallya's shoulder, knowing there was nothing he could say to console her. Then he turned to Golfen and asked quietly, 'Is its corpse any good to you?'

'No. But I will take some of the venom. When diluted, it serves as a fast-acting poison for which there's no antidote. It's impossible even for Menders to stop its spread if not done immediately. Even a few seconds will make it too late.'

Golfen removed heavy gloves and a couple of earthenware jars from the bag he carried. He approached the spider and bent to grasp one of the pincers, careful not to touch anything else. He squeezed venom into first one and then another jar. He then took a step back and threw the gloves he had used onto the corpse. With another pair, he closed the jars securely and then threw those gloves as well. He packed the jars in the bag and moved back.

'You've seen how the coating of venom from its webs kills trees. The pure venom from its pincers will burn through any container except earthenware. And now there's only one thing to do.'

'What?' Gadryl asked.

'We must burn everything: both the spider and the girl.'

'No,' Thallya protested as she spoke for the first time. Peryst hadn't even noticed that Fiona had joined her. Voice trembling, Thallya stretched a hand as if to touch Gena but stopped herself. 'We cannot burn her body. We don't use the method divined by the Hand of Reason to exterminate the Touched in Forglenden. We'll give her a burial and do brysk for her spirit.'

'We'll celebrate our girl's life, acknowledging her bravery,' Fiona spoke on a sob. 'And we'll describe and name her so that any gods or spirits she comes across in her afterlife wanderings will recognise her and guide her to the halls of the fallen.'

'And kill us all in the process?' Golfen asked shortly.

Peryst shifted his attention to him.

'I suspect you saw how quickly Gena died. That is just how quickly any of you will die if you touch her or that fluid,' Golfen added.

Thallya came to her feet with difficulty before helping Fiona up. Both looked shrivelled, husks of the women Peryst had known till then. Thallya spoke in a strained voice. 'Then we'll make a trench so the fire won't spread and keep watch from a distance.' She turned to Olli and Jai. 'Olli, go and wake Tam. He's an Air Primal and will be able to keep the wind blowing upwards so that no fumes come into the camp. Jai, you and Tandy get shovels and axes so we can dig a trench.' She rubbed her face, gulped, and added, 'And we'll do brysk for Gena once we've eliminated the danger. Gena wouldn't want it otherwise.' She pointed down to a small plant that grew next to where Gena lay that had withered and died in the time since she had fallen. Fiona stifled a sob and placed her arm over Thallya's shoulders.

'I'll bring lempasanct potion to sprinkle round the clearing so that the poison doesn't spread through the earth,' Golfen said and turned back to the camp.

More came to cut down trees and gather stacks of dry leaves and branches. Others came to dig a trench to surround Gena and the thoxutria. It would stop the fire from spreading into the forest. They threw the chopped wood, branches, and leaves into the small clearing they'd made within the trench and made a makeshift pyre over Gena and the monster. Once it was done, Peryst and Olli concentrated more energy than they normally would have at lighting the fire. Golfen said the monster wouldn't burn at normal temperatures, so they made it hot enough to consume the cold and wet branches with ease. After the fire started, people began making their way back to the camp, except for Thallya, Fiona, and Jai, who stayed with Peryst, Olli, Golfen, and Tam.

Peryst and Olli kept their focus and concentration on the fire, while Tam and Jai kept theirs on the air above the pyre, and Golfen circled the area sprinkling his potion into the trench. Tam and Jai whirled and twirled the mix of smoke and fumes straight up, pushing till the smoke was out of sight, then letting it all loose where it would cause no harm.

Tears coursing down their faces, Thallya and Fiona took turns in speaking of the girl they'd reared and damned the Hand for driving them from Ros, where Gena would never have met such a beast.

The late afternoon slunk into evening and still Peryst, Olli, Jai, and Tam kept their focus on the pyre. Peryst could think of nothing else but the fire. His mind was so focused it was almost as if he were the fire. All he saw were flames, burning hotter than any other made by man. At regular intervals, Golfen slipped small fragments of umasu root into Peryst's hand. He chewed them slowly to replenish enough Touched energy to keep the flames burning.

It was past midnight when there was nothing left to burn, and the fire started dying down of its own accord. Of Gena, all that was left were a few fragments, broken and porous, barely like bones at all; and of the thoxutria, there was nothing, not even a fragment. Only then, once everything had ended, did Thallya approach Peryst. He turned, disoriented, and feeling the cold of the winter night. He hadn't even realised that Golfen had left.

'You are needed, Peryst. Maia is upset. Sacha came to tell us some time ago, and Golfen went back to camp to see what he could do.'

Exhausted by his steady outpouring of Touched power and with shaking hands, Peryst nodded once and set off at a slow, wavering run with the rest close behind. His mind could barely function from the effort, and his body struggled to respond to his orders, but all he could think was that Maia needed him.

He could hear Maia's wailing and Nela's howls before he could even see the camp, and the sound of her distress made him take strength from some hidden corner to run faster to reach his screaming child. Sacha stopped him as he ran like a madman through the wide-awake camp.

'Peryst! Wait. The child is unharmed. Wait!' She held him by the arm and forced him to stop and listen.

'What is it?' he asked, his voice hoarse and strained.

'We don't know. The camp was in uproar, and all the children were unsettled. When you didn't come for her at the usual time and Golfen didn't come either, Maia became inconsolable. When I tried to pick her up, she pushed me back.'

'She's a baby, Sacha, how could she push you?' Thallya asked.

'She lifted her hands and threw a strong gust of air at me,' Sacha said. 'Enough to push me across the clearing.'

'Why. Is. She. Still. Screaming?' Peryst asked, trying to loosen Sacha's grasp on his arm. 'And why is Nela howling?'

'Because, when I tried to approach Maia again, she reached for Nela and pushed me away a second time. She won't let anyone get close, bringing up a barrier of air when we try. Not even Golfen.'

Peryst thrust Sacha from him and ran to Maia, ignoring everything else. He stopped when he reached Golfen, who tried from a distance to get Maia to listen to him. Nela sat, howling incessantly, but stopped when Peryst came close. Her face tear-stained and puffy, Maia leaned against the wolf as sobs racked her little body. Peryst, only thinking of her anguish, went down onto his knees and shuffled to her, hand upraised. And then Maia was in his arms crying quietly as Nela rubbed herself against him.

'Did you think I'd left you, little one? Is that what this was? Didn't you hear me say that I'd be with you till I drew my last breath? I'm your father, Maia. I will always come for you. Always.' Peryst whispered disjointed phrases as he rocked the exhausted child with one hand and stroked Nela with the other.

'That child is more powerful than any Touched I have ever known, but she carries a great insecurity, Peryst,' Thallya said quietly. 'Only an immense fear of loss could have brought about such a strong reaction.'

'She lost her mother,' Peryst replied.

'It has to be more than that,' Thallya said thoughtfully. She peered searchingly at Peryst. 'Was there another child? One that didn't survive?'

Peryst brushed his lips over Maia's sweat-matted hair. 'There was another child,' he said softly.

Thallya nodded. 'The loss of a parent and a twin. It's a pain she'll carry forever.'

'Oh Maia,' Peryst said, his heart twisting in his chest as he held her tighter. 'You'll always have Nela and me.'

'Take her to bed, Peryst. And get some rest. I'll get you some ale and some milk for the child.'

'Just water, Thallya. I couldn't drink ale tonight.'

'Fair enough.'

Peryst moved Maia's cot next to his bed and lay with his arm over her. Both slept deeply and long, exhausted as they were from their different ordeals. Peryst woke naturally in the late-morning light to Maia's contented chattering.

He took water from a barrel and washed himself and Maia before dressing and taking her in search of food. He came across some of those who cared for the youngsters, but all turned away, so he was perplexed by the time he reached the food area.

'Peryst!' Thallya joined him. 'How is she?'

'Hungry.'

Thallya smiled and helped ready a plate for Peryst and another for Maia.

'Will you let me feed you, Maia, so that your father may eat as well? We'll sit right next to him.' Thallya smiled at the little girl, who clasped her hands about Peryst's neck tightly.

Peryst took Maia's hands from his neck and sat on the bench sideways, setting her onto his lap. 'There. Now we can both eat.'

As Peryst placed the cuts of meat between bread, Thallya silently fed Maia her puree.

'Everyone I met from my hut to the table averted their gazes. Why?'

'They're afraid.'

'Of me?'

'Of the child.'

'We've been here two months, Thallya. They haven't been afraid before.'

'No, they haven't, but they hadn't seen Maia lose control. She's very powerful, Peryst. Sacha wasn't merely pushed back but thrown across the clearing when she tried to approach. And she wouldn't listen to any of us, not even to Golfen, whom she knows and loves.'

Peryst carried on eating.

'I don't know enough to help train one so young and so powerful, Peryst. None in the camp is capable of such training. And Maia is a danger to herself and others till she learns control, but I wouldn't know how to start to guide her.'

Maia held onto the end of his belt with one hand. Peryst stared blindly at the little white knuckles and confessed to himself that he didn't either. He wanted above all to do the right thing by Maia but didn't know how or what to do. And even if he wanted to react angrily and rail at Thallya, he had no energy to do so as he was scared himself. Scared of failing this child who depended on him.

'There's a powerful Mas south of the Ramu, in Deragaz. Her name is Lexya Elmcrest. She'll be able to help you both. There is none more powerful than her south of the Kunlan Range.'

'We'll leave at daybreak tomorrow,' Peryst said finally, smiling wryly. He didn't need to decide. Leaving had been decided for him.

DERAGAZ

YEAR 5162 OF THE NEW ERA – SPRING

LEXYA USHERED PERYST into the cottage that stood just beyond the shadow extending from the south-eastern border of Forglenden. Twisting his neck before entering, he caught sight of the walls of Deragaz and a guard pacing back and forth in front of one of the arches into the town.

The front room, as white as the exterior of the small cottage, doubled as kitchen and sitting room.

'Thallya was right to send you here,' Lexya said as she gestured for Peryst to place Maia on a multi-coloured rug that covered the rough floorboards in front of the well-cushioned armchair onto which she lowered herself.

The moment Peryst set Maia down, she turned back to him. Peryst realised she was checking that he would go nowhere without her. Whatever she saw in his face reassured her enough to crawl off to investigate her new surroundings.

'What type of Touched are you? And what is she?' Lexya asked.

'I'm a Sight and Touch Sensal with a hint of Primal abilities. I have an affinity with fire, but I don't know about Maia. So far, she's manipulated air, so she's an Air Primal, but she has also lit a fire, so she's also a Fire Primal.'

Lexya nodded and observed Maia thoughtfully. 'When did you first notice that she had Touched abilities?'

Peryst hesitated. It had all started just before the Lithe Fair, according to Marie, so Maia would have been shy of six months, but could there have been signs before that none noticed? 'When she was six months,' he said, 'but perhaps she had used her powers earlier and I just didn't notice.'

Lexya watched intently as Maia touched the wooden floor with her fingers and crawled to the cold stone hearth. When she came up to a wooden armchair, she grabbed hold of the leg and pulled herself to a teetering upright position. Peryst made a convulsive move to stabilise her, but Lexya held him back with a gesture. Maia passed a hand over the soft cushion on the seat and then lowered herself slowly. She did the same with every chair, with the wooden table, and with the brick cooker. Once she had touched every surface, she returned to the rug in front of the hearth and traced its patterns with her fingers.

'Maia,' Lexya said quietly.

Maia raised her head to the Mas then frowned and turned away.

'Maia,' Lexya said again, sternly, staring intently at the child.

Maia turned back and this time didn't shift her gaze till the Mas did. Lexya repeated the exercise over and over again, always stopping first.

'What are you doing?' Peryst asked.

'I am establishing obedience. For Maia to learn control, she must learn respect. She must know that there are boundaries and rules. Most important, she must learn her own boundaries and rules. You're so blinded by your love and fear for her wellbeing that you will run to her whenever she is vulnerable instead of letting her fall and learn to pull herself up again.'

'Is that not my role as her father?'

'Not at all. She must learn to fall and stand again. She must learn to stop herself before she falls. And with a child this powerful, you must be her father and her teacher. She cannot be allowed to manipulate your love, or she could cause great damage to herself and others.'

'Have you seen many children whose powers manifest this early?'

Lexya took some time to answer. 'All children born in the Isles of Vel and in the southern continent of Glannafel are like her. In Vel it's thanks to their

Glannafel ancestry, of course, but it is very rare to find such a child in Ankisua. I have never seen another but have read of children like Maia,' she said as she moved to prepare an infusion with the water she had left heating on the stove. Ramrod straight, the grey-haired woman poured water onto a bundle of herbs so that a pungent, sweet, and bark-like aroma filled the cottage.

Peryst winced as the aroma pushed at his mind's eye, urging it to open even further and triggering a slight headache between his brows. 'What's that scent?'

Lexya chuckled. 'A herbal mix of my own that can extend the reach of the mind's eye.'

'In what way?'

'What can you do with your mind's eye, Peryst de Arranu?'

Peryst shrugged. 'I see the weakness in things living and not living. My sense of touch is enhanced.' He paused. 'I can play with fire.'

She smiled. 'With my tea, your mind's eye would move beyond those boundaries, possibly even stretching to others of your senses. You would see more, feel more, and perhaps even smell and hear more. Effects can vary from person to person, but the reach of the mind's eye is always extended.'

He lifted both hands, pushing the idea away. 'I don't think I would want that.'

She nodded. 'Many feel as you do, but if I am to help you with your daughter, I must see the extent of her powers. Will you allow me to focus on her with my mind's eye?'

Peryst hesitated. It implied extreme trust to open oneself completely and allow another to look into them with their mind's eye. Everything was there to be seen and evaluated: every weakness, every foible, every dream. He had only done so with Sanjia, and even with her, the love of his life, it had left him trembling, vulnerable, and exposed.

What will Lexya see? Will she find Reba in Maia? Will she see Raf? I can't teach Maia to control her powers, and her life depends on her learning to manage them. But she needs to know she's my daughter, with no doubts and no confusion. She needs a clear identity.

Peryst sighed. He was up against a wall but knew he would take the risk. He had to. He needed Lexya's help.

'Do it,' he said quietly.

Lexya drank deeply and let her eyelids fall. When she turned back to him, her pupils had grown larger, blending into the black of her eyes. She centred her gaze on Maia, who sat with her back to the Mas, and called to her in a gentle voice. 'Maia.'

The child lifted her head as if hearing a call from afar, and, dropping the toy, she twisted her body till she was facing Lexya, her gaze fixed on the Mas. They stared at each other, still as stone. Her long, grey hair piled on the top of her head and her back straight, arms at her sides, and wrinkled face unmoving and stern, Lexya appeared to concentrate her being on the child. Maia lifted her head, extended her neck, and, with her face serious and almost adultlike, concentrated on Lexya.

After a time during which Peryst fought himself not to pick up his daughter, a faint moan escaped Maia's throat, but she didn't move or shift her gaze till Lexya leaned back. Then whatever had held Maia up suddenly let her go. She slumped down and, whimpering, crawled to Peryst, who met her halfway and cradled her as he whispered soothing words. Within seconds she was fast asleep in his arms.

Lexya sat crumpled in her wooden chair. Her hands shook, and she breathed lightly.

'What was that?' Peryst asked quietly.

She didn't reply immediately but sat slowing her breathing. She returned his gaze slowly with an exhausted expression. 'Maia looked back at me,' she said.

'You asked her to,' he replied.

'I asked her to show me her eyes, so I could see into them with my mind's eye. She did and I did, but then she focused her own mind's eye on mine, Peryst, to see in me.'

He regarded the sleeping child but said nothing.

'She's a Primal, but she's also a Sensal and maybe even a Mender. Her power is such that I have rarely seen before. Though not unheard of, very few children can command their mind's eye from infancy and without training.'

Peryst nodded. He remembered his time in Genai under Glauca's instruction and then the months with the Fellowship in Lukur, under the instruction of a powerful Touched who taught him how to combine the use of his different powers. 'There is a type of Touched that runs through my mother's line that develops skills in all three aspects of Touched powers. One hasn't been heard of in a couple of generations, but they were all Menders, Sensals, and Primals. Maia must be like them.'

'It's possible. But for power to manifest so strongly and so early in your daughter, either you or her mother must have had Glannafel roots.'

'There's a story in our branch of Clan de Arranu that says that our particular shade of green eyes comes from a Glannafel woman who partnered with a remote ancestor. And there's always been Touched in our family, but nothing out of the ordinary in recent generations. I don't know about the other side.'

'Maia's powers, whatever they may be and wherever they came from, seem to be governed by grief and fear,' Lexya added. 'The loss of mother and sibling may explain part of it, but the grief goes beyond that, and her fear is overwhelming.'

'Fear of what?'

Lexya shook her head. 'I couldn't see. Maia used her mind's eye to block mine. I have never had that happen with one untrained.'

'What now then?' he asked, both frightened at the level of Maia's power and relieved that Lexya had seen nothing further in the child.

Lexya moved her head from side to side and up and down, rubbing the back of her neck. 'Now I will teach your daughter what I can, but before that I will give you a warning.'

Peryst, reeling with relief that his secret was safe, stiffened. He needed no one to warn him of the danger Maia could be in. He'd taken responsibility for the child, making her his own, knowing that she would be in danger from the Hand, but also that she would be viewed with distrust by those who had little education in the ways of the mind's eye.

'Maia's power is deeper than I've ever seen, but it's surrounded by a well of fear. Her reaction in Forglenden came from the fear that you wouldn't return to her.'

Peryst nodded. That much had been obvious.

'The line between fear and anger is a fine one, Peryst. You'll need to watch her carefully. There will be periods in her life when her dominant emotion will be fear or anger born of frustration: first as a young child, when she struggles to communicate but knows what she wants; then later when she's older, when her body and spirit are changing, and she cannot control that change. At these times, her fear will mix with anger.'

'What will that do?'

Lexya shook her head. 'You tell me. What were you taught when you were trained in Genai?'

Peryst sighed. 'Never use power in anger, never for revenge, never for selfish gain. Never use your mind's eye on another living being without consent unless there is danger of imminent death.'

'Do you know why we don't use power in anger?'

'I always assumed it was a basic rule of *do no harm*.'

'No. It's more than that. Anger amplifies power, Peryst. As do grief and fear. You tell me that this baby, who cannot walk or talk, pushed an adult across a clearing out of fear.'

He assented and peered down at Maia's lashes quivering on her little flushed face.

'Can you imagine what she could have done to that woman had she been angry?'

Peryst blanched.

'She will need to learn to control her emotions before she controls her power, and she will need to learn to live with fear and grief in such a way that it isn't at the forefront of each of her reactions.'

'How can a child so young learn to do this?'

'I'll help you both. She's young, but all her senses are active. I'll use her mind's eye to teach her.'

'How long before it's safe for me to take her to Lis?'

Lexya shrugged. 'If she responds exceptionally well, by eighteen months. If not, perhaps by the time she's two years old.'

'She's a year old! What will I do till then?' Peryst sighed.

'You'll join the Deragaz Guard and help them with the wave of bandits we've had in the area.'

'Are there many?'

'Enough for them to be a problem. We have bands of thugs who roam the wilderness. So, you'll go to Deragaz and seek accommodation at Sava's within the walls. Tell her I've sent you. Then speak to the Agazi. Tell him I sent you, too.'

'What about Maia?'

'You'll take her with you till the end of the week. On the morning of the sixth day, bring her to me and I'll begin her training.'

He scrutinised the cottage. It boasted thick, whitewashed walls, deep-set windows with diamond panes, and reddish shutters. Inside, two open doors led from the main room where they sat to a larger bedroom and a smaller one. Through a tidy orchard behind the cottage ran a small stream, and to the side was a chicken coop and a lean-to where a cow had been lying in the shade when he and Maia arrived. It was surrounded by trees that cocooned the cottage like the fingers of caring hands.

'How safe are you here? You're outside the walls, and if you say these thugs roam the countryside, I wouldn't leave my daughter out here unguarded.'

Lexya chuckled. 'We are visible from the walls, Peryst de Arranu. The Deragaz Guard watches for me but, in any event, more than walls and guards protect this house. You came with good intentions and, thus, could approach safely. Your child will be secure with me.'

'So be it.' Peryst fastened a still sleeping Maia to his back. 'But I'll bring Nela with her. Nela will protect Maia with her life.'

'If that's what you desire,' Lexya replied.

'You will need payment,' Peryst added firmly.

'I will send you for herbs or other ingredients I can't source myself and ask you to make repairs that I'm unable to do. That will be payment enough. Now, go into Deragaz before evening comes.'

Herbs he could collect and roofs he could fix easily. It was a small price to pay for Lexya to help with Maia's training. He gathered his belongings as Lexya, brow furrowed, gazed at the deeply slumbering child. 'She'll sleep for a few more hours and will wake ravenous. Then she'll sleep again all night and wake her usual self.'

Peryst bowed his head and departed, calling the faithful Nela to his side from where she had waited near the cottage door.

Mounting Roan, he experienced again the sorrow that had haunted him since leaving Forglenden. It had been long since he'd enjoyed another's company, longer still since he'd had a friend. Golfen had become one. Their relationship had been cemented in Forglenden, when both were at a certain peace and had been able to talk long into the nights, laugh carelessly with shared humour, and listen to each other's plans. Golfen had been shocked when Peryst announced his departure, but he'd found his place with his fellow Rohinians in the camp. He had a purpose now—fighting the Hand of Reason in the hope of preventing them forever taking his homeland—and Peryst could respect that. Golfen was no longer a fugitive separated from the Dreaming. He had no need to carry on roaming the wilds and, though Golfen loved Maia dearly, he'd decided to make a life in the forest.

'Promise me you won't wrap yourself in silence again,' Golfen had begged as they said their farewells. 'Maia needs words.'

Golfen had filled Peryst's days with conversation and, in doing so, had reminded him how to act with other people. By the time Peryst was ready to leave the forest, he knew he would've reminded those who'd known him of the clear-eyed man from before Sanjia's death. He was once again a Klaevani willing to strike up conversation with anyone and learn what he could from others. 'I promise.'

'If you have nothing to say, describe what you see, but talk incessantly to her,' Golfen insisted. 'Promise.'

'I will, Golfen. I promise.'

'I will see you again, Peryst and Maia de Arranu,' he said with a quivering voice as he kissed Maia's little hand and ruffled Nela's ears.

'That you will!' Peryst replied, hoping it would be so.

True to his word, he narrated their surroundings, told tales of his childhood with Marie, described plants and flowers, conveyed his hopes and fears, and spoke of Sanjia. His voice, which had been silenced by his wife's absence, rang again. Maia, in turn, tried replying in her nonsensical babbling till the day when she pointed at him with 'Dada' and at Nela with 'Lela'.

As he left Lexya's cottage, Peryst remained silent and alert. He hadn't expected to be fearful this far south and once again felt vulnerable with a child on his back. He heaved a sigh of relief when he glimpsed the welcoming western arch of the white town of Deragaz, set in the shape of a cross like most Mehruvian towns.

'Welcome to Deragaz, traveller!' a guard called out from the shadow of the thick, whitewashed arch from which the town walls stemmed on either side. Deragaz's walls were taller than those he'd seen in northern Mehru and had a central walkway where a guard watched the surroundings from above.

'Where are you headed? Deragaz for the duration or passing through?' the guard asked in a cheerful tone.

'Deragaz for now. Lexya, the Mas, has told me to speak to Sava about accommodation and to the Agazi about occupation.'

The guard chuckled and then took a startled step back when he caught sight of Nela. 'Is that a wolf?'

'It is indeed. She's Nela, our faithful defender and companion.'

'Our? Are you so big that you count for two?' the guard retorted with a grin.

Peryst laughed and half turned in his saddle.

'A baby! A Klaevani monster hunter with a baby strapped to his back is a sight I've never seen.'

'There's a first time for everything,' Peryst replied.

'Yours?'

'My daughter. We lost her mother and brother at birth, so it's just the two of us, Nela, and Roan,' Peryst replied, patting his mare.

The guard nodded. 'For Sava's, follow the main road east till you've crossed the green. Then turn into the fifth road to your right. Sava's is at the end.'

'How long will it take me?'

'At this time? With everyone on the streets stopping you for conversation and news? An hour, maybe.'

'Thank you, guard. Yours is the warmest welcome I have had in Mehru so far.'

The guard's face darkened. 'Ah, well, you've come from north of here. Northern Mehru is Mehru in name only these days.'

Peryst nodded once and guided Roan carefully through the arch and into a town much bigger than Ros. This was the Mehru he remembered, teeming with people and cheerful voices calling out to one another. Whitewashed houses with domed reddish roofs lined the streets. Doors were open and windows were decorated with cheerful flowerpots on their sills. Dark-haired children dressed in bright colours darted between adults who went about their business of knowing everybody else's business. As he expected, Peryst was stopped every few steps with questions about Nela, about Maia, and about how things were going in the North. He smiled to himself. Golfen would be relieved to know that there would be no danger of him retreating into silence in Deragaz: he wouldn't be allowed to!

Where the four main roads met was the green, home to a lively market, with the town hall, the guard house, the Temple to Gal, and the Deragaz emporium, each on a corner like in every Mehruvian town. Again, Peryst sighed in relief that southern Mehru remained as he remembered. He made his way carefully through the market, intent on not running over a child, a dog, or a distracted adult, till he came to the alley the guard described.

Sava's was a large, double-fronted boarding house with a stable to one side. As on every house he'd passed, its shutters, windows, and doors were open. On his approach, a young lad ran out, lanky and tall with the same colouring as his daughter but with a thatch of bright red hair that spoke of Tamad ancestry.

'Will you be lodging with us, traveller? Shall I take care of your horse?'

Peryst smiled at him as he dismounted. 'Not yet, lad. I'll speak to Sava first.'

The lad nodded and pointed the way into the house.

A bright room greeted Peryst, with tables and benches set to the front of a wide wooden bar. Behind the bar reigned a large woman with bright red hair tied in a knot behind her head, its wisps surrounding her cheerful red-cheeked face, and swathed in a wide red apron that complemented her colouring.

'Welcome, welcome,' she called, wiping her hands on the apron.

'Sava? I have come on the advice of Lexya in search of accommodation for myself, my daughter, and my beasts.'

'A Klaevani? What would you be doing in these parts?'

Peryst knew her query was from friendliness and not idle curiosity. 'I'm Peryst de Arranu and I have brought my daughter, Maia, to train with Lexya before I carry on to her grandfather's house in Lis, where I'll rejoin my company in the Southern Mehruvian Army. In the meantime, I intend to seek occupation with the Deragaz Guard.'

'Your daughter?' Confused, Sava swivelled her gaze and then came back to Peryst.

When he half turned, her expression softened. 'A baby! She is beautiful. Mehruvian colouring. Her mother was Mehruvian?'

'She was. And what would a Tamad like you be doing in Mehru?'

Sava chuckled. 'Love of a man brought me east from Tamadal, but love of Deragaz has kept me here.' She lifted a hinged section of the bar and walked out into the room while calling loudly up the stairs. Two young girls clattered down. They were like the boy outside: tall and Mehruvian, if he ignored the red hair.

Sava gestured towards the girls. 'My daughters. They help me run the guesthouse. We have one other guest—merchant from northern Usur—but he's due to leave soon.' She turned to the girls. 'Enna, add a cot to the front room for Peryst and his daughter, and you, Anna, go and see to the evening meal. Set aside some for mashing for the baby.'

She turned to Peryst and pointed at Nela, who sat patiently at his side. 'The wolf stays with you?'

'With Maia.'

Sava nodded. 'You have a horse?'

'Outside.'

Sava moved to the door and called the lanky lad into the room. 'My son, Pan, will care for your horse.'

'Thank you. Her name is Roan. Let me get my bags.' Peryst approached Roan and patted her flank after removing the saddlebags. 'You'll have a well-deserved rest, Roan,' he said before passing the reins to Pan, who led the mare into the stables.

'Give that horse a good rubdown, Pan, and make her comfortable,' Sava instructed over her shoulder as she led Peryst back into the room and up the stairs.

The front room was an airy chamber with a large bed barely visible under a gleaming white feather coverlet. At its side sat a wooden cot. Given the slight chill of the spring afternoon, a fire roared behind a grate on the hearth and the windows were fastened shut, but the sun shone through the panes.

'We serve the evening meal two bells after sundown, which is still late this time of year but will start getting earlier soon enough, and breakfast at sunrise. The midday meal is served with the town hall's bells.'

'Thank you,' Peryst said.

'You can leave your daughter with us when you seek out the Agazi. I've raised four youngsters, the eldest of which you will meet if you work with the guard.'

Peryst bowed his head. 'Thank you again. I would be grateful for that once she has met you all. Now she still sleeps, so I'll take her with me. I wouldn't like her to wake in an unknown place with strangers.'

'You said she's to train with Lexya. It's unusual for one so young to need such training. Touched powers tend to manifest later.'

'Indeed,' Peryst agreed. 'Lexya tells me it's not unheard of for power to manifest so young when there are Glannafel roots. In any event, Maia can't yet control her powers. I wouldn't like her to cause harm to any of you out of fear.'

Sava chuckled. 'My Pan was like that when his powers flowered. Older, it's true, but when nervous, his power would flare. He almost burnt down the guesthouse when a girl he liked came in with her parents.'

As Sava wiped the counter, the chuckle still at her lips, Peryst thought all Ankisua should be like this, where any could talk about the Touched without lowering their voices.

Peryst bowed his head. 'Where can I find the Agazi?'

'At this time of day? He'll be at the guard house on the green at the intersection of the four ways. It's the building to the right of the town hall.'

'Thank you, Mistress Sava.'

'The pleasure is mine, Master Peryst.'

Peryst walked up the alley, heading to the eastern way with Maia still fast asleep on his back and Nela padding along at his side. He calculated another hour of Maia's slumber before she woke. The baby on his back attracted curious comments and questions, but all so friendly and cheerful that the pain he'd carried since Usur—and the fear since Reor—dispersed a little.

A guard dressed in a worn leather cuirass with a sword on his side and a bow on his back stood at the guard house's heavy and copper studded open doors. He nodded as Peryst approached. 'Well met, traveller. What can I do for you?'

'I would like to speak with the Agazi. I've been sent by Lexya, the Mas on the fringe of Forglenden.'

'Aye, we all know Lexya.' The guard turned and beckoned to another who approached from inside the cool hall and asked him to lead Peryst to the Agazi, who was out back in the training grounds.

'Follow me.' The second guard, with a thatch of red hair, was younger.

'You must be Sava's son,' Peryst said.

'Aye, my name is Can Spicehart.' He stretched his hand out to Nela. 'A wolf?'

'Well met, Can. I'm Peryst de Arranu and this is Nela, my longtime faithful companion. We're staying at your mother's guesthouse.'

Can nodded, pride in his expression. 'You'll both be well cared for. My mother is an excellent cook, one of the best in Deragaz.'

'It's been weeks since I've had a proper cooked meal.' Peryst followed Can down a wide hall lined with doors and then out a side door to a large central patio where targets, dummies, and sparring partners assisted in training what were obviously the newest Deragaz Guard recruits.

'Peryst de Arranu! Blessed be Gal! You are the last person I expected to see here!'

A tall Mehruvian dressed in leather armour like the others stalked in Peryst's direction and enveloped him in a hug. Laughing, Peryst hugged his old friend Gintras of Barges, almost choking at the other's yelp of surprise when he encountered the sleeping child on his back.

'A baby and a wolf? This calls for an ale. How long has it been?'

'Almost eight years, Gintras.'

'Indeed, when you carried the lovely Sanjia away to the North, to the desolation of her father and of every red-blooded man in the vicinity, and not a few women.' Gintras chuckled.

Peryst remembered the lively days of courtship and joy and almost wished he hadn't succeeded because then Sanjia would still be alive.

'Is she well?' Gintras asked.

'She is no longer of the living. I lost her more than a year ago in the wilds of northern Usur. All I have left is my daughter, Maia, and her wolf, Nela.'

'Ahh, that is ill news indeed. I am sorry to hear it, Peryst. Her father will be distraught.'

'I bring him the worst news a father can hear.' Peryst shook his head sadly. 'It's not natural that a parent should hear of their child's death.'

'Aye. You're right.' Gintras clapped Peryst on the shoulder. 'It's good to see you regardless. I've thought of you often, remembering our times in the army.'

'They were good days when we did well.'

'I remember the day you joined our battalion as a mercenary recruit. How old were we?' Gintras scratched his head.

'It was in spring of 5147. I was just seventeen,' Peryst replied. They'd both been mere lads when they joined, later serving under Anil, the youngest Agazi in the army and only daughter of the High Luk, who led one of the six battalions that formed the Southern Mehruvian Army.

'Such nights of revelry! Remember the nights of Lis? Stumbling from tavern to tavern?' Gintras chuckled, a faraway expression on his face.

'I remember.' Peryst recalled days of hard training and nights of carousing as he rose through the ranks of his company quickly in happy competition with Gintras till Anil named them joint captains of their own company.

'And then when we joined Agazi Anil's company to deal with the pirates from Vel? When was that?'

'I think it was in early 5154.' Peryst shook his head, lost in the memories of their trip to the Isles of Vel. It was where the Touched that escaped from Reor when the Hand first arose had taken refuge. They'd joined with the inhabitants of the islands—originally from Glannafel—and developed into a people who became fearsome pirates and who made crossing the Erian Waters a dangerous venture for merchants.

Gintras chuckled to himself. 'Remember how nervous we were? How convinced that we would go into battle with the Velans?'

Peryst nodded. 'And how surprised when instead Anil signed a peace agreement with them?'

Gintras let out a bark of laughter. 'That agreement was signed beneath the sheets, as we all know.'

Peryst laughed in turn. Gintras's affirmation was not entirely untrue as Anil had eventually wed Klaust of Lugal and Eridia, only son and heir to the Pirate Chief of Vel, and, even in that first meeting on the Velan capital's jetty, Peryst had watched sparks fly between them.

'Enough of the past! What are you doing here?' Gintras asked.

'What would a Klaevani be doing? I need coin, so I'm after the Agazi to offer my services. My daughter is Touched and will train with Lexya for a few months at least.' Peryst pointed at his weapons. 'In the meantime, they need use and I need exercise and coin.'

Gintras laughed happily. 'You are speaking to the Agazi, Peryst.' He grew serious. 'What have you done since I last saw you?'

'I've killed monsters, human and animal, and joined the army in Kurbal on Agazi Anil's orders. In Genai and Usur, I mainly dealt with monsters: suraru and wyverns. Since losing Sanjia and one of the babies, I've been travelling with the intention of reaching Lis. On the way, I killed a cockatrice and joined a rebel cell in Forglenden, where I killed a thoxutria.'

Gintras shrugged. 'Business as usual.'

'And you? How is it that you're here and not climbing the army ranks? I left you as captain to one of the companies in Anil's battalion and would have expected you to be an Agazi in the army by now and not leading a provincial guard on the borders of southern Mehru. Not quite the upward army progression I'd have expected for one such as you!'

Gintras's face darkened momentarily and then cleared as he replied with a wink and a grin. 'Bad decisions that at the time I thought were excellent. A tale for another day.' He opened his arms. 'Welcome to the Deragaz Guard. We have occasional run-ins with bandits and the odd beast.'

'So I've heard.'

'Do you intend to fight with the child on your back?' Gintras asked seriously.

'Have you such little faith in me? I've hunted with the child on my back and could fight without an issue.' Which was only a very light lie.

Gintras nodded. 'I don't doubt you. I've fought by your side before.'

'But,' Peryst added, 'I'll leave her with Sava and Lexya once she's become acclimatised. This child is Touched as I am, but her power has manifested very early, and she has no control. I would have her cause harm to none.'

Gintras peered curiously at the sleeping baby. 'This is fair. Settle your child and come back.'

Peryst nodded. 'I will.'

It was almost sundown when he walked back into Sava's, and Maia was beginning to stir. He took her up to his room and changed her, still drowsy, and then carried her back down to the front room where a long table was set with a wooden highchair.

He had barely set foot on the ground floor when Maia woke fully, complaining fretfully, and buried her face in Peryst's neck.

'Ah, hello, Maia. Welcome to Deragaz.' Sava smiled at the child and placed a plate in front of the highchair. 'After an encounter with Lexya and her mind's eye, you must be ravenous. My Pan almost ate the entire family's meal after that first day with the Mas.' Chattering and smiling, she reached for Maia.

Maia raised a bewildered face to Peryst, but he handed her to Sava, ruffled the baby's damp hair, and gave her an encouraging smile.

Sava sat Maia in the chair and immediately began feeding her. Enna and Anna came in, each bearing a large pot, as Pan carried a carafe of wine.

The sounds of Maia's eating were drowned by a booming voice from the stairs.

'My last meal in Deragaz! I doubt I will find better victuals elsewhere in Mehru.' A portly Usurian followed Sava's children into the room then stopped and bowed upon spotting Peryst. 'A Klaevani! Well met. Rustian of Grolliat, at your service.'

'Peryst de Arranu, at yours.'

The meal was a cheerful affair, with Nela at the foot of Maia's chair gnawing a bone thoughtfully provided by Pan and everyone making a fuss of the child.

Peryst and Maia soon settled into the routine of Sava's guesthouse, with Peryst making himself useful by assisting Pan with maintenance issues. Though never bustling, the establishment served a regular stream of guests, the majority of whom were merchants who'd once sampled Sava's cooking and were led back by the memory of its flavours. Maia was cared for by all, and when Peryst made his daily visits to train at the guard house she was happy to spend time at the inn with Nela and Sava's family.

Thinking of Golfen, Peryst asked them to talk to Maia, and the family took his words to heart. Pan took her into the stables where he would talk incessantly about the care of animals, showing her the different creatures and explaining their needs. Enna and Anna were not much different. They played with Maia, told her tales, and showed her the herbs they dried and how they could be used. Sava did the same. If she absorbed just a fraction of Sava's chatter on food and recipes, thought Peryst, the child would be a treasure in Klaevan, which wasn't known for the quality of its food.

On the sixth day, Peryst took Maia back to Lexya's cottage. He rode with her sitting in front of him, holding her with one hand and the reins with the other. Nela paced by Roan, flicking her tail and smelling the forest air.

As they approached the cottage, Maia tensed. Filled with alarm at his child's discomfort, he wondered whether to turn back, but forced himself to carry on, murmuring words of encouragement to her.

Lexya greeted them cheerfully and, once they were inside, pointed Peryst to the same chair he had occupied the week before.

Lexya fixed her gaze on Maia. 'Maia, I see you remember last week's experience.'

Bottom lip trembling, Maia glanced back at her.

'I won't hurt you, Maia, nor will I hurt your father, whom you seem to want to protect.'

Peryst straightened with a start. 'Me?'

'Yes. When she lashed back at me with her mind's eye, I had tried to delve into her fear of losing you. She wouldn't let me see anything related to her early days and the loss of mother and twin.'

Peryst passed a hand over Maia's head. It had been half a year since they'd left Lost Corner. *How much does Maia remember of her life before me? Are her fears rooted in specific memories or in a vague insecurity born of waking in the depths of the wilds with me instead of her mother? Does her mind's eye know that I'm not her father? Does she? Did she block Lexya to prevent her from learning the truth? Or did she simply react in rebellion at the mental invasion?*

'She must accept that I won't hurt either of you so that she'll trust in my teaching.'

Peryst knelt on the floor in front of Maia and, with his large hand, moved her face up so that she could see into his. Slightly focusing his mind's eye—not for the purpose of looking into the child but to have her see into him and understand the meaning of his words—he spoke softly. 'You are a child of great power, daughter of mine. While there is much I will teach you, there is much more I don't know. Lexya will be the first of your many teachers. You'll learn everything she has to give because I ask you to. Everything you learn from her, from Pan, from Enna, from Anna, and from Sava now, and from others later will make your mind's eye—and you—stronger and better.' He hesitated and added, 'One day, perhaps, we'll find a place to live without fear of the Hand of Reason. Or else, we'll join those who strive to push them back into Reor. But to do that, you must learn to be strong, my daughter, and I must do what I must keep us both safe.'

Maia was a year old. She spoke only a few words and had just started pulling herself up against table legs and chairs to take two or three unaided steps before falling on her well-padded rear. But Peryst knew her mind's eye was different: older and more mysterious than Maia herself. There were many conflicting beliefs, but Peryst's Genaian teacher, Glauca, had believed the mind's eye was connected to an ever-powerful consciousness, Lu, which slept beneath the world, older than time itself, and which sought to share itself with every person. Glauca had waited for the day when every sentient being would be Touched, and then Lu would awaken and lead the world to utmost bliss. Subsequent teachers had different beliefs with different endings, many not so positive, but all agreed on one thing: the mind's eye was somehow older and wiser than its bearer. Counting on that, Peryst had spoken to Maia's and hoped she would understand.

He sensed that she relaxed physically as he finished speaking, and, taking his hand from her chin, he eased back into his chair. The child pulled herself up with the aid of Peryst's leg and took stumbling and wavering steps across the room in Lexya's direction. She almost fell at the third step but stabilised herself and advanced another few steps before rocking dangerously and stabilising again. She did this till she teetered forwards to rest against Lexya's legs, her face tilted upwards to the old Mas's.

Lexya smiled warmly. 'I've been accepted.'

'Indeed, you have.' Watching his daughter, Peryst knew she had told him, as well as she could, that she accepted his words.

YEAR 5162 OF THE NEW ERA – SUMMER

Though Maia had accepted Lexya as her teacher and, a couple of months later, was progressing nicely in learning to control herself, Peryst would not leave her with the Mas for more than a few hours each day.

'It's time, Peryst,' Lexya said gently.

Though he thought he knew exactly what she was saying, he questioned her. 'Time for what?'

'Time for you to take up your post with the Deragaz Guard in full instead of this part-time affair of dedicating a few half days to them and the rest to the child.' Lexya spoke over Maia's head as his daughter played with her toy dragon.

'Did Gintras set you up for this?' Peryst asked. 'He thinks I'm still the one he used to go revelling with in Lis taverns. I'm not that man any more. I have Maia now. I can't leave her! The last time I did, she nearly killed Sacha.' Even as he spoke, he almost heard Golfen murmur in his head reminding him not to forget himself.

'I haven't spoken to Gintras,' Lexya replied, 'nor am I this Sacha. I'm not a rebel chit in the forest, Peryst. I've been training people in the use of their powers since before you were born. And Maia is powerful, but she's no monster and not the child she was in Forglenden. She's learning control and knows that you love her above all things.'

'Of course she knows, but it's because she's learnt that I'm here for her each day and always.'

'You cannot spend the rest of your days by her side.'

'I can and I will. It's my duty as she has no mother.'

Lexya shook her head. 'Your duty as her father is to help her become the best she can be, and that will mean letting others more powerful than you teach her. It will mean knowing when to let her go so that she can grow and develop apart from you. It will also mean you carry on growing and developing yourself. She will need to have a father to admire, to show her the way, to demonstrate that you never stop learning. If you carry on like this, you'll be smoothing her path her whole life and never teaching her to build one for herself.'

Peryst said nothing.

'The more you are, the more you can give. You're a Klaevani monster hunter and soldier, Touched, and have a post of captain waiting for you in the Southern Mehruvian Army. Though you've done much, there is always more to do and more to learn. It's the Klaevani way for a child to be brought up by many, not only by its mother and father. Remember what you said to Maia the first day you brought her to me.'

He knew Lexya was right and remembered every word he'd said. He also remembered his and Marie's childhood during which they were cared for and taught by family and friends while their parents carried out their own activities and missions. He and his twin sister had not just been brought up by a village, as they said in Klaevan, but by hordes! Everyone they met in their family's travels had a hand in forming them.

'Maia has no mother,' he whispered. She had nobody but him. If something happened to him, she would be alone. The thought haunted him.

'And because of that you wish to make her wholly dependent on you?' Lexya asked in a mordant tone, ignoring his anguish. 'You want her to lean on you always, never taking a step on her own?'

A flash of memory pierced Peryst's mind: Marie lighting up in hope at his urging her to pack and leave and then the light dying as Felim argued against it. Marie as a child would've fought, would've argued, would've bundled up both her children and ran if need be. She wouldn't have bowed and given in. She wouldn't have been a subservient young woman depending on her husband for guidance and always agreeing with him. *Is that what I want for Maia? Do I want her to look up to me and only to me? What kind of person will she then become?*

'No, no. It's not that. But I want her to know that she is loved and the most important thing in my life,' he replied with urgency.

'She knows,' Lexya responded. Then she leaned over and placed a wrinkled hand on his. 'I'll teach you both to communicate mind to mind.'

'No,' Peryst interrupted. 'How can you even suggest such a thing for a child so young?'

Lexya observed him in amusement. 'What do you know of mind-to-mind communication?'

'I know how to do it,' he replied shortly.

'Where did you learn? It is not a practice common to the South.'

'With good reason. It's excruciating to learn.'

Lexya tilted her head to the side. '*When* did you learn?'

'A few years ago. In Kurbal. I trained with an Idhan in Seyan.'

Lexya nodded with a chuckle. 'Yes, I can imagine it would've been a very painful exercise for you to learn the skill. The reason it's so painful for an adult to learn is because your channels of communication have been set since childhood. When you're learning this new way of communication, your mind's eye must shift and adapt. It's similar to when your Touched powers come in.'

'It was very unpleasant.'

'It's not as bad these days. A Rohinian, during experiments with hirim grass to aid non-halflings to join in the Dreaming, discovered that when brewed as a tisane, the grass can ease mind-to-mind communication and all but eliminate the pains suffered when learning the skill.'

'You could give some to Maia?'

'There's no need for it. Children like her learn to communicate with voice and mind simultaneously. To them, it's no different. As babbling doesn't hurt, neither does mind-to-mind communication for such children. Those who rear children in Vel or Glannafel find it much easier given that they're able to communicate with their infants before they can speak with their voices.'

'Convenient. And something I wish I'd known,' Peryst mumbled.

Lexya chuckled. 'If I'd known that you practiced the skill, I would've told you earlier. I'm assuming you've never tried speaking into her mind?'

'I haven't.'

'You should. Then you'll always be able to know that she's safe, and she'll know that you haven't forgotten her. Then the father can become Peryst de Arranu again and Maia de Arranu will have a chance to find herself.' She smiled. 'You want your daughter to be all she can be in terms of her power and all she can in terms of womanhood. Right now, we know she can manipulate air and fire like a Primal, and she has some enhanced senses which make her a Sensal. But you also want her to know who Maia is. You want her to be proud of her Klaevani father and proud to be Klaevani herself, independent and sure.'

Maia, who'd initially raised her head in concern at the clipped tones, went back to her game. Peryst clasped his hands between his knees and watched her guide the wooden dragon along the patterns on the carpet. *Lexya is right. But it'll be a wrench to let this child follow her own path, whether she's a year old or twenty. I never thought I'd be capable of such love after losing Sanjia and the babies, but all that love has grown into a tidal wave for Maia, one so big and so powerful I can barely contain it within me.*

'Try it, Peryst. Talk to your daughter in her mind.'

'Doesn't she have to want to?'

'Which baby won't want to communicate with her parent? With adults, both need to want and deliberately open their minds to each other for mind-to-mind communication. It's different in youngsters because they haven't yet differentiated one way of communicating with another. Try it and you'll see.'

Focusing his mind's eye, Peryst spoke into Maia's mind.

> *That's a lovely dragon, Maia. Do you remember Amanda? She gave it to you when you were younger.*

Peryst expected his words to fall into a void and almost fell off his chair when Maia raised her face and beamed at him as he encountered an image in his mind that came from her. There were no words, but a likeness of Amanda passing her the wooden dragon.

'Now that she knows that she can speak to you in this way, she'll be able to explain aches and pains, tell you when she's hungry or tired, and make your caring of her that bit easier,' Lexya explained.

Rearing Maia became inordinately easier, as Lexya had announced, but it was difficult for Peryst to fully let go. At first, he came and went with her every morning and evening till the day came when he was able to leave her for a few days at a time to fulfil his obligations to the Deragaz Guard.

'I'm appointing you as my advisor, Peryst, now that you're with us full time. It makes no sense for one of your seniority to be doing watches in the countryside,' Gintras said over an ale at the tavern closest to the green, where he tended to go at the end of the day.

'I'd be surprised if that didn't cause comment or resentment amongst your guards, my friend. I'm sure you have many worthy locals vying for the post who'll wonder at your choice, particularly as I won't be here forever.'

Gintras waved away Peryst's concerns with an airy hand as he called for two more ales. 'My guards trust my judgement like we trusted Anil's. Would you rather march through farms at dawn? I'd much prefer us to put our heads together to face the trouble that's coming. I hear that the Hand is getting greedy in northern Mehru. It's a matter of time before they turn our way. We're not that far from Ros, you know.'

Peryst took a deep drink. Another who saw the threat. How was it that those on the ground could see it so clearly and those above couldn't? He shook his head, banishing the dark thoughts.

'So how is it that you're here, Gintras? What did you do? This is obviously a punishment for a rising star like you were.'

Gintras passed a finger down his tankard and gave a sidelong glance at a couple of women at another table. One winked at him saucily and whispered something to her companion. Gintras sighed. 'A woman, Peryst.'

Peryst thought back to their nights in Lis, before Sanjia, when they were both young and free and enjoyed days of soldiering and nights of revelry and passion in rooms reached by climbing trellises and trees, sometimes escaping barely dressed as a husband or a father made their untimely appearance.

'The fickle Gintras lost his heart? She must have been quite the woman!'

'Heart? Never! But my, Peryst, was she a wonder! In appearance she would have surpassed your Sanjia, and in bed, well, courtesy prevents me from saying more.'

'What went wrong?' Peryst asked. 'She sounds near perfect.'

'Her honesty wasn't quite at the standard of her other virtues. She was involved with another.'

'A lady of varied interests, it seems.' Peryst chuckled. 'You would've been well matched, then,' he added.

'Indeed. I would've been willing to share, with the three of us content, but the other was more possessive and … powerful.'

Peryst drained his ale and waved for another. 'Who was he? Or were they a she?'

'The second son of the High Luk—Anil's older half-brother, Atul.'

Peryst couldn't prevent a wince. Anil was the daughter of the High Luk's second wife of later years, a Mehruvian of good but humble birth. She had been brought up by her mother to never forget that she was merely a daughter of Mehru and that the accident of her birth didn't make her better than anyone else. Her older brothers, on the other hand, had been reared by their mother, a princess of Tamadal, who was not loved by the populace. Though the marriage had been advantageous for both realms, the princess had made it very clear that she thought she had married down. In Mehru, the High Luk observed none of the pomp and ceremony she had grown up with in Tamadal. Despite the High Luk's efforts to the contrary, his sons had been taught by their mother to be haughty and proud, never letting anyone forget who they were.

'That must've been awkward.'

Gintras grimaced. 'Understatement. It cost me my post. Anil tried to help, but I told her to keep out of it. The whole thing got very ugly, and so I find myself in a backwater stopping bandits and ruffians instead of as a commander in the Southern Mehruvian Army, which I would be by now.'

'What happened to the lady?'

Gintras laughed. 'She had served her time and was duly discarded, of course. She fared better than I, though, and now runs a leading musical establishment in Vel, or so I've heard.'

'There should be a lesson in that somewhere.' Peryst chuckled.

'Perhaps, but now we're being summoned by those two lovely ladies in yonder table. Shall we?'

Peryst shook his head. 'All yours, my friend.'

'You can't mourn Sanjia forever, Peryst,' Gintras said. 'That fiery and beautiful girl wouldn't want you to turn into a husk of yourself.'

'Maybe a day will come when I can want a woman, but now even the thought is clouded by pain … and by the image of her bleeding to death.' He truly wondered whether a day would come when he would enjoy a light-hearted and carefree encounter. Today, he didn't think so.

Gintras made a grimace of distaste. 'And that was an image I certainly didn't need.' He clasped Peryst on the shoulder. 'I will erase it with the help of two lovely ladies!'

YEAR 5162 OF THE NEW ERA – AUTUMN

Six months to the day since Maia's first in Lexya's cottage, Peryst walked into the guard house to find Gintras reading a letter sporting the High Luk's seal. Sayla Maynefield, Gintras's second-in-command, stood at his side.

'Peryst, your battalion is stationed along the banks of the Ramu in Gallya,' Gintras said.

'No chance of the Hand getting through them to southern Mehru, then,' Peryst replied, wondering what that meant for him. He had expected Anil to be flitting between Lis and Vel as she usually did between her obligations as a military leader for Mehru and time with Klaust and their boys. He had planned to rejoin her company in the capital, not elsewhere.

Gintras chuckled. 'None while Anil is in Mehru.'

'Anil?' Sayla asked incredulously. 'That Anil?'

Gintras frowned. 'The Agazi of our old battalion, under which Peryst and I served,' he said drily, not quite answering Sayla's question before picking up the letter again. He whistled as he progressed down the missive.

'What is it?' she asked.

'The High Luk has sent emissaries to all northern cities east of Ros and Ilia for the first time in decades,' he said.

'Emissaries for what?' Peryst asked.

Gintras passed a hand through his thick, dark hair before replying with one word that was met with awed silence. 'Reunification.'

'It will never happen,' Sayla said bluntly after a beat.

Gintras re-read the letter as he replied absently. 'Don't be so sure. It's not even half a century since Mehru was one. And the eastern towns of northern Mehru are those with a higher proportion of Touched population. They'll be feeling particularly vulnerable. Think of Min, where the nephew of the High Luk is Alkaid and where most authorities are Touched!'

'Does the letter say anything about the outcome of the emissaries' visits?' Peryst asked.

'It does. They have apparently been met with initial approval,' Gintras replied.

'What does the High Luk offer them?'

Gintras scanned the letter again. 'Full defence of their towns and lands in exchange for representatives in each town and a Mehru united against the Hand of Reason.'

'Will they take the offer?' Peryst asked.

Gintras thought before replying. 'They might. The Hand started slowly on the west side of northern Mehru, preaching, dividing populations, and providing their gadgets, but wherever they met with resistance, things got ugly very quickly. In Fallya and Gyllia, for instance, alchemists were burnt as were any vocally against Reor. The eastern towns have watched with alarm as the Hand edges closer, but now the High Luk is giving them an alternative.'

'Do we have instructions?' Sayla asked.

'We do. We're asked to defend Leyandale from the advance of the Hand,' Gintras said, beaming.

Peryst realised that an order like this would give Gintras far more satisfaction than dealing with common bandits and the occasional dangerous creature from Forglenden.

Gintras pulled out a second letter with a different, less elaborate seal and perused it quickly before glancing up at Peryst.

'From Anil. Their scouts say that if Leyandale falls, the reunification will fail. The High Luk needs the eastern towns united against the Hand before we start trying to take back the western ones under the Hand's control. The Agazis of the Selkirk and Folchester battalions have sent companies west and north respectively, but they'll take time in reaching the city. If we keep Leyandale safe till their arrival, says Anil, her battalion could start the march of liberation from Fallya.'

'No small thing to ask,' Sayla replied.

Gintras sat back in his chair and stared at the ceiling. Peryst remembered the position: Gintras was playing different scenarios out in his head. He had always been an excellent Citadel player. The game of strategy popular in Mehru required analysing every possible alternative before making a decision. In his youth, Peryst had been a more impulsive player, thus losing out to Gintras each time. His friend had taught him the value of making decisions slowly based on thought instead of instinct. Peryst's grin widened as he watched his friend shuffle alternatives in his mind.

'Sayla, you'll be in charge of the Deragaz Guard in my absence,' Gintras said finally.

She frowned. 'I would be of more use in Leyandale.'

He shook his head slowly. 'I'll take two dozen with me and leave you the rest.'

'You'll need more. Twenty-five soldiers won't be enough to hold Leyandale if it's overrun by the Hand,' she protested.

'I don't think it's indeed overrun, but twenty-five is all I can afford and all I need. I won't leave Deragaz undefended. There are bandits and beasts to deal with locally. We have an obligation to the town and the countryside as well, which you'll need to meet with the guards that will remain and any more you can recruit and train from the townspeople. Remember the packs of wolves from two years ago?'

Not sure whether to interrupt given the mutinous expression on Sayla's face, Peryst cleared his throat.

'Anything to add, Peryst?' Gintras asked with a furrowed brow.

Peryst replied mildly, 'I know where to find more to join in a Leyandale venture.'

Gintras and Sayla shared a bemused glance.

'If we ignore those on their way already, there are no more trained soldiers this far east,' Sayla snapped.

'There are,' Peryst said. 'There's a faction in Forglenden to the southeast of Leyandale. They'll know what goes on in the city and will doubtlessly welcome our venture.'

Gintras frowned. 'Is this the rebel cell you spoke about?'

Peryst stifled a grin of amusement at the thought of the rebel leaders and Gintras head-to-head, each reluctant to cede control to another. Their interaction would be interesting to watch. 'Indeed, it is.'

'Rebels?' Sayla interjected with a scowl at Peryst and a loaded glance at Gintras. 'You'd have untrained rebels in your company?'

'Oh, they're trained, extremely well trained, but they wouldn't be in your company, Gintras. They're led by strong leaders of their own, and I think they'd support your venture and aid the Deragaz Guard, but if they did, they'd do so under their own terms.'

Sayla snorted. 'And you'd accept that, Gintras? It sounds like madness. Why not wait for our own companies from Selkirk and Folchester?'

'Because by their arrival it may be too late,' Peryst said quietly.

LEYANDALE

YEAR 5162 OF THE NEW ERA – AUTUMN

PERYST LED THE Deragaz Guard north towards the Ramu. The forest was coloured from the lightest of yellows to the darkest of reds and the ground thick with fallen leaves. Bushes loaded with late autumn berries and yellowing vines hugged the trees, and branches bowed under the weight of their soon to be lost leaves. The ground, damp and muddy after the recent rains, made their progress slower than it had been when Peryst had followed the same route with Maia in the opposite direction. It was almost three weeks before they were challenged from above.

'Again, Peryst?' Tam's clear voice rang out two days after the Deragaz Guard had braved fording the Ramu.

Peering up into the branches, Peryst laughed. 'Well met, Tam. I bring reinforcements.'

Tam lowered himself from a branch with an agile jump and landed in front of Peryst with his bow in his hand. 'Reinforcements for what, exactly?'

Showing he was very much the leader of his small company, Gintras took a step forwards. 'We march to Leyandale to defend them from Reordans that approach from the west.'

Tam turned back to Peryst, ignoring Gintras. 'Who are your friends, Peryst, and where is Maia?'

Peryst knew Tam was demonstrating that while Gintras could be the leader of his own band, in Forglenden he was nobody. He half turned to Gintras. 'Tam, this is Gintras of Barges, head of the Deragaz Guard and a very old friend and companion in many battles.' Then he pointed at Tam. 'And Gintras, this is Tam Ashweaver, head of the Forglenden Watch. Don't let his youth and acrobatics mislead you. Tam is a deadly companion in battle, an excellent tracker, a valuable ally, and a good friend.'

Both Tam and Gintras lowered their heads, with mirrored expressions of suspicion.

'We need to see Thallya and Fiona, Tam,' Peryst added quietly.

Tam paused. 'Only Thallya, Peryst. Fiona died a short time after you left.'

'I'm sorry to hear that. So many losses for Thallya in such little time.'

Tam nodded and, turning into the trees, emitted a short whistle. Replies rang back from different directions. He then asked again, 'Where's Maia?'

'She's safe with the Mas in Deragaz.'

Tam nodded. 'Lexya! Good. She'll learn much from her.' He grew serious and spoke for only Peryst to hear. 'I was sorry to come back and find you both gone, Peryst. Not all in the Gluok agreed with Thallya's view regarding Maia. Some were very upset at your leaving.'

Peryst bowed. 'It's not my place to comment on your matters of government, but seeing Maia with Lexya has led me to believe that Thallya's recommendation was correct. Maia does need to learn control, and I can't teach her.'

Tam nodded. 'With Lexya, she'll learn more than control. I did.'

With a light step, he turned into the thickest part of the forest, where a barrier of foliage made it all but impossible to pass. Moving aside a thick branch, he exposed a well-trodden path. The Deragaz Guard followed in silence.

'Peryst!' Golfen raced across the camp as soon as the group entered. To the sounds of muffled amusement from the Deragaz Guard, he threw himself at Peryst's legs. Peryst, laughing, crouched down and returned the hug.

'Good to see you, too, Golfen.'

Then Golfen took a step back, a dark frown on his face and hands on his hips. 'Where's the princess?'

Peryst lifted both hands in defence. 'She's with Nela in Deragaz, Golfen. The Mas is caring for her. She walks, Golfen, and talks and sings. She communicates mind to mind. I speak to her every night!'

Golfen didn't seem convinced. 'The princess will have been upset to see you leave. You should have brought her with you!'

Peryst's affection for his friend surged. 'She is learning so much, Golfen. It's good for her to be with Lexya. She's safe in Deragaz and will be ready for our journey to Lis when I get back.' He thought of the moment before he left, when Peryst focused his mind's eye on Maia's and explained the situation in her mind.

> *It's your role to learn and grow, Maia, and it's mine to push back the Hand of Reason. Every step the Hand takes forwards means a smaller area of safety for the likes of you and me. But I'll be back for you, never doubt that. Even if I should have to crawl to reach you, I will return, Maia. So, stay safe, grow, and learn, my child.*

Another voice intervened from behind. 'It gives me great joy to hear that.'

Peryst turned quickly, hands outstretched. 'Thallya! Tam told me about Fiona. I'm so sorry for your loss. I understand the pain of losing your soul mate and your child.'

Thallya squeezed his hands tight. 'Of all, you would. Thank you.'

Peryst kept his hold on her hands. 'I will be ever grateful that you sent me to Lexya. Maia thrives. I communicate with her mind daily.'

Thallya's face opened in relief. 'I'm so glad, Peryst. I feared I'd been mistaken in telling you to go.'

In a loud voice for all to hear, Peryst replied, 'You weren't mistaken. Neither you nor I could reach Maia the way Lexya has been able to reach her.'

'What brings you back to Forglenden?' she asked.

He nodded towards Gintras. 'I will let the Agazi of the Deragaz Guard explain.'

Gintras bowed his head. 'Mistress Thallya. I am Gintras of Barges, Agazi of the Deragaz Guard,' he said, one leader to another. Peryst was gratified that his trust in his friend's sagaciousness had not been misplaced. Unlike Sayla, who'd been full of disdain, Gintras was willing to grant the Forglenden rebels the same respect he expected to be granted to his own guards.

Thallya bowed her head in response but waved a deprecatory hand. 'Thallya is enough.'

Gintras nodded. 'We've received notice that Leyandale teeters on the edge of falling to the Hand. As we speak, companies from Selkirk and Folchester travel in this direction to aid the east of northern Mehru in its defence against the armies of the Hand that are said to march from the west. We've come from Deragaz to prevent Leyandale from falling to the enemy. I understand from Peryst that we're aligned in this matter and invite your band to join us in this endeavour as I realise that, together, we would make a fearful team.'

Thallya betrayed no emotion, but Peryst could see that she was thinking furiously.

'Your proposal is interesting, Gintras of Barges, but we will need to discuss it in our Gluok.' She turned to Golfen. 'Golfen, please make our guests comfortable while I convene the Gluok.'

Golfen nodded and turned to Peryst. 'Bring your friends to the food hut. I'm sure you could do with refreshments.'

As they walked through the camp, many approached asking after Maia. Peryst searched the faces he could see, seeking those he knew. 'Where are Sacha and Gadryl?'

'Sacha is on watch and Gadryl represents the elves on the Gluok,' Golfen said before changing the subject to innumerable questions about Maia.

When Gintras and Peryst were summoned before the Gluok, Peryst turned back briefly to glance at the Deragaz soldiers who'd already discovered much in common with those from the camp. A stranger would've been hard pressed to say who came from where because they all seemed like part of the same band.

'Peryst. It's good to have you back!' Gadryl said, clasping Peryst by the shoulders in the traditional elven greeting.

'It's good to be back,' Peryst replied before turning to Gintras. 'This is Gintras of Barges, Agazi of the Deragaz Guard.'

'So we've heard,' Neeva replied for the Rohinians.

Gadryl considered Gintras. 'Are you at liberty to share the motivation behind southern Mehru aiding northern Mehru? This hasn't happened before. Every town and village between Fallya and Ros has fallen to the Hand of Reason without southern Mehru lifting a finger. What's changed?'

Gintras pursed his lips and thought for a beat before answering. 'I have limited information regarding the High Luk's plans, but I can say that it's in everyone's interest that the east of northern Mehru remains free of the Hand. Only if that is so will we have a chance of retaking the western towns already under the Hand.'

The members of the Gluok glanced at each other, some frowning, some with slight smiles.

'Are you saying that retaking the western towns is a possibility?' Neeva asked.

'Possibilities are endless,' Gintras replied diplomatically, 'but if the eastern region is fractured, they become more remote.'

'Is that a threat? Are you saying that if we don't join you, the High Luk won't aid the retaking?' a grizzled man asked, sitting straighter in his chair and glaring at Gintras.

Peryst raised both hands. 'Of course it isn't a threat, Petras! It's merely common sense! If Leyandale falls to the Hand of Reason, Reor will send part of its army to hold it and start its advance into the eastern reaches of northern Mehru. The chances of smaller villages and towns to the southeast of Ros remaining free will diminish. Reclaiming anything with the Hand in place will be virtually impossible.'

Thallya intervened in the steely tone Peryst remembered so well. 'Reor hasn't expanded its reach by force before. Their control in western towns and villages has been accomplished by stealth and manipulation, by instilling fear after dividing the population and pitting them against each other, and now you speak of them coming with armies! Is this a fact or are they rumours like the many that seem to swirl regarding the Hand?'

Gintras lifted his hands. 'I have no facts other than that a battalion from the Southern Mehruvian Army is stationed in Gallya, that two other companies travel to Leyandale's defence but will take time to arrive, and that some sort of threat lies over the city.'

'So, the Hand mobilising its Defence is another rumour?' Thallya barked. 'It would be unlike them to order a full-scale invasion. It would pit the general population against them, and they like their people cowed, not rebellious.'

'Perhaps the Five who lead the Hand are changing their tactics. Perhaps they're tired of doing things slowly and have grown greedy. Reor is landlocked but for the tiny strip of Mirah. Perhaps the Five want a coastline.' Peryst had wondered about this as they rode from Deragaz and shared his thoughts aloud. 'Or perhaps they're reacting to Anil stationing her battalion in Gallya, worried that she'll start moving east.'

Gadryl nodded thoughtfully before saying in an even voice, 'If we join you, we would do so under our own command as equal partners in battle and not in any way subservient to the Deragaz Guard.'

'We wouldn't accept you any other way. I only command those I've trained myself,' Gintras replied.

Gadryl and Thallya exchanged a glance.

'Thank you, Gintras of Barges. If you'll excuse us, we'll now discuss your proposal amongst ourselves,' Thallya said.

Peryst led Gintras back to where the evening bonfire crackled and groups lounged near its glow as on the nights that he remembered.

'Do you think they'll join us?' Gintras asked quietly.

Peryst shook his head. 'I can't tell. When I was here last, Thallya and Fiona were full of talk of revolution and aiding the resistance in Ilia. I don't know what's happened since then.'

Gintras sighed. 'I'll wait till midnight for an answer. If none is forthcoming, we'll remain for the night and march towards Leyandale at dawn with whatever knowledge they can share about the city.'

'This is fair,' Peryst replied.

Sacha appeared suddenly, her form lit from behind by the fire. 'Peryst! I was told you'd come! I'm so sorry. I was devastated when I heard you and Maia left us because of me. I didn't want that.'

Gintras, whom Peryst had told of Gena's death, moved to sit by Golfen, leaving Peryst alone with Sacha.

Peryst took both her hands. 'I know, Sacha. Please, don't dwell on this. It was the right decision. Maia is with an extremely powerful Mas, and I'm very pleased with her progress.'

She smiled crookedly. 'What are you doing here?'

He angled his chin at the Gluok's tent as he replied, 'You'll know soon enough.'

As the fire died down, Gintras acquired a set expression and Peryst began doubting his predictions of a united front in Leyandale. Their troop was given space for their bed mats and retired one by one till only Peryst, Gintras, and Golfen sat by the fire.

'It seems that the situation ran away with the Hand in Leyandale,' Golfen said, staring moodily into the fire. 'It would be folly of the Gluok not to take advantage of that now.'

'What do you mean?' Peryst asked. 'Ran away how?'

Golfen grinned wryly. 'In most places they start slowly, pitching the population against each other with rumours and stories.'

Gintras nodded. 'That is how the Hand succeeds.'

'We hear that they became impatient in Leyandale,' Golfen said.

'What do you mean? Is the Hand already in Leyandale?' Peryst asked. This wasn't what Gintras had been told in his letters, and the Gluok hadn't mentioned it earlier.

'From what we've heard, a handful came from Ros. We think they want to take Leyandale quickly and so have foregone their usual system.'

'What have they done?'

'It's a bit like that Alkaid in Ilia, remember?' Golfen asked Peryst. 'The leader of the band, a lad of high ambitions, wants Leyandale to fall quickly to advance his position within the Hand.'

'How do you know this, Golfen?' Peryst asked.

Golfen shrugged as he pushed at the embers with a stick. 'Gavrel sent word. We only learnt of it two days ago.'

'So, what's the situation now?' Gintras asked.

So engrossed were they in Golfen's tale that Peryst didn't notice that the Gluok had disbanded till Gadryl replied to Gintras's question. 'At a stalemate. Leyandale, like most of the east of northern Mehru, is a city in which nearly every family has a Touched member. The Hand didn't stand a chance of convincing anyone quickly, so it seems they've instead resorted to violence.'

'The Hand always uses violence,' Peryst said.

'This is true,' Thallya replied, approaching. 'But from what we've heard, they keep Leyandale in a stalemate by holding the Alkaid's daughter, a lass who isn't even Touched, and threatening to burn her if the Alkaid won't give them control of the city.'

'Blackmail? The Hand of Reason? Not that I'd be surprised at any villainy coming from them, but it's unlike any method they've used before,' Gintras said.

'Is it?' Thallya asked. 'They got rid of the Alkaid in Ros by beating her daughter almost to death.'

'And it'll give them the upper hand if it's true that a company of Defenders comes from Reor,' Gadryl said.

Gintras wiped his hands on his trousers. 'I don't know whether you've decided, but regardless, we march to Leyandale at dawn. We won't let Leyandale fall to blackmailers, whoever they may be.'

Thallya smiled. 'Indeed, we won't. We've instructed Tam to designate a skeleton watch to guard the camp. The rest, under Tam, march with you.'

Gintras gave a curt nod. 'How many?'

'Forty.'

Peryst simply leaned in and hugged Thallya as relief flooded him. 'You won't regret this, Thallya.' Then he rubbed his face in exhaustion. 'Now I will sleep.'

Upon waking to the shouts and clanging weapons of a group preparing to march, Peryst focused his mind's eye, reaching for Maia. While he was sure she had understood that he'd be back, he wanted to show her that she was constantly on his mind.

> *I'm here with Golfen, who loves you. Rosie is well, still bucking him off when she gets excited. The rest of the camp have asked after you. I miss you and love you very much.*

As usual, he received a flash in his mind: the image of Nela and a grinning Lexya. But then he was shocked when she spoke back.

> *Dada.*

Reassured, and even slightly frightened at the child's power, he rose to prepare for the march, pleased that soon he'd be able to hold conversations with his daughter.

'Olli and some others are in Leyandale,' Tam explained. 'We sent them ahead when we heard what was going on. We hadn't yet figured out how best to aid them.' He gestured at the large band that fastened armours and weapons in preparation for the march. 'They'll be shocked at what I bring with me.'

'So I should hope,' Gintras replied tightly.

Seeing in his friend's face the internal struggle of a leader forced to follow, Peryst clapped him on the shoulder.

The week-long march east brought about an unexpected blending. By their arrival in Leyandale they'd all declared themselves to be the New Watch for Mehru. To Peryst's astonishment, even Tam and Gintras had reached a tentative agreement and gave orders jointly after discussion between themselves.

Leyandale sat in a shallow valley on Forglenden's north-eastern border under the shadow of a vast plateau. On its outskirts, the edges of the forest were soft. Instead of an abrupt end of cover, Forglenden provided them with thinning copses and groves from where they could survey the city, which lay eerily quiet in the twilight. Only a few lights flickered, and the silence had a loaded and heavy quality. The city was arranged in the usual Mehruvian cross-shape but on a much larger scale than any of the towns that Peryst had seen in northern Mehru.

Sacha, who knew Leyandale well, stole in under cover of darkness to find Olli and Jai.

Sometime later, an almost invisible cluster of shadows moved out through the southern arch and crept across the long grasses, taking cover from grove to grove. They soon reached the safety of the trees opposite the city, where the rest waited impatiently in the growing dark.

Peryst recognised Olli and Jai as the leaders of the group. Jai was both thinner and stronger than when Peryst had seen him last. More man than boy, his encounter with the thoxutria and Gena's death, together with whatever had occurred later, had doubtlessly forced adulthood on the boy, as suffering usually did. Olli nodded with a grim smile at Peryst from under his dark grey hood and, in an undertone, spoke to Tam. 'There's a place further into the trees where we can talk. It would be best for no sound to carry into the city. We don't know if the Defenders have spies.'

Tam glanced at Gintras, who nodded. Olli turned into the forest and led everyone further into the woods to a large clearing.

Tam and Gintras conferred with Olli briefly before ordering everyone to sit where they could. The clanking of weapons and rustling of leather was almost deafening as they sat. Peryst leaned back against a tree trunk, curiously observing Olli's five hooded companions.

Olli turned deferentially to them, and they lowered their hoods to reveal three women and two men of varying ages: four humans; one elf. It was difficult for Peryst to know from her appearance whether she was from Kurbal or

Sahar, but he guessed Kurbali given the reluctance of Sahari to settle beyond elven lands.

The eldest woman, of indeterminate age, tall, and bearing a face lined with worry and lack of sleep, nodded at Olli. 'I am Nuva Houseridge, Alkaid of Leyandale.' She spoke in a gravelly voice. 'Three weeks ago, the Hand of Reason took a group of Leyandale children.'

Tam frowned. 'Children? We were told that they'd taken one child, your daughter, who isn't Touched.'

Nuva sighed. 'They took my daughter but also children of each and every person of any influence in Leyandale: the Agazi, post masters, shop owners, everyone.'

'This isn't how the Hand usually operates,' Gintras intervened.

Another of the newcomers replied, 'No, it isn't.' He nodded round, greeting everyone wordlessly. 'I am Velin Honeywell, Agazi of the Leyandale Guard.' He shook his head. 'Nothing in this situation is usual.'

'Can you explain what's going on?' Tam asked patiently.

Nuva nodded. 'One of ours, Bryn Faymelden, has grandparents in Ros. Each year his mother sent him and his sister to visit with them. She wished her children to form strong bonds with her family in Ros as well as with her husband's in Leyandale. Bryn's father has been dead for a few years now, and his mother died recently. The boy, who was very close to her, was devastated. He blamed our Mas for being unable to save her.'

Velin added, 'From what we've gathered from his younger sister—who is Touched and has refused to visit Ros since it came under the sphere of the Hand—in his distress, Bryn was influenced by Reordans who've settled in Ros.'

'Though we've had Guardians of the Hand come to Leyandale in the past, we've always been on guard against them, but we didn't expect an attack from one of our own,' Nuva said sadly.

'What did he do?' Tam asked.

'Bryn came back from Ros a month ago. Unbeknownst to the guard, he guided a group of Defenders into the city and hid them in an abandoned warehouse. Afterwards, they took the children. The children all knew Bryn as a friend of older siblings, a neighbour, or as the son of Bryanna, the candlemaker. So, the unsuspecting children went with him,' Nuva explained.

Peryst spoke for the first time. 'What do they want them for?'

Velin replied in a tight voice, 'To tie our hands and for Bryn to curry favour with the Hand.'

'Bryn found consolation for his mother's death by rejecting Touched power and, thus, the Hand was the logical progression,' Nuva said. 'If Bryn and his band subdue Leyandale, they'll be heroes to the Hand of Reason.'

'Why haven't you taken the children back?' Tam asked.

Nuva and Velin glanced at each other. 'They threatened to burn a child alive if we tried.'

'Nonsense!' Tam replied.

Velin shook his head slowly as a moan escaped the elven woman's throat. 'They're barricaded inside the town hall. Never heavily guarded, as there's never been a need, they stormed it, killed those inside, and locked themselves in there with the children. We had no intention of taking any of this sitting down. The Leyandale Guard tried to knock down the front doors that same day.'

'A little after the guard began to storm the front doors, smoke rose from the town hall's patio. We heard a child screaming in agony. I obviously ordered Velin to stop the assault. Hours later, after everything went silent and the smoke cleared, they hung a charred body from a window for all Leyandale to see,' Nuva said hoarsely.

'We don't know whose child it was,' the elven woman said in a strained voice. 'And have been too frightened of them hurting another to try anything further.'

Nuva straightened her back. 'We do know, Rima. It was a child of Leyandale that they burnt alive in agony. It was my child and your child and every child.'

Velin smiled grimly. 'Leyandale cannot stand for this. Those who objected to our initial attack have realised that we've no choice. We can't bow to blackmail, so at dawn we're storming the town hall regardless of the consequences.'

Rima added, 'We won't be held hostage by ten members of the Hand of Reason and wait, wringing our hands, till an army comes to mow our city down.'

Tam, Peryst, and Gintras shared glances.

'We came to push you to do this,' Gintras said, 'but you need no pushing.' He bowed his head in respect. 'You have the Deragaz Guard at your command.'

Gadryl cleared his throat. 'There's no Deragaz Guard, Agazi.'

Those from Deragaz concurred in strong voices, with Can adding, 'What you have is the New Watch for Mehru.'

'What's your plan for tomorrow?' Peryst asked.

It soon became clear that there was no plan and that the Leyandale Guard would simply try to force themselves into the town hall through doors they already knew to be barricaded.

Peryst gave a stick to Velin and pointed to the ground. 'Draw us a plan of the town hall and its location, please.'

Leyandale's town hall was located on the north-east corner of the intersection of the four main roads. The building itself was simple: a large square two-level box with a central courtyard that couldn't be seen from outside.

'Where in the building would they keep the children?' Peryst asked. 'And how many children are we talking about?'

'There are twenty children missing.' Nuva gulped noisily. 'Now nineteen. And they could be anywhere in the building.'

'No,' Peryst disagreed. 'It would need to be a large room where they had no access to windows. They wouldn't want to risk them escaping.'

Nuva considered. 'Then they must be in the cellar. There's only one, where we keep stores, but it's a large space that covers a section of the underbelly of the building.'

'Is there a back entrance? Or any other ways in apart from the front?'

'There's no back entrance, but there are back windows.'

Peryst pointed at the rough drawing in the dirt. 'Show me.'

At sunrise, the Leyandale Guard and many of Leyandale's adults—those whose children had been taken and many whose children had not—faced the town hall's closed doors armed with what they had: weapons, axes, and even brooms. Amongst them were half of the New Watch. The swarthiest carried a large tree trunk as a battering ram.

A young Mehruvian, not twenty, leaned out the window where the charred body hung and shouted down, 'Are you asking for another one?'

The crowd roared. An arrow flew and grazed the youth's temple. He lifted a hand to his head and took it away stained with blood. 'You asked for it!' he yelled. 'You cannot say you weren't warned.' He turned back into the building.

Stones crashed against the windows, archers let arrows fly through the broken glass, and the trunk rammed against the doors as, from the inside, projectiles flew back: arrows, glass paperweights, doorstops and, to the horror of those below, a burnt skull.

Peryst knew they had limited time to carry out the plan they'd concocted because inside the town hall they'd be preparing and lighting the pyre to burn another child.

He led twenty—ten from Deragaz and ten from the forest—to a storage room's small side window at the back of the building. Under cover of the noise coming from the front, Tam prised open the window. One by one, they slithered through the tight opening and landed in a cramped storage room. Once all were inside, Can, a Matter Primal, manipulated the lock so that Peryst could inch open the door to the arcade that surrounded the courtyard. Through the crack, he saw two people with their backs to him. By their severe black uniforms with purple piping, he recognised them as Defenders, members of the martial arm of the Hand of Reason: the soldiers who formed the Reordan army and led the advance of the Hand. Their purple cloaks lay discarded on a bench as they piled wood onto the remains of a fire in the centre of what had once been a small pond surrounded by stone benches.

Turning back to his companions, Peryst lifted two fingers.

Slowly, he pushed the door open and stole out into the arcade in silence, the rest following and holding their hands over their weapons to avoid any noise. They hid behind the columns that held up the arches through which they could see the growing pile of wood.

Exchanging a nod, Peryst and Gintras began the same manoeuvre they'd used as rookie soldiers when invading a town in southern Tamadal. Peryst went left as Gintras went right. When they were almost touching the two preparing the pyre, Peryst caught sight of a boy of about seven. Hands and ankles bound, with a gag in his mouth, he lay on a bench and stared at them from wide and terrified eyes. He'd seen enough horrors for such a short life, and the horrors to come weren't images that should haunt a child, so Peryst gestured silently in his direction. Gintras nodded and pressed his fingers onto a pressure point in the child's temple to send him into a deep sleep.

Peryst and Gintras simultaneously yanked the Defenders' heads back by the hair, exposing their throats above their purple collars. Before the men had time to open their mouths to scream, they were silenced with quick slashes from carved bone knives. Peryst felt a twinge at taking a life, even if it was that of a monster, but silenced his misgivings when his gaze shifted to the little boy on the bench.

Quickly, they placed the bodies on the pyre. Peryst threw the cloaks on top of them and, with a flick of his fingers, lit the pyre before reaching for the still sleeping child. He carried him gently back to the storage room where he lowered him through the window to those who waited below.

Peryst warned, 'Keep him quiet.'

From Velin's explanation, they knew the entrance to the cellar lay straight down the corridor. In silence, Tam led the team down the arcade to a heavy wooden door. Testament to the extreme confidence—or carelessness—of the band, a metal key stuck out proudly from the lock. Peryst followed Tam down the dark stairs with half of the team. Gintras and the rest guarded from the top.

In Peryst's time as a mercenary, he'd witnessed scenes of torture and death; he knew what people could do to each other in the name of power or belief and knew it was easy to strip the veneer of humanity and reveal the monster within. But he'd never forget what he saw in that cellar. Perhaps it was because he was now a father, but the sight of eighteen children huddled like small animals in their own filth, the oldest no more than ten and the youngest about the same age as Maia, filled him with a horror beyond what he'd expected.

Placing a finger in front of his mouth, he lit a taper. The younger ones were simply dazed, but the older ones nodded as he moved down onto the floor. Crouching by the children, he said in a whisper, 'Keep very, very, quiet. We're here to take you to your mamas.'

Most of the watch members took two children in their arms. Peryst saw in the tight lips and set faces of his companions, who moved quietly with little arms clasped tightly about their necks, the same overwhelming anger that threatened to drown him at the cruelty of what had been done to the children.

One by one, they climbed the stairs and made their way down the corridor to the storage room, where they lowered the children to those waiting below. Peryst prised the tight little hands from his neck with a pang and passed the child he carried to Sacha and Olli, repeating his earlier entreaty to keep them quiet. Then he turned back to the corridor where Gintras and the rest were watching the fire.

The pyre was burning well, emitting a thick plume of smoke that made its way straight upwards in the windless morning. Peryst hated the thought of Leyandale parents seeing the plume and thinking another child burnt but hoped they would stick to the plan, keeping their onslaught to the front of the town hall.

'They've barricaded the front door from the inside, piling heavy furniture against it,' Gintras whispered. 'There's no chance of the townspeople breaking through without us removing the piles, but that will take time.'

'How many Defenders do we have inside?' Peryst asked.

'Conflicting information. If we believe what they said last night, there should be eight or nine upstairs. They're so confident about their barricade that no one is guarding the doors.'

'So, we send some to dismantle it,' Peryst said.

Tam agreed. 'While they do, we'll need to deal with the Defenders upstairs. If we don't, they'll hear ours moving the furniture and attack them from behind.'

'We'll do that. Where are the stairs?' Peryst asked.

Gintras pointed across the patio to the corner opposite to the cellar door as Tam ordered four to the barricade.

Before they moved, a high voice rang out from the stairway.

'Excellent, and a thick plume, but did you knock the child senseless? I'm missing the screams.'

'Not for long,' Peryst replied loudly. He leapt to the side of the pyre as he took his sword from his back, and came face to face with a tall, startled Defender of the Hand. *How does she not look like a monster? How can she be young, graceful, and beautiful? How does the evil not show?*

She screamed as she drew a sword from the scabbard hanging at her side.

'And there's the scream,' Peryst said as she slashed at him, screaming again. He jumped back nimbly and said, 'This doesn't have to end in your death. Put down your weapon and submit to the judgement of the people of Leyandale.'

'We'll go for the rest,' Gintras called as he led a band to the stairs.

The woman laughed, showing even, white teeth and again making Peryst wonder how evil could be so fair. 'Instead, we'll cleanse them of power and submit them to the Hand of Reason's judgement.' She winked at Peryst. 'But first, you'll die for raising a weapon against a Defender as your friends will die upstairs.'

'Such arrogance,' Peryst said drily.

'Not arrogance. Truth.'

Peryst and the Defender circled each other. He breathed slowly, trying to bring his still boiling anger under control because he knew any emotion would cloud his judgement. Focusing his mind's eye, he flew at her, his light sword moving quickly in a blur. The Defender tried to block him, but Peryst had come in too fast and strong for anything but a substantial jump back, which she didn't have time to do. She died surprised, which was always better than dying in fear.

Without stopping to dwell on another life he'd taken, Peryst leapt over her body and raced to the stairs with a quick glance at those who were pushing and pulling at the heavy wardrobes, tables, and chairs piled in front of the town hall's doors. Wide, with ornately carved banisters, the staircase curved left, leading to an upstairs arcade that mirrored the one below and overlooked the courtyard.

Peryst took the steps two by two and followed the sounds of battle coming from the large room facing the green.

He sighed as he saw the chaos that raged within. Knowing Gintras, he had no doubt that an offer of clemency and judgement had been made. As with his recent foe, such offer had undoubtedly been declined.

Gintras was locked in close battle with an older Defender. An excellent swordswoman, she was making Gintras work for the victory Peryst knew he would eventually achieve. Gadryl, a sword in each hand, fought two in front—who kept backing away and would soon run out of room—and one on his right. Tam fought a man who was older, bigger, and with a longer sword, but who was no match for the agile younger boy who flew over and under the heavy weapon to slash at wrists and knees. The rest all clashed and slashed in a chaos of flashing weapons. Their intelligence had been wrong. Instead of eight, there were fifteen: nine Defenders, three Mehruvians, and three Reordans.

'As was undoubtedly offered to you already, I repeat the entreaty. Surrender and submit yourselves to the judgement of Leyandale. You've already lost three of your number, and the children have been liberated. You're all facing death.' Peryst's loud voice carried through the room.

Without pausing, the Defender who fought Gintras yelled, 'The Hand of Reason has come to free Leyandale of the Touched. The Hand of Reason places us above the likes of you. The Hand of Reason does not surrender! We fight to the death! Your death!'

Peryst grimaced. 'So be it.'

He jumped into the fray, sword whirling, to even the odds by dealing with the Defender to Gadryl's right. An accomplished swordswoman, she was nevertheless not as accomplished as Peryst, who exploited the weakness he saw in her left shoulder to press his advantage. He wanted to merely disarm her, but when parrying an unexpected thrust, he miscalculated and slashed at her neck, severing the artery. But he suffered no remorse. He was a monster hunter and she'd clearly been one.

Though the Hand didn't surrender, most of the Reordan and Mehruvian acolytes did. Five put down their weapons. Bryn tried to emulate his Defender companions yelling that he would never yield but, not having their skill in weaponry, was easily disarmed by Gadryl. Of the Defenders, four were killed, two injured, and two disarmed. Gintras and the woman were the only ones who still fought, both bleeding lightly and still circling and thrusting.

'Why don't you and Gadryl lead the prisoners downstairs and help those clearing the barricade?' Peryst said to Tam. 'I'll keep watch in case Gintras should need assistance.'

Tam glanced at Gintras. 'He won't.'

Peryst leaned against the wall. He knew Gintras wouldn't, but he would remain just in case. That's what friends did for friends.

Gintras and the woman seemed engaged in a dance, coming together, clashing, rolling, and leaping apart. Peryst knew what would come before Gintras had completed the movement. He'd seen his friend do the same feint before, and, as usual, his foe fell for it and ended up against the wall with no weapon and Gintras's sword at her throat.

'The Hand of Reason may not surrender, but it can be defeated,' Gintras panted in her face.

'Never,' the woman replied, pushing herself forcefully into Gintras's blade.

'No!' Gintras pulled his sword back and in doing so released her. The woman slid to the ground, blood spurting from her throat.

'Why would did she do that?' Gintras growled.

'Quickest way to immortality,' Peryst replied drily. 'An instant martyr for the Hand of Reason. She's made sure her name will never be forgotten.'

Gintras frowned. 'Not on my watch.' He pointed to one of the dead Defenders. 'Bring him, too.' Then, as Peryst heaved the body onto his shoulder, Gintras covered the woman's head with her purple cloak and, ignoring the blood, lifted the body over his own shoulder and marched out of the room.

Peryst followed.

The pyre was burning well and welcomed with loud crackling the two more bodies that Gintras and Peryst thrust on it.

When the barricade was finally cleared and the Leyandale Guard streamed into the town hall, Gintras and Peryst made their way back upstairs for the rest of the dead and placed each of them on the pyre. None would do brysk for monsters or give them honourable burials.

'No martyrs for the Hand,' Gintras said tersely.

Overjoyed and grateful for the outcome, Peryst was encouraged to see that the good people of Leyandale concluded that the life of the Alkaid's child had been too high a price to pay. Their judgement of the Hand's supporters was swift and, to their minds, fair. To some, the quick executions of Bryn and his companions were overly compassionate compared to the agony they'd imposed on an innocent girl, but Leyandale had a strict criminal code that they followed despite the rawness of the situation.

Gintras sent messengers east in search of the High Luk's companies, warning of the rumours regarding the coming of Reordan troops and urging them to hurry because the Leyandale Watch, even with the assistance of the New Watch, would be unable to hold the city against the full force of a company of Reordan Defenders. Following a suggestion from Peryst and in the hope of dissuading the local factions of the Hand from a better organised attempt, the Alkaid also sent emissaries to Ros and Ilia communicating the Hand's defeat in Leyandale and the imminent arrival of an army of defence.

Peryst could feel the tension as Leyandale waited on edge but united against the Hand. Any doubts that remained in its inhabitants had been completely erased by the agonising screams of that child in which every parent had heard their own and, afterwards, by Bryn and his companions' complete lack of remorse. A system that could justify such an atrocity had no place in Leyandale and, thus, each adult of arm-bearing age had taken down weapons previously used only as decoration, sharpened axes and carving knives, and repurposed tools as they started a training of sorts.

'This was a simple skirmish, Gintras,' Peryst mused a few days later over ale at Brendan the Voyager, the tavern Velin had recommended. 'What comes next will be nothing like.'

'I'm aware of this, my friend.'

'The whole town supported us here.'

'I'm aware of this,' Gintras repeated wearily.

'We won't find that anywhere to the west.'

'Again, Peryst, I know.'

Peryst took a deep drink of ale. 'We'll be facing trained soldiers next time, not a majority of enthusiastic amateurs.'

'Yes, I know. It will be carnage, and these Leyandale butchers and bakers with their carving knives and rolling pins will be cut down like dry grass if the High Luk's companies don't arrive in time. They're not like southern Mehruvians, who train regularly and are always ready to be called to arms. But what would you have us do? Tell them to cower in their houses and wait for the Hand to burn them down? At least now they have a purpose.'

Peryst sighed. 'Retaking northern Mehru will take years, Gintras.'

'It will.'

Peryst rubbed his hands over his face and turned back to his thoughts since he'd connected his mind's eye to Maia's the night before. His child was well and seemingly learning faster than Lexya had thought possible, as witnessed by the growing ease with which he could share thoughts with her, but she was in the care of one who was not family. In the past he would've dropped everything to join Gintras in the campaign of liberation that loomed, but he now first needed to provide for Maia properly. Only when he could be sure that she was where she should be could he take up his weapons and march on.

'A Klaevani child is brought up by a community of many,' Peryst said suddenly to Gintras, following his own train of thought. 'Infancy is when older, less mobile family members take charge of their upbringing and teach defence skills while the parents make a living, often away from the child.'

Gintras nodded but didn't interrupt.

'Once a child is four or five, they'll come with the parents and learn to be a Klaevani monster hunter and fighter. These days, Klaevani infants have their mind's eyes opened at birth, so all Klaevani children are Touched. Once their power manifests they'll also learn to harness and control that power, sometimes with the Fellowship in Lukur. Usually, the time with the Fellowship will be the one period in a Klaevani's life, apart from infancy, when they're relatively sedentary.'

'And you tell me this why?' Gintras finally asked.

'I crave to join in the liberation march, but I can't leave Maia in Deragaz indefinitely, Gintras.'

'Why not? She's well cared for.'

'Lexya isn't family. Maia has learnt some control, so I should take her to Sanjia's father in Lis.'

'Will he be able to do for her what Lexya can?'

'Perhaps not, but he'll hold her dear above all things and not for pay.'

Gintras shrugged. 'I have no child so cannot advise you.'

More quietly, Peryst added, 'And Lis is further from where the front will be.'

Gintras snorted. 'We have no idea where the front will be, but you will be of little use if your mind is taken up with worry for your child.'

'I suspect my mind will be taken up with worry for Maia till the day I die, but I'll be able to manage it better if I know she's with Ishab.'

'What does this mean?'

'It means that I'll collect my daughter and take her to her grandfather in Lis and will re-join Anil and meet you wherever the front may be after that.'

Gintras sighed, stroking the pommel of the sword at his side. 'May my sword never be shackled by a child.'

Peryst placed a hand on his friend's shoulder. 'May it be that one day you feel enough love for another that you may reconsider when to use your sword.'

Gintras laughed as he tipped back his ale. 'May Gal preserve me from your wish.'

LIS

YEAR 5163 OF THE NEW ERA – SUMMER

PERYST WAITED TILL spring loomed before leaving Deragaz, so as not to submit Maia to the rigours of winter in the wilds. The trip south proved easier than earlier trips Peryst had done with her. The weather was warm and she could communicate her needs, though he still needed to stop more often than he would've if he'd been alone. With his weapons on his back again, he carried Maia in front of him on a double saddle made by an Usurian saddler in Deragaz. It was of camyl leather, padded with sheepskin and with a smaller saddle attached to the front with a rigid handle for Maia to hold onto for stability and pegs for her feet instead of stirrups. She held onto the handle firmly, repeating whatever names Peryst pointed out and expressing wonder at every sight.

He followed the Old Forest Way that bordered Forglenden Forest and found a welcome in each village, hamlet, and farmhouse. Maia enjoyed the attention bestowed on her by friendly Mehruvians and mingled happily with local children, learning new words and eating new foods under Nela's watch. Peryst was interested to see that she rarely used her powers when she was with other children.

Almost four months had passed when they came within sight of Lis in the early afternoon of a sunny day.

From the top of a hill, Peryst pointed at the coast.

'Can you see the water, Maia? The blue is the sea, and that city below is Lis, the jewel of southern Mehru. Can you see the shape of the land on which it's built? Doesn't it seem like two fingers pointing into the blue?'

Maia nodded enthusiastically, repeating his words.

'It points at the Isles of Vel, but you can't see them from here. But sometimes, when the days are very clear, you can. In Lis, Maia, we'll find Grandda. It may be your and Nela's home for a time. Isn't it beautiful?'

Peryst pointed at the Lis Plaza, where the High Luk's turreted palace faced inland to remind all that his people came first; and the High Temple to Gal faced the sea to remind all that Gal was the goddess of sun, earth, sea, and sky. As in other Mehruvian towns, the buildings were all white and had domed roofs. Instead of tiled like elsewhere in Mehru, the roofs of Lis were covered in copper and glinted orange in the sunlight.

'See the parks and promenades near the palace. I'll take you there to visit the statues of the old kings of Mehru. And you can see the four quarters. Can you see the highest point, to the north, greener and with wider roads? That's where the wealthiest live. Then there's the west. See the tangle of alleys and narrow streets curving back on themselves? That's where we'll get you a new pair of boots that fit, my growing girl.'

Maia pointed at her feet and exclaimed loudly, 'Boots for Maia!'

'The orderly area in the east is where the High Luk's barracks are. That's where I'll be spending my time when I rejoin my company. And that other area'—Peryst leaned over Maia's shoulder and grasped her waving hand and pointed it towards the south of the city—'is where I courted Sanjia.' He heard the rasp in his voice. 'There, on the sandy beaches and the port of the seven bridges. There is where we'll find Grandda.'

'Gada,' Maia repeated. 'Gada.'

Seeing the city below and showing it to his daughter made Peryst quake at the painful errand he was to complete upon meeting his father-in-law, but he straightened, bracing himself for what was to come and, slowly, guided Roan down the hill to the closest arch into the capital. As in all Mehruvian towns, it remained open, but unlike other places it boasted heavy studded wooden doors and was guarded.

'Can it be the one and only Peryst de Arranu? With a wolf?'

Peryst grinned at the distinctly featured woman who'd been speaking to one of the guards. 'Liria Fulmight! Well met. I see you, at least, have risen in the ranks.'

Liria, dark hair tied into a thick braid and shoulders shaking in laughter, opened her arms, showing off her gleaming black armour and blue cape. 'Agazi of the Lis Guard to you, my friend.'

'Congratulations! Highly deserved, I'm sure,' Peryst replied to his and Gintras's former companion-in-arms. 'I come from Deragaz, where I was with Gintras.'

Liria shook her head. 'Some of us have moved up in the last years, Peryst; not all have followed Gintras's dubious trajectory. But it must have been like old times for the both of you.' She pointed at Nela. 'And where is the lovely Sanjia? Has she shifted into a wolf?'

Peryst knew he would be asked this time and again, more now that he was in Sanjia's hometown. He'd thought it would get easier to explain his loss the more he had to do so, but it wasn't the case. Every time he said the words, the sob that had lain lodged in his throat since northern Usur threatened to choke him. He knew it would be worse in Lis, where everyone had their own memories of his wife. He realised Maia sensed his distress when she placed both her little hands on the one with which he held her, twisted her small body to him, and said, 'Dada.'

'Sanjia is no longer, Liria,' he replied and then leaned to brush his lips over Maia's head. 'This is Maia, my daughter, and the wolf Nela is her protector.'

'I'm very sorry to hear this, Peryst,' Liria said softly, reaching up and placing a hand on his arm. 'I'm so sorry.'

Peryst bowed his head, not trusting himself to speak.

'Does Ishab know?' she asked.

'He does not,' he managed.

Liria spoke gravely. 'I don't envy you the task of giving him such news.'

'And I don't relish the giving of it.'

'Will you be rejoining your company?'

'I had meant to do so but hear that Anil's in Gallya,' he replied.

'Come by the Wrestlers three days from now in the evening, and we'll talk about your options.'

'Thank you, Liria. I'll do so.'

He made his way slowly through the city's old northern way, a wide cobbled street lined with trees and grand white buildings with arched doorways and windows, cool interior patios, and potted orange and olive trees. But instead of following the northern way straight to the Lis Plaza, he made his way west, heading further from places where he risked meeting one who knew Ishab. It wouldn't do for someone else to break the news to him before Peryst had a chance to do so. He followed a winding route south through markets and alleys and then crossed over to reach the eastern side of the peninsula where Ishab's tavern, The Fiery Camyl, faced the coastal promenade where the population of Lis walked at sundown.

It was with a heavy heart that Peryst guided Roan down the promenade, keeping well to the left to avoid mowing down people who, grand and not so grand, took the sea air every evening.

The Fiery Camyl was a long, white building with a wide main room that Peryst remembered filled with customers. It had been in the hands of the Meadfield family for generations. On the upper floors, the family lived on one side and Ishab had comfortable guest rooms on the other, perhaps not as large and airy as other inns but impeccably clean and with views to the sea and, on clear days, to the Isles of Vel. The tavern had made a brisk business when Sanjia served behind the bar, mainly due to her charms, but he had to admit that the location and excellent food made by Sanjia's aunt Hana also helped.

He made his way to the stables behind the tavern. Dismounting, he found that the stableboy was one he hadn't met. He lifted Maia down and removed the saddlebags.

'Please rub down my horse and feed her generously. We've travelled from afar. Her name is Roan.'

The boy took Roan's reins and stroked her nose.

'Is Ishab inside?' Peryst asked.

'Aye,' the boy replied as he led Roan further into the stables.

Another boy came out. 'Welcome to The Fiery Camyl. Will you be lodging with us, master? Shall I take your saddlebags while you carry the child?' He hesitated, staring at Nela. 'Does the animal come with you?'

'She does. Thank you.' Peryst gathered strength within and entered the tavern from the side door with Maia, who peered round. The tavern seemed exactly as it had been when he saw Sanjia for the first time. The long oak bar stood to his right, behind which his beloved had once served ale or wine from the casks and bottles lining the wall. Regulars made conversation from the stools facing the bar and others shared tables in the long room that looked out onto the promenade.

Searching for his father-in-law, he spotted the tall man quickly. With the same colouring as his daughter and coal-black hair with only hints of grey, Ishab moved swiftly, showing a young woman how to take orders and serve while Hana helped a young man at the bar.

Peryst suddenly couldn't face telling this family of Sanjia's death and waited uncertainly at the door with Nela watchful at his side.

'What are you doing there?' another serving woman asked. 'Are you after a table?' She pointed to an empty one by the window. 'There's one from which the child can look out onto the sea.' She looked doubtfully at Nela. 'Is the animal safe near people?'

Ishab heard her speak and paused as he wiped a table. Slowly, he straightened, an expression of unmitigated joy on his face. Dropping the cloth, he rushed through the tables towards his son-in-law. 'Peryst! Son!' He opened his arms and froze. Without moving his eyes from Peryst's stricken face, he lowered his arms slowly. Very quietly, he asked, 'Where's Sanjia? Where's my daughter?'

Peryst tried to speak but couldn't. He closed his eyes briefly and tried again, but the sob still lodged in his throat broke free and tears coursed slowly down his face. Finally, images of Sanjia laughing, lifting her lips to his, singing and dancing, came back in a rush. Sobbing and speaking with a broken voice, he said, 'I buried her more than two years ago in northern Usur. The birthing came early. I lost them.' Maia whimpered, frightened at the emotions raging through him, so Peryst lifted a hand to comfort her as he continued haltingly. 'This is Maia. She, Sanjia's wolf, Nela, and a letter to you is all I have.'

Peryst could see he'd dealt Ishab a bodily blow. The man paled, took a step back, and leaned against a table. A heavy silence descended onto the tavern as Peryst shook with sobs while helplessly holding Maia, who crumpled her face, too, and started to cry.

Hana came out from behind the bar. She grasped Peryst's face and lowered it to her height. She kissed his forehead and then did the same with Maia, who stopped crying, bewildered. 'Welcome home, Peryst and Maia. Follow me.' Then she turned to her brother and, placing a supporting arm round him, led him back through the tables to a door by the bar that led to the snug. Empty and spent, Peryst followed without a word.

Hana pulled Ishab to the only table in the little room and helped lower him onto a chair. He sat and put his head in his hands, sobbing quietly as Hana went out into the main room and returned with a small glass of brandy, which she put on the table in front of him. She then sat beside him, patting his back.

Peryst put Maia down onto the floor by his feet and reached to undo the buckles on the side of his leather cuirass. From the inside pocket he'd charged an Usurian leatherworker to add, he removed a folded, worn, and badly stained piece of paper. Meanwhile, Maia pulled herself up. Clutching her wooden dragon in one hand, she made her way to Ishab and held onto his knees, her face angled up at him.

'Gada.'

Ishab lifted his tear-stained face and saw Maia, so like Peryst and so different from his late daughter. But in her bright little face surrounded by riotous black curls, Peryst watched him search for the echoes of the daughter he had lost. He passed a gentle finger down her face, and Maia lifted her small hand and held it, babbling and smiling. Peryst lowered himself to the chair opposite and placed the letter on the table. He knew every word because he'd watched Sanjia painstakingly write it with the last of her energy, but he couldn't bear to read it again.

My dearest Da,

If you're reading this, I didn't survive what should have been the happiest day of my life. The birthing started unexpectedly, and Peryst has tried everything to no avail. He wanted to go for help but I asked him not to leave me because I sense the end is near. I feel the babies inside me striving to emerge, but I'm so tired, I don't know now if I have the energy to help them.

I hope my children will live, even if I don't. They're a boy and a girl. I know it. Love them as you loved me, Da, and teach them that they're of Mehru as well as from Klaevan. Peryst has promised that he'll take them to you as infants. I've asked him to wait till they're four before he takes them to Klaevan so they can find their Mehruvian essence, wherever they go later.

I love you, Da. Teach my children as you taught me, and don't grieve too much as I hope to leave you with those that come from me.

Your loving daughter,
Sanjia

Ishab read the letter without picking it up. Then he read it again before asking in a broken voice. 'Where are they?'

'They lie on the slope of a hill on the eastern coast of northern Usur,' Peryst said.

'What happened?'

Peryst lifted his hands with a gesture of helplessness. 'I don't know. All was well, and we were near Skinweave, where we'd planned to settle till after the birthing, which was at least eight weeks away. Sanjia woke losing blood and water. The pains started suddenly. I tried to stem the bleeding with herbs, but it only got worse. I'm no Mender, so when I realised that there was nothing I could do, I decided to travel into the city for a healer, but Sanjia couldn't move and wouldn't let me leave her.' He paused, seeing Sanjia in the cave where they'd passed the night, lying in a pool of spreading blood, growing weaker and paler by the minute. 'I watched her fade away in hours.'

'How long ago was this?' Ishab asked.

'Maia is two and three months.'

Ishab frowned. 'It's taken you that long to travel from northern Usur?'

Peryst straightened and passed a hand over his face. 'It has. I came through Lost Corner, in Reor, where my twin sister lives and recently lost a child. The trip through Reor and northern Mehru took much longer than I expected. It became dangerous for both of us when I realised that Maia is an unusually powerful Touched.'

'Impossible to know with one so young, Peryst,' Ishab said harshly.

'So I thought, till she almost killed someone out of fear.'

'Nonsense! She's a baby.'

Peryst leaned over, took the dragon from Maia, and placed it on the mantle above the fireplace on the other end of the snug. Maia cried out in protest, but Peryst sat back down in front of Ishab. Maia turned back to Peryst and repeated, 'Dada, dago.' But Peryst didn't give her the toy.

Ishab frowned at Peryst. 'Why take it from her?'

'Wait,' Peryst answered and focused his mind's eye a little, telling Maia to take back the dragon. 'Take the dragon, Maia,' he said again out loud.

She shifted her gaze from the dragon to him doubtfully.

'Take it, Maia. Use the air,' Peryst repeated gently, nodding.

Ishab's mouth fell open as he watched the wooden dragon sail on a cushion of air to Maia's outstretched hands.

'Dago,' she said in satisfaction as she placed the wooden tail in her mouth and turned back to Peryst, who smiled encouragingly.

Ishab stared at Maia and then up at Peryst, dumb with shock.

'I detoured through Deragaz where a powerful Mas taught Maia to listen through her mind's eye. I can now communicate with her, mind to mind, and she has better control than she had.'

Ishab shook his head in wonder. 'I've not heard of a child so young with developed powers in Ankisua.'

Peryst shrugged. 'I'm blaming a remote ancestor from Glannafel. My aim is for the Fellowship in Lukur to train her when she's older. If she has this much power now, I fear to imagine what'll happen when she reaches womanhood.'

Ishab hesitated before asking, 'Will you follow Sanjia's wish and remain in Mehru till she's four?'

Peryst nodded. 'We'd always planned for me to rejoin my company, and now that there's talk of the liberation of northern Mehru, I might participate in that effort as I'll do anything to keep the Hand of Reason as far from Maia as possible. But I can only do so if I leave Maia with you. Only then would I be confident that she would be as loved and cared for as with me.'

Ishab grew straighter with each of Peryst's words, and when he spoke it was firmly. 'Maia is of Sanjia, and therefore she is mine to care for as I did her mother.'

Peryst was a de Arranu, whose motto was *In Light, we see Light*, and for whom truth was a guiding beacon, so he knew he should have suffered some discomfort at Ishab's words, but he didn't. For Peryst, the truth of Maia's real parentage paled in importance when faced with her wellbeing. That was his only concern.

'Thank you, Ishab.' Peryst bowed his head. 'Nela will watch Maia as well.' He placed a heavy hand on the wolf's head. 'She was hand-reared by your daughter. It was she who kept me alive when I was driven mad by grief after Sanjia's death. And it is she who's taken Maia as her new mistress.'

Ishab's hand replaced Peryst's on the wolf's head. Staring into Nela's yellow eyes, he said, 'You cared for my daughter. You and I together will care for hers.'

'Why, Peryst?' Hana asked. 'Why would a Klaevani join the liberation of northern Mehru instead of heading to the safety of beyond the Kunlan Range?'

Peryst had asked himself the same as he rode from Deragaz. 'I gave my soul to Sanjia. We'd planned to return to Lis together, where I'd rejoin my company. We'd rear our children here with you for a time. With her dying breath, she begged me to keep her children safe. Maia is Touched, and no Touched will ever be safe in

Ankisua if the Hand of Reason is allowed to spread its venom. That's part of it. The other is what I saw in Leyandale. It's what I do, Hana. I kill monsters.' Peryst sighed. 'But some masquerade as people. The Hand of Reason is full of them, and they kill those born different. A regime of monsters that justifies such cruelty cannot be allowed to exist. And yes, I could turn and take my child to Klaevan. I could ignore the Hand of Reason, focusing only on myself. But if we all did that, the Hand would eventually reach us there, too. If all think only of themselves instead of standing up to the Hand, then we're lost. And if I did, what example would I set for my child? How can I face myself if I don't fight those who would kill me and my daughter?'

Ishab nodded slowly. 'There may come a time when you will have to choose, Peryst. There may come a time when your daughter's safety will come first.'

'Her safety will always come first, Ishab. But where will she be safer in Mehru than in Lis and with you?'

'There's one condition,' Ishab said as he lifted a finger.

'Which is?'

'No teachers, no Mas, no training. In Mehru, Maia will be the child that she is. She'll play with her cousins, she'll learn her letters and numbers as her mother did, she'll play with mud, paddle in the sea, and be foolish. She'll be loved and cared for, but she won't be trained like a performing beast.'

The implied criticism was a tangible pain for Peryst. 'Any training has been for her safety and that of others.'

'This is fair, but you say she's gained control. This is both good and enough,' Ishab replied. 'Sanjia wished her daughter to know she is of Mehru. A Mehruvian child is a child. I know your Klaevani ways. Your children are barely out of wraps when they're trained to fight. Your young are given weapons in infancy, with little chance of childhood and play!'

Peryst opened his mouth to retort angrily but paused as images of his childhood flashed through his mind: he and Marie, little older than Maia, bows in hand; his birthday gift at five, a maqtarum knife, sharp as his father's sword and the blue metal tinged with toxins; his first beast kill a few months after that birthday; his time in Genai and later in Lukur learning to master his powers; and his travels to earn his keep by hunting and killing monsters. Klaevani were considered adults at fifteen. He frowned. He'd been happy but certainly not carefree. Games in Klaevan always had a purpose: to teach the players to survive.

Peryst watched Maia happily walking her dragon up and down Ishab's thigh as she babbled into the older man's face. Peryst had nothing material to leave his daughter, but he would make sure she had every skill that he had. She would be able to earn her keep with bow, knife, and sword. She would use her powers for herself or for gain so she would never, ever depend on another for survival. Maia would be trained in every way possible, for that training would give her freedom, and that at least Peryst could and would leave her. But he could wait a little to start and give Maia a few years of the childhood he'd never had. He would do that for Ishab.

A few days later, after Maia had settled in happily to life in the tavern under Ishab and Hana's doting care and Nela's watchful protection, Peryst made his way to the Wrestlers, the regular drinking hole for the different factions of the Lis Guard and the Southern Mehruvian Army.

Coming from a land that had no organised army, Peryst admired the structure of the Southern Mehruvian Army and, more, the story of its origins. In the beginning, the Lis Guard had been mostly ceremonial and there'd been no organised army. With the rise of the Hand, however, the High Luk of the unified Mehru of then had thought ahead to a day when the Hand would be done with Reor and would set its sights on the lands beyond. The High Luk then formed a professional army made up of six battalions stationed all over Mehru. Each battalion was made up of three or four regiments that worked together and were comprised of five or six companies each. Unlike other realms, the Mehruvian companies tended to be specialised, thus a regiment could have a cavalry company, an infantry company, and a company made up of archers and crossbows.

But what Peryst most admired was that after the split of Mehru, the current High Luk had kept the structure of the army as it had been. He had also established mandatory training for all in southern Mehru whereby every southern Mehruvian spent two years training with the army in their youth and a month every year thereafter, men and women alike. The current High Luk's second wife had championed the cause and joined the army herself, taking her daughter on training exercises since she was a child. Since then, it had been the southern Mehruvian way. After their two years of mandatory training anyone could be called upon by the High Luk to serve again at any time of their lives if the need should arise. Some, like Gintras and Liria, chose to make a career with the army, but many others only returned for their annual training.

Peryst stopped at the door. The Wrestlers hadn't changed at all. As ever, he could barely hear himself think amongst the voices and laughter. Ale flowed liberally as the younger recruits flaunted their new uniforms in the front room or sat by the windows facing the street, hoping to see and to be seen, as he and Gintras had done all those years before. The older soldiers—regulars and those doing their annual training—tended to find a place in the back. Peryst elbowed his way to the bar through the crowd of youngsters and collected a tankard of ale and then turned to the archway that led to the quieter back room.

Liria, in earnest conversation with a hooded companion, suddenly saw Peryst. Her face lit up in a wide smile, and she beckoned him over to her table against the back wall. Peryst made his way through the room and sat next to Liria. The woman in the hood shook her head slightly and lifted her index finger to her lips. Peryst was startled to recognise Anil, whom he thought with her battalion in Gallya. The High Luk's youngest daughter and Agazi of one of the six battalions in his army was ten years Peryst's junior. Despite her being his commanding officer, they'd become close friends perhaps thanks to both being Touched and because of the easy ways of Mehruvians. He made no sign of recognition.

'I am so sorry about Sanjia,' Anil said, grasping his hand tightly. 'Liria told me the news.'

Peryst gave a brief nod of appreciation at the depth of her feeling. 'I thank you.' He took a sip of the dark ale, speciality of the house, and asked, 'I thought you were in Gallya. Why the secrecy?'

Anil kept the hood low over her face to hide the strong, straight nose, so like her father's, and the stubborn chin that would be recognised immediately by all. 'Most believe me to be either there or in Vel, and I'd rather it remains that way.'

'Why?' he asked again.

She changed the subject. 'I heard you participated in the defence of Leyandale.'

'I did. With Gintras. It was no big thing.'

'Not in execution, perhaps, but in effect it was immense,' Anil said. 'It's cemented Mehru's hold on the area and will permit us to begin taking back the western towns. I hear the companies from Folchester and Selkirk have joined those in Leyandale and an assault on Ilia is underway.'

'This is news to me. It's more than four months since I left Leyandale, and then they were waiting with bated breath.'

'No longer,' Anil replied. 'You've heard of the efforts for reunification.'

'I have,' Peryst replied, catching Liria's eye. Did Liria have any idea where the conversation was heading? Because he certainly didn't. But she merely smiled briefly and reassuringly at him.

'My father seeks to give new life to the Mehru of old and unite it against the Hand of Reason.'

'A worthy aspiration,' Peryst replied. 'And one that will reassure the rest of Ankisua.'

'Indeed,' Anil replied. He spied a closed expression and tightened lips.

Confused, he asked, 'What is it? Is the idea of reunification not to your liking? Or to that of our allies in Vel?' He referred carefully to the Pirate Chief, as the leader of the isles was called, whose son was Anil's longtime partner and father of her two sons.

'The union with northern Mehru is very much to my liking and Vel's, as it is to most at my father's court, but for different reasons. Traders see it as an opportunity for new markets, others as a resurrection of Mehru's ancient glories, and yet others as our only chance to keep the Hand away from our lands.'

'All truths, and all valid,' Peryst replied pragmatically.

'Some, though, would prefer to attract and not repel the Hand,' she added quietly.

'What do you mean? Who could wish that? Only those with no knowledge of the Hand's methods could ever find ways to justify their existence.'

'Some at my father's court see the reunification as a means to negotiate with the Hand. They think once Mehru is whole, we'll be able to deal with the Hand as equals and share their advances even if it means respecting their ideology.'

'The Hand of Reason doesn't share,' he stated.

'Do you think I don't know that?'

'It's of no consequence, however, because the High Luk would never negotiate with the Hand of Reason,' he said reassuringly.

Anil lowered her hooded head. 'What if the High Luk were not there to negotiate?'

The shock of Anil's words robbed him of speech for a second. He cleared his throat. 'Is the High Luk dead?'

'Not yet, but I fear that once he's achieved reunification, he will be. Perhaps even before.'

'You speak in riddles.'

Anil raised her troubled gaze to Peryst. 'The High Luk has sons from his first wife who tire of waiting for the throne. They see the future of southern Ankisua as united under the umbrella of Reor's advances.'

'Reor's gadgets come hand in hand with the Hand of Reason, with death for all those who are different, particularly the Touched, like you,' he replied, pointing between Anil's brows.

She shrugged. 'Neither of them is Touched. None in their mother's line were.'

'Do you really think the High Luk is in danger from his own sons?'

'I don't know. He won't hear a word against them, but I discovered—Klaust did really—a secret trip to Stonehelve. Why would the High Luk's sons travel to Stonehelve?'

'Who knows? Are you in your father's confidence?'

'Partially. I am with regards to the reunification plans because I'm one of his six army commanders. But with respect to other court intrigues or political decisions, I'm not. The High Luk doesn't keep all his eggs in one basket.'

Peryst sighed, believing that, as a younger child removed from her father's court, she harboured some resentment towards her older brothers.

'The High Luk is no fool. He's not in his dotage and is as strong as ever. Any secret you've heard he doubtlessly has heard as well. I would trust he won't be taken in by petty intrigue, even if it's led by his own sons.'

'I hope you're right,' Anil replied heavily.

'Will you be in Lis long?' he asked, trying to distract her from her disturbing thoughts.

'I leave tonight. I was in Vel briefly to see Klaust and the boys but came back when the intelligence of my brothers' visit to Stonehelve reached Vel. I wanted to consult with my father before I return to my battalion in Gallya.' Anil sighed. 'I never cease to feel impotence that my husband is able to learn more of the state of Mehru than I can. His vast network of Touched spies deliver information in a heartbeat that would take weeks for us to uncover.'

Peryst knew the heartbreak her words covered. He knew what she sacrificed for Mehru and her father. He knew of the all-too-brief moments with her husband and children, always under the shadow of her imminent departure to fulfil her obligations as the Agazi of the battalion that protected the Mehruvian capital from Reor's reaching fingers.

Liria gave Peryst an imperceptible shrug before speaking. 'What about you, Peryst? I've heard through the grapevine that Ishab will care for your daughter while you rejoin your company.'

'That was my plan,' Peryst replied with a smile at Anil.

'Good,' said Anil. 'It's taken longer than we expected, but you can add a company to my battalion: an Idhan that'll gather the many Touched spread amongst my soldiers. You'll train them and be their captain, their Idhani.'

'I'll be happy to help train them but surely you have able captains who can lead them,' Peryst replied. He didn't want to ruffle any of her captains' feathers.

Anil lifted her pointed chin. 'I do, but none has your experience in the matter. It's not just that you are you and that Klaust and I love you. You're not only Touched yourself, but you've served in an Idhan in Kurbal. I know of none other who's done this.'

Peryst shook his head. 'Your captains won't want a Klaevani taking the Touched from their sections to form a new faction. And they'll object to you giving me such a role. Is this what you need right now? A battalion divided by resentment?'

Anil shook her head. 'I need the best battalion I can make, and that involves a strong cavalry, an infantry with excellent archers and organised swords, and a powerful Idhan.'

'You would need to gather truly committed Touched willing to suffer for your cause. It's necessary for the members of an Idhan to be capable of mind-to-mind communication for it to be effective. And to learn the skill is excruciating.'

'I expected you to come up with exactly that issue, my friend. Though Klaust paid dearly for it, I had him source a stash of hirim grass from Kurbal for me. I have it set aside to make the tisane for your Idhan.'

Peryst raised both his hands with a snort of laughter. Of course she had. Anil's stubbornness was legendary.

'I intend to cross the Ramu and start retaking the western towns of Mehru that suffer under the Hand, beginning with Fallya,' Anil said. 'Once we've done that, we'll march east, liberating as we go along till we meet those doing the same from Leyandale.'

'Some of those towns and cities have been under the Hand for close to a decade. They may see your march more as conquest than liberation,' he said.

'Perhaps at first, but they'll come to see that under Mehruvian rule they'll no longer live in fear.'

'I wonder what my brother-in-law would feel about a *liberation* led by Mehru. I suspect that he'd fight any such liberation fiercely to protect his way of life, established for generations. You'll encounter similar in the western towns of northern Mehru.'

'You're right, of course,' Anil replied. 'It will be more of a challenge than your little foray in Leyandale. Will it be too much of a challenge for Peryst de Arranu?' she asked in a lightly mocking tone.

He placed his tankard on the table and spoke in a low tone that throbbed as he pictured the days, months, and years that would come. 'Don't fool yourself. Retaking northern Mehru will be no march to freedom. It'll be an uphill struggle that'll take years, with victories and setbacks for all of us. Will you sacrifice your family for this?' Peryst thought of Klaust and her boys, little older than Maia, who lived in the Citadel of Vel while Anil came and went from the Isle.

Anil grew serious. 'I know this, but, like the most pragmatic faction of my father's court, I also know that the only way for Mehru to resist the Hand of Reason is if we're united against Reor, so I'll do what I can to make the High Luk's wishes a reality and to make Mehru safe for my children, Touched as they are. My brothers won't, and so, despite what I sacrifice, it's what I must do. You of all people should understand this. To liberate Leyandale did you not leave your child with the Mas in Deragaz?'

Peryst sighed and bowed his head in acquiescence. 'Once my child is settled with her grandfather, it will be my honour to serve you and the High Luk in any way I can.'

GALLYA

YEAR 5163 OF THE NEW ERA – SUMMER

PERYST ENCOUNTERED THE resistance he'd expected when Anil announced the creation of an Idhan from the Touched scattered throughout the different companies in the battalion stationed in Gallya.

'The Southern Mehruvian Army has never had Idhans. Why do we need them now?' cavalry captain Seg Kaelblade asked from his seat across from Anil at the table in the Gallya town hall, where the Agazi had called a meeting of captains.

'Because we'll be engaging in a campaign that might take years, and we'll need as much talent and expertise as we can muster. Reor is a powerful enemy with a well-organised and ruthless army,' Anil replied.

'We have all such talent already, just spread out within the different sections of our army,' Seg insisted. 'That makes us stronger.'

Anil shook her short curls and struck her fist on the table. 'Would your riders be such a powerful force if they were scattered amongst the rest, Seg? Are they not powerful because you command them as a unit so they defend or attack like different parts of one body, all working for the same purpose?'

Kasu Ironver, the captain of the archers, intervened from the other end. 'It'll mean taking some of our soldiers to form a different company. Some of the Touched may be essential to their current sections, but you'd have Peryst rifle through our companies and take the best for his Idhan.'

Anil nodded and made a note on a document in front of her. 'This may be an issue, it's true. No one shall be forced to join Peryst, but all will be given the option to do so.' With a wave of her hand, she invited Peryst, who sat to her left, to speak.

'Sahar and Kurbal have Idhans in their armies. But not all soldiers with power join them as many have other talents that are better, more powerful, or even more to their liking. So, in such armies it's possible to find an excellent archer who's Touched but who prefers to do battle with the archers,' Peryst said. 'And this choice must be respected. Each knows where their real strengths lie.'

'Why should we even listen to a Klaevani mercenary?' Seg snapped.

'Because I'm asking you to,' Anil replied drily.

'If the High Luk had wanted his army to have Idhans, he'd have formed them ages ago. There's a reason the Southern Mehruvian Army doesn't have them,' Seg insisted.

Anil stiffened. 'The High Luk formed the army he could at a time when we had none. Circumstances have changed since. We now fight for the survival of our homeland as Reor marches taking defenceless towns and villages. We'll need every advantage we can muster to prevent Reor conquering the whole of Mehru.'

'There have always been Touched in Mehru, and the High Luk would've given them more power if he'd deemed it necessary or appropriate,' Seg insisted. 'Would you even be considering this if you weren't Touched yourself?'

Most of those at the table gasped at Seg's temerity, and Anil's face tightened imperceptibly. The only Touched of her siblings, taking after her father, she'd been belittled by her brothers for being Touched. Peryst knew Seg's words would've infuriated her, but he also knew she wouldn't let her anger show.

'It's attitudes like this that sit at the root of the Hand of Reason's rise, Seg. The High Luk gave me, his *Touched* daughter, the command of the most important battalion of his army, which has been charged with protecting Lis and retaking northern Mehru. Don't you think that's enough power to the Touched?' Anil asked.

'No, I think it's power to his daughter, whom he loves and considers a valuable army commander. It has nothing to do with you being Touched,' Seg replied recklessly.

Peryst had seen Anil lose her temper only once, and that had been enough to teach him and all those who'd borne witness never to underestimate the High Luk's daughter, young and mild though she seemed.

Anil lifted her chin and suddenly so resembled her father that it was uncanny. 'As the High Luk's commander, daughter or not, I am charged to make the decisions I deem most appropriate for the battalion I command. As such, I have decided to form an Idhan. Now.' Anil's jaw was clenched as she made an obvious effort to speak without raising her voice. 'There is a fine line between treason and insubordination, Seg, and you are walking it now. There is no place for either in the Southern Mehruvian Army but ample space under the hangman's noose.' She let her gaze rove, briefly stopping at every single captain, all of whom lowered their faces and stared at the wood.

Seg paled and stammered. 'I did not mean it like that, Agazi. I would never disrespect your command, but good captains should always question their superiors' decisions.'

'Good captains should question, it's true, yet your intention was not to question but to cast doubt. I am not a fool, Seg,' Anil said witheringly. 'I won't tolerate insubordination on this or any other matter. Not now, not ever. You have been a valuable captain till now, but you are a breath away from the noose.'

His face pale and set, Seg stated, 'I will face execution with a high head, Agazi, if you should decide that my motives in questioning were to humiliate or disrupt your plans. If, however, you can see the truth—that I will always question to make sure the decision reached is sound—then allow me to remain as your faithful captain.'

Peryst didn't let his incredulity pass over his face. Seg had spoken the exact words Anil needed to hear. Perhaps they were, in fact, truth, but Peryst vowed from then on to watch Seg; he feared Anil would forgive and forget, both a virtue and a flaw. Peryst, though, wouldn't forget.

But perhaps Anil wouldn't forget either, he considered, as she pierced Seg with her gaze before speaking again. 'I want you all to listen to Peryst.'

'He knows what he's talking about,' Asruel Charmilder, a captain of the infantry, intervened. 'Peryst served under me in the raids on Tamadal. He's an able and brave captain, loyal to Mehru.'

'He's a mercenary, not a Mehruvian,' Seg said quietly. 'There are plenty of able Touched within our own ranks who could lead the Idhan.'

'So that's what bothers you?' Anil asked Seg. 'Is it not enough that he served in our army for years and later commanded a company jointly with a Mehruvian? Is it not enough that he married a Mehruvian and has a Mehruvian child?' Anil's voice rose. 'Is it not enough that I, your Agazi, have chosen him for qualities you may know nothing about?'

Peryst resisted the urge to place a calming hand on Anil's arm. In no way would he undermine her authority, but he needed to be accepted on his own merits. He knew full well that for their plan to work, the new Idhan would need to be welcomed by the whole battalion and he, as the Idhani, would need not only to be accepted but respected as an equal by all the captains in the regiment.

'I have chosen this regiment to start with because it is you who will retake Fallya,' Anil said quietly. 'Later, we will establish Idhans in each regiment of the battalion and, eventually, in the whole army. It's the High Luk's wish to ensure that our army uses every tool it has to fight against the Hand of Reason, but, even so, know that our battle will be fraught and difficult.'

Seg lowered his head. 'I will listen, Agazi.'

Anil turned to Kasu. 'And you?'

Kasu raised her chin. 'I will listen, Agazi.'

Anil then gestured again at Peryst as noise from the green below sounded in the background and light streamed in through the windows. The meeting room, save for different tapestries and wood trim, could have been in any town hall. Peryst studied the circle of closed faces. Seg and Kasu sat together with rebellious expressions. Next to Kasu sat Mabian Lightreathe, another cavalry captain, and whom, like Asruel, Peryst knew from the past. She winked at him, one light in a room of mostly stern faces.

Peryst cleared his throat. 'I'm Peryst de Arranu. I had the honour of joining the Southern Mehruvian Army in 5147, when I was seventeen years old. I rose through the ranks like all of you, and, when I left Mehru eight years ago, I had been commanding a company jointly with Gintras of Barges—the Agazi who recently retook Leyandale—for two years. Some of you will remember me from those days.'

Mabian, Asruel, and the Alkaid of Gallya nodded.

Mabian chuckled. 'The good times and the bad.'

'Why did you leave?' Kasu asked.

'I was charged by Agazi Anil to study the Idhans in Kurbal to bring such knowledge to Mehru.'

'He married Sanjia, the daughter of Ishab Meadfield, owner of The Fiery Camyl in the southern quarter of Lis,' Mabian added.

Most nodded, even Seg. The tavern was popular in Lis, and many had known Ishab's laughing, black-eyed daughter.

'Sanjia and I travelled to Kurbal, where we both joined Idhans. I shadowed the Idhani for four years, learning both how to train the members and what they could do to support the rest of the army in their maritime battle with Sahar.'

Again, those at the table nodded, all with the same air of perplexity at the unending battles on the Revan Sea. Despite time spent in Kurbal, Peryst could still not quite understand the elven war. Both nations had been involved in a horrific war when they agreed, after an entire century of visiting destruction and death upon one another, only ever to battle at sea so that the only dead would be those who chose to fight and no destruction would ever fall on the innocent. For another century, they'd waged ferocious naval battles, and both countries lived in peace and prosperity while the waters of the Revan Sea roiled with blood. Then, decades before Peryst's birth, they'd changed their approach again and only did battle at sea on alternate days, some days with Sahar defending and Kurbal attacking, and the next the other way round. The war between them had become a kind of war-training exercise in which both nations honed their skills. Meanwhile, on land their populations mixed and thrived.

'Only four years in Kurbal?' Asruel asked. 'That's unlike you, Peryst.'

Peryst shrugged. 'I'd learnt all I needed, and Sanjia missed her family. We decided to return to Lis and journeyed through Genai very slowly because Sanjia was pregnant at the time.' Peryst smiled sadly.

'Congratulations!' Mabian clapped her hands silently.

Peryst continued painfully, avoiding catching Mabian's gaze as she would doubtless feel terrible after he finished. 'I lost Sanjia and one of the babies in northern Usur and afterwards made my way south with my daughter.'

'He joined Gintras in the liberation of Leyandale,' Anil intervened.

Peryst nodded. 'That's my background, but it tells you little other than my history. I can tell you what I saw in Kurbal. Idhans there sometimes operate on their own, sometimes as support for other companies, but always as another part of the army, following their respective high command's plan.'

'How are they structured, and what can they do?' Seg asked grudgingly.

'They're structured like any army company, with a captain they call Idhani and ranks, but what they can do depends on the powers their members possess.'

'I don't understand,' Seg replied.

'You will once the Idhan is formed,' Anil said and added sternly, 'and I will not tolerate interference with its formation.'

After the meeting at the town hall, Anil convened the entirety of her battalion in turns at the mess of the barracks built on the city's outskirts. Flanked by her captains, she announced the plan to create an Idhan in the first regiment initially and later in the rest. Then she introduced Peryst.

Peryst spoke briefly but sought to address the captains' fears. 'I don't come to diminish any part of the battalion, but the opposite. By creating powerful Idhans, we'll be able to centralise our powers and abilities in support of the rest of the companies in each regiment so archers, infantry, and cavalry are more powerful. Any Touched ability can be used to enhance the abilities of others. The Idhan will make us better in unexpected ways.'

A voice rang out from the back of the barn-like structure. 'Do all Touched have to join the Idhan?'

'No. I only want those who wish to join, who aspire to make Agazi Anil's battalion renowned in the Southern Mehruvian Army, regardless of their abilities.'

Peryst's words were met with deep silence and none of the roar of applause he would have wanted. Maybe he hadn't been persuasive enough; maybe Seg and Kasu had spread too deep a distrust in him.

'Those who wish to join the first Idhan should let me know by sundown. I'll be by the arms tent till full dark. We'll start training tomorrow with however many come, whether three or forty. Even three could make a difference.'

All afternoon Peryst waited by the arms tent with his arms crossed, trying to look confident.

Will anybody come? Please, Ilu, let some come. Let me show them that an Idhan can make a difference. Let them come.

Peryst didn't try to convince any who asked questions but waited till the end of the day, when he was relieved that twenty-one of the younger soldiers, unhappy where they were for different reasons, signed up with him.

Peryst began simply by trying to create an identity for his company of twenty-two, including himself, by placing their tents together in a separate area of the camp and by adding a copper woven letter *I* to their upper sleeves.

'Why follow the instructions of a Klaevani? I like my tent where it is,' a young woman spat in frustration when told that she would have to move her tent to the new area. It was a question Peryst was getting used to hearing.

'Because this Klaevani has served in the Kurbali army and has seen how their Touched are a force that actually counts,' Peryst replied mildly.

'Are you saying that we don't count?'

Peryst studied her intently. She was tall and dark, with the usual Mehruvian colouring, and glared at him.

'Why did you join the Idhan?'

'Why is that your concern?'

'Because I'm the Idhani, responsible for the performance of every one of its members.'

Lana Falltreader, a soldier whose father had served under Peryst and Gintras many years earlier, placed a placating hand on the woman's arm. 'Answer him.'

She snorted. 'Why shouldn't I have joined?'

'You certainly should have, but I'd like to know why,' Peryst insisted. 'What's your name and where were you till now?'

'Ria Hart. And I was with the archers.'

'Why did you leave?'

Ria glowered, a snarl on her face, till Lana put her arm over her shoulders and whispered in her ear. The anger seeped out of Ria's face as her shoulders lowered. She shook her head and raised her chin defiantly. 'I left the archers because I was no good. I'm a mediocre archer at best and would never make a difference. I hate horses, so no good for the cavalry, and have even less skill with the sword. I thought maybe it would be different with the Idhan.'

Peryst nodded but gave no consolatory speech or encouraging words. The other recruits listened, all with abashed demeanours. He guessed they'd all joined for similar reasons. He had a group of frustrated soldiers who thought they were no good plus one who'd joined because her father had spoken well of him: not the best foundation for a fearsome Idhan. But this was what he had, so this was what he'd use, and he'd show Seg, Kasu, and the rest that an Idhan *could* make a difference. He would start by memorising their names and skills.

'What are you?' Peryst asked Ria.

'What do you mean?'

'What type of Touched?'

'I'm an Air Primal.'

'Good. Have you ever used your powers in battle?'

Ria frowned. 'Never.'

Peryst nodded and turned to Lana. 'And you?'

Lana shrugged. 'I'm also a Primal. Matter.'

'Wonderful. Have you used your powers in battle?'

As Lana grinned, he knew he had her; at least one!

'Very few of us use our powers in combat, Idhani. The only ones who do are the Menders, for obvious reasons. The rest of us tend to use other talents.' She pointed at the sword at her side.

'And that, Ria, is why you need to listen to me. Every one of you has a talent that can be used to enhance the effectiveness of this company. I have seen this done in Kurbal and Sahar and believe we can do it even better in Mehru.'

The fight was still in Ria, who replied crossly, 'And why would a Klaevani mercenary be interested in Mehru doing things better?'

Peryst smiled, almost liking the girl for her abrasiveness. She had spirit and asked a fair question.

'Am I a mercenary? I was once, like many Klaevani. Mercenaries don't think beyond the coin, but it's different for me with Mehru because my child is Mehruvian, like all of you, and keeping her home safe is part of what a father is meant to do. And because if we don't all rise to stop the Hand of Reason, before long pyres will be burning all over Ankisua.'

Ria nodded and asked, still in an aggressive tone, 'How do you intend to make us into a force that counts, then?'

Peryst scanned his new recruits. 'We'll sleep and eat together. We'll determine who we are and discuss what we can use in battle. Together. We'll become a team. I'm a Sight and Touch Sensal with a slight Fire Primal ability. When I focus my mind's eye, I can see weakness in all things. If I'm facing a monster, I see exactly where I need to hit to defeat it. If I gaze at a wall, I see where the bricks have moved and made a vulnerability. If I focus my sight on a person, I see where their armour is too tight, where their shoulder pains them, or where their own sight is weak. All this allows me to better plan my attack.'

'That's more useful than my power,' a lanky young man replied.

Peryst turned to him. 'What's your name?'

'Benat Clayvein.'

'What are you, Benat?'

'I'm also a Sight Sensal, but when I focus my mind's eye, I can see what's far away as if very close.' He grimaced. 'Good for spotting my young son when he wanders off and for bird watching but little else.'

'Not only good for that,' Peryst replied. 'That's an excellent power when surveying a battlefield or access to a city. I can see weakness, but I can only do so when close enough to see naturally, but you can observe from afar, so you could, for instance, show me mind to mind so I can search for weaknesses in what you see.' He picked up a stick and drew on the dusty earth as he spoke. 'Our battalion is located here, on the outskirts of a city, any city. Agazi Anil's scouts try to approach but are seen and must draw back. Long-view glasses work but can only be focused on small areas at a time.'

The group nodded, pushing closer to study the scenario he was drawing in the dirt.

'Benat, however, can see it all. He can see where the long-range enemy archers position themselves on the walls, here and here, and he can see how many guards they have.'

Peryst turned to a grinning Benat and spoke with more intention. 'Benat can tell our archers where to aim their arrows to rid us of the long-range archers, or he can show me, mind to mind, so I can spot specific weaknesses and tell them where to aim.'

Lana shook her head. 'Archers can be good, Idhani, but I have never known one who could hit a target at such a distance.'

'And that is where Ria comes in.' Peryst turned to Ria with a smile. 'You, Ria, would use your mind's eye to manipulate and push the air behind a flight of arrows so that they reach their target, however far away.'

The awe on the faces of his Touched were all Peryst could have hoped for in terms of enthusiasm, but he knew that he'd have an uphill struggle to make them into a true Idhan.

'If we all work together, if we all know what each of us can do and use those skills properly, if we all keep thinking in new ways, we'll make our Idhan an invaluable ally to the first regiment and something for the rest of the battalion to envy. But you'll need to trust me to guide you and remember that my first obligation will be to each of you because I am Touched, just like you are. I'll support and protect you any way I can.'

Later that day, Peryst gazed out the window of the town hall, where Anil held her weekly meeting with the captains of her battalion and the authorities of Gallya. Perched on the northern branch of the Ramu delta, Fallya was clearly visible across the water.

'Were Gallya and Fallya ever one city?' he asked Asruel.

'Not quite,' Asruel replied. 'After the division of Mehru, the two towns' north-to-south roads were connected by the bridge till the coming of the Hand.'

Peryst leaned forwards to see the stone bridge with its four half-moon arches. A low parapet lined its sides, and in the exact middle rose a tall and more graceful arch carved with wolves. From its highest point hung a banner with the howling wolf of Mehru on the side facing Gallya and another that depicted a hand holding a solar torch on the side facing Fallya.

'So, the links between both towns will have been strong,' Peryst affirmed.

'Very,' Asruel agreed. 'Families lived and worked on either side of the river, and joint festivals, markets, and fairs were held on the bridge itself. Fallya and Gallya acted like sister cities till the first crossing of the Hand of Reason from Mirah thirteen years ago.'

'How is it that Fallya fell and Gallya didn't?'

'The Alkaid of Gallya, following orders from the High Luk, had been wary of the Hand's overtures, whereas her companion to the north welcomed them with open arms. Fallya fell quickly into the Hand's clutches.'

'Were there purges?'

'Some, but the Defenders started slowly. They began by forcing the Touched to wear a *T* on their chests then confiscating their property. They soon expanded their sphere of hate to include anyone related to a Touched or who could be deemed to use power for any purpose, even healing, and finally all who followed the Temple of Gal's teachings. By then, most of those with Touched family members had crossed the bridge to join us, so when the Hand began building pyres Gallya was a haven for those who fled Fallya.'

'Was that when the High Luk sent this battalion to guard the southern banks of the Ramu?' Peryst asked.

Asruel nodded. 'We came four years ago. Anil has come and gone from Vel, and here we remain protecting access to Lis.'

Peryst observed the bridge. 'It's heavily fortified on the southern side.'

'Anil's doing. As are the sentinels and beacons all the way east up to the edges of Forglenden. There's little chance of anyone crossing from the north without

Anil's knowledge and no chance of Gallya succumbing to the wiles of the Hand after they've watched friends and family members first driven from their homes and later burnt to death.'

'It must have placed a heavy burden on Gallya, though,' Peryst mused.

'It did. The city had to expand quickly to provide refuge for kin from Fallya. And then we came along to defend them, placing an even heavier burden on the city and its resources.'

When Anil cleared her throat, Peryst and Asruel sat at the table with the other captains. Anil stared out the window at Fallya. She turned abruptly, interrupting the quiet conversation.

'Now is the time to take Fallya back,' Anil said.

'Why now?' Feran Bouldert, the Agazi of the Gallya Guard, asked.

'The Hand of Reason first rose to power in Reor in 5011, more than a hundred and fifty years ago. During the purges, their methods were met with horror, and it took a couple of generations for Reordans to cooperate willingly with the Hand.' Anil said what they all knew.

Peryst thought of Felim and those at the Lithe Fair in Belfane who knew no Touched or, given the fewer born in Reor these days, rarely saw them being burnt alive and, thus, could forget that their prosperity and way of life rested on those who'd been persecuted and tortured before them.

Anil said out loud what he was thinking. 'Today, four or five generations since the purges, Reordans wouldn't join us if we came to drive out the Hand of Reason. On the contrary, they'd fight us.'

Peryst chuckled wryly. 'It's the Hand that feeds them.'

'Surely not,' Mabian protested. 'They know what the Hand does.'

Peryst shook his head. 'No. They've forgotten.' He paused. 'Or perhaps forgotten is not the right word. They've forced themselves not to think of how they've got to where they are, because if they did, they'd despise themselves.' He thought again of the fear in his sister's face when he saw her last. 'And because they have families with mouths to feed. And blood comes first.' Or should. But for Felim it hadn't. It made him angry every time he thought of his brother-in-law, so he willed himself to concentrate on Anil.

'Fallya, however, is different,' Anil said.

'Of course it is. The Hand started its takeover thirteen years ago. I appreciate what you're saying.' Feran nodded. 'They've not yet fully settled into life under the Hand and still harbour rebellion. Five to ten years from now, they'll probably fight us too if we come to liberate them.'

'They and the other western towns have been seduced by more than what seduced Reor a hundred and fifty years ago. Reordan inventions have developed tenfold, making day-to-day life easier and more comfortable. The Academy provides these towns with all sorts of gadgets and tells them that only if they comply might their children reach the heights of the Academy,' Anil explained.

'By getting rid of the Touched.' Mabian scowled.

'Not just the Touched,' Peryst intervened. 'The Touched, the halflings, the elves, alchemists, healers, weavers of tales, of music, or of anything that can keep the old ways alive. Reor bases its progress on destruction of what came before instead of building upon and improving what's there.'

'Why?' Pinta Reeves, the Alkaid of Gallya, asked.

Anil sighed. 'The age-old yearning for power, Pinta. The elimination of the Touched in Reor was an excuse for the Five to topple the previous regime of the Kissar. There had been some truly horrible Kissars with no power at all throughout Reordan history, but the Hand chose the elimination of the Touched as their cornerstone. It was easy to stir hatred of a minority that was different. But their inventions and Touched power can coexist, improving each other, and it is well known that we learn from the errors of the past. Southern Mehru, Usur, Kurbal, Klaevan, and Genai are proof of this, as are Meyan and Sahar. It need not be one or the other as the Hand of Reason insists.'

'What can we do to help Fallya?' Pinta asked.

'You're already helping, Pinta. Gallya faces Fallya. Despite the pressure put upon your city by the refugees from across the river and the presence of the army, you've been able to expand the town and keep its spirit and at the same time remind Fallya of who they are,' Anil stated.

Pinta wrinkled her nose in confusion.

'You play the old music to Fallya, Pinta, you shine bright, colourful lights, and you remind them of what it means to be of Mehru. Every market and every music festival that you hold on the bridge reminds Fallya of what they're missing. The Air Primals who magnify sound and throw music and joy across the river and the light displays visible from Fallya all show we haven't forgotten those who are still across the border.'

'They could've crossed the bridge,' Kasu muttered. 'They could've turned their back on the Hand like so many from Fallya have done, but they chose not to. I'm not sure we need to expend so much energy reminding them of what they're missing as they obviously don't care.'

'None can know what lives inside another, Kasu. Fear, attachment to property, ill health, and confusion are all valid reasons not to leave, and those who made such choices deserve sympathy and not contempt,' Pinta replied.

'We've watched Fallya from across the river for years, so they won't expect us to cross now, but when we do, I suspect not all will receive us with lances and swords,' Anil said thoughtfully.

'At this time, the Five are facing east, where the Southern Mehruvian Army has already met Reor's army of Defenders,' Peryst said quietly. The Five led the Hand of Reason from their fortress in Shya on the Reordan side of the Kunlan Range. They were a mysterious quintet—three women and two men—elected for life by and from the elite group of High Defenders of Shya within the Reordan army. On election, they took the names of the first Five to make themselves eternal and godlike.

'They won't expect us to come from this direction, so our time is now. Our role is to reclaim the western towns so we leave the Hand with nowhere to go but back to Reor,' Anil said.

Through the window of the large airy town-hall room, Peryst could see across the river to the roofs of Fallya. He could just glimpse wide streets and many empty buildings. The green, of which he could see only a corner, held a small market, and where the temple had once towered was a deserted, overgrown plot with stone ruins. All in the room could see Gallya's green with its market of multicoloured awnings, overflowing baskets of produce, and children running in between the adults trying to glean the latest news from their neighbours, and, across the green, the Temple of Gal with its doors wide open in welcome to any who wanted the solace given by the music that spilled from within its walls.

'How will we do it?' Feran asked.

Anil leaned on her hands. 'We'll think. We'll plan. And then, we'll cross the bridge.'

'How soon?' Peryst asked.

'How soon can you get your Idhan in shape?' Anil countered.

'Two months?'

Anil chuckled. 'I'll give you three. Then, with every step carefully planned, we cross the bridge.'

Peryst listened and kept his own counsel as the other captains argued and debated. He knew he wasn't yet one of them and it would take time, and possibly even substantial loss of blood, before they considered him as such, but he would bide his time till he proved to them that the Touched could make a difference.

OUTSKIRTS OF GALLYA

YEAR 5163 OF THE NEW ERA – SUMMER

ANIL'S BATTALION HAD their barracks to the west, well beyond the town walls. But Peryst marched the Idhan even further west and through a grove of trees to the last clearing before a copse by the narrower southern branch of the Ramu. There, they'd be far enough away from gawkers to train uninterrupted.

Peryst was gratified to find that he had recruits from all three recognised branches of Touched. Three were Menders of the usual type, all healers, and a fourth declared herself to be a very weak healer. Seven were Sensals, covering four of the remaining senses: four had sight enhancements, one had enhanced hearing, another enhanced touch and sight—like Peryst—and one had a sense of smell that rivalled that of the best tracker dog. Of the ten Primals, three manipulated water, two air and wind, three matter, and the last two were proficient with fire.

'We have a good breadth of powers,' Peryst said from the middle of the circle of Touched early on the first morning of training. 'Though the company is small, I believe you can make a difference to any battle.'

'What kind of training will we need?' Sada Stonvale, a Fire Primal, asked.

Peryst turned to the three stronger Menders. 'Are any of you archers, even if mediocre?'

Mech Grant and Pena Pebbleford raised their hands.

'Good, grab your bows.'

Peryst pointed at the grove beyond the camp and spoke to Benat. 'We'll aim at the trees. Observe them carefully and find me a worthy target.'

Benat focused his mind's eye on the trees.

'What do you see?' Peryst asked.

'I can see the trees right in front of me. One has a darker knot about three quarters of the way up the trunk.'

'One of the most important things members of an Idhan must learn is to be able to communicate mind to mind with their Idhani and their companions.'

'How do we do that?' Benat asked.

'I'll teach you, and the tisane you all drank this morning, which you will drink till you master the skill, will ease the learning and prevent you from suffering headaches as you do so. Now, which of you were trained when you were younger?'

They all looked at each other and shrugged.

Lana replied for them. 'It's different in Mehru, Idhani. Touched are not trained like you are in the North. There's such fear of creating a situation like that in Reor that Touched here are mostly left to their own devices. If we're lucky, there'll be another Touched in the family or a local Mas who'll give guidance in controlling our powers. If not, we figure things out ourselves as well as we can.'

Peryst sighed. 'This will make things slightly more complicated.' He placed a hand on Benat's shoulder and signalled for everyone to sit in a circle.

'The first thing a young Touched is taught as soon as they come into their powers is to control the mind's eye. You all can do that? You all can focus your mind's eye at will?'

All twenty-one nodded.

'That's something,' Peryst said in relief. 'To learn to communicate mind to mind you will need to learn to compartmentalise.'

Their confused features told him they'd never even heard the term. Peryst stifled a frustrated sigh and tried again. 'What would happen if all my awareness were given to, say, that rock ahead?'

Lana giggled. 'You'd get to know the rock very well?'

'I would leave myself vulnerable to attack from elsewhere. To keep safe, I need to be able to focus on more than one thing at a time. I'll find the rock's weakness, but at the same time I'll be alert to my surroundings and even, if needed, communicate with another soldier and also strike with my sword.'

'How do you do all that at the same time?' Benat asked.

'You breathe and speak, see and hear at the same time, do you not?' Peryst asked.

Benat nodded.

'You need to imagine that your mind's eye is separate from yourself, and you need to use the same skill you use to focus at will to divide it into as many compartments as you need.' The recruits waited eagerly for him to continue.

'Communicating mind to mind is an essential skill in an Idhan. Things change rapidly, and either your companions will need warning or we'll be acting in a situation in which silence is required.'

'But how do we do it?' Benat insisted.

'We'll start with an exercise given to an Idhan in Kurbal,' Peryst said, injecting his voice with positivity. 'All of you, close your physical eyes and go back to your youth. Remember how and when you learnt to focus your mind's eye. I want each of you to focus your attention on whatever your skill may be but, at the same time, order your mind's eye to show me an image of what you had for breakfast. No voices.'

'That's impossible!' Sada exclaimed.

'Not only is it not impossible, but it's what each of you can do with practice. At first, you'll only be able to send pictures, but you'll progress to full conversations. Don't concentrate too much. Instead, in the same way you can see and hear at the same time, order your mind's eye to focus on your power as you also order it to send me the image. It's like when you sing and groom your horse at the same time.'

Peryst had expected the Sensals to succeed first so was surprised when he received a clear image of scrambled eggs from Ria as her moving hands created a small whirlwind that raised her hair round the satisfied expression on her face. The others followed one by one, some clearer, others less so, and some lasting a mere instant, others longer, till the only one left was Benat, who, with a frown of fierce concentration, kept trying to no avail.

'Stop, Benat,' Peryst said.

'No. I can do it,' Benat replied, wrinkling his brow and clenching his fists.

'Just stop. Turn back to me.'

Benat reluctantly lifted a pained face to Peryst.

'Raise your hands,' Peryst told him.

Benat grimaced in confusion but raised both hands.

'Good. Now lower your left.'

Benat lowered his left hand.

'Did you need to concentrate to do that?'

Benat shook his head.

'Now observe the trees with your mind's eye focused.'

Benat turned back to the grove. The moment when all his attention was focused on the trees, Peryst said softly, 'Lift your right hand.'

Benat lifted it. Peryst barely moved—he didn't want to break Benat's concentration on the trees—and instead sent into Benat's mind an image of the roast rabbit he wished to have had for breakfast. Benat's mouth opened in surprise. Seconds later, Peryst saw a shadowy image of bread and the smooth spreadable cheese that Mehruvians enjoyed for breakfast.

'I did it!' Benat lifted both fists in victory.

Peryst grinned. 'You did. Sometimes concentrating too much will hinder you.'

He gave his team the exercise he'd been given by his irascible Idhani, Nova Seaborn, when he was struggling with mind-to-mind communication in Kurbal. 'Practice with the person to your left till you can send messages, use your power, and pick up stones, stir the air, or do whatever you want at the same time with no pauses. Over and over again.'

By the end of the morning, each of them could divide their mind to a certain degree, some more easily than others, and all could communicate images without words.

'You'll carry out this same exercise every morning and every evening for the next three months till it becomes as easy as focusing your mind's eye.' Peryst turned to Benat. 'And you'll do it again each midday.'

'Now we'll try the target again, Benat. Concentrate on the target and send me the image.' He told the two archer Menders, 'Be ready for me.' And then to the two Air Primals, Ria and Tatya Mainfel, he said, 'Stand behind the archers.'

Benat took a deep breath and fixed his attention on the trees that were just starting to lose their leaves. Slowly, a blurry image of the darker knot of wood came into Peryst's mind. He shared the image with the Menders and the Air Primals.

'Can you see it?'

At their nods, Peryst gave further instructions. 'Ria and Tatya, I want you to form a column of wind to push the arrows towards the target as soon as they're released.' He lifted a hand. 'Now!'

The Menders, concentrating on the target, let their arrows fly. Ria and Tatya, hands raised, manipulated the air, trying to form a shaft to envelope the arrows and push them to the tree. Their timing was too slow, and the arrows landed in the grass some distance from the trees.

'For this to work, the timing must be perfect. The moment you have the image, you let the arrows fly and you, Ria and Tatya, must be in mind-to-mind communication to make sure you push your air shafts at the same time. We'll do this again and again. The rest of you will practice doing more than one thing at a time.'

The more they tried, the easier it became for Benat to send his image to Peryst, with it becoming more defined with each try. The Menders sent their arrows flying immediately, but Ria and Tatya struggled.

'I can't do it!' Ria despaired when the arrow she was pushing fell flat for the fifth time as Tatya's reached the tree but not the target.

'Yes, you can,' Peryst said. 'You need to act quickly when you get the image identifying the target. It'll be easier if you place yourselves immediately behind the archer so that you're in line with the arrow.' He smiled in encouragement. 'Again. Till you do it. And then again, till there is never a time you *don't* do it.'

While Ria and Tatya kept trying with Benat and the two Menders, Peryst turned to the two Fire Primals, Al Ironbound and Sada. 'I need fire on my blades,' he said, sword in one hand and knife in the other.

Al hesitated. 'I can make fire, expand a fire, and keep one burning, but I don't know how to set your blades on fire.'

Sada nodded. 'I don't know how to do that, either. I can't attach fire to things.'

Peryst sighed, privately wondering whether he'd bitten off more than he could chew. Idhanis in Kurbal started out with fully trained Touched who could communicate mind to mind and who were already trained with others, learning to work in teams even as they were learning the boundaries of their own abilities. 'It's similar to what we did earlier. Though you aren't Menders, who can bind things together, you can create your fires on anything or even anyone,' Peryst explained. 'Follow the steps you normally take in lighting a fire but do so while seeing your swords with your mind's eye. Then light the fire on them.'

Peryst sheathed his knife. He passed a finger slowly down the blade of the sword he held in his right hand, and where he touched a line of fire appeared, burning brightly. He then closed his hand and the fire went out. He did it again, but merely by looking at the blade.

'Do it till you manage. Repetition is key.'

Swords in hand, Al and Sada took a step back.

'Perhaps it would be better if you moved nearer to the ruins.' Peryst pointed at the remnants of a wall of an ancient building. 'And maybe have a Water Primal on standby?' He beckoned for Madi Cragmind, the eldest of the three Water Primals, to join them.

Al and Sada conjured fires everywhere but on the blades till a dubious success was reached by late afternoon when Sada, still desperately trying to set her blade alight, missed and instead set Madi on fire. The Water Primal's sleeves were enveloped in flames when she raised her arms like an avenging goddess and called water from a low-lying cloud to rain over her head. Peryst ran to them as the fire was doused, calling to another of the Menders, Kir, to come and attend the angry burns climbing from Madi's fingers to her shoulders.

'Keep still, Madi. I'll take care of your burns.' Kir Kliffridge ran his fingers up and down Madi's right arm. Peryst knew he was focusing his mind's eye and seeing the skin knitting itself back together.

Madi paled as the healing progressed. Having been subject to the ministrations of Menders, Peryst could remember the pain increasing till almost unbearable, then throbbing and finally cooling till nothing was left, sometimes not even a scar. When there was only a slight pinkness where the wounds had been, Kir turned to the other arm and repeated the process.

'Though unintentional, Sada, you've set someone alight. This is a useful skill to have. I'll ask you to do it again when we cook our dinner this evening.' Peryst paused. 'With a hare.' He turned to Madi. 'Perhaps you should step a little further away from them.'

A chagrined Sada grimaced worriedly at Madi as she focused her mind's eye again and ran her fingertips lightly down her sword. Irregular spots of fire rose where her fingers had been. 'I did it! I did it!'

Peryst clapped. 'Again, Sada. Till we finish for the day. Explain to Al exactly what you've done and how.'

Peryst passed both hands through his hair while trying not to show his recruits how overwhelmed he was feeling.

This is like dealing with a school of Maias before she could talk mind to mind. How will I ever manage to turn them into an efficient Idhan?

With an encouraging smile, he instructed the two remaining Water Primals, Fen Minefist and Bika Grithaven to practice bringing a localised drizzle down from the clouds and also using water from the nearby Ramu to conjure a mist. Both, he explained, could be used to obscure visibility and aid an advance on the enemy. As he expected, both ended up soaked to the skin in full visibility. They managed to make rain pour either over themselves, just nearby, or even over the other groups, or they generated a patchy, ankle-level mist that, at most, disguised their boots.

It's going to be a very long three months.

Peryst turned to the last three Primals: Lana, Fyn Miles, and Egast Slatebound. 'Matter Primals? How does it manifest?'

Lana spoke for her and Fyn. 'We have a similar ability and can move things. The most useful thing I've ever done is unlock a door,' she giggled.

'An excellent ability. And moving things is always useful. What about you, Egast?'

'I'm almost a Mender but of Matter. I can fix and attach things or take them apart.'

'Again, a very useful skill.' Peryst beckoned to Lyn Fernridge, a Sight Sensal who could see through things as well as having the same developed sense of touch as Peryst.

'I'd like you four to work together.'

'Doing what?' Lana asked.

'Lyn, you'll find the most evenly shaped rocks under water and direct Lana and Fyn to bring them up from the river's depths. And you, Egast, build us a bridge over which we can cross the river.'

Lana laughed delightedly. 'We'll try.'

Peryst gave thanks that Lana's father had spoken well enough of him to his daughter that she was willing not only to trust him but to do so joyfully.

He turned to the rest of the Sensals.

'What have we got left?' Peryst knew from experience that there were always obscure powers or some that were very light. All could be used and useful provided the wielder believed so.

A red-headed youth called Barg Hollyborn raised a hand as he spoke. 'I am an Olfactory Sensal.'

Peryst nodded. 'How does it manifest?'

'I can distinguish any scent, whether living or not.' Barg grinned. 'I'm basically a hound.'

'This is no bad skill to have, Barg. You can aid in tracking the enemy or a lost patrol in unknown terrain.' He turned to the remaining four. 'What else?'

'Hearing Sensal,' Holya Sage replied apologetically.

Peryst nodded. 'Another excellent skill, very useful in an army!' The girl flushed a bright red. 'Show me.'

'I can determine how much I hear.' She pointed at Benat, Ria, and Tatya, who were furthest away. 'I could hear them if I wanted to or even hear what happens on the fringes of the camp.'

'Excellent, Holya. You can be a spy at a distance. This is very good.'

At Peryst's words, Holya's cheeks grew so bright they were luminous. 'No one has ever said my skill is useful before,' she said.

'You haven't been in an Idhan before,' Peryst replied.

Barg placed a hand on her arm. 'I bet you were like me. Did people tease you for the uselessness of your skill?'

Holya nodded. 'I was branded nosy and a cheat for hearing what wasn't meant for me.'

'I very much hope you will hear much that's not meant for you. Doing so may save lives,' Peryst said, turning to the remainder of the recruits.

'I'm a Sight Sensal,' a tall young man called Mei Mosskin said. 'I, like Lyn, can see through things, but instead of just seeing what's there, I see the force of life like a lightly throbbing colour.'

'What do you mean?' Peryst asked.

Mei pointed at the grove behind them where the trees were thickest. After a few moments of silence, he said, 'There are five or six rabbits sheltered amongst the bushes to the right, a serpent curled underneath a fallen trunk, numerous birds amongst the branches, and two humans hidden behind the tree closest to the edge of the clearing, the one with the yellowing leaves.'

'Impressive!' Peryst replied. 'The animals will be our meal for this evening, and the humans are doubtlessly spying on our progress or lack thereof. Can you tell who they are?'

Mei shook his head. 'No. I can see their outlines in a warm kind of light. I see life pulsing through them. If they were ill or close to death, the light would be different, paler and pulsing slowly.'

Peryst asked, 'Holya, can you hear what they say?'

Holya turned to the trees and turned back with a chuckle a moment later.

'They were scared that we kept staring in their direction, wondering whether we'd spotted them.'

Mei added, 'They're backing away from us now.'

'Excellent, both of you. See how your skills could be used in a real battle?'

Including Barg, Peryst told the three trackers to use their combined sight, hearing, and smell to procure dinner for all of them and then turned to the remaining two Sensals who had kept themselves apart from the others. They held hands, knuckles white, and neither would look at him directly.

'You both joined the Idhan, so you clearly have a skill you think may be of use, but neither of you have volunteered information about it, which makes me wonder whether you are embarrassed or afraid. I won't share what you tell me unless you authorise me to.'

Both Mehruvian in appearance, one slight and the other taller, the girls shared a glance. The taller one was called Graia Thornglade, Peryst remembered, and the smaller, Fra Ruskin. They were unusual names in the South. He wondered whether they'd come from somewhere in northern Mehru.

Graia spoke first. 'I'm from a village east of Ros. I ran away soon after my powers came in, when I was twelve. I was luckier than many here because our local Mas was good, and she helped me learn some control.'

'Why did you leave your home?' Peryst asked.

Graia grimaced. 'Because they would have turned me into a whore.'

Peryst's face betrayed his surprise as he tried to think of a Touched skill that would have given the girl such an idea.

'A mind whore, Idhani, not a physical one, but I still would've been forced to sell myself for a living.'

'I don't understand,' Peryst said quietly.

'I'm a Sight Sensal,' Graia said, 'but I see the future.'

Peryst knew of Touched with such powers, but normally only amongst the seers in Genai. He could see why it could become a problem for one who was not one of them.

'Show me.'

Graia turned back to where Lyn, Lana, Fyn, and Egast toiled by the water. As Graia glanced at them, an involuntary giggle escaped her as she spoke. 'You will need to get one of the Menders over there quickly.'

She hadn't finished speaking when screams followed a sharp yell: a rock had crashed straight into Egast's face.

Peryst ran up, calling for Mech. The two arrived at a scene of chaos. Blood streaming from a broken nose and numerous cuts and bruises on his erstwhile handsome face, Egast sat on the riverbank moaning and rocking back and forth. In tears, Lana apologised repeatedly and kept blaming herself as Fyn berated her for interfering when he was doing fine on his own.

'Enough, you two,' Peryst ordered to Lana and Fyn. 'How bad is it, Mech?'

Mech went down on his knees and coaxed Egast to lie back. 'This will hurt, Egast.'

Peryst stole a glance at Lana, who bit her lip, pale and stricken, as Egast clenched his teeth and fists till his knuckles were white. Mech passed his fingers over the bloodied face.

'Cheekbone cracked, slash across temple, nose crushed, and numerous cuts, but never fear, your handsome face will be lovely again when I'm done with you.'

Mech was quick but brutal, going step by step from the forehead down and healing the nose and cheekbone at the same time. Egast paled and couldn't bite back a moan but swiftly relaxed when the healing progressed. A little shakily, he sat back up, ashen and bloody but handsome as ever.

'Thank you, Mech. That was … unpleasant.'

'Not as unpleasant as your face would've been without me,' Mech replied as he climbed back to his feet.

'Are you all right?' Peryst asked the Mender. 'It wasn't too much for you?' Power was like a muscle that used up energy. Even in the peak of health and youth, Touched had to learn their boundaries and limits so they didn't overtax themselves. Peryst had seen it happen. Stretched too thin, Touched would be too tired and weak to defend themselves; at worst, they'd pass out or even die.

'I'm fine!' Mech brushed his knees. 'Mind your rocks,' he said to Lana as he turned back to the target where his companions waited.

Lana fell on her knees by Egast. 'I'm so sorry, Egast. That was all my fault.' Her voice shook.

Egast smiled at her, his perfect white teeth terrifying in his bloodied face. 'Accidents happen, Lana.'

Peryst intervened. 'They do. And we practice to make sure they don't. What went wrong?'

Fyn replied sullenly, 'I was lifting a rock without problem when Lana decided to help me. I didn't expect her interference, and the rock changed direction too quickly for me to control it.'

Peryst nodded. 'Lana?'

'I thought the rock was too heavy for Fyn so tried to help guide it.' She flushed. 'I got distracted.' She lowered her face.

'Lesson: always communicate your actions. You're a team. And *never* get distracted when you have a heavy object aloft,' Peryst said. 'Now, carry on.'

He rejoined Graia. 'What was that, Graia? You saw that happening before it did?' The implications of having such power rushed through Peryst's mind.

'In a way,' Graia replied. 'I can see the immediate consequence of a decision.'

'Can you please explain exactly what that means?'

'I saw Fyn decide to lift a larger stone than he previously had. The consequence of that was that Lana decided to help. The consequence of her decision was the rock careering out of control into Egast's face.' Graia grimaced. 'I can only see the immediate consequences of one decision.'

'I could see how it would become annoying if everyone knew you had such power.'

'It did.'

'What about you?' Peryst asked Fra.

Graia replied for her. 'She's my partner. We do things together.'

Peryst noted that Fra kept her attention on the ground as she twisted her hands. 'There's more to it, isn't there?'

Fra's hand tightened on Graia's arm. 'We have to trust someone. We can't hide forever,' she whispered.

'We can,' Graia growled.

'My power is useless, Idhani,' Fra muttered.

'Why did you join the Idhan, then?'

Graia placed an arm round Fra. 'She joined because I did. We've been together since we met and will be forever. And I won't let anyone hurt her.'

'I would never hurt you, Fra.' Peryst said quietly.

'I'm a Sight Sensal, Idhani.'

'What do you see?'

'Death,' Fra whispered.

Frowning, Peryst asked, 'What do you mean?'

'Just that,' Fra replied. 'When I focus my mind's eye on any living being, I see how it will die. Not when, not where, but just how.' She shook her head. 'I can't even warn anyone. It's a horrible ability that only serves to make people angry at me.'

'I met a Mas in the east. She brewed a tea that could push the limits of the mind's eye. If you drank that tea, maybe you could see more.' Peryst said. *Knowing the circumstances of another's death? Would I want to know? I don't think so. Even if it gave me time to prepare, I think I'd become driven only by the thought of my death.*

Fra smiled ruefully. 'I don't think I'd want that. Maybe one day I'll find a use for this skill, but I wouldn't relish being the messenger of death, nor do I think it would endear me to others.'

'I can't disagree,' Peryst replied. 'But we need an excuse for you being part of the Idhan. It's always best never to tell a lie if you can avoid it. We'll make an exception in this case and say that, despite having no powers, you have joined because Graia has.' He looked to Graia. 'She, as your partner, goes where you go.'

Graia shrugged. 'It's not a lie.'

Peryst walked back to where the last Mender, Bei Cedarwell, remained, alone near the edge of the forest, watching as the others practiced.

'A weak healer, Bei?'

Bei, a small girl who didn't reach his shoulder and had the appearance of childhood barely left behind, sighed softly. 'I'm no healer, Idhani.'

'I thought not,' Peryst replied. 'What are you, then?'

Bei hesitated. 'I would've been killed if I had stayed in my village. Those like me rarely grow old.'

Peryst swallowed. 'You're a Mental?' Peryst had never met one of the fourth type of Touched that even the Touched preferred to forget. Very few had ever existed. They could control the mind of another living being. The latest known Mental in Ankisuan history had been advisor to the last Kissar in Reor. He was sometimes cited as the ultimate cause for the rise of the Hand of Reason thanks to his cruelty and corruption. He'd used his power to abuse others, but Peryst thought any use of such a power was abuse. No Mentals had been known for a century at least, and if there were any, they kept it very quiet. Could he be facing one now?

Bei shook her head. 'No, not as bad as that, but close. I'm the opposite of a healer.'

'What do you mean?' Peryst was overwhelmed with relief. He didn't care what the girl was as long as she wasn't a Mental. Nothing could rival such a thing for horror.

'I am a Mender of the unbinding sort. You could probably call me an *unmender*.'

'You take things apart?'

Bei faced Peryst with a frightened expression before turning and entering the forest. Peryst followed her, intrigued. With a finger to her lips, Bei froze. Peryst did the same. After a few minutes, a snake slithered across the raised roots of a tree. Bei pointed at the snake, twisting her wrist. The snake instantly stopped dead.

'I unbind life,' Bei whispered. 'I can stop a beating heart with a twist of my wrist.'

Peryst put a hand on the girl's shoulder. 'I can see why you keep this quiet, and I advise you to carry on doing so because there will be those who won't understand that ending a life with a bow or a sword is no different to ending it with your mind. You're merely using a different tool for the same end.'

For the first time since he'd seen her, Bei's face cleared of fear. 'You're the first person who hasn't shown disgust towards me and my power.'

'Bei, your power is simply another part of you, like your sight, your hearing, your more or less developed ability to sing. Any such ability is in itself neutral. It's what you choose to do with it that makes you worthy of admiration or disgust.'

Bei listened with mouth slightly open, appearing even more like a child.

'If you killed everyone and everything that annoyed you without consideration, if you used your power for revenge, and if you turned into an assassin for hire, then you'd be worthy of contempt. Killing is never what we wish to do, but it's sometimes necessary to defend ourselves or our homeland. You'll learn to use your ability to protect those who cannot protect themselves, to guard yourself and others, so you'll be worthy of admiration,' Peryst said gently.

Bei nodded solemnly. 'Thank you, Idhani.'

He ached at the thought of her living in fear. It didn't surprise him, though. South of the mountains the great majority wasn't Touched, and any more unusual power was feared with good reason because, without training, accidents happened.

'How is it that you decided to join the Idhan? You must've known that you'd have to explain yourself to me. What led you to trust me with your secret?'

'Lana's father told her of a boy whose life you saved: a Primal who lost control and burnt down the shrine to Gal somewhere near Lis.'

Peryst remembered the day well. He'd been on his way with Gintras and their company to join Anil in Lis. They'd marched through a hamlet so small it had no name but boasted a small shrine to Gal. The boy hadn't known he was Touched and knew of no power in his family. His powers had manifested suddenly in the fervour of his praise to Gal during a local festival. Peryst remembered being grateful that the fire had started when the boy was singing and not when engaging in other activities that involved passion and fervour. The villagers, distraught at the destruction of their shrine and at the injuries of those nearby, were set to lynch the lad. Peryst and his company marched through as the shrine smouldered, the parents screamed, and the village bayed for the boy's blood. Peryst intervened as captain of the Southern Mehruvian Army. He calmed the villagers, and as with his recruits, he gave the boy rudimentary training, enough for him to be able to control his skill and cause no more accidents. Before continuing on his way to Lis, Peryst had advised the parents to take the boy to a Mas for further training.

'Unlike that boy's, yours is a very useful skill for hunting dinner quickly and cleanly!'

Giggling, Bei followed Peryst out of the forest.

Guffaws rang out suddenly. 'This is what will turn the tide of our army? These are the soldiers that will make a difference?'

Seg, Kasu, and a few others Peryst didn't know watched from the outskirts of the clearing, pointing and jeering at the Touched. They were, even Peryst had to admit, a pitiful sight. Arrows fell far from the target as the Air Primals struggled to guide them; the Fire Primals set everything but the weapons alight; drizzle fell on the Water Primal who failed to direct it anywhere else; and the beginning of the stone bridge had collapsed into a messy rock pile. Fighting to control his anger, he faced his critics. He knew very well that as well as training their skills he was giving his recruits faith in themselves, and any mockery would kill whatever he'd managed to instil in them so far.

'Did you hit a target the first time you held a bow?' Peryst asked Kasu. 'And were you not taught to ride by someone, Seg, or were you born on a horse? These soldiers have raw, untrained power that will make a difference once harnessed, just as your abilities became useful once learnt. Give them time and you will see.' Peryst took a menacing step in their direction, fists clenched in fury. 'And in the meantime, I'd advise you to remove yourselves from my training grounds.'

Peryst turned back to his Touched. 'Each of you has the power to make a difference, whatever others may say. All you need is confidence and practice. I know you can do it because I've seen it done before. You've already been part of a team, part of a company, so you know how to work together. That is already half your training done. You have, in the little time we've been together, learnt to communicate mind to mind. Keep working hard. I have utmost faith in every single one of you.'

The jeers and taunts of the departing group rang out but didn't manage to drown Peryst's strong voice.

Instead of breaking his recruits, the scorn and derision brought out a strength and determination Peryst hadn't known his Touched had. Each of them tried harder and longer. Soft and gentle to start with, they grew leaner and stronger by the day, with the light of resolve in their eyes and a sense of pride in their Idhani, who publicly defended and believed in them. And so, Peryst saw, they began to believe in themselves, too.

FALLYA

YEAR 5163 OF THE NEW ERA – AUTUMN

WARM AUTUMNAL LIGHT streamed in through the town hall windows where the captains of Anil's first regiment waited for their Agazi. Peryst surveyed them one by one. He still felt, and was treated as, an outsider. But he vowed that would change.

'How is your Idhan progressing, Peryst?' Anil asked once she took her seat and arranged a pile of documents and maps before her.

Peryst squinted at a flash of sunlight. 'Very well, Agazi. They'll provide great support to the battalion.'

Seg mumbled under his breath to Kasu, who sniggered, earning them both a frown from Anil. It was a month since Peryst had started training the Touched, and she'd convened a meeting of the captains of the first regiment to plan the assault on Fallya.

'In what way?' Mabian asked, conciliatory as ever.

'There are two who can manipulate air,' Peryst replied.

Seg stifled a laugh. 'Useful to keep cool when summer comes.'

Peryst swallowed a sharp retort and replied calmly, 'Useful to help boost arrows so they go further and truer than they otherwise would. My two Air Primals could aid about twenty to thirty archers.'

Kasu dropped the look of derision and, ignoring Seg's elbow in the ribs, appeared to be interested. 'Really? They could do that?'

'Yes. It would be ideal if they could train with your archers, as the timing must be perfect.'

'Are we talking a good increased distance?' Kasu asked eagerly.

'We're talking four to five times the original distance of an arrow, maybe even more.'

'What else, Peryst?' Anil asked with a slight smile as she caught Kasu's thoughtful expression.

'One of my Sight Sensals has wide-range telescopic vision. He would be able to see across to Fallya, for instance, as if he were overlooking the green from that window. He could see every detail and relay it to me, mind to mind.' He lifted his hands. 'I am also a Sight Sensal, and I can see where there's weakness in all things. So, I could tell Kasu where to shoot the arrows for maximum effect and, with the boost of air, make sure they hit.'

The captains, barring the still-incredulous Seg, were all leaning forwards.

'Anything else?' Mabian asked.

'Plenty,' Peryst told her. 'My Olfactory Sensal can warn us of horses so riders don't surprise us. Water Primals could create mist to hide our troops or bring down rain to interfere with the enemy's aim.'

Anil tapped her lips thoughtfully. 'Could they disguise us all? So that we could cross the bridge undetected?'

'They could, Agazi,' Peryst replied. 'And the Fire Primals could light arrow tips and sword blades for more damage. My Hearing Sensal could tell exactly how many soldiers march in our direction.'

'Do we have any Menders in the Idhan?' Anil asked.

'There are three Menders who are exceptional healers, and we also have powerful Matter Primals.'

'What would be the use of that?' Seg asked.

'Egast can fix a broken bridge or block a passage with debris, for instance.'

Peryst kept the abilities of Bei, Graia, and Fra to himself. Although they'd eventually be useful—maybe not Fra as much as the others—making them public could create terrible consequences for the women. Peryst had seen Felim's distrust and fear of his powers, which weren't too far out of the ordinary. Stranger powers would doubtlessly turn their wielders into puppets to be used. He'd do all he could to create a useful Idhan for Anil, but he wouldn't expose abilities that would put individual Touched in any sort of danger.

'How would these abilities be used in practice?' Kasu asked.

'Any attack or battle will need to be planned carefully. If you tell me what you intend, we can make our suggestions.'

Benat and Peryst spent the weeks prior to the crossing spying out the town to spot sentinels and weaknesses. Mei swam under the bridge to the other side and, from the cover of the last stone arch, focused his mind's eye on Fallya to see where there was life within the walls, human and otherwise. Anil and Pinta had a fair idea that about seventy Mehruvians—men, women, and children—were left in the town, far fewer than the close to two hundred live bodies Mei counted, mostly gathered in two buildings on the town green.

'Defenders must have come in secret,' Pinta mused. 'Why would they do that?'

'Because they aren't fools and, even if they can see the risk is now further to the east, they wouldn't want to lose what they've gained,' Kasu stated. 'With Gallya across the bridge and our army in full sight, they'd have to be witless to leave Fallya unguarded.'

'Kasu's right,' Anil said. 'But we're richer for knowing and can plan better.' She turned to Peryst. 'Thank you, Idhani.'

Peryst bowed his head, a small smile betraying the pride he felt at the difference his Idhan would make to Anil's planned assault.

Anil regarded her captains. 'We'll take Fallya with as little loss of life as we can manage. I want no deaths of innocents. I want no sacking and no taking of spoils. Fallya is our sister town, and we'll treat her with respect and care. Is that understood?'

'Soldiers expect spoils after a victory, Agazi. Our companies have been stuck in Gallya for months. They'll want to let go after battle,' Seg replied.

'Perhaps. But it'll be your role to remind them that they will not do so. We'll be battling our kin. This isn't a battle in Reor or Tamadal where we're up against enemies alone. Here, we're simply helping our brothers and sisters to recover their homes.'

'Brothers and sisters who chose to flourish under the Hand of Reason instead of joining us in Gallya,' Kasu muttered.

'As Pinta said to you when we first talked of taking Fallya, none knows what lives in another, Kasu. I'll hold each captain responsible for the actions of those under them. And I will not be lenient.' Anil waited a beat. 'I hope this is clear.'

The captains nodded.

'We'll use whatever the Idhan can give us to ensure the secrecy of our approach.' Anil glanced at Peryst, who nodded, immediately thinking that a thick mist conjured by the Water Primals would disguise them crossing the bridge.

Feran intervened. 'They'll have sentinels and guards on all the arches. No disguise can be so complete to prevent them warning of our coming.'

'The sentinels will be silenced,' Anil said with another glance at Peryst.

Seg snorted. 'How many are we talking about? At least four at each arch? Disposed of without a noise? How is that possible?'

'Kasu's archers will deal with them,' Anil insisted.

'You ask too much, Agazi,' Kasu replied. 'My archers are good, but even with this help from the Idhan, eight simultaneous bows through the eye with no noise is impossible.'

'Not impossible,' Peryst said mildly. 'Only difficult.'

Kasu frowned, her incredulity very obvious.

'Choose your eight best archers to train with my Air Primals. They'll need to shoot arrows with long sharp heads as opposed to their usual triangular-bladed ones.'

Kasu let her breath out slowly. 'I know what instructions to give my archers, Peryst.'

'This is fair,' Peryst replied, bowing his head slightly and realising he'd made a mistake that had alienated Kasu, who still didn't recognise him as an equal. 'But let them train with the Air Primals. We need timings to be perfect for it to work.'

'Let's assume that the guards are silenced and we enter the town without being spotted,' Feran said. 'What then?'

Pinta intervened. 'Mei says that the majority of Reordans, if they are Reordans, are in or near the green, so they must be in the guard house and town hall.'

Kasu spoke up. 'So, we divide our forces into four sections and come in from the cardinal points, convene on the green, and block all access and escape.'

'That means no cavalry,' Seg stated. 'Horses don't fare well within narrow streets.'

'That means that the cavalry, also divided in four, will wait at each of the arches, guarding access and escape from the town,' Anil clarified.

Pinta frowned. 'Agazi, it'll be a bloodbath. If you block all escape from the green, the battle will be concentrated there. They'll have no chance.'

'Isn't that the objective?' Seg asked.

'The objective is to take back Fallya, not to have a bloodbath,' Anil said sternly. 'I will offer clemency to those who put down their arms. I have no intention of killing for the sake of it.'

'Why not?' Seg muttered. 'We're soldiers; it's what we do.'

'No, Seg, there's more to being a soldier than killing, and if you haven't yet learnt that you should,' Anil said sternly.

Peryst cleared his throat. 'I'm afraid Pinta's right. It will be a bloodbath.'

Anil frowned and turned back to Peryst. 'Why would you say that?'

'Because the Defenders of the Hand never surrender, Agazi. They prefer to die for the Hand than live in defeat. I saw it in Leyandale. Every Defender who wasn't disarmed fought to the death and, when cornered, fell on their own weapons. I saw one even cut her own throat on Gintras's sword.'

'We don't know whether there are Defenders of the Hand within Fallya's walls,' Anil argued.

'No, we don't, but we can assume there are. And we can assume they won't surrender. And we can assume that the only way to defeat them will be by their death,' Peryst replied.

Anil lifted her chin. 'So be it. I have no qualms about ridding Mehru of Defenders. It is to the Fallyans and Mehruvians I would grant clemency.'

Peryst caught some of the captains' quickly hidden grimaces of disgust. They mistook Anil's compassion for weakness. Peryst knew better. Anil was a shrewd strategist and a wise leader. While merciful, she'd mete out justice or punishment when deserved, and she was a fiend on the battlefield.

The day planned for the attack began overcast and cold, with low clouds blotting out the still dark sky. Thus, the three Water Primals had plenty to work with to mask the advance of Anil's troops. From the Ramu, they raised a mist that first covered the northern banks and the bridge, making visibility difficult. Slowly, they spread the mist across Fallya's surroundings. From the clouds, they brought down a solid drizzle that further disguised the soldiers and dulled the inevitable sounds of their advance.

Anil had chosen four factions of sixty or so from her different companies, including the most accurate of her archers and the best soldiers of her infantry. She allocated even numbers amongst the four groups, led by herself, Feran, Asruel, and Mabian. Seg led one of the four sections of the cavalry that would prevent anyone from leaving Fallya.

In the still and damp darkness, Anil led her faction across the bridge to a spot just past the halfway point.

The eight best archers chosen by Kasu, with whom Ria and Tatya had practiced incessantly in the previous days, waited, arrows nocked and aims fixed on the sentinel posts on either side of Fallya's southern arch. Behind them were Peryst and Benat with the two Air Primals, who had their hands raised and fingers moving as they sensed and caught at the air. They were attuned to each other and to the air surrounding them. They and the archers watched Kasu for the sign to let their arrows fly. Upon Kasu lowering her hand, the long metal arrows left the eight bows at the same time, and Ria and Tatya surrounded them with streams of air that pushed them unerringly towards the eight sentinels watching from behind the waist-high parapet on either side of the arch.

It was over in seconds. Without so much as a breath, the eight guards disappeared from view, each pierced straight through the left eye.

Kasu bowed to Peryst. 'I owe you an apology, Idhani.'

Peryst shook his head and held out his hand, which Kasu shook fervently. 'None required. It's difficult to believe without seeing.'

Under the blanket of mist and rain, Peryst, Benat, the Air Primals, and the eight archers made their way round the outskirts of the town. They were surprised to discover only two guards on each of the other three arches and promptly dispatched them without so much as a sigh. Fallya had expected no trouble from anywhere but the bridge.

Shrouded by mist and rain, each of the four captains waited with their factions outside the four arches that led to Fallya's centre. Near each was a Sensal and behind, in a heavy silence, the infantry and archers listened for the order to enter the city.

With all the guards gone, and back with Anil's faction, Peryst spoke to the minds of the three other Sensals, relaying Anil's orders to enter through the four arches as silently as they could. They'd learnt from Feran that the change of guard in Fallya occurred at full dawn, so they counted on being able to creep into the green before the next set of guards emerged to make their way to the arches.

Peryst gestured at Mei, who was a step behind Anil. Mei spun slowly in a circle at the entry to the still-sleeping town.

> *Many buildings are empty. Those that aren't have what are probably families within as I see smaller bodies. Two of the buildings on the green, however, house most of the people in Fallya—at least a hundred and twenty.* He relayed the information to both Peryst and Anil, who had been proficient in mind-to-mind communication since meeting Klaust in her youth.
>
> *Those are the town hall and the guard house,* Anil said. *Can you sense whether those that are inside are awake or asleep, Mei?*
>
> Mei considered. *The most I can say is that the majority are motionless. Maybe they're still sleeping?*
>
> Peryst turned to Graia and spoke in her mind. *Can you tell me the immediate outcome of us entering the green simultaneously from the four cardinal points?*
>
> Graia considered and then replied. *Even before anyone is in position at the entrance of the four ways, they'll be spotted by a man leaning out the window of the guard house. At his shouts, Defenders will stream into the green and attack as we scramble to get in position. Vials filled with smoke will be thrown, shattering and obscuring our vision. The battle will be chaotic and bloody with great loss of life on both sides.*
>
> Peryst pursed his lips, turned to Bei, and relayed into her mind what Graia had said.
>
> *There's only one thing to do then,* Bei replied.

Peryst and Bei crept through the slumbering town down to the green, hugging the walls and hiding in the shadows and the steady drizzle.

The green was clear and quiet, but at a window, Peryst could glimpse a tall middle-aged man wearing a black shirt with an open purple collar. He leaned on the windowsill as he took slow puffs of a long-stemmed pipe and gazed out at the still far-off dawn.

Peryst watched the expression of disgust on Bei's face. He understood. The idea of killing an unsuspecting man for watching the sunrise was horrific and one he'd struggle with too, but he hoped she would remember what he'd said when she first joined the Idhan: her mind was just a tool with which she was defending her own. Her face reflected her thoughts: fear of letting Peryst down and, more, the fear of Graia's words coming true. The doubts raced over her face, and he wondered whether she'd be able to conquer the horror and twist her wrist.

He saw when Bei reached her decision. She bit her lip and faced the man and his steadily beating heart and twisted her hand. He fell without a sound. With a slight green tinge to her face, Bei turned back to Peryst.

She gave a brief nod as he squeezed her shoulder.

> *I understand. Every normal person chokes with a mixture of disgust and despair at their first killing. I still do. But you will learn that your ability, like a sword or a bow, will help you defend your homeland from the Hand. It's that or death, and not just your own.*

Peryst and Bei stole back to where the others waited. He nodded at Graia.

> *The way is clear*, he said in Anil's mind.

Anil instructed Peryst to signal mentally to the other Sensals that the captains at the other sides of the green were to guide their factions to their positions at the mouths of each of the four ways. The rearguard faced backwards in case they were rushed from behind, and small additional patrols marched the streets of Fallya to thwart any other uprisings that could happen outside the green.

Once everyone was in position, Anil lifted the horn of Mehru to her lips. It was one of six, each borne by the Agazis of the battalions that made up the Southern Mehruvian Army. Glinting in the rain, the horn let out a clear and bright sound, which, to all who'd heard it before, heralded hope.

Pulling on armour and clutching weapons, half-awake soldiers—mostly Defenders but also apprentices and a few Mehruvians—streamed out of the town hall and the guard house onto the green without order or reason. Many drew to a stop upon spying Anil's forces silently surrounding them. A Defender with the red collar and piping on her uniform marking her as a High Defender of Shya appeared at a window and called out orders to organise the defence as a multitude of other Defenders rushed out.

'Put down your weapons. Relinquish your hold on Fallya, and your lives will be spared. We want not loss of life but Fallya's return to Mehru,' Anil called out in a voice that reverberated throughout the green.

The High Defender at the window laughed derisively. 'The Hand of Reason doesn't bow to a filthy Touched. Fallya is under the rule of Reor and, thus, marks the beginning of the end of Mehru.' She called down to the green. 'To arms, Defenders of the Hand, to arms, for Reor and the Rule of Reason with which we shall vanquish the darkness of the Touched from all over Ankisua!'

Anil gave a brief nod to Peryst, who waved at Ria. She whispered an instruction in the ear of the archer who stood by her and pointed at the High Defender who shouted orders from the window. As the archer released his arrow, Ria enveloped it in a shaft of air. The arrow through her left eye, the High Defender flew back in a blur of black and red. But even left without a leader, the Defenders on the ground managed to organise themselves into a four-pronged formation to face Anil's divided company. Anil didn't give them time enough and blew the horn again, the signal for all factions to attack.

The Hand put up a creditable defence on the green despite the unexpectedness of the assault. Their four rough factions of forty soldiers each were made up of Defenders, a few grey-clad apprentices, and even fewer Fallyans. The Fallyans surrendered before the fighting had even begun, so Anil's forces battled only Defenders who fought viciously despite Anil's renewed offers of clemency.

As Idhani, Peryst coordinated his troops, instructing them with his mind as he observed the green with his enhanced sight, searching for weaknesses to exploit. Amidst the shouts and clashing of weapons, he signalled to the Water Primals to focus their mist to surround the more effective Defenders, confusing them and causing them to attack their own. He'd placed Sada and Al further back, where they'd be more protected, and had them lighting swords but no arrows because Anil had asked them to keep damage to the town to a minimum. The Matter Primals were also restricted in their performance. Peryst would've wanted to instruct Egast to take stones from buildings so others could use them as projectiles, but he respected Anil's instructions to cause as little damage as possible. When the smoke vials Graia predicted soared from a high window on the guard house, blinding the Mehruvians and causing them to double over coughing, Peryst had Ria and Tatya prepared and on hand to disperse the smoke quickly.

And when there wasn't much more he could add as an Idhani, Peryst did what he'd been itching to do since the beginning and, with a mental invitation to the rest of his Touched, he removed his sword from his back and leapt into the fray with the Matter Primals and many of the Sensals at his side, including Fra, who he'd discovered was a very competent swordswoman.

When one of the two Defenders he was fighting suddenly collapsed before him, he realised Bei was in the background using her skill in his defence. He gratefully concentrated on parrying the blows from the remaining Defender.

He had instructed the Menders to rush from one corner to the other to heal only the most severe injuries but only enough for survival and in order for Anil's soldiers to carry on fighting. He didn't want the Menders to use up all their energy before the end of the battle when they'd have more injured to deal with.

As he thrust and parried, sweat running down his back, Peryst saw his warnings had been fair as Defenders refused to surrender and kept up a sustained attack from an ever-smaller circle who preferred to die on their own swords than to accept defeat. As in Leyandale, when finally cornered, most turned their weapons on themselves and died with a full-throated cry to the Hand. Horrified, he saw even a couple of apprentices, little more than children, do the same.

Early dawn revealed Fallya's green littered with a mix of bodies in black and grey as well as a few in Mehruvian blues. Peryst was pleased that though Anil's company had suffered some losses, they were minimal, the Menders having mostly intervened in time. The Fallyans who put down arms before the battle had been shepherded into the town hall, and the roughly thirty apprentices who'd been defeated were led into the guard house prison block together with one remaining Defender, who, neck bent, cried silently. Peryst assumed it was in disgust for his own survival.

As the sun rose high, Anil ordered her company to gather the Reordan dead in the centre of the green. Their own were taken back to Gallya by Seg and the riders, where they'd be placed on biers on that green. They would be mourned for a night the Mehruvian way: brysk would be done in their honours with singing, dancing, and rejoicing for their lives and honourable deaths. At the first light of dawn the next day, graves would be dug, and they would be buried to rejoin Gal's creation in peace.

Like the rest, Peryst carried the bodies of dead Reordans to a hastily prepared pyre in the centre of Fallya, where the battle had raged. Townspeople, many still in their nightclothes, watched from the four corners of the green as the bodies of those who'd controlled their town were placed on an ever-growing pile. Once the green was clear of the dead and the injured had been moved to the guard house, Anil stood, slight but strong, to the left of the pyre and bellowed, 'Fallya has dwelt in the darkness brought by the Hand of Reason, who, despite claiming the light as its own, brings only shadow, fear, and despair. By this cleansing fire, we bring the light of Gal's creation back to Fallya and banish the darkness of the so-called Rule of Reason. The Reordan dead we send back with respect through the flames into Gal's creation, where they may serve a better role than the one they did in life.'

She nodded at Peryst, who approached the pyre with Sada and Al. With a flick of their hands, the wood ignited, and flames rose.

'It needs to burn stronger and brighter than a usual fire to turn so many bodies quickly to ashes,' Peryst instructed before glancing back to Madi and the other two Water Primals.

'Watch for sparks. We've managed not to damage the town so far, so it would be somewhat ironic to burn it down at this stage.'

Once the fire was burning well, bringing Peryst memories of the night of Gena's death in Forglenden, he instructed Sada and Al to take turns with him so that none of them used too much of their energy because he was running low on umasu root, which helped replenish Touched energy but came from the North so was hard to get these days.

Anil remained on guard for five hours till the fire burnt itself out. 'It's easy to grant respect to a dead enemy,' she sighed once the fire was spent and all that was left were fragments of bone and grey ash. 'Much more difficult to deal with the defeated living.'

Straightening her shoulders, Anil turned to Peryst. 'Peryst, please have your Menders deal with the injured, both ours and theirs.'

'This has been done, Anil, though many Reordans have rejected healing by Touched.'

'Their loss. It's that or nothing.'

In the early afternoon of the same day, followed by Feran and Pinta, Anil entered the great room of the town hall. She sat at the centre of the long table that looked down from a low dais. With Feran on her left and Pinta on her right, Anil called for the sole remaining Defender to be brought before them.

Fallyans and members of her battalion lined the sides of the room, and Peryst watched from amongst the captains as Kasu led the Defender in front of Anil.

'You and yours came into our lands to impose your creed. Where you saw anyone different to yourselves, you meted out violence and cruelty. Fallya will now see the light once again. And this is just the beginning! Light will rush across our lands, lifting the curtain of your darkness.'

The Defender lifted his tear-stained face and laughed. 'Little do you know, Purveyor of Shadows. The Rule of Reason will not be dulled, your hopes will be dashed, and Mehru will be cleansed of the likes of you.'

Anil shook her head and gestured at Pinta, who said, 'As interim Alkaid of Fallya and following the laws of said city, for the deaths of all Touched fallen under your rule, for all Fallyans driven to exile, and for all damage caused to this town, I sentence you to death.'

When he saw the Defender's relief and that the man welcomed death, Peryst almost had pity. But he knew Anil would also see the look and make sure his relief was short lived.

It didn't surprise him when Anil took up the word with heavy sarcasm. 'Yes, Defender, you'll have your death, but it won't be the honourable death you crave.' The Defender paled as Anil carried on. 'No, Defender, yours won't be the death of glorious martyrdom on the town green. It will be like the death of the mangy animal that you are, tucked away in a corner, hands tied, covered in your own filth, with none to witness and none to exalt.' With a wave of her hand, she ordered him to be left in a dungeon at her pleasure. Death would come when Pinta pleased.

The fate of the rest was varied. Those who'd been known for their cruelty to Fallyans or as authors of dark deeds were summarily executed by hanging in accordance with Fallyan laws. Others who expressed no remorse for their actions and poured only vitriol on the victors were also executed. Anil didn't interfere with Pinta's judgements till it was time to address the fifteen apprentices who'd put down their arms early and who had gratefully received the attentions of the Menders.

Leaning against the wall, arms crossed, Peryst watched Anil speak to them sternly. 'I don't know what twisted pathways of fate led you to Fallya. None may truly know the hidden corners of another's spirit. I don't know whether in yours you harbour a real hatred of those like me or whether you've simply followed the orders given by leaders who had your lives in their hands.'

Some kept their attention on Anil and others on their boots, but all were still and quiet.

At that moment, Peryst saw them as the children they were under their grey uniforms. Adulthood in Klaevan was at fifteen, in Mehru, also at fifteen, and in Reor at sixteen, but many of these children reared in hatred and intolerance, as his nephew Raf and so many others would be, appeared younger than that. He was filled with zeal to smash up the Hand, to prevent other children from growing up like this and dying on battlefields for a twisted and cruel regime.

'The laws of Fallya would sentence you to death, but I have requested the Alkaid to grant you a form of mercy.' The apprentices—boys and girls—stared, open mouthed, and so young that Peryst's chest tightened at the thought of the hate that had been bred into them. 'You will either join my company in the lowest position and aid in Fallya's restoration, or you will be escorted to the closest border with Reor. You have till the end of the day to decide.'

As they prepared the brysk for their dead, Seg argued strongly against giving the apprentices this option, but Anil remained firm in her decision. 'Not all will join me, but those who do will give me their loyalty for the rest of their days. They expected an ignominious death and instead have been given a second chance. That is in my favour. Those who don't join me will take the news to Reor that Mehru has raised its head. That no Defender remains in Fallya. And that the retaking of northern Mehru is underway. I'm using them as the harbingers of fear. It's the only thing Reor understands: fear.'

Of the fifteen, only eight decided to join Anil's company.

'They'll escape as soon as they can and take any information they can glean back to Reor,' Seg said, shaking his head.

Anil smiled. 'Perhaps, but perhaps not.' She placed them in different factions and paired them up with another of a similar age who, unlike Seg and others, believed in second chances.

The others were kept confined but comfortable till the dead had been mourned, the injured healed, and Fallya had been cleansed of even the smallest stain left by the Hand of Reason. Then Seg instructed a group from the cavalry to escort them to the nearest border with Reor, a few days ride west of Fallya.

And though Anil's battalion enjoyed no pillaging or spoils of battle, the feasting and celebrations that spilled from Gallya to Fallya and back again made up for it so that even Seg was satisfied with the result.

LIS

YEAR 5164 OF THE NEW ERA – SPRING

PERYST'S DAILY COMMUNICATIONS with Maia showed that she was healthy and happy, growing in the confidence of a child who knows they are loved unconditionally. At times he wondered whether leaving her in Lis had been the right decision but then told himself that giving her that window of carefree childhood was also a way of showing her his love. And he knew she was aware of it, at least in her mind's eye.

'With the victory in Fallya we've begun the retaking of northern Mehru. The eastern battalions are marching in this direction, liberating as they come.' Anil pointed at the map on the table in Gallya's town hall and at the latest communications from the east. 'We'll have an arduous journey to meet them.'

'Why do you think that?' Pinta asked.

'Fallya was an easy win partly because of the Idhan but mainly because we had no resistance from the Fallyans,' Peryst intervened. 'It won't be the same further east, where they've lived under the Hand for much longer and are isolated from others. They'll be like regular Reordans and will most probably consider us invaders, not liberators.'

'But your battalion will be much stronger now with the Idhan,' Pinta said to Anil and nodded to Peryst.

'After seeing the success of the Idhan's performance in the taking of Fallya, more of the Touched interspersed in the various companies have joined us,' Peryst said. 'Most are Primals, though a few additional Menders and Sensals have also joined, none with powers out of the ordinary. My original twenty-one recruits are making great strides in training the newcomers.'

Even Seg had grudgingly admitted that the Idhan was what turned the tide in their favour in Fallya, so Peryst was finally accepted on an equal status with the rest of the captains. It was liberating not to have to guard his words any more and to be able to snap back at his fellow captains without the constant fear of alienating them.

'They're also aiding the guards of both towns in training some of their local recruits. Both the Agazis of the Gallya and Fallya Town Guards have embraced the concept of an Idhan to help protect them from further Reordan incursions,' Anil told her captains. 'Which leads me to the next step in our campaign. I intend to leave two mixed companies to support the town guards and defend the road to Lis. It's been two months since the retaking of Fallya, and it's time for the rest of us to march east to meet those who head this way. I know that it will be wrenching for some of you, but it's time. Please prepare your troops.'

Anil's battalion had been stationed in the vicinity of the Ramu for years. Many of its members had made families in Gallya, and all had made lifelong relationships, so the leave-taking was fraught with tears and pain. Peryst suffered for them, but he, too, was impatient to reach the rest of the army in victory. Even knowing the campaign would be long and difficult, he could already see a Mehru united under the High Luk and free from the Hand. So even if it was a subdued army that marched east, Peryst rode cheerfully, filled with hope.

At sundown a week into the march, Holya alerted Peryst to the sound of hoofbeats advancing towards the camp. At Peryst's order, Benat raced to where the guards waited and, focusing his mind's eye, studied the terrain behind them. 'A single rider on a spent horse. Mehruvian blues.'

Covered in mud and with bloodshot eyes, the rider in the so-called Mehruvian blue of the Lis Guard uniform reined in his horse when challenged by the guards. 'Message from Lis for Agazi Anil.'

'We'll take your mount,' one of the guards said, taking in the horse's sweat-covered coat and foaming mouth. 'How long have you been riding?'

'Long enough,' the rider replied, sliding out of his saddle and handing the reins to the guard. 'I changed horses in Gallya, where I expected to find Agazi Anil, and have rested little since then.'

'Follow me.' Peryst led the rider to Anil's tent, where she was studying a map of Fisjen and making notes of the ways in which the Idhan could aid in taking back the town.

'Agazi Anil.' The rider bowed his head and removed a thick envelope sealed with a distinctive wax seal. 'Message from the High Luk.'

Anil frowned as she examined the rider's obvious exhaustion. 'Do you come straight from Lis?'

'No, Agazi. I was sent to Gallya, where I expected to find you. I missed you by little more than three days. There, they told me you'd begun your march east. I've followed in your tracks since then.'

Anil broke the seal and read the letter from her father. Peryst watched as colour drained from her face. She passed a hand over her eyes and read the letter again before passing it to Peryst.

'Do you know the contents of this letter?' Anil asked the rider.

'No, Agazi. I was merely told to ride like the wind till I reached you.'

Anil turned to the guard who'd remained just inside the tent. 'Please take this man and see to his comfort and to that of his mount.'

'Yes, Agazi.' The guard and the messenger went out into the camp.

Anil turned to Peryst, who was reading the letter from the High Luk.

Lis, Realm of Southern Mehru

First day of the Third Month of the Year 5164 of the New Era

My dear daughter,

I write both as your father and as your High Luk with dire tidings I would rather not have to impart. The rejoicing in your victory in Fallya has unfortunately been short-lived. By the time you read this, all in Mehru will have become aware that our doom is nigh. Tidings will doubtlessly not reach you till my messenger does that Tamadal has joined forces with Reor. In exchange for an illusory independence, which I have no doubt the Hand of Reason will thwart once Mehru has been subdued, Tamadal has ceded its army to the Hand.

The joint Reordan and Tamad army have retaken Ilia, and Leyandale is now under Reordan rule. Our losses were heavy, but that is not all. The erstwhile free east of northern Mehru has been taken by the Hand with the support of the two eastern battalions of the Southern Mehruvian Army led by your brothers. The Hand of Reason has crossed the Ramu. As I write, Selkirk and Deragaz fight bravely, but their fall is inevitable because the remaining companies faithful to Lis and the High Luk have been driven south towards Folchester.

Our four remaining battalions cannot defeat the joint forces of Tamadal, Reor, and two of our own battalions, so I've taken the painful decision to recall those still faithful to defend Lis. While I weep at the idea of leaving the eastern reaches to their own defence, I live in hope that if Lis can withstand the onslaught—with Vel's aid—we may take back our land before too much damage is done to our kin.

Make haste, Anil. The fate of the jewel of Mehru lies in the hands of my four faithful Agazis. Please do not let Lis fall to the Hand of Reason.

Your father,
Galo of Belu and Taskal

Seal and print of the High Luk.

Peryst, feeling as pale as Anil had turned, asked, 'Is this truly from your father?'

Anil nodded. 'I've no doubt it's his hand and style but cannot vouch for the truth of the words.' She passed her hands through her hair. 'If they are true, however, my fears regarding my brothers will not have been unfounded.' Her voice trembled. 'All we have done will have been for nought.'

'Could they be untrue?'

Anil shrugged and rubbed her face with both hands. 'You communicate with your daughter every night, Peryst. Ask her. Ask her about Lis. Klaust has said nothing about all this when I've spoken to him in the last few days, but I'll check with him. Perhaps news will have come to Vel, and he will know. How I wish my father had learnt how to communicate mind to mind so I could ask him directly, but he never would. He thought it would alienate his subjects. Go, Peryst, check with your daughter!'

'Maia is a very young child, Anil. She'll know nothing of the politics of war.'

'Perhaps, but I don't wish to sacrifice our plans if this is a ploy to distract us. If it's true we must make haste.'

Peryst nodded. 'I'll return shortly.'

Fear gripped his stomach. If what the letter said was true, Maia would be in danger again, and his first obligation was to her. Cross-legged on the floor of his tent, Peryst focused his mind on Maia's, trying not to let his fear shine through as mind-to-mind communication tended to show not just the words but the emotions behind them. As always, Maia's mind opened to his with a flash of joy but was different from the previous night.

> *Come back Dada.* She showed him Ishab beckoning.
>
> *I'll start back as soon as I can, Maia. Tell Grandda that I'm coming.* He made sure to infuse his communication with a reassurance he did not feel.

He burst into Anil's quarters, inwardly shaking. Anil was leaning against the table with the slightly absent expression of one conversing with another mind to mind, as she did daily with Klaust and her boys. But unlike the usual peace Peryst had seen on her face when her husband touched her mind, Anil's expression was tight and drawn.

When she finally spoke, Peryst knew Klaust had confirmed the High Luk's letter.

'I had no time to contact him. As I was preparing to do so, Klaust did so himself. His regular intelligence-gathering party in Mehru communicated with him today. They confirm my brothers' betrayal. Klaust says that the joint Reordan forces march towards the capital. They plan an imminent siege of Lis.'

'Then we have to get to Lis before them,' Peryst replied with the same dismay and hopelessness he saw in Anil.

When she called a council of captains from the whole battalion, her face was set with determination.

'How can the High Luk ask us to abandon Mehru?' Kasu asked after hearing the news.

'He doesn't ask us to abandon Mehru, Kasu, he asks us to save that which can be saved, when even his own have betrayed him,' Anil replied. 'I like this as little as you do.'

'Many of ours have families in Gallya,' Kasu said.

Anil winced and then hardened. Peryst knew that as Agazi of the High Luk she would obey her orders, but as the mother of two young boys she would ache for those who would need to leave their loved ones.

'My orders, as you have seen, are to fly to Lis. I will do so by the shortest route possible. I will force none to follow me but will ask everyone to examine the oaths they've taken before they decide not to do so. Relay my orders to each member of your factions. I march at dawn with those who will come.'

Dawn saw a different company ride south. Grim faced and silent, most of Anil's battalion rode to the aid of Lis where many had left their families. The few who'd chosen not to follow rode back towards Gallya.

Peryst was almost reeling with the shock of the sudden change. He'd been so filled with hope, so certain that they'd be victorious, that he was lost and despairing. Despite knowing the times ahead would be darker than any he'd yet seen, he fought against the desolation that threatened to overwhelm him.

Anil addressed the battalion before they left the camp. 'We will ride hard, only stopping when necessary so we reach our destination ready to face what will come. The High Luk's missive was at least three weeks old by the time the messenger arrived. We need to reach the capital before the Hand of Reason. If we don't, Lis will fall, and we'll all be slaughtered. So, ride firm. Ride hard.'

Peryst rode Roan alongside his own demons. He'd taken Maia out of Reor to save her from the Hand only to place her within their reach once again. Guilt and fear kept pace, and he swore that upon arriving in Lis he'd take Maia to the safety of the North by any means possible.

In little more than three weeks, they reached the opposite side of the hill where Peryst had stopped with Maia almost ten months earlier. The capital seemed as tranquil as it had been on that day: copper roofs glinted in the sunset, and white walls were grey in the growing shadows. The only difference was that, instead of housing cattle and other grazing beasts, the wide esplanade in front of the walls housed a fierce army facing threateningly outwards.

Peryst heaved a sigh of relief. Not all the Southern Mehruvian Army had forsaken the High Luk. From the hill, Peryst could just see the blue of three battalions. With Anil's, they'd be able protect Lis to the death.

Met by cheers, Anil's battalion marched into Lis. Shouts of welcome rang out as their colours were spotted. Peryst read surprise on many faces as they recognised the High Luk's daughter at the head of her battalion. He turned quickly to Anil and caught her horror as she realised the city hadn't expected her: those who didn't know her well would've assumed that she sided with her brothers.

Once the battalion was settled in their barracks in the eastern quarter, Anil went to pay her respects to her father and gather news, and Peryst once again guided Roan through the southern quarter to The Fiery Camel.

Dismounting behind the tavern, he had barely passed Roan's reins to the stableboy when the back door burst open and Ishab rushed out to embrace him. 'We've been watching for you since we heard of the arrival of the fourth battalion.' He reached a hand to his son-in-law's face. 'You look exhausted.'

Peryst knew he smelled of sweat, fear, and horse. He passed a weary hand over his face. 'Maia?'

'She's well and happy, Peryst. I haven't let the tension in the city touch her.'

'We've been riding since the High Luk's missive reached us.'

Ishab sighed. 'Thank the heavens! Lis has been waiting to see whether the daughter would join the father, join the brothers, or simply flee to Vel.'

'How could any have doubts about that? Anil has proved time and again her loyalty to her father.' He shook his head. 'Even now, when she could be safely with her family in Vel, she's been facing the Hand and striving to take back what Reor had occupied. She is first and foremost her father's daughter.'

'As Maia is yours. Come, lad, see how much she has grown.' But then he let his gaze rove over Peryst. 'Perhaps you should bathe first.'

Ishab led Peryst through the tavern and up to the family quarters, where Peryst washed himself gratefully, shaved, and changed into a clean uniform. The last thing he wanted was to frighten his daughter by appearing haggard and soiled before her. With dripping hair and still tired, but feeling more human, he paused at the door to Ishab's wood-panelled study and spied Maia sitting on a brightly patterned rug and leaning against Nela as she built a castle with coloured blocks. His breath caught as he took in the dark curls held back by a bright ribbon and the frown of concentration as she placed her blocks on a tower. Nela spotted him first and, without moving, let out a little whine of recognition and a single thump of her tail. Slowly, green eyes turned to his, and Maia's face lit up in a smile, so like Marie's and his own that it gave him a shock. Knocking over the tower in her haste, she ran to Peryst. He scooped her into his arms and held her close as she repeated, 'Dada's come, Nela. I told you he was coming.'

'Look how big you've grown!' Peryst saw only the clear, untroubled gaze of a child who knew she was loved. Nela rubbed her head against his leg as he crouched and, still holding his daughter with one arm, hugged the wolf with the other.

'She won't leave the child, Peryst. Nela guards her always, and woe to any strangers who dare approach her,' Ishab said, patting the wolf fondly.

Peryst ruffled Nela's ears affectionately. 'Thank you for guarding my child.'

Nela made a sound between a bark and a yelp and licked his face.

Peryst passed his hand down her back warmly while still holding Maia, who'd settled against his chest with her arms tight about his neck.

'What's your plan, son?' Ishab asked.

'Anil has gone to the High Luk's palace. I will return to the barracks to hear the news and then decide.'

Touching Maia's face, Ishab nodded. 'It's Maia's bedtime. Why don't you bring her?'

As Peryst followed, Maia chattered about Nela, about the sand, and about her toys. Peryst was relieved to see that she was simply a little girl excited to see her father. In the middle of the chattering, she let out a yawn and rubbed her face with her chubby little hands.

'Are you tired, Princess?'

Confused, she stopped rubbing.

'That's what Golfen used to call you, Maia. Do you remember him and Rosie? Golfen also loved you.' Peryst thought briefly of Golfen and wished him safe, though he knew full well that none would be safe in Mehru in the coming times.

Ishab had placed Maia in Sanjia's old room. Peryst's heart contracted at the sight of the familiar window with pale blue curtains through which he had climbed in the dead of night to Sanjia's quiet giggling. Her bed with the blue coverlet that had once buried their silent lovemaking and whispered confidences had been replaced by a wooden cot covered with a cheerful patchwork blanket he knew Hana had made. The pictures were the ones he remembered: Sanjia's mother smiled from above the cot, and scenes from Mehru decorated the other walls.

Peryst lowered Maia into the cot and bent to place a kiss on her brow. Slowly, and almost without meaning to, he began singing the lullaby his own mother had sung to him and Marie when they were infants. It was a song of Klaevani wanderers, of restlessness, goodbyes, and discoveries. He hadn't known that he remembered it, and, when he finished, he was surprised to find Maia's hand lax in his and her fast asleep.

As Ishab beckoned from the door, Nela settled herself under the cot with a contented whine.

Ishab clasped Peryst's arm as they made their way down the stairs. 'I know I've not had the four years Sanjia would have wanted, but I want you to take Maia from Lis. Take her to your people. Even with Anil's battalion, Lis won't withstand an extended siege. Take my granddaughter far away from here to where she'll be safe.'

Peryst put his hand reassuringly on Ishab's. 'I'll head back and learn what there is to learn. Then I'll decide. But never fear, Maia's security will come above everything.' He sighed. 'I'll see you later, probably at daybreak.'

Ishab nodded curtly.

Peryst made his way back to the eastern quarter. The warm spring night felt heavy, like his thoughts. If Ishab was asking him to take Maia, rumours in Lis must be dire indeed. He hoped, therefore, that Anil would have gathered facts and not hearsay on which he could base a balanced decision. He smiled grimly. He was starting to sound like Thallya!

As he dismounted near the stable blocks, a soldier recognised him. 'Idhani, Agazi Anil has called for all captains to attend council in her quarters.'

Peryst nodded and made his way up through the tidy streets to the section where the six Agazis had their quarters, only four now occupied.

Upon being allowed admittance by the two guards at the door, he came upon Anil pacing in front of a table filled with her captains. 'Ah, Peryst! Good. We're waiting for Seg and Asruel,' she said.

'Only Asruel,' Seg quipped as he walked in behind Peryst.

'You mentioned me?' Asruel sauntered in last.

Anil stopped her pacing and leaned on her hands. She studied her captains, her brow furrowed and her expression strained.

'It doesn't bode well for Lis,' she said darkly. 'My brothers' treachery has destroyed any hope we had of keeping Reor from southern Mehru.' With a grimace of pain she added, 'Deragaz and Folchester have fallen.'

Peryst thought of all those who'd helped care for Maia in Deragaz. He didn't want to imagine what would be done to Lexya if the Hand of Reason began rounding up the Touched.

'We're not sure of the situation on the ground or whether it will be Reordans or my brothers who will govern this new Mehru,' Anil admitted.

'What does the High Luk plan?' Asruel asked quietly.

'The High Luk has given orders to prepare for a siege. We have the ocean and small holdings within the city limits but will be cut off from any produce or people from outside the walls.'

'How long can Lis last under siege?' Mabian asked.

'We have four battalions, impregnable walls, and numerous Touched to defend the capital. We have sources of water and food: the ocean will feed us, and the silos and warehouses are still full after a mild winter. We have Vel to provide what we lack. Lis can survive for a long period physically, but I don't know how long it'll take to break our spirits,' Anil replied heavily.

'Mehruvian spirits do not break,' Peryst said.

'I hope this is true.' Anil gave him a ghost of a smile.

'What are our orders?' Kasu asked.

Anil passed a hand over her face. 'You're to prepare your companies for both a possible siege and battle from within and without the walls.' She turned to Peryst. 'I'll need you to name a replacement Idhani because the High Luk has requested your assistance in a different matter.'

The other captains gasped.

'Peryst is to leave us?' Mabian asked.

Anil shrugged. 'I've been asked that you report at the palace, Peryst, after leaving the Idhan in order. You'll now be under the High Luk's direct command. He will ask you to travel north once again to raise awareness of our plight and garner support from the northern realms. You are to go to him tonight.'

Peryst bowed his head. 'The High Luk's orders are mine to obey.'

'Who would you name as replacement? Though, of course, none could really replace you,' Anil said.

Peryst had been wondering about this since the beginning of the ride back to Lis. He had thought hard about the best way to protect Graia, Fra, and Bei and had concluded that there was only one way to keep the Idhan running smoothly and not expose the three women. 'I'd have joint Idhanis. Benat and Graia, both Sensals, should command the Idhan together, and Ria, a Primal, should deal with training new recruits.'

Anil nodded. 'I'll trust your judgement on this. Will they be capable of helping the other regiments and then the other battalions to form their own Idhans?'

'More than capable. They've helped train all newcomers since Fallya. The current Idhan headcount in the first regiment is a company of forty-five Touched and growing.'

'Please tell them and make your way to the palace as soon as you're able.' She spoke sternly but with a very slight tremor of emotion. 'I'm truly grateful for what you have done for this battalion, Peryst. Despite distrust and derision, you've made us stronger and more efficient. I wish for your next mission to be equally successful.' She paused. 'And that we may meet again.'

'That sounds like goodbye, Agazi.'

Anil smiled sadly. 'It is goodbye, Peryst. You'll be given your orders, and I already have mine. I'll defend Lis to the death: mine or that of the Hand of Reason.' She lifted her chin stubbornly. 'You said the Defenders of the Hand do not surrender. I won't either.'

Ignoring protocol, Peryst approached Anil. 'You're a strong and powerful Agazi, loyal to your blood and homeland. I've been honoured to serve under you and be your friend. I'm now honoured to serve under the High Luk. Mehru will emerge victorious even if it takes years of bloodshed. As I said, the Mehruvian spirit does not break. It will not do so now or ever.' He bowed to her.

Chin high but eyes shining with tears, Anil ignored protocol as well and hugged him tightly as she whispered, 'I doubt we'll see each other again. Travel safe and keep Mehru and me in your heart.'

'Always.'

The Idhan—crammed into their new accommodations in the eastern quarter, where it was six to a room, so different from their airy tent village on the outskirts of Gallya—received Peryst's news with sombre expressions. Graia and Fra clutched each other's hands, and Bei paled and bit her lips.

'I promised to turn you into a section that would count. I said that you would be a fearsome company and fulfilled my vow, as you amply demonstrated in the taking of Fallya,' Peryst said proudly.

'We only managed because you led us,' Lana said tearfully.

'No. You managed because you had the power to do so. I merely showed you what you could do with what you had. You no longer need me for this.'

'So, you abandon us when things get difficult?' Ria snapped. 'What kind of leader are you?'

'Even leaders must obey their superiors, Ria. I've been summoned by the High Luk and ordered to leave the Idhan in the best hands possible. I don't know what the High Luk wants of me, but whatever it may be, I will fulfil it to the best of my ability. And each of you will follow your Idhani and Agazi Anil to the best of your abilities.'

Scowling, Ria wouldn't meet his gaze.

'I've told Agazi Anil that the Idhan will be led by joint Idhanis. Benat and Graia will replace me in leading. Ria, with a team of her choosing, will oversee training both new recruits and the new Idhans to be formed in the other regiments of this battalion and in the other three battalions stationed in Lis.'

Graia, Fra, and Bei dropped their shoulders in relief.

'Me?' Ria asked in amazement.

'You're strong and quick in learning. Your impatience and stubbornness will make you come up with creative uses of power, and your pride will not allow you to accept mediocrity. Idhans formed under your tutelage will be fierce, Ria. And this is what the High Luk needs.'

Ria lifted her face. 'I will make you proud, Idhani.'

'I know.' Peryst turned to Benat and Graia and raised his eyebrows slightly at the woman. 'You will need to trust each other fully.' Graia gave an imperceptible nod.

'I've named you joint Idhanis because the basis of an Idhan is cooperation. One Touched can do a little, but a team of Touched cooperating with an army can do so much more. Reor, Tamadal, and the two traitor battalions don't have Idhans. Use what you have, and fight for each of your members. Remember you have Agazi Anil's support, and, though her captains didn't think we would amount to much, Fallya proved them wrong. Show them what you can do.'

Peryst picked up the satchel that held his few belongings. 'It's been my honour to work with each of you. May we meet again.'

Without a backward glance, Peryst strode to the stable block through streets still teeming with soldiers returning from their evening meals. As he waited for Roan to be brought out, he felt a hand on his shoulder. Turning, he was surprised to see Seg. 'Seg?'

Seg said nothing but held out both hands and clasped Peryst's forearms. It was an old-fashioned Mehruvian salutation that showed respect. 'May Gal light your way, Klaevani.'

Peryst bowed his head. It was all he would get from the abrasive captain of the cavalry, but he realised that it represented an apology and appreciation. 'May Gal light yours, Seg, and may we meet again in happier times.'

Seg nodded and released Peryst's arms as the stableboy appeared with Roan. Without another word, Seg stole away into the night as Peryst mounted, wondering at the vagaries of people. He had to acknowledge that the gesture had even more value because it had been made privately rather than to impress Anil in front of the other captains. Peryst hadn't liked Seg in the past but was sure he could've grown to do so.

The Lis Plaza was busy despite the late hour. Peryst left Roan at the palace stables before the guards ushered him through the heavy doors in the high arch of the main entrance to the High Luk's palace. It had been years since Peryst had last made his way into the courtyard from where he could see the great hall straight ahead and the four towers at each corner. As palaces went, the High Luk's residence in Lis was humble and plain, nothing like the ornate and gigantic palace of Sintra or the glass palaces of Stonehelve and Kalvech. Its sole claim to luxury came from the pristine white of its walls and shining roofs.

'Peryst de Arranu,' he announced to a questioning courtier who approached.

The courtier nodded as a clock somewhere nearby rang the midnight bells. 'The High Luk awaits you.'

Peryst followed him silently through the great hall, which was dark and quiet, with a few wolves lying under tables. Lifting their heads, they followed the marching men with their amber eyes. The courtier led Peryst up the stairs to the tower where the High Luk's council room looked out over the city and lands beyond.

At a large table, thick with papers and maps, stood the High Luk with his closest advisor, the Malik. Dressed simply in a soldier's blue uniform and with a few grey strands amongst his thick black curls, the Mehruvian ruler seemed strained and older than Peryst remembered. As Peryst walked in, the man lifted bloodshot dark eyes and a stubborn chin much like his daughter's and smiled warmly in greeting. 'Peryst de Arranu,' he said in his deep voice, 'welcome to Lis.'

Peryst raised his fisted right hand to his chest. 'It's both a sadness and an honour to be here, my lord.'

'Thank you for attending my call.'

Peryst bowed his head.

'My daughter has always spoken highly of you, Peryst de Arranu.' The High Luk observed him curiously. 'I have no doubt you are aware of our current predicament.' The High Luk beckoned him over to the table where a detailed map of Mehru dominated. Marks showed the cities and towns that had fallen, and counters showed the armies advancing towards Lis. It made for a sobering sight.

The High Luk pointed at the towns that dotted the southern coast.

'Folchester fell yesterday. As soon as they have the city secure, they will advance west. I anticipate that they'll find little resistance before Lis because none of the cities have much more than local guards, and the battalions usually stationed at Owestry and southwest of Forglenden have already reached Lis.'

Peryst nodded and tried not to imagine the cheerful towns on the southern coast falling as silent as Fallya.

'You have a daughter in Lis.'

It didn't surprise Peryst that the High Luk knew about Maia, but he wondered why he mentioned her, and defensiveness rose within him.

The High Luk continued. 'In less time than I would like, the Hand of Reason will control all Mehru's ports except Lis. Reor has no maritime abilities, but Tamadal has an able and powerful fleet. They will aid the Hand of Reason in setting up blockades with the aim of cutting us off from the rest of Ankisua.'

The Malik nodded in agreement.

'It would be natural for a Klaevani mercenary to cut his losses while he still can and leave Lis with his daughter.'

Peryst frowned. The High Luk must have read his mind.

The High Luk smiled grimly. 'You could start by sailing to Vel with a missive to the Pirate Chief.'

'With respect, my lord, would there not be a faster way to reach the Pirate Chief?' Considering that Anil communicated mind to mind daily with the Pirate Chief's son, it seemed absurd to rely on a slow-moving ship if urgent communication was required.

'Indeed, there is, but requests for aid between nations must be made in a formal manner,' the High Luk replied. 'But it is more than that. I would request that, with Vel's aid and as an esteemed captain in my army with a deep knowledge of the situation in Mehru, you make your way to Usur and then further north as my emissary to the realms beyond the Kunlan Range. Though for now they shelter behind the mountains, Reor will be planning a way to eventually extend its fingers to reach the northern realms. Reor's ambition will not end with Mehru, Peryst de Arranu. The Hand of Reason aims to rule the entirety of Ankisua.'

Peryst knew the High Luk was right. 'It will be an honour to serve the High Luk,' he said firmly.

The High Luk nodded briefly. 'I will prepare the documentation and have my treasurer prepare compensation in a form easy to carry and hide.'

'Thank you, my lord.'

The High Luk nodded. 'A ship sails at sundown today for Vel. You will be on board with your daughter.' In an undertone he added, 'I only wish you could also take mine.'

VEL

YEAR 5164 OF THE NEW ERA – SPRING

KLAUST, THE ONLY son and heir of the Pirate Chief, husband of Anil, and father of her two sons, leaned his long frame against the rail on the Arya jetty. 'What an unexpected surprise,' he drawled.

Peryst found himself grinning as he usually did at Klaust's insolence. Klaust had been first an enemy, then a grudging ally, and finally a good friend. At least a head taller than Peryst, the younger tawny-haired man considered him and then, with curiosity, Maia.

Her interested green eyes met his almost clear ones, bright against his dark skin. Peryst knew Vel would be yet another new experience for Maia to encounter since he'd taken her from Lis and exposed her to a creaking ship full of loud sailors as well as to rocking seas instead of a peaceful room, doting grandfather, and loving Hana. But Nela was at her side, and Peryst, solid and reassuring, held her safe and close.

'The eye is strong in your daughter,' Klaust said. 'Welcome to Vel.'

'I come as emissary of the High Luk,' Peryst replied.

'I know. Anil told me.' Klaust smiled his predator smile. 'Hence my presence on the jetty. It's not everyone I receive personally.' Klaust laughed and clasped Peryst in a tight hug. 'It's good to see you, though I wish you'd dragged Anil with you.' He clapped Peryst on the shoulder and sauntered up the steps leading to the second level of Arya, which rose in terraces above the port. 'Come, we'll talk in the Citadel.'

Peryst craned his neck back and let his gaze take in the expanse of Arya, the capital city of the Isles of Vel, as it towered proudly over the port at the base of the mountain facing the Lis peninsula. It was hard to believe that since the Hand of Reason first arose in Reor Arya had grown from a wooden jetty where the Touched who managed to flee sought refuge. He could picture them arriving however they could in rickety boats and makeshift rafts. There were stories of those who'd even tried to swim across the Velan Strait. Many had drowned in their quest for freedom and safety from the flames of the Hand. But those who'd reached the Isles had discovered a mountainous archipelago of fair-haired people who'd come from Glannafel decades earlier. They welcomed the Reordan refugees as fellows. And not a generation later, they were all from Vel no matter what they looked like.

The Isles were hard on their inhabitants. Peryst remembered stories of the earlier days when the Velans, after struggling for decades to eke a living from the jungle-like and mountainous archipelago, took up pirating on passing ships and eventually the coastland nearby. He glanced sideways at Klaust, who sauntered at his side with feline grace and the air of an unscrupulous pirate. And then Peryst gazed up again at the city built from the proceeds of the raids, which had achieved legendary status in Ankisua's history. Velans stole widely but didn't kill and only took what they needed. Theirs was not a piracy of sacking, rape, and pillaging, but one of gentlefolk who took with a bow and an apology. Peryst laughed to himself and then furrowed his brow, thinking back.

'When was it that you dropped your nefarious pirating ways?' he asked his companion.

Klaust grinned. 'But have we? Some would say trade is merely the other face of piracy.'

Peryst elbowed him lightly.

'The year before you came to Arya with Anil: in 5153, after we discovered that the reefs of the Isles are heavy with blood pearls and, quickly after, that there are extensive diamond-dust deposits in the mountains of southern Vel and also in the western islets.'

Blood pearls, the rarest and most valuable of jewels, were sought after all over Ankisua and Glannafel, and the deposits on Vel were larger than any found elsewhere. His mother had worn a ring with the slightly uneven pearl of a red so deep it lived up to its name. And diamond dust, essential to strengthen glass, was scarce in Ankisua and previously only sourced from a single deposit deep in the Tujauve Desert. One single grain of diamond dust in the manufacturing process was enough to make any glass as strong as diamond and essential for the use given to glass both in Genai and Reor.

'Not that long ago, though it seems aeons in the past that Tamadal began bowing and scraping to Reor.'

Klaust snorted. 'That first overture from Tamadal to Reor will prove their undoing, you'll see. Wanting our treasures, they partnered with the Hand for trade and never knew that, in so doing, they were preparing their downfall.' He sighed. 'Look at them now, getting into bed with the Five. They'll come to regret it.'

'Not before they cause a great deal of damage, though it does seem like they've been in league forever.'

'It does. It's only ten years ago, but so much has happened since that it could be a lifetime.'

'I remember you well: a cocky sixteen-year-old reared as heir, standing at the head of your welcoming party when we docked.' Peryst chuckled. 'Though I wonder if *welcoming* is the right word?'

'Some of them might have been welcoming, but I was not. Though I agreed with my father that we needed to ally ourselves with Mehru, I wished to have driven a harder bargain.'

'The shock on your face when you realised it was Anil who'd been sent to negotiate!' Peryst couldn't keep the amusement from his voice. At fifteen, Anil had been a newly appointed Agazi to one of her father's battalions. She'd served in the army since childhood and, as the only daughter of the High Luk, he'd sent her to Vel as proof of the importance the High Luk granted to an alliance with the Velans.

'How could I not be shocked? There was I, heir to the newly established main trading hub of the South expecting to be treated with utmost respect, and instead of the older sons or a senior Agazi of the High Luk, I'm faced with Anil!' Klaust let out a rolling and easy laugh. 'Despite being a year younger than I was,

I deemed her a child! Sent to negotiate with *me*, the heir and only son of Ellias, the Pirate Chief of Vel!'

Peryst laughed, recalling them circle one another like suspicious dogs: both Sensals, both with a strong control over their mind's eye, and both so sure of themselves. He'd held his breath as he waited for the bite that would surely follow the snarl and send any possible negotiations up in smoke.

'Does the High Luk always send his smallest dog to do his bidding?' Klaust had taunted.

'The High Luk knows the value of each of his curs. He sent the best,' Anil had replied.

Klaust had raised his fair eyebrows with feigned surprise. 'Best? As defined by who?'

Peryst heard Anil's clear laughter again as she'd ignored Klaust's taunts and had focused her mind's eye on him. 'Myself. And I would know best.' Klaust had made as if to reject Anil but then changed his mind, focusing his own on her.

They'd connected. From the outside, it had seemed like a lightning strike between the two.

Years later, they'd each told Peryst that in that connection, they'd truly seen each other, naked of posturing, titles, uniforms, and weapons. They'd discovered in each other an extreme loyalty to their respective fathers, an entrenched sense of fairness, a deep hatred for the Hand of Reason, and an unexpected vulnerability and loneliness. A knowing that would have taken years was completed in seconds, and the bite that Peryst had expected never came. Instead, they were truly welcomed, ideas were shared, and a treaty was signed. Mehru and Vel became staunch allies against any who extolled the Hand of Reason, and Klaust and Anil became lovers.

Peryst had watched as their mutual respect and physical enjoyment of each other grew into a profound and enduring love in a union so complete that each felt empty without the other. He knew it was a terrible fate for both, as neither could or would forsake their responsibilities, and so they were doomed to what stolen time they could find and to sharing what they could daily, mind to mind, even after their two children had been born.

'I think I fell in love with her then,' Klaust said, a softening in his face. 'Probably when she set one foot on the jetty, her chin high as she glared at me.'

And loved her still, Peryst could plainly see, with the same fervour as then. A pang of envy pierced him at the memory of his own such love. But he shook his head. It was not the time to dwell on his heartbreak. He angled his neck back.

'Arya is looking well,' Peryst observed. 'Wider, like a settled matron.'

With his hands on his hips, Klaust peered up at the terraces that led to the Citadel. Unlike the white and graceful Lis, Arya was built of grey stone, and, like a crouching animal, each level hugged the rocky escarpment from where it weathered the salt air and storms that hit from every direction. Peryst would never describe it as beautiful, but it was imposing in its own way.

He twisted back to the simple port where only three ships lay at anchor. It was greatly misleading as to the Velan maritime capacity: the rest of the mighty Velan fleet lay off the southeastern coast, where towns spread over land reclaimed from the jungle and reached down to the sea's wide bays.

Peryst grunted and shifted his pack as the straps dug in painfully. He put Maia down. It was hot and there was a long climb up to the Citadel so he would let her walk some of it but held her hand tightly as they advanced through the terrace filled with warehouses, taverns, and inns where the business of maritime trade flourished. It was heaving with activity, and Touched power flowed freely everywhere.

'How's trade?' he asked Klaust, who led the way but was stopped every few steps by Velans inquiring about his father's health.

Peryst admired Klaust's easy interactions with his people. When he'd first met Klaust, he'd thought him arrogant. And he was. Very. But his arrogance was shared by every Velan Peryst had subsequently met. It was born of pride in being Velan—a mix of two very different peoples—and hatred. Velans never forgot that their ancestors had been driven from their homes by fire and had vowed they never would be again. It was that hatred that had spurred them to build their city, to protect their new home, and to form a society where power flowed unfettered and proud.

'Excellent. Demand for our goods is ever high.' Klaust lowered his voice for only Peryst to hear. 'And my side business of information gathering is growing well.'

'Diamond dust must be coveted by Reor. Do you trade with them?'

'Never. We trade freely with all Ankisua except Reor. And if we learn one of our buyers sells our goods to Reor, we won't trade with them again. Vel does not forget, Peryst.'

Once they reached the second terrace, where local business reigned, Klaust was stopped frequently by shopkeepers and marketgoers. Peryst was grateful for the slowing down as Maia's short legs couldn't match pace with the two of them.

It was as they were leaving the second terrace and climbing the wide stone stairs leading to the three residential terraces above that Maia suddenly stopped under one of the flower laden trees that clung to the mountain itself. With a moan, she placed her small hands over her ears and shut her eyes tightly.

Peryst crouched to her level. 'What is it, Maia?'

The little girl shook her head, eyes screwed shut.

Klaust turned back to them, his initial concerned expression clearing as he observed the child. 'The Isles can be a bit much for those not accustomed,' he drawled.

Peryst realised there was nothing truly wrong and that Maia was simply overwhelmed. As a Sensal, to her sluggish mind's eye, the power in Arya would seem like a deafening commotion.

He lifted her gently into his arms and she immediately tried to bury her head in his shoulder, but he eased back, holding her away from him. He fixed his eyes on hers, focusing his mind's eye and reminded her of what she had learnt with Lexya, instructing her to compartmentalise her mind's eye and turn off the excess so she wasn't bombarded by stimuli. 'Wake up your mind's eye, Maia. You can do this. Then see this wonderful place filled with power.'

Maia obeyed slowly, very clearly struggling to wake up her mind's eye, which had been largely dormant for many months. After a couple of false starts during which she leaned forwards to shelter against Peryst's chest, she lifted a wet face filled with wonder.

For the remainder of the climb, Peryst was proud that Maia skipped ahead, exclaiming at the occasional drooping vines trailing from upper terraces, at the Velans who carried heavy parcels by manipulating air, and at children playing with floating marbles.

He was sweating lightly and ready to put down his pack when they finally reached the Citadel—square, grey, and imposing, more fort than castle—that watched the surrounding seas from the highest point of the island.

Klaust led them straight to the nursery. It was a large room at the top of the building, with high ceilings and light streaming in from the windows. Peryst smiled down at Maia. It would be unlike anywhere she'd seen before: the bright blue sky contrasted with the rolling grey sea beyond the windows and within, the children of Vel played and laughed as they used their powers freely. Peryst waited with Maia by the door, watching children, many younger than Maia, using their powers.

They're like you, Maia. Peryst pointed at floating toys and pictures in the air.

Welcome, Maia and Peryst. Maia flinched and moved closer to Peryst when the Mas of the Citadel spoke in their minds.

This is how Velans speak to each other much of the time, Peryst explained. *Like you did with Lexya and like you do with me.*

Slowly, more curious faces turned to Maia, and the children opened their minds to her. The children of Vel had never been taught to curtail or hide their power; on the contrary, it was encouraged, so they approached her in the only way they knew: mind to mind. The slow smile on his daughter's face told Peryst that bringing her to Vel had been the right decision. She took one step and then another into the bright room. In no time, she was making toys fly, creating castles in the air, and playing with Anil's sons under the careful watch of the Citadel's Mas. With no concern, Peryst left her when she waved distractedly at him as her laughter rang out.

ELLIAS GREETED PERYST in the Citadel's council room from where every approach to the Isles could be watched. Peryst bowed, fist to chest, greeting him with words of respect. He was much older than Peryst remembered, with his face heavily lined and a vague expression in the clear eyes so like his son's. Ellias, seated behind a large desk, initially responded with a welcoming smile but suddenly became confused and turned away. Caring and reassuring, Klaust quickly went to him.

'Peryst de Arranu comes to pay his respects, Father. He's the emissary of the High Luk.'

Hands shaking, frowning, and biting his lip, Ellias asked his tall son, 'Are they coming, Klaust? Has he come to say they're coming for us?'

'No, Father. None come from Reor. We're safe in Vel.'

'Good, son. We must keep it that way,' Ellias mumbled in relief.

'We will, Father.' Klaust made a gesture to one of the guards, who carefully helped the elderly man hobble out of the room.

'Your father seems feeble,' Peryst observed as Klaust watched the door close behind him.

'I fear his days draw to an end,' Klaust replied sadly. 'His life has been long and rich. As the only son, born late in his life, I've shared only the latter end of it, but regardless, we'll rejoice much when he passes.' Instead of mourning the dead, Vel, like Glannafel, celebrated them with a joyful brysk where no tears were shed while recounting their lives with songs and stories.

'I bring a letter from Anil for you and one from the High Luk for the Pirate Chief of Vel. Are you him now? Do I give it to you?'

'I'm not the Pirate Chief and will not be so till my father is gone, but it's to me that you will give the missive as my father's eyes have grown cloudy, both those on his face and those in his mind.'

Peryst nodded and removed both letters from his satchel.

Klaust placed Anil's in his pocket to read later. 'It's always strange to read Anil's words on paper, so different to our daily mind-to-mind communication. But there's joy in touching what she's touched recently.'

'How long since you were last together?' Peryst had often wondered whether he would've been able to sustain as strong a relationship with Sanjia if they'd been apart as often as Anil and Klaust.

'Too long. With my father's condition, it's been difficult for me to join her on the continent. It would be entirely possible that he could wake one morning and decide that the outline of the Lis peninsula in the distance is a Reordan fleet and order a full-scale attack.'

'It must be very trying.'

'We knew when we came together that it would be thus,' Klaust said with a smile. 'I would always have my obligations to my people and she to hers. But even in the times when all we have is our connection of minds and only a few scattered meetings, it's worth it. Without each other, we are so much less. But it's hard on the boys, so, as soon as I'm able, I'll cross over to Lis with them.' He winked. 'We all need time with Anil. I with my wife, and they with their mother.'

He turned to the High Luk's missive. 'What I expected.' He sighed. 'We've watched Reor move its pieces on the game board of southern Ankisua and cannot understand how they do it. How can a nation without Touched power get as far as they have and keep going?'

Peryst frowned. 'They use a power stronger than ours, Klaust, and much more deadly. Fear is the strongest power of all. It'll turn brother against brother and son against father.'

'How long since you left Mehru? How long were you at sea?'

'The crossing from Lis took a week. Though we had six Air Primals channelling the wind to make haste, one of the usual spring storms delayed us.'

Klaust leaned back against the window. 'So, you won't know that southern Mehru has fallen to the Hand of Reason, and Lis is under siege.'

Peryst slowly sat on an armchair in the small seating area near the desk and placed his head in his hands. His mind wailed though no sound escaped his lips.

'I've been running from the Hand since I left my sister's house in Reor. Always a step ahead, I joined each who stood against them in my journey. We won every battle, Klaust! We pushed the Hand back and reclaimed towns for Mehru every single time! How is it that once again I am merely a step ahead of them as they close in?'

Klaust placed a hand on his shoulder.

'Lis will fall. Four battalions are not enough against the whole of Tamadal and Reor. Worst, the sons of the High Luk will erode the confidence of those still loyal to their father. They'll paint him as behind the times, old fashioned, and feeble, hiding behind his Touched daughter as they advocate for what Reor can give them,' Peryst said dully.

'Yes. Lis will fall,' Klaust agreed. 'That time will come eventually, but not yet. In the meantime, Vel will stand shoulder to shoulder with Lis against Reor and Tamadal. I've already told Anil and the High Luk but will send an official reply to that respect. We will aid in her defence from the sea, but they both know that if a time should come when the Isles are threatened, we will have to turn all our power towards our own defence and leave Lis to hers. Vel cannot fall under the Hand of Reason. However much I wish to aid Anil, my first duty has to be to my people.'

'This is fair.'

'And you? What'll you do?' Klaust sat on the facing armchair.

Peryst felt a wave of desolation as he clasped his hands between his knees. 'I'll run. What else can I do? I've lost. We've lost. Lis will fall, and Reor will swallow southern Usur and southern Rohin. The Hand of Reason will rise higher and higher till it covers all southern Ankisua, and then the Five will reach their hand to the North, and I will keep running to save my daughter from their clutches.'

'No, Peryst, we haven't lost.' Klaust leaned back, stretched his legs, and crossed his ankles. 'We may have lost a battle, perhaps many battles, but this war will be one of ages. It won't end in my lifetime or in yours. Perhaps in that of our sons and daughters or their sons and daughters. The Hand of Reason will fail. Not today and not tomorrow, but it will fail, and the likes of you and I will die fighting against them and will teach our children and our children's children to die fighting against them, because any regime of such cruelty must and will fail.'

'I wanted to keep Maia safe, yet all I've managed is to keep half a step ahead of the Hand.' Peryst passed his hands through his hair, grown too long again since he'd had it cut by Hana before leaving for Gallya. 'I should never have brought her to Mehru.'

'Make your home here. The ocean protects us. Stay where your daughter will thrive under our teaching, and you will be amongst your kind.'

'Careful,' Peryst said quietly as he moved towards the window. 'It is *your kind* and *my kind* that began the end of Reor.'

'You're so right. It's a dangerous thing to forget.'

'Therein lies the danger. History turns into a story, and the same mistakes are made again.' Peryst peered out at the dark ocean that surrounded Vel far below. He craned his sight beyond where, on a clear day, the peninsula of Lis could be glimpsed. Leaning against the sill, he spun back to Klaust, who sat in his chair watching him.

'I would enjoy a time in Vel, and, as you say, Maia could find a place here and develop further, but I can't remain eternally. I made a commitment with the High Luk and with myself. I'll travel in search of allies against the Hand of Reason.'

'You won't find them, Peryst. Behind the Kunlan Range they all feel safe. The northern realms have no need to fight the Hand of Reason. Not yet.'

'Perhaps, but now that Reor and Tamadal have joined, it's only a matter of time till rest of southern Ankisua is overrun. Then, mountains or not, the Hand will reach the North and also here. You know this.'

Klaust nodded thoughtfully. 'I do. Our navy and maritime defences are strong, and none could ever land on our Isles without our agreement, but if the whole of southern Ankisua is under the Hand, our northern trading routes will be severely curtailed.'

'Is Vel still trading northwards these days?'

Klaust grinned. 'Of course. Tamadal has been slow in setting up maritime blockades. It's focused on taking Mehru by land and has been careless with the seas. Meyan and Sahar are still within our reach, but not for long, I fear.'

'They'll remember the sea once they realise that Lis will not fall without a lengthy siege,' Peryst said drily. 'Then they'll leave the siege in the hands of the Mehruvian traitors who will break their kin quicker and more efficiently. The

Reordan and Tamad forces will head east to Usur. Once southern Usur falls, your traders will be blocked from Ankisua.'

Klaust shrugged. 'And so, it's a good thing our trade links with Glannafel are strong and flourishing. If the Hand won't let us sail north, then Vel will face south.'

'Will some question the financial aspect of that decision?' Peryst mused.

'Not in Vel. In another couple of generations perhaps, but not yet. Our resentment towards the Hand of Reason is still alive and strong.'

'Long may it last,' Peryst said fervently.

'Stay, Peryst, till your daughter is older. Make a new life here where the Hand has never ventured. We're good people. And I, as the soon-to-be Pirate Chief of Vel, will grant my welcome to you and your daughter for however long you would wish to make your home on the Isles.'

Peryst put off his departure because Maia was indeed thriving in Vel. She used her power without limits, only curtailed by the Mas when she went too far.

'She and Kindu need to be watched closely,' the Mas of the nursery declared to Peryst and Klaust as she reported on their children.

'Kindu? He's the older of your sons, isn't he? I'd have thought she'd connect better with the younger one,' Peryst said to Klaust.

'Gael has no time for her.' The Mas chuckled. 'But Kindu, though the eldest at four, is another matter. To be fair, I think it started with the wolf. Paying attention to Maia meant he could get close to Nela. He'd never seen one before, and many in the Citadel have taken to calling him *wolf cub*.'

Peryst could see why. Gael was fair like his father, but Kindu resembled Anil and, even more, his grandfather. These boys would be heirs to Vel and Mehru. Could it be that their parents had determined which would take each throne based on their colouring? The High Luk was known as the *Wolf of Mehru*, and any heir was the *wolf cub*.

The Mas was still talking. 'They get up to all sorts of mischief together, most of it harmless, but this morning Nela dragged me downstairs to where they were trying to reach the iron chandelier in the great hall. They'd stolen out of the nursery when one of the nurses was distracted. Kindu removed a cord from a curtain, and Maia fashioned a rough stairway with it. They were both climbing when I stopped them.'

Klaust laughed. 'Who leads and who follows?'

'I think it's very much a joint effort, but there's no deceit in them at all. Both happily shared their plan of swinging from the lamp.'

Peryst covered his face in mock horror. 'How will I ever survive this child?'

'Maia's very powerful. As you said, Master Peryst, she's a Sensal and a Primal, but, when Gael fell this morning, she helped Kindu heal his knee. Maia's also a Mender.'

'A Touched that's all three? That's rare,' Klaust said.

'The combination of powers runs in my family line,' Peryst replied. 'My grandmother combined the three as well, but it seems to have skipped two generations.'

'There was one like her in my great-grandmother's village in Reor,' the Mas said quietly. 'She was the first burnt by the Hand of Reason. They feared her power as greatly as they would fear Maia today. Take good care of her, Master Peryst, and keep her far away from the Hand.'

'I intend to,' Peryst replied, watching Maia stare into Klaust's face in wonder as the future Pirate Chief of Vel told her and his two sons a story while making pictures in the air with their toy ships and blocks.

YEAR 5164 OF THE NEW ERA – SUMMER

The death of Ellias delayed Peryst's departure yet further. The celebration of his life lasted a week, with music, light shows, and feasting during which the Isles ignored all but their own affairs. Once Klaust was officially named Pirate Chief of the United Isles of Vel, on the fifteenth day of the sixth month of 5164 of the New Era, the Velans woke up to the outside again.

While music had played and toasts to Ellias had rung out, the siege of Lis had grown tighter and the Agazi of the third battalion had led his troops to join the sons of the High Luk.

As Peryst had announced, it was only then that Tamadal set up a blockade west of the Lis peninsula, preventing Mehruvian vessels from westward travel and any other vessels from approaching Lis. News then came of a Tamad diplomatic ship heading to Vel. Klaust gave orders for it to be met at high sea. No ally of the Hand of Reason would land in Arya under his watch or even come within its coastal waters, and he wouldn't deign to meet them himself. They weren't worthy of his time and presence. A delegation was dispatched to meet with them in the waters south of Guzal.

'If you still plan to leave, Peryst, it's probably time,' Klaust said in his Council Room a few days after his father's burial and before the meeting with the Tamad ship. 'Reor has already turned to Usur and west to Rohin. The latest communication from the continent says Defenders are on the march east and west. Our days of trade in those directions are undoubtedly numbered, but I'll be sending one last ship to fulfil our commitments with Usur. I suspect it will be the last to travel north from Vel openly.'

'A pirate is always a pirate?' Peryst smirked.

'Exactly. We'll simply revert to our licentious ways of old and take to smuggling.' Klaust winked. 'I'm almost looking forward to it!'

In appearance, Klaust was far more suited to smuggling and piracy. His air of power was a little dangerous and his impudent delivery nothing like the expected sternness of a leader. But it was as misleading as Anil's youth and perceived gentleness. Like his wife, Klaust was no fool and an able and far-seeing strategist who would lead his people well. Peryst would sorely miss his company.

'I can give you a place on the last official ship from Vel if you're still bent on reaching the North by sea,' Klaust offered. 'Now that Vel is safe from the danger of an unstable ruler...' Peryst mouthed, *is it*? with a grin, but Klaust waved away the comment and continued. 'Once this tedious little Tamad affair is settled, I'll cross over to Lis with the boys to see Anil.'

It was with a heavy heart that Peryst agreed, and a few days later he stood on the deck of the *Creaking Goodbye* and watched the Isles of Vel disappear into the sea. Peryst gazed down at Maia, who'd fallen asleep placidly in his arms. Kissing her brow softly, he thought back onto her first three years. He smiled grimly.

Her future will be no different: we will fight against and run from the Hand of Reason till I have no breath left.

She's a Klaevani, after all. As such, she's doomed or perhaps blessed to wander from one place to the next, first by my side and then on her own, learning from any who can teach.

Here, still at the beginning of her road, I swear that I will give her all the knowledge I have so she will never deem herself weak and in need of protection. I'll teach her to know when it's time to ask for aid and when it's time to give up. As best I can, I'll teach her to use her powers to harm none. And I'll teach her that freedom lies in being able to choose her way, whichever that may be.

She is my daughter after all.

Keep reading for an excerpt from

RULE OF REASON

Book 2 of the Hand of Reason

Coming Summer 2026

PROLOGUE

YEAR 5162 OF THE NEW ERA – WINTER

WITH A SHAKING hand, Marie handed the letter to her husband as she held her young son on her hip. She tried to keep her voice from shaking, but couldn't. 'It's come, Felim.'

Felim carefully opened the thick envelope. Over his shoulder, she read the official text and lifted her gaze to his wan skin that, she knew, was no different to her own. She was no longer the confident and happy mother of twins from barely six months before. In the mirror every morning she saw dull skin and dark smudges that indicated sleepless nights of tossing and turning.

Marie mourned the loss of their daughter in her own way: alone and in the privacy of her heart while accusing herself and Felim for the decisions they'd made. At first, she had found excuses for her husband. He was Reordan after all, and this was his family's home, but lately she'd begun resenting his seeming lack of remorse and his apparent relief that Reba was no longer with them. She couldn't fathom how Felim was able to carry on without breaking into a million pieces, like she was.

Their gazes locked on Raf, who was struggling to be let down from his mother's hip to investigate the fascinating colours and textures of the glass workshop.

'We can't go on like this, Marie,' Felim said in a murmur. 'If not for us, for Raf.'

Marie tried to find in him the Reordan boy for whom she'd left behind her roaming Klaevani life and everything she had known. Together they had put the old farm that had been in his family for generations on the map with their glassmaking facilities, the envy of those nearby. Their contracts with the Academy in the capital had brought them prosperity, comfort, and prestige. And together they'd made a family. A family with two children. Two! Not just the one she held on her hip.

Marie buried her face in the struggling Raf's curls.

'They'll be in Lost Corner for the testing by the end of the week, Marie.'

From the depths of her son's hair, she choked out, 'What if they find something in him, too?'

Felim took the child, lifted his wife's face, and kissed her gently on the forehead. 'If they find traces of power in him, Raf will go to the Lost Corner lyceum instead of to the Academy. We'll train him to take over our business. He'll be a prosperous son of Reor! He'll have contracts with the Academy and will inherit a thriving glassmaking business.'

Barricades broke in Marie, and the torrent of despair escaped into words she could finally speak aloud. 'I can't think, Felim. I can't sleep. I watch him day and night, expecting to see a flare of power.'

Felim placed the child on the floor, grasped Marie by her arms and shook her lightly. 'Watching him won't make power disappear if it's in him, Marie.'

'What if he's Touched, too? What if he's like Reba?' She couldn't control her rising voice. 'What if he is? They'll take him! They'll kill him!' Her voice broke on a sob. 'They'll make everything we did worthless.'

'He isn't Touched. He can't be.' She heard in his voice a desperate will to believe his own words.

'But what if he is? Reba was.' *Reba is. Reba is. I can't and won't think of my daughter as dead.*

'Six days, Marie. Six days and we'll know.'

'Six days,' she whispered. 'I don't know if I'll survive another six days.' She didn't know if she would survive the rest of her life with the burden of what she had done.

'You will and you must. We can't give Raf less than he deserves. Losing Reba can't haunt our son however much it may haunt you. And we can't make him afraid of his world. We're not in your native Klaevan where all are Touched. We're Reordans, Marie. Our son is Reordan, and, as such, subject to the Hand of Reason.'

Marie fought back tears as the exhaustion and fear that had haunted her for six months closed in. But, for the first time since losing Reba, she felt a hard core of resolve as she crouched by her son: the same core that had helped save her daughter. She straightened slowly, a hand in the small of her back, and spoke aloud of Reba for the first time since she'd bundled her into her brother's arms. 'A part of me died when we lost Reba, and all I've had left is guilt, fear, and resentment since then. But I'll use what I can find within for Raf. We'll never be who we were, and we can't have more children, but if Raf survives, I'll do my best by him and you.' *No matter how much it'll cost me.*

Felim stooped to pick up Raf, who was crawling close to one of the kilns.

'It was not only you who lost a daughter. Even if I don't show it like you do, I lost her, too. And I also fear for our son.' He passed his lips over Raf's hair. 'But I won't let it kill what we've built together, and I won't let it mark Raf. We swore to give him the life he deserved and I, at least, will do so.' He added desperately, 'We must, Marie. There's more we can build, you and I, for ourselves and for Raf. There must be more.'

Smiling tentatively, Marie studied her husband. Could it be that the relief she had seen in him wasn't that at all? Could it be that he'd been just as sad and lost as she? Could it be that the man who had seemed to so blithely choose his lands and name over his child was also suffering over his choice?

For the first time in six months, Marie turned to Felim in the night and welcomed his touch. They loved and slept together that night, limbs entangled instead of separated by a wall of guilt, resentment, and pain.

'They've come, Mistress Lengahr. I'm thinking young Raf will be their last stop,' said one of their three glassworkers when he came in for a warm cup of trega after walking all the way down the winding road from the village to work under Felim's careful supervision.

'How many?' Marie asked, feeling her mouth dry.

'Seven at first. One of them is a Defender with a white collar, the ones who don't speak.'

Marie remembered one such Defender from her own testing, before she was allowed to marry Felim, but hadn't realised at the time that they didn't speak. 'I've never seen an infant testing party before.'

'The testing party is made up of two Guardians,' Felim explained. 'Like the ones who run the lyceum in the village. They're escorted by Defenders, but their numbers vary. There's always one dressed differently who doesn't speak. I'm not sure why.'

'The Defenders came in handy this time, Mister Lengahr. Given the disturbance.'

With shaking hands and filled with foreboding, Marie asked, 'Which disturbance? What happened?'

'You missed a lot of drama in the village this morning. Ban, the son of the emporium owner, was found to have some power.' The glassworker chuckled. 'You should've heard his mother's wailing that her precious boy won't make the Academy! Sounded like they were skinning a cat!'

'They had high ambitions for the boy,' Felim replied.

Marie resisted the urge to say, *Like yours, Felim. Like the ambitions you have for Raf.* She twisted back to see Raf happily pulling himself up in the playpen Felim had made for the twins, too large for only one child.

'They did. And now will have to find some more modest ones.' The glassworker had lowered his voice and schooled his expression into seriousness, but Marie could see he was relishing the telling. 'It was with the blacksmith's daughter, the one called Claya, that the Defenders came in handy.'

Marie gulped at the glassworker's obviously deliberate pause and slight glee. She wanted to cover her ears and not hear his next words, but Felim asked, 'What of her?'

'Touched.'

Marie leaned back against the doorjamb so she wouldn't fall. She forced herself to remain impassive and not scream through the roaring in her ears.

'As they took the child, the Defenders had to fight the parents off. The mother was scratching and screaming, and the blacksmith attacked them with a hammer. One of the Defenders is keeping guard over her for now.'

For now. Till they see Raf. She wanted to laugh hysterically. Or cry. Or both.

'What will be done with her?' Felim asked. Marie saw the worry in his sidelong glance. He thought she would scream. She wanted to. Oh, how she wanted to. But she kept herself upright, listening as if none of it affected her.

'They've got her in the constabulary for now. I guess they're waiting to see what they find in young Raf,' the glassworker said and craned his neck to catch a glimpse of Raf as he played in his wooden pen. 'They're building a pyre on the green for the burning this evening. It's been years since a monster was discovered in Lost Corner.' The glassworker spat on the ground. 'The Defenders are saying that Claya would have been exceptionally powerful, one of them that kills with a thought.' He shuddered. 'Good riddance!'

Marie wanted to be sick. Defenders couldn't know what powers baby Claya would have. Till the powers manifested, *nobody* could know. She tried to find indignation for that lie. It was better than facing the horror that the whole village would be forced to watch. *That would have been Reba* drummed in her mind over and over again.

And Marie knew what would happen next. The blacksmith would be stripped of his post, the family's lands requisitioned, and his other newborn son excluded there and then from the Academy till the third generation. The family would survive on charity from the villagers for a few days, maybe a week, but the goodwill would only last while the horror of Claya's screams was fresh. Then the villagers would begin to find the begging blacksmith and his family a nuisance because it would remind them that their prosperity and comfort had been built upon destroyed families, intolerance, and piles of dead Touched, most of them innocent babies like Claya. The blacksmith and his family would eventually leave Lost Corner, their home for generations, and beg along their way till they reached a place where the Hand of Reason had no hold yet. There they'd rebuild their lives with the image of Claya ever in their minds.

Marie excused herself and went through the arch to the kitchen. She could barely keep herself upright as she blindly opened the back door and stepped into the back yard where she was violently sick.

Just after midday, the two Guardians and four Defenders rode down the lane through what had once been fields but now were yellowing bush-covered lands of cracked earth. Marie and Felim waited at the front door between the pair of small olive trees planted in glass pots.

'Felim and Marie Lengahr?' the first Guardian asked once all had dismounted.

Felim bowed his head as Marie, unable to make a sound, nodded.

The testing party gestured towards the house. Felim ushered them into their great room lit by Academy-manufactured solar lamps. Marie watched them inspect her home. They peered at the empty hearth to the left before noting that beyond the heavy trestle table an arch led to the kitchen. As they observed the dust-free shelves heavy with books, glass ornaments, and an intricate clock she had made, Marie felt they were rating her cleanliness, her tidiness, and her performance as a non-Reordan housewife. She would've been angry if she'd had room for anything other than fear.

Pointing at the clock, a young man dressed in black with a telltale red collar under the red-lined purple cloak of the High Defenders of Shya turned to Marie. 'Your handiwork, I assume. You have a growing reputation in Reor for clockmaking. I've seen one of your clocks at the Academy. It's a work of art.'

Marie used the glass left over from the manufacture of the Academy's vials to make clocks and jewellery. Each year, her glass clocks sold for more than the year before at the Lithe Fair. At any other time, she would've been ecstatic at the praise, but now she merely mumbled her thanks, unable to speak properly through the waves of panic that surged inside her.

Grasping the bars of his playpen, Raf peered curiously at the newcomers but was quiet. Marie wondered whether he sensed her fear.

'You must be Raf.' The youngest of the Guardians was little more than a boy. He crouched by the pen and smiled at Raf, who babbled back. 'And where is the other child? I thought you had twins?'

Marie would've fallen had Felim not held her up with a strong arm.

His voice tight, Felim replied, 'We lost our daughter, Reba, six months ago. You should have a record of the notice we sent to Stonehelve.'

The eldest Guardian, a stern-faced woman with greying hair, nodded. 'We do. I apologise for my colleague's lack of diplomacy and sympathise with your loss.' She then proceeded to ask questions about Raf's eating habits, development, and sleeping patterns. Marie replied with a shaking voice.

'I notice he is not overly verbal,' the High Defender observed as a pale, white-collared Defender studied Raf intently.

'He and his sister suffered a usual childhood ailment that should've passed without consequence. He recovered to a world without his twin, and I believe his development has suffered because of it, as we've all suffered,' Felim replied. Marie lowered her lashes so none could see the emotion swirling in her face.

She couldn't have given such an explanation—or any explanation for that matter—without breaking down.

The Guardian nodded and made a note in a ledger. 'Please wait outside. When we have finished our examination, we will let you know the outcome.'

Marie crouched by the pen and passed her hand over Raf's untidy curls. 'They will do some tests on you, my love. Mama will be just outside.' She kissed his head and followed Felim into the cold winter afternoon.

One of the Defenders closed the door behind them.

Straining to listen through the thick blue door, Marie bit her lip and twisted her hands as Felim faced their dry lands, hands clasped behind his back and humming. *How can he be so calm when I'm going to pieces?* She leaned her ear against the door. There was a deep silence followed by low voices. Another silence, more voices, and a sharp squeal from Raf. Marie made a convulsive movement to open the door, but Felim held her firmly.

A few minutes later, the youngest Guardian appeared and passed a whimpering Raf to Marie.

'Congratulations. Raf Lengahr is hereby given a place at the Academy in Stonehelve. A true son of the Rule of Reason, he will grow to join us and aid in the eradication of every whisper of the Shadow of Unreason from Reor and the liberated lands,' the grey-haired Guardian said.

Limp with relief that he was safe, Marie hugged Raf so tightly he cried and squirmed in protest. That her son would study at the Academy didn't matter to her. That he was safe and would live was all she cared about.

'He has nothing?' Felim asked the Guardian in a trembling voice.

'Your son is free from the taint that is Touched power.'

Felim's posture and tone expressed pride as he thanked the delegation that had opened the way for Raf to achieve the greatness that Felim had so hoped for him.

Relief so strong it tightened her chest engulfed Marie as she tried not to think of the blacksmith and his wife and of what she would witness come evening. She buried her face in Raf's hair and whispered her thanks to Ilu. She only lifted her head when she heard Felim speak. All that was left of the testing party was a cloud of whirling dust far down the lane.

'We cannot burden Raf more than he will already be burdened, Marie.'

Confused at her husband's words, Marie furrowed her brow. 'What do you mean? He has no power. You heard them say so.'

Felim lifted Raf's face, his darker hand a contrast against the child's lighter skin. 'Our child is the perfect blend of you and I, Marie. And he is beautiful. His eyes are beautiful. But.'

They were a mirror of her own, as Reba's had been, too.

'In Lost Corner he's Raf Lengahr, and Lengahrs have lived on this farm since Reor had a name. His physical appearance will have less importance here because of his name, but he'll suffer for them regardless because children can be cruel. At the Academy it'll be different, Marie. He will need to prove himself to be the perfect Reordan when his appearance will scream Klaevani.'

Marie grew cold. The welcome relief that had flooded her swept out, replaced by dread and a growing dullness. 'There was a time when you loved my eyes,' she whispered.

Felim grasped her hands tightly. 'I still do. I always will. Yours and Raf's. But others will not. Others will use his appearance to make my son less.'

Marie put Raf down to play with the dog and lifted her hands, wishing she could push away this new threat. *My* son. Not *our* son. Not a boy who was half and half, not one who was also of Clan de Arranu, but one who was Lengahr and only Lengahr.

She heard the coldness when she replied. 'What will you have me do? Gouge them out? Because I can't change his appearance. I'm no Mender.'

'I never meant anything like *that*, Marie,' Felim barked with disgust at her choice of words. 'I meant that we cannot let Raf be anything other than the perfect Reordan.'

'Isn't that what he'll become at the Academy?' she asked. 'Isn't that what they do there? Turn children into the perfect tools of the Hand? How much more of a Reordan do you want him to be?'

'He'll need to be one before then. He must arrive at the Academy with a perfect record, with no doubts and no confusion about who he is.'

Suddenly exasperated, she asked, 'And what doubts are you implying I will give him?' She spoke louder than she intended, surprising Raf, who screwed up his face to cry. She crouched by him and smiled stiffly to distract him.

'At the local lyceum, he'll be taught what all Reordans learn, but there must be no tales of nomads, no gods, no Touched, and no powers. You can't share your songs and legends with him. You cannot make him different in any way. He must be like every other Reordan boy. Better than any of them.'

'But he's also part of me, Felim. He's also Klaevani,' she whispered.

'He can't be. To counteract his appearance, Raf must be more Reordan than any Reordan.'

Marie smiled mechanically at Raf, who was calling her attention to the dog's matted tail. Empty and exhausted, she'd thought the testing ordeal would be the last before she could try to enjoy her son's childhood. But now she would never be able to truly do so, and the Hand of Reason's shadow would always hover above her as she double guessed her words and actions to make sure she *instilled no doubts* in Raf. The Hand had already taken her daughter, and now it would take all she had planned to give her son, who'd grow up to be what most terrified her. She wasn't stupid. If it were known that Raf had Touched in his bloodline, his chances within the Hand would be marred and he would always be suspect in Reor. She'd seen what happened to the few who spoke out against the Hand: the jailings, the exile, the appropriations of land.

'We made the utmost sacrifice to give each of our children the life they deserved. For Raf to have his, you'll need to sacrifice a little more, Marie.' Felim spoke gently, and she knew the sympathy in his voice was only for her pain and not because Raf wouldn't own his Klaevani heritage.

She raised her face and, keeping pain from her expression and voice, said, 'I won't do anything to hurt Raf or make him vulnerable.' Marie paused then said what were the most difficult words she had ever uttered: 'I won't share my background with Raf. He'll be the perfect Reordan boy, whatever it costs me, as I've been the perfect Reordan wife. I sacrificed all for Reba, and I'll sacrifice this small thing for Raf.' But it was no small thing, and she would struggle daily.

'Promise me,' Felim insisted.

'I promise.' But as Raf pulled at her earrings she wondered whether as a mother she'd be able to unconditionally love a son who would believe with all his heart that his sister would have deserved to die.

ACKOWLEDGEMENTS

As a true believer in causation, this section could go back a couple of centuries and take up half the book, while I thank the adventurous ancestors that got me here and the authors of every book I've read. But I'll be brief. Kind of.

First, I'd like to thank my parents for always having books in the house, for giving me books for every birthday, and for making trips to the bookshop into adventures. And my grandmother, Isabel Edwards Cruchaga, also an author and a woman who read widely, who gave me my first Ray Bradbury and then, *The Hobbit* and *The Master and Margarita*. She set an already voracious reader on the road to fantasy.

Then John Byrne, in my lawyer days—my first editor—who, with his red pen, tried to teach me to make my point clearly, with short sentences and fewer words.

Much later, my cousin Mary Ann Hudson, who with a well-timed quote about being a writer showed me who I truly was and kept my fingers on the keyboard.

And then my husband, Presley, who pushed me on, always believing that I could do it. And who, though not a reader of fantasy, read my drafts and asked science-related questions that plugged holes and made my systems work.

My first and most stalwart readers, my children. Scott and Katya, fantasy lovers, who read and critiqued, questioned and badgered, so that Ankisua grew into a clearer and more layered world. Alexia, who focused on emotions and personalities, and who, when I worried about the lack of romance in this book, insisted that *Touched by Light* had the greatest romance of all time in Peryst's enduring love for Sanjia. And Christina, who told everyone she knew that her mother was a writer and who gave my dialogues the highest praise I could have wished for.

Huge thanks go to Maria Iglesias, who, with infinite patience, read every scrap I wrote as I struggled to find my voice many years ago, giving feedback and commentary, and then reading it all again, and again, and again.

To Scott Walker, author of the Little Yokai Urban Fantasy Series, a good friend who has pushed me to take the plunge for years over zoom calls.

To Garrick Bainbridge, Ross Coyne, and Franco Paoletti, my good friends and *Dungeons & Dragons* companions, with whom I roll dice and slay monsters every week and who have supported and cheered me on for the last two years.

To my brother, Pat Hudson, with whom I did my first ever fantasy seminar such a long time ago and who believed in me when I said I was a writer.

To Brooke Harlander, who was the first to cry with *Touched by Light* when it was just a first draft.

To Jon Oliver, my developmental editor, for his insightful comments and for introducing me to Tiffani Angus, extraordinary copy-editor, hand holder, friend, conference mamma, and incredible author who's pushed me to become the best I can be. Huge thanks to Tiff, who said: 'It's time.' And I always do what Tiff says. So if you enjoyed the book, you too owe her thanks. Left to my own devices, I'd still be editing.

To Nastasia Bishop, Jonas Spokas, Elyot Veillon, Frederick Kroner, and Fakel Barros at Stardust Book Services, for my wonderful maps, covers, and illustrations.

To Craig Martelle, who gave a presentation which spurred me to get my act together and start taking my writing seriously and not as a hobby.

To Luke Gygax, for his lovely blurb and kind words of encouragement, as well as the long-ago *Dungeons & Dragons* games where I managed not to die.

To Sebastien de Castell, who persevered through tech issues till he could read my manuscript and who only had good things to say.

To the many I missed, for comments and smiles, and for support when they never even knew they were giving it!

And finally, to Echo, my Great Dane sidekick, who lies by my side at home or at the pub or plods along listening to my rantings when I'm stuck. She looks wise but never replies.

BERNA HUDSON was born in Chile, grew up in Australia, then returned to Chile for her teenage years before moving to Spain. She moved to England in 1999 and stayed. Daughter of a true nomad, she's proved to be less so in practice but very much so in her mind.

Berna's first job was as a money collector from butchers. Side payments in steak kept her alive when funds were short. Her next experience was working for the legal department of a Drug Rehab centre, much less dangerous than the first job. The third was in aircraft financing, which gave her way too much information about aeroplanes, which she has actively tried to forget. The fourth and last in the legal world was in shipping, where she gave her whole salary over to childcare and realised it wasn't worth it so packed up the files.

The Hand of Reason came about by accident. Berna started writing a short story about a girl called Maia. It turned into the story of her father and went on from there. It was a long time later that she realised that it was a story that tried to make sense of her youth, looking at the insidiousness of totalitarianism from all sides.

Berna lives in London with her husband and her Great Dane, Echo. Her children come and go, but never too far.

You can find out more at www.bernahudson.com

DID YOU ENJOY THIS BOOK?

Reviews are the most important way for a book to get noticed. I don't have a big-name publishing house behind me, but I have something better: YOU, my reader!

If you enjoyed this book, I would be eternally grateful if you spent some time writing a review wherever you bought it. It doesn't have to be long, it doesn't have to be detailed, but a few positive words will make a huge difference to me.

Thank you so very much.

DO YOU WANT EXCLUSIVE MATERIALS AND NEWS?

An author writes for a variety of reasons. In my case, I can't help it: the compulsion to write is unavoidable. That's the internal force that makes my ideas churn and my fingers type. But there's another aspect: I write stories for you to spend an afternoon, or many afternoons, in a world that is different to the messed-up one we live in.

If you want to know more about that world, if you'd like to have access to exclusive stories, or if you'd like to simply find out more about me and where my stories come from, check out my website. While there, join my newsletter to get a free novella, *Farewell to the Hunter*, in which you'll discover how Marie ended up in Lost Corner...

Just visit www.bernahudson.com